Praise for *Sophomores*

"What a vibrant, propulsive, wildly intelligent, and big-hearted slice of life *Sophomores* is, an intricate portrait of a family in crisis rendered with a great deal of humor and compassion. I loved this family, this corner of the world, this novel."
—Claire Lombardo, author of *The Most Fun We Ever Had*

"This book is excellent. It's such a great story. It takes place in the '80s, in Dallas; think *Dead Poets Society*, coming of age. It's funny, it's also sad . . . Highly recommend it."
—Dana Perino, host of "The Five"

"Sean Desmond mined his experiences growing up in the 1980s in Dallas for his new novel, *Sophomores*." —*Dallas Morning News*

"With *Sophomores*, Sean Desmond (*Adams Fall*) evokes late-1980s Dallas and its suburbs with eerie precision. . . . A rich, subtle story of family grief and love, teenaged seeking and adult angst . . . *Sophomores* is a sharp, crystalline look at a few months in the lives of a 'regular' family. With a keen gaze, it captures a city in transition and a boy just coming of age. Dan and his parents will stay with the reader long after the story is finished. . . . [A] poignant and searching novel." —*Shelf Awareness*

"*Sophomores* is a raw, honest coming of age story. . . . It is heartfelt and raw and portrays a family traveling through a challenging period in their lives, hoping to break the cycle, but not sure how to accomplish it." —*Fresh Fiction*

"Like Anne Tyler's fiction, Desmond's tale simmers as it shifts among members of the family, and an unspoken tension is present throughout. Infused with a dry and mournful humor, this slice of late 1980s nostalgia is a quietly fascinating exploration of coming of age, faith, and heritage." —*Booklist*

"Desmond is good at conveying suburban angst."
—*Publishers Weekly*

"Desmond's novel is smartly written and structured."
—*Kirkus Reviews*

"A witty, melancholic, and affecting story about a family that struggles with the curse of knowing their own failings. *Sophomores* is a smart and beautiful novel about growing up and getting through that readers will savor."
—Sarah Bird, author of *Alamo House*

"With sensitivity and great wit, Sean Desmond brings the 1980s to life in a big-hearted family saga that knows and loves its characters from deep within. An enthralling read."
—Bruce Holsinger, author of *The Gifted School*

"*Sophomores* is the most mature adventure in immaturity I've ever read, a mordantly funny year in the life of a teenage boy who, true to his Irish-Catholic origins, sees and feels everything. Despite what the world heaped on this kid's shoulders, I found myself laughing every other page and wishing I was a part of the crew Sean Desmond manufactured to make the world a more interesting place." —Eric Dezenhall, author of *The Devil Himself*

"Few writers have the talent to bring off a book like this—a Tom-Wolfe-on-the-Trinity, wittily observed, affectionate skewering of a particular time and place, in this instance Dallas in the '80s—but Sean Desmond succeeds brilliantly. It's by turns funny and touching, and always entertaining, with nods to *Bonfire of the Vanities*, *Dead Poets Society*, *The Catcher in the Rye*, and your favorite '80s high school movie. I was sad upon reaching the last page."

—James Donovan, author of *The Blood of Heroes*

ALSO BY SEAN DESMOND

Adams Fall

SOPHOMORES

A NOVEL

[from the Greek: *sophos* wise + *mōros* foolish]

SEAN DESMOND

G. P. PUTNAM'S SONS

NEW YORK

PUTNAM
— EST. 1838 —

G. P. Putnam's Sons
Publishers Since 1838
An imprint of Penguin Random House LLC
penguinrandomhouse.com

The Library of Congress has catalogued the G. P. Putnam's Sons hardcover edition as follows:

Names: Desmond, Sean, 1973– author.
Title: Sophomores: a novel / Sean Desmond.
Description: New York: G. P. Putnam's Sons, [2021] |
Identifiers: LCCN 2020022043 (print) | LCCN 2020022044 (ebook) |
ISBN 9780525542681 (hardcover) | ISBN 9780593084847 (ebook)
Subjects: LCSH: Domestic fiction.
Classification: LCC PS3554.E842 S67 2021 (print) |
LCC PS3554.E842 (ebook) | DDC 813/.54—dc23
LC record available at https://lccn.loc.gov/2020022043
LC ebook record available at https://lccn.loc.gov/2020022044
p.   cm.

G. P. Putnam's Sons hardcover edition / January 2021
First G. P. Putnam's Sons trade paperback edition / December 2021
G. P. Putnam's Sons trade paperback edition ISBN: 9780593084854

Printed in the United States of America
1st Printing

Book design by Pauline Neuwirth

For my mother and father

SOPHOMORES

"ODYSSEUS IS A MAN WHO IS NEVER AT A LOSS. THE GODS STRIP HIM like bark, separate him from his men, exile him from his family. Yet he persists—travels to hell and back, always with a plan, without doubt, never baffled. He is ever at the ready despite his many trials."

Mr. Oglesby looked over the class of sophomores, steadying himself in a lean against Teddy Boudreaux's desk. The next quiver of questions was a deliberate digression from the lesson plan, and he shot them out rapid fire.

"So why does Homer ascribe contradictions to his hero? How can he never be at fault yet decide that taunting a Cyclops is a good idea? Why would someone smart enough to win the Trojan War be so stupid as to anger the gods?"

Oglesby returned to the blackboard, raising one of his many teaching sticks—this one named Keisaku—and pointed to the words he had written earlier: *The myth of the hero.*

"Mr. Humphrey, what kind of a hero is Odysseus?"

"Mythic?"

Oglesby shook his head and stared out the window at the faded green of the courtyard. "Don't regurgitate, Mr. Humphrey. Mr. Atherton?"

"Uh . . . he's a classic hero."

"Next you'll tell me he's Greek."

A discomforting five seconds passed as Oglesby stalked the center aisle of the classroom, punching Keisaku at the carpet like he was on a mountain trail.

"Gentlemen, stop guessing and start thinking. Can someone actually prove to me that they've read this book and not Dr. Cliff's summary of the plot?"

Oglesby exhaled through his nose, his disappointment as subtle as a vaudeville act. He lowered his head and considered what remedial assignment he would have to resort to. A hand went up from the front row.

"Yes, Mr. Gilchrist."

"He's a hero because his greatness can contain contradictions."

"Yes, and . . . ?"

"And he is searching for something he probably won't find."

"What do you mean?"

"The hero has a quest."

"Thank you." A wave of relief passed across the teacher's face, and he started a peripatetic shuffle up and down the center aisle. "Gentlemen, Mr. Gilchrist is correct. The hero is defined by his journey. A hero isn't perfect. Every man has flaws that he must confront and overcome. That is the internal quest of the hero. And the eternal quest of literature."

Daniel Malone frowned. He knew that answer and should have raised his hand.

o o o

THIS WAS SECOND PERIOD, SOPHOMORE HONORS ENGLISH, TAUGHT BY Mr. David Oglesby at the Jesuit College Preparatory School of Dallas. The course and its teacher were legendary for their rigor and Socratic curveballs. Each morning, Oglesby walked into class purposefully, carrying his "persuasion stick"—today it was the black-and-maroon Keisaku; he had many others—and an olive-drab backpack slung over one shoulder. The pack was government issue and a reminder to the sophomores that their teacher had once been an army medic on a search-and-destroy team in a place we used to call Indochina. For this version of boot camp, Oglesby dressed sharply—Hickey Freeman sports coats, button-down oxfords, cuffed Brooks Brothers slacks, cordovan penny loafers, and a sequence of solid knit ties that were in fashion the fall of 1987.

For the first two weeks, Mr. Oglesby was quick to prove command and control. He had two default modes: stern and strict. Each day, twenty new vocabulary words, and each night, a journal-writing assignment—at least one hundred words on weird topics that included: epic simile, Venetian blinds, Pyrrhic victory, and something called the Paraclete. Oglesby's class came with a minor catechism of standard-issue rules—*"Organization is the key to high school," "Think before you speak"*—and absurd ones—*"Never give a gun to a duck." ("After all,"* he'd say, *"the duck might be a quack shot.")*

Each class was at once a performance and an inquisition aimed at startling sophomores into effort. Dan Malone certainly was intimidated. Oglesby had a booming teaching voice, dactylic in cadence. He had wide, searching gray-blue eyes that were quick to appraise whether the light was on or not with a student. He also had the reflexes of a black belt and was quantum quick to grab a wisecracking ephebe by his tie knot *(Oglesby synonyms: cravat, foulard)* or bring his teaching stick down with an emphatic near miss of a sophomore skull.

Dan had strong marks from freshman English and had moved up to the honors class with his crew—namely, Rick Dowlearn, Rob McGhee, and Steve "Sticky" O'Donnell. None of the boys knew what to make of Oglesby's strange temperament. Rick admittedly did the best Texas Brahmin impression (*"Misterh DAWH-learn, de-FINE mimesis"*), along with a mea culpa beating of the breast with a copy of Strunk and White, which ended in a back-of-the-hand-to-the-temple half swoon. But all the sophomores were on

guard for when Oglesby's class turned into a close-reading cross
between *Jeopardy!* and *Press Your Luck.*

○ ○ ○

"Gentlemen, I'm returning your journals," Mr. Oglesby said,
his back to the class. He whirled around and peered at them one by
one. "Let me say this: Your parents are not paying tuition for you to
scribble such narcissistic drivel. Writing begins with thinking.
Thinking begins with asking questions. Rule number four: your
journal is your life-force."

Oglesby dropped Dan's journal onto his desk in the back row
without pause or comment and continued on to Cameron Coleman, then Jay Blaylock. Already this early into the school year,
the last row was a nose-picking, catnapping affair, and Dan felt a
bit of exile on these back benches. Dan was a solid, if uninspired,
student; mostly A's, but that came at the hectoring of his mother,
herself a teacher baptized and confirmed in the pre–Vatican II
rote academy. Dan had always taken the path of least resistance
with reading and writing, while math, like most boys, he gleaned
from the sports page. He wasn't exactly lazy, but in class, he didn't
try to show off or even engage much. Part of this was fear of being
teased or labeled a nerd, but he was cleverly unefforted and un-
motivated, and his talents had lain under the bushel. Until he
came face-to-face with Oglesby, who seemed to have the drop on
this routine from day one. Dan opened his journal and leafed
through his entries. *Check, check, check.* And one comment:
Fine but not fine.

"My compliments to Mr. O'Donnell," Oglesby said. Sticky
tucked the long bangs of his dark brown hair behind his ear and
sat up nervously. "Who actually did some inquiry on Venetian
blinds and postulated a connection to Botticelli."

There was a pause while the sophomores shot glances at each

other and wondered why they hadn't thought of opening a *World Book* encyclopedia and doing a lick of research.

"Gentlemen, writing is a muscle. The more you use it, the stronger it gets. One hundred words—Mr. Deangelis, are you listening?—does not mean padding out an assignment with adjectives and articles. I want ideas. Brains running, not jogging."

Finished with the pass-back, Oglesby returned to the front of the classroom, closed his eyes in fake meditation, and waved Keisaku back and forth across the room like a blind samurai. "Rule number eight: writing is thinking. And reading is paying attention. Our rule number seven. Mr. Lamberty, what is the reason I assigned *The Odyssey*?"

Troy Lamberty hesitated, the simple answers fluttering into an ontological void. Oglesby took two steps forward and stomped on Mark Flanagan's tapping foot.

"Mr. Dowlearn?"

"Um, to study the hero?"

"Keep going."

"And this is one of the first stories about heroes."

"Can anyone help him?"

Mark Flanagan, writhing in pain with his foot still impaled by the heel of Oglesby's loafer, looked up at him. "Because Odysseus will win in the end."

A few snorted at Flanagan's suffering. Oglesby poked the sophomore in the chest with his stick. "I've given you all too much credit. Forget the discussion of heroes. Gentlemen, that is beyond the capabilities of this class."

"But we did the reading," Colin Indovina whined with his hand up, as if arguing an offsides by the line judge.

"Mr. Indovina, no doubt you moved your eyes over the pages of this book, but what do you really know?" Oglesby returned to the front of the class and opened his planner. "Prove to me you read this book."

Indovina spoke in a slow, perplexed pitch, as if bringing his teacher up to speed. "Odysseus returns to Ithaca. He kills the suit—"

"Yes, yes, yes. We know that. Everyone who listened to Homer sing his alexandrines for the first time knew that already. Okay." Oglesby closed his eyes again and held up his hand. "I have two tests in mind for next week. The first is a multiple-choice test on the themes of the hero, which will be fairly easy if you've been paying attention in this classroom. The second test will be a comprehensive essay, examination, and close reading about every character and event that took place in *The Odyssey*. That test will be near impossible.

"We're going to play a game. How well this class answers my questions in the final ten minutes of this period will determine which test I prepare and how much suffering your weekend will entail. Now, the class as a whole will be given five strikes—five wrong answers, your fate is sealed, and the close-reading test guaranteed."

"Can we play Monday—after we've prepped for this?" Liam Plimmer, a big grade hound, was worried about the ruin of his GPA at the hands of others.

"No."

"But that's not fair."

"Rule number one, Mr. Plimmer: life is unfair." Oglesby picked up his well-creased copy of the Rouse translation.

"Mr. McGhee, let's start with an easy one. What does it mean to keep the Bear or Wagoner on your left as you sail the sea at night?"

Rob was good at stalling until answers came to him, but not today. "Well, in ancient times, the currents of the Mediterranean—"

"It refers to the Big Dipper," Oglesby said with dirgelike certainty. "Strike one. Mr. Tsao."

Ethan Tsao rubbed his eyes behind his glasses, annoyed at getting called on.

"Name me three of the four rivers of the underworld."

"Uh, the Styx, the Aching—"

"Acheron. Continue."

"Uh . . ."

"Strike two." It was clear Oglesby wasn't kidding around. "The Pyriphlegethon and Cocytos are the other two. Mr. Warner—"

"Pass." A doomed laughter spread through the sophomores.

"Strike three. Mr. Hardy?"

"Strike four. Pass."

Oglesby shook his head and grabbed his chin. "Gentlemen, this is *honors* English. If you don't do the reading, if you want to be babied like a bunch of freshman smart-asses, I have a hundred exercises in vocabulary and grammar." Oglesby pounded the teacher's desk with Keisaku. "Reading is paying attention! I can't teach you to think about the big questions when you can't command the basic details. Four strikes. And I'm going to be benevolent and pick someone who thinks they've done the reading. Mr. Dowlearn."

"Come on, Rick."

"Don't screw this up."

"Dude"—Rick shook them off—"don't put this all on me."

"Mr. Dowlearn, who is the Crookshank God?"

"Poseidon," Deangelis stage-whispered. "He carries a shank."

"That's a trident, you idiot," McGhee corrected him.

Rick exhaled through his teeth in frustration. "It's not Zeus or Ares, but it might be—"

"Sir!" It was Dan with his hand up in the back.

"Yes, Mr. Malone."

"Permission to steal the question."

"Excuse me?"

"Let Mr. Dowlearn pass to me."

"Do you know the answer?"

"Yes."

"Very well, Mr. Malone, who is the Crookshank God?"

"Hephaestus."

"Correct."

"Malone saved us." Mike Torkel collapsed back into his seat.

"With one right answer, Mr. Torkel? I assure you I have many more questions." Oglesby thumbed over pages annealed with years of annotation.

"All right, Mr. Coleman." Cameron stretched—he was just waking up from a midperiod snooze interrupted by the smack of Keisaku on his desk. "In the hall of Alcinous, what is the name of the minstrel—the blind man many think is a stand-in for Homer himself?"

Cameron was out of it. "Is this before or after the *Odyssey* guy kills everyone?"

"Welcome back, Mr. Coleman, I hope you're well rested. Okay, that's strike—"

Dan's hand went up again.

"Yes, Mr. Malone."

"The minstrel is Demodocus."

"Correct." A barely perceptible grin ticked across Oglesby's face.

"Mr. Oglesby, sir?"

"Yes, Flanagan."

"I'd like to nominate Malone as our class representative for the remainder of this game."

Several heads nodded and affirmed.

"Mr. Malone, do you want to demonstrate what close reading means to your classmates?"

"Uh, okay."

"Your men are counting on you, do you want to be the hero—or the goat? Remember, class, *tragos*—tragedy—is Greek for 'goat song.'"

"I'll try." Dan felt the pressure as everyone turned in their chairs. *Aww crap,* he thought. *Stay calm, gotta focus.* He had read the book, and years ago, his father had given him D'Aulaires' *Greek Myths,* which he had devoured. He knew his mythology but had been lucky that Oglesby had hit on familiar trivia with the last two questions.

"Here we go then. The name of the Cyclops is . . ."

"Polyphemos."

"The name of the swineherd?"

"Eumaios."

"Who are the Spinners?"

"The Fates."

"The seer who is half—"

"Tiresias."

"The following questions involve Odysseus's trip to the underworld. When he goes, name three queens he meets."

"In order?"

Oglesby looked up from his book. "Of course . . ."

"Tyro, Antiope, Alcmene, Epicaste, Chloris, Leda . . ."

"Christ, Malone," Sticky muttered.

Oglesby flipped pages rapidly. Dan's classmates just stared at him with disbelief. Rob McGhee was silently pumping his fist.

"Our hero smiles twice in the course of *The Odyssey.* When and why?"

"Once when Telemachos tells him to spare his servant Medon, and the second time when Penelope still doubts it's him."

"What does Homer describe as 'all-conquering'?"

Sleep or death, Dan thought, and then guessed: "Sleep."

"What must Odysseus do to right things with Poseidon?"

"Plant an oar in a land where no man knows what it's for."

Oglesby looked up again from the Rouse translation. "Very good, Mr. Malone. One last question, which no one in the history of this class has answered on the first try. You get it right, we talk about heroes, and the class takes the easy test. You get it wrong, and I will have Professor Spiridakos at SMU write the essay questions in ancient Greek. Are you ready?"

Holy shit, Dan thought.

"Do it for Johnny!" Jay Blaylock was a movie-line jukebox, and Oglesby's whipping boy.

"Mr. Blaylock—you can write a five-hundred-word essay on outbursts for tomorrow."

"Thank you, sir." A snappy Boy Scout salute.

"Make it a thousand."

Oglesby slammed his stick on Blaylock's desk. It broke some of the tension Dan felt. His hands were trembling as he gripped the edge of his desk.

"Okay, Mr. Malone. What drunk companion of Odysseus's fell off Circe's roof?"

Dan threw his chin down in concentration. *C'mon, you know this.* "It's not Eurylochus."

"No."

"It's not Perimedes."

Confident, Oglesby closed his book. "No."

"Ahhh . . ."

"Well, Mr. Malone, I must say, that was the closest . . ."

Then it came to him, like a gift from the gods.

"Elpenor!" Dan shouted. "It's Elpenor. Odysseus sees him again in the underworld!"

Mr. Oglesby bowed. The bell rang, and a great cheer went up among the sophomores.

o o o

THAT SATURDAY EVENING ROB MCGHEE WAS STILL CROWING ABOUT Dan's epic trivia battle. As the sun set and all the ways of the day went dark, Dan and Rob sat on the concrete retaining wall in front of the Malone house on Crown Shore Drive. The wall was the one signature element to the property—although you could only park half your ass on it, it was reminiscent of the wall in *Charlie Brown* and was a well-placed caesura in the familiar beat of Fox and Jacobs tract housing. In the fifties, the North Dallas developer had laid out the lots with a simple repeat of ranch houses and given all these side streets their generic marine and littoral appellations—Crown Shore, Boca Bay, Cold Harbor, and so on. The irony that the subdivision sat on a high prairie hundreds of miles from the sea seemed unintended. Nonetheless, the wall was a good spot for cigarettes, conversations, and watching the western skies.

"C'mon, Malone—what was that?" Rob teased his hand through his moussed hair; he had stolen the Perma Soft from his older sister Lexy. They were waiting for Steve O'Donnell to pick them up—Sticky was the first to get his license—and take them to the dance at Ursuline, the girls' high school.

"Just read a lot of mythology, I guess," Dan said.

"That was some *Real Genius* shit."

With cupped hands Dan chased a cricket along the retaining wall until it hopped toward the sewer grate. "Nah, I'm a really slow reader."

They stood there in the gloaming, the day's swelter leaching from the asphalt, until the square headlights of the O'Donnell family station wagon flashed around the bend. The tape deck was murmuring "Radio Free Europe" as the Nissan Stanza rolled up.

Dan peered inside the car. Sticky at the wheel and Rick riding shotgun. Rob grabbed the seat behind Rick, and with the car seat for Stick's baby sister glued into the other backseat with a resin of Hi-C and Cheerios, Dan tumbled into the way back and sniffed. *Christ, the smell is 4-H back here.*

"Hey, asswipes . . ." Rick reached over and sucker-punched Rob in the chest.

"Son of a . . . ow."

"That was for racking me before Latin."

Sticky pulled away. It was a breezy Indian-summer night. Windows down, they glided through the halos of light along Forest Lane, Rick mumbling along with the music.

"So, gentlemen, what's our plan for the night?" Rick was the crew's unofficial social chair and the only one with any significant game—i.e., he could flirt with a girl longer than one slow song. Freshman year Rick had the same class schedule as Dan, and osmotically they had become friends. Before Jesuit Prep, Rick was a child actor (he played Spalding Gray's son in the movie *True Stories* and was backslapped by Bobby Valentine in a Whataburger commercial), but his personality veered far from the philothespic pretensions of the drama nerds. His looks were a little elfin, like a young Jack Lemmon with ash-brown hair that had a natural part to its curls, followed by baby blues, freckles, dimples, and a jaw-drop smile. The girls fell for this big-time.

"I'm dancing with Jenny O'Meara, I tell you what." Rob put it out there.

"Dude, she's going with deMarini," Sticky replied in a here-we-go cadence.

"So?"

"So, he can hurt you without even trying. And she is so out of your league."

"We've got a thing. We went to camp together."

"Jesus, McGhee, that was Bible camp five fuckin' years ago."

Rob McGhee was the son of Reverend Robert McGhee, the pastor of Good Shepherd Episcopal. Father McGhee was so high church that you could argue Rob was more Catholic than anyone else in the car. (Especially since Rick was a Methodist.) Rob went to high school at Jesuit over Episcopal for a number of reasons—but most likely because his father was close to leaving his flock (or vice versa). Rob had been raised so Christian it was almost untenable, but he wasn't naïve or saintly, just anxious, high-strung, a confused vineyard worker. Under a mop of dirty-blond hair cropped new wave, Rob was a manic dreamer, a guitar pick tucked between his teeth, fidgety, his fingers folding, drumming, knuckles cracking, fingernails in constant chaw as the preacher's son imagined what John Lennon meant by "no religion." His worry-wart tendencies were antagonized to the hilt by the bathtub cynicism of Steve O'Donnell.

"I'm telling you I can get there."

"Yeah, get her to pity you."

"Stick, it's sad that you are so lonely that you have to lash out at others like this."

Sticky—a nickname earned for an incident freshman year involving pocket pool, a melted Jolly Rancher, and fingers glued to his algebra test in Chaplinesque fashion—loved to talk shit. He was the best athlete of the bunch but was close to dropping JV football and basketball for music. When not suffering from a case of the fuck-its, he was going to be Jimmy Page, and he and Rob— who, well, he wasn't Robert Plant, more like Robert Smith—had plans that extended well past their third, breakout album. Sticky had a wide, pied-Irish face, real caterpillar brows, and a great widow's peak of Kennedy hair lacquered in *Outsiders* style. He affected lazy punk and too-cool-for-school. He did care; he just didn't let you know.

"Lexy said this is the dance where girls pick their guy for the year." Rob belched out a fat cloud of Dr Pepper. "Winter Snowball, Sadie Hawkins, prom. Tonight's the night you have to get all that going."

"Fuck that noise," Rick said.

"I'm not getting married. But I'd settle for some boobs in my face," Sticky announced to the floor mats of his driver's seat. The car swerved as he felt around for his Cult tape. He was doing fifty in a thirty, driving over the lane bumpers, but traffic was light and death not imminent.

Sticky's family was an interesting case. His brother Dennis "Rabbit" O'Donnell was a senior at Jesuit, third in his class, all-state in cross-country, and for whom early admission to Stanford felt like a done deal. Dennis had hectored Sticky into a myriad (*Oglesby word*) of second-banana complexes. Sticky was also five deviations bright, but with family issues like tissues, one after the next, the foremost being his father had left Sticky's mother, and not for another woman. Sticky, who was the second oldest of six, didn't talk about this, ever.

The rest of the crew groaned as he found the tape along the floorboards and the screaming guitar came in off *Electric*. It was Stick's car and Stick's stereo, but the Cult?

God, this music sucks and blows, Dan thought as he stared up at the dome light like he was making some last petition for an unanswered prayer. As the station wagon turned on Inwood, Rob stretched out in the backseat and kicked his Kaepas next to the headrest for Rick's seat.

"I bet five dollars that Malone doesn't talk to Cady Bloom."

"Fuck you," Dan said.

"You know, Lexy told me Cady is going out for cheerleading this year." Rob had all the cheerleader gossip via his sister.

"So?"

"So she'll be over at Jesuit every afternoon for practice. Your competition is about to go school-wide. I'm just saying you got to lock it down early."

"She doesn't even know—"

"Bullshit." Rick was trying to buck him up in his smart-ass way. "She knows you from St. Rita's. Get on it, Malone."

Fuckin'-a, Rick's right.

"Where are we going after this?" Rob asked.

"You and Malone here can go on a magical double date with girls you'll never speak to," Rick riffed. The rest of the car cackled with gleeful agreement. *Cruel*, Dan smarted, *and probably true.*

For it was known throughout the Nissan Stanza, if not the entire realm of North Dallas: Dan Malone was rattled by girls.

Dan tapped his pack of cigarettes, wanting to get a smoke in before the dance. *Am I really such a coward?* he wondered as he stared out the back window, watching the road disappear into the Dallas night.

o o o

FIVE MINUTES AT THE URSULINE DANCE PROVED THAT THE BOYS WERE as socially inept as expected. Jesuit kids ran in the normal, awkward cliques (jocks, greasers, anti-socs, headbangers, artsy fartsies, band geeks, etc.)—but Dan's crew flew apart in a multitude of directions. Rick spotted Lili Villeneuve, the French foreign exchange student, and that was the last they saw of Rick that night. Rob shadowed Jenny O'Meara while pretending not to. Stick got into an argument with his cousin Tara, who, with a bevy of froshgirls, wanted full backgrounds on impending lettermen. "When Smokey Sings" leapt out of the speakers, and all the girls started pulling taffy and stutter-stepping aerobics like Molly Ringwald in detention. And just that quickly, Dan was left alone on the sidelines. "I gotta hit the head . . . ," he said to no one, and slipped away. The boys' room in an all-girls Catholic high school was three floors down in some subbasement where he was sure he'd be murdered by a member of the janitorial staff. But the long halls on the way attracted a curious if disaffected element. There was Eddie Rivera in front of the mirror, dragging his bangs across his face. Between rounds of grab-ass, Devin Osweiler and a couple of his good ole boys from the wrestling team were dippin' and had covered one urinal in brown loogies. Lalo da Silva was yelling at his twin brother, Memo, in Spanish about *una chica*, and uber-nerd Peter Winkleman muttered to himself, lost in some Bakshi version of reality.

Dan washed his hands and stared into the mirror. *No major acne disasters, but don't pick at that. Mop top kind of hopeless. Why did you wear this Benetton rugby shirt? You look like a flag for an African country. Stop it, man up, go chat up girls, not including Jenny Nowicki, who talks nonstop about swim team. Find Cady Bloom before the next slow song.*

Unable to muster or convince himself, Dan dawdled back to the dance. The Ursuline dining hall was lit low, but he had no problem spotting Cady. She was enveloped by deep blue banners that read, TWILIGHT STARDUST, some sort of confusing, half-baked theme for this mixer. *Mary Mother of God, she is cute*, Dan thought—big brown eyes, brown hair teased and crimped, and pulling off a checkered-skirt-and-black-tights look that was somewhere between Winona Ryder and Lisa Bonet. The good news: she wasn't dancing but gazing toward the floor to do so. The bad news: there was that giant dickface Brad McQuivers making his way over.

The window for approach was closing fast, and Dan was about to veer off when McQuivers was accosted by Samantha Schimmel. Dan almost broke into a skip. The DJ was slip-cueing to the synth whining of Tears for Fears. Dan started across the brazen threshold. *Act cool, don't make a beeline.* Three steps away, he caught her dark eyes, and she smiled bright. He moved under the heavenly banners with her now. Two steps away.

"Cady, oh my Gawd, come, come, come!"

The piano for "Head over Heels" crashed in, and Julie Houlihan practically tackled Cady from behind, turning her away from Dan, who found himself on a barren tundra as everyone else paired off. *Goddamn it.*

Dan circled the outskirts of the dance floor, pretending to have purpose but really orbiting like a sad, lost satellite. After a couple of forlorn passes, he headed out to the balcony off the dining hall. The balcony was crowded with upper-class assholes, and Dan wandered down the steps to the back lawn of the school, which rolled to a break of cedars.

Dan lit his cigarette and watched the smoke silver in the moonlight. He paced around the lawn and then parked himself below the balcony—just in case a chaperone or one of the Ursuline sisters was doing their rounds. The other kids' shadows bobbed like crows on the lawn. Standing where he was, Dan could eavesdrop on all the adolescent back-and-forth bullshit. Like the swineherd listening in on the suitors in the hall. Then he heard:

"Oh my Gawd, he was totally coming over."

"Totally . . ."

It was Cady and Julie. They had ducked Dan on purpose. And now he knew. Dan put out his cigarette and hugged the wall. *Lord, if they see me now—complete social suicide.*

"He's been in love with you since like seventh grade."

Julie Houlihan had no business but your business, and she had had it in for Dan since he beat her in the St. Rita's spelling bee.

"Okay, so now I'm starting to feel bad. I should have danced with him."

"You dance with him and then you can rule out Charlie Corlett, who I'm telling you told Janie, who told me, that he thought he might like you . . ."

"He's like shy, right? It's like so late in the dance, what was he waiting for?"

There was no way he could be seen overhearing all this. Dan looked up at the Big Dipper, trying to muster a plan. *Okay, asshole, run away.* Dan stayed tight to the wall, crab-walking until he was clear of the balcony. *Cady Bloom feels kind of sorry for me. That's something I can work with, right?* He rambled his way through bushes, a drainage ditch, and the side lawns of Ursuline Academy to burst forth into the parking lot. The kids hanging out there just assumed he was smoking pot and asked if he was Holden Caulfield.

Within the hour Dan had rounded up his shameless crew: Rick, who was in a vague penalty/power-play situation with Lili for eyeing another girl or some other petty *merde*; Sticky, who was ranting at poor Agatha Torres about the Cowboys' flex defense; and Rob, who was serving up the nice-boy shoulder to cry on with Jenny O'Meara. (Jason deMarini had apparently told her they needed to "take it easy," and what did that really mean?) They had all basically struck out but gotten through unscathed by major rejection or drawing unwanted attention to themselves.

So after a minor success of a night, the boys hit the skids, piling into Sticky's station wagon to cruise Forest Lane. The dance wound down to "Stairway to Heaven," and then lights up, hands coming off butts and bras quick. At ten p.m., Mother Pauline came over from the convent to lock up. She led the DJ toward the music room to stow the speakers and the turntables.

As they placed all the equipment in the A/V closet, Mother Pauline gazed around her music teacher's classroom with a deep sadness. This was Margaret Raleigh's class, and it was her usual job to close down the dances. The reason she wasn't there was terrible: in April, Peggy had been brutally attacked and strangled in the driveway of her Lake Highlands home. This left the Ursuline music teacher in a coma, lying in a bed of Presbyterian Hospital. Her husband was Reverend Standing Raleigh, the pastor of First United Methodist, whom the Dallas police had arrested and charged with attempted murder. His Park Cities congregation put up his bail as he awaited trial.

As she flicked out the lights in the music room, Mother Pauline said a prayer for Peggy and whispered to no one: "Heaven help us."

IN THE FIRST QUARTER OF 1987, AMERICAN AIRLINES SAVED $40,000 by eliminating one olive from each salad served in first class. Pat Malone considered this as he sucked the brine and vodka out of the pit of the olive he had drowned and then salvaged from his martini. The memory of the financials meeting, an exhausting carousel of fiscal slides, shuffled forward in his mind as Pat replayed a god-awful long day. Pat's boss, Robert Crandall, the lugubrious leader of the largest airline in the free world, was hunting and pecking for cuts all over the place.

"Do you know how much overhead was saved by not painting the hulls on the new craft silver or white?"

Crandall was an hour into the managers' summit in the airline's old New York HQ, 633 Third Avenue, and started to chain-smoke.

"The cost of the paint is two-point-three-million dollars, plus the weight of that paint on the aircraft is on average a hundred fifty-four pounds. That's a weight savings of point oh three percent compared to the painted fleet. Now multiply that over the new MD-80s, Airbus 300s, and 757s, and that's thirty-four less tons of weight we are carrying per mile, with an average itinerary of four hundred thirty-six miles and total revenue passenger miles of one hundred twenty-three billion, that's one hundred sixty-three million dollars to this year's bottom line and close to a one-point-five-billion projection over the life of the new fleet."

"Riles, again," Pat called to the bartender at Sweeney's. He pulled at his button-down collar and loosened a dark blue company tie. A warm mid-September day in New York, and the far end of the bar was a stifled ozone of flat beer, ash, and stale piss. But that was no bother to Pat, who had time to kill before dinner with his cousin Bill. And with Jimmy Reilly behind the bar, he was killing time in familiar fashion—Sweeney's, his old local, was a couple of blocks from the American offices.

God, I missed this place. How did I become some sort of out-of-town asshole? Pat blamed airline deregulation, which had hit in 1978, sending everything straight to hell. The unions became greedy, the management more so. Losses were cut, profits dwindled, the stock price yo-yoed, and American hubbed itself in North Texas, relocating the Malones from the Bronx to Dallas in the summer of 1982.

All morning had been cost-cutting reports and budget run-throughs. Markets were shaky again, ridership was down despite a host of up indicators, and then 3Q came in down 11 percent, 18 percent off capacity, and up 4.3 percent on expenses. That required the Pharaoh Crandall—a nickname Pat had coined with his coworkers—to convene the entire pyramid-building enterprise and figure out how to correct before the holidays and make the numbers "fly right."

Reilly placed a fresh vodka on ice in front of Pat, with a napkin of three cents' worth of olives, skewered by a tiny red sword to hilt and tang. It was a martini if you counted thinking about France as the vermouth. Pat took a long swig of relief. Sweeney's had somehow kept the compressor going on its antediluvian ice machine, which spat out the good oval chips Pat liked to crack against his molars.

The final meeting of the day was to preset strategy for dealing with (i.e., piano-wiring) the unions. The contracts were all in order, but the mechanics were the next ones out, and they were part of the Transport Workers Union, and that meant AFL-CIO and Crandall's nemesis Lane Kirkland, and that meant hostage and holler tactics. Unbothered to look up, Crandall fired questions into the blue folder of Pat's report. *How many mechanics on disability? Overall liabilities are totaled on lines F and G? So what does AMR owe the pension in the next eighteen months? Break this out for over forty, and then over fifty, what's that? Twenty-two percent of the cohort? And where does it factor the '88 and '89 cost-of-living adjustments?* Finally he took off his glasses and held them up to the fluorescents and blew at the dust and smudges.

"So the number I need is at what age—if we bought out everyone—can I knock the teeth out of Kirkland's jaw and divide the younger membership against the executive council?"

Pat slurped rather than sipped his drink. The Pharaoh Crandall relished this kind of corporate warfare. *But gut too hard and what's left?* Pat worried. *A bunch of junior mechanics, aging planes in disrepair traveling at five hundred miles an hour, horrific accidents, NTSB investigations, FAA penalties, and then bankrupting insurance premiums.* But despite being chief actuary to the airline, Pat couldn't bottom-line in his reports to Crandall the causation and cost of sticking it to the pinkos at the AFL-CIO.

"Pat, how's Texas treating you? Did you buy any horses?" From the other side of the bar Reilly grinned like a joker, a cigarette pursed at his lips.

"I traded all my horses."

"To the Injuns?"

"Something like that."

Pat slid his empty rocks glass six inches toward his bartender.

"Good luck with this, Paddy." Reilly poured Smirnoff heavy over the old ice and knocked on this third drink.

Pat gasped a bit at the strength of the martini. It was that ecstatic moment a drinker seeks, like the pins and needles after a sneeze, followed by a warm shudder.

Five years since Pat had left New York and the city did seem different. Sweeney's was still hunkered down on the east side of Third Avenue between Thirty-Eighth and Thirty-Ninth, a half-out-of-the-way spot from the arteries that coursed toward Grand Central. No frills, just bottles and chasers, and a cast of shirt-sleeves from the offices of the *Daily News*, Mobil Oil, and the Con Ed plant tucked behind Tudor City. It also drew the brass from Engine 21 and the scrubs from Bellevue (minus butterfly nets, as Reilly always joked). Plenty of Bronx and Queens Irish on turvy wooden stools below the typical bric-a-brac of Yankees pennants and road signs from County Monaghan.

Despite the familiar buzz of the barflies at Sweeney's, New York was invariably alien when you came back as a visitor. Pat couldn't quite put his finger on it, but the city didn't allow for something; it was flowing too fast, and when you got out of the slipstream of it, you were gone.

Pat took another gulp of poteen and tapped the bar with his ring finger, shave and a haircut. *Where to go with Billy boy?* His cousin had wanted Pat to train up to Katonah. *To hell with jackassing all that way.* Besides, Pat could still expense a strip and potato. *Pharaoh Crandall hasn't crimped the expense accounts . . . yet.* Another swig and rattle of the ice and the glow was full-on. Pat stood to stretch and hit the john. He took one hitched step, and there it was: numbness all down the leg. *Give it a minute.*

"I thought that was you, Paddy boy!" It was Richie DeNuccio, from Cardinal Hayes High School. Now Sergeant DeNuccio in his patrol blues.

"Holy shit, Richie, how are you?" Pat awkwardly braced against the bar and threw an arm around him.

"Fuckin' sixes and sevens, Paddy. Where you been?" Richie had a cop's squint that made you feel like a perp. He had a beer

gut, no surprise, and looked fat faced from his desk job but overall pretty hearty—not too far gone from the pulling guard for
Hayes's varsity. "Didn't you move to Texas?"

"That's the story the Feds have me telling."

"Jesus Christ. Cowboy Malone on the range."

"How's the finest?"

"Hanging in . . ." Richie guzzled a Löwenbräu and waved at his
lieutenant and a couple of patrolmen to rack the pool table and
start without him. "Hanging in by a thread. I'm about to retire.
They wanted to switch me out from operations downtown back up
to Webster Avenue. I said go fuck yourself. I know all the criminals in the North Bronx, and they ain't going nowhere. I'm done,
fully vested. And my pal Vinnie—you know Vincent Intondi? Went
to Bergen Catholic and used to crawl around this hole-in-the-
wall?—well, he's on Nixon's detail in Saddle River and thinks he
can get me in there."

Pat let go of the bar, his leg still unresponsive, and lurched toward Richie, who put a hand up to catch him.

"Whoa, cowboy. You all right?"

"Sorry, leg fell asleep."

Pat was half in the bag, and Richie gave himself a quick hook
and made like he was catching the next train to Fordham Road.

"You're a good man, Malone—like Gary Cooper heading out to
the territories. Reilly, what the fuck was the name of that movie?"

"*Sound of Music?*"

"No, asshole, the one where he's the hanging judge?"

"*Pride of the Yankees?*" The regulars howled at that one.

"Such a cocksucker, this one. Good to see you, Paddy. Take care."
And with that Richie turned tail to the front of the bar.

Pat faked a smile and tried to shake the sleep out of his left leg.

"Riles, while you're in the neighborhood."

"Gotcha, sir." And he lifted the Smirnoff out of the well again.

Jesus—Richie the cop is well past his twenty-and-out. Pat hobbled to the bathroom and took a piss and then returned to his dark corner. The bar was starting to fill in, and Pat realized his glow was gone. He needed to slow down, but that thought seemed to make him drink twice as fast. Pat hoisted himself back onto his stool as Reilly lit another cigarette and parked it in an ashtray below the bar. "You okay over there?"

"Just tired, stiff legs."

"Stretch it out, Malone. And let me know when to call the ambulance."

Pat poured the vodka into his thoughts. *Forget the ambulance, call the hearse.* It had started with a hitch in his step, which he chalked up to a childhood injury, a busted play at the stoop. That became tendinitis from jogging. Well, maybe it was arthritis, which his mother, Hannah, had. But in the past two years his left leg had gotten worse, not just stiff but aching, sometimes numb or tingly, and it didn't move right, always behind the rest of his stride, never catching up. Then, three months ago, Pat first heard the term "multiple sclerosis."

The day before his meetings at American, he had gone to his old doctor, Hugh MacNeill, another Hayes classmate, who had a good general practice going on East Eighty-Fourth balancing the sensitive humors of the upper class. It was to get a second—no, third—opinion on his MS diagnosis, but he wanted the no-bullshit version, which he got as soon as MacNeill saw his recent history.

"Pat, I could charge your insurance a bunch of money running tests to confirm it, but this Dr. Landis has done them, and these scans . . ." MacNeill sucked on his cheek. *Not good.* "Rather than poke and prod you to find out what we know, I think we should talk about how to deal with this."

Pat tried to let the bluntness of that pass by, but his chin sank into his chest. He got mad at himself for that: *What were you hoping for?*

"You have a chronic disease, and no one can tell how it will progress. The mystery here is that MS treats everyone different. You have to take care of yourself and get stronger. You're losing weight; you got to drink less, a glass or two of wine at most. You never smoked, right, Pat?"

"Never."

"That's great, no nicotine. And you're already doing PT with bikes and weights. Keep at that. You have to build up the muscles and the nerves that go with them. And there's diet—cut the caffeine, cut the fat, cut the salt. Vegetables, greens, more chicken and fish, less red meat."

"Already on that one, doc." Pat thought of all the flavorless, skinless chicken breasts his wife, Anne, had stacked in the freezer. *Miserable.*

"Attaboy. So, Pat, I'll be honest—this condition will frustrate you. Some days it will flare up and you will think you're a cripple. And then a few days where it goes away. You need to be ready for that. I'm not trying to give you false hope, but the right outlook and regimen can add years to your life. This is not great news, but it's not a death sentence. It's a fight against decline."

Pat stood again. The feeling in his leg was returning. He took five quick, hinky steps to the pay phone at the back of Sweeney's. Reilly in his absence freshened his drink. Pat plunked down on the bench and fished in his pockets for a quarter. Billy worked for Ma Bell, now called NYNEX, and Pat pulled the number for his Wall Street office from the blue pages.

"The homecoming of Patrick Francis Fitzgerald Aloysius Xavier Malone." Billy sounded ready to ring the bell, and Pat felt mortified. "What do you say, boyo?"

"Bill, I'm so sorry, but they're riding us tonight."

"Ah, that's awful. Where you calling from?"

"Uh, I'm at Sweeney's, a few of us stepped out for a beer before we head back into a night session."

"Okay . . ."

"Sorry, Bill, dinner's out. I'm stuck with a bunch of Chicken Littles here. The fare wars and all that—and we're running around like chickens without heads."

"That's a lot of chickens. You okay, Pat? You sound . . . tired."

Bill knew, and Pat knew he knew.

"I'll be fine, I'm tired of this crap with chickenshit management." He followed that one with a hollow laugh. "Sorry. But we'll prevail. Listen, I'll be back up soon enough, and we'll get together. I want to hear how Billy's doing. What's he playing these days?"

"He's fierce at field hockey. The Villanova coach came up to scout—"

"What the hell is field hockey?" *Too sharp, off-key. Get off the phone, Malone.*

"It's like hurling—remember when Uncle Aiden would play hurling up at Iona?"

"Ah, so sticks and drinking, then. Followed by beatings, no doubt."

"Not quite, cuz. How's Anne and Dan?"

"The queen and the prince live life without surcease, sir." *Christ, I sound unfunny.* "Listen, I'm sorry, give my love to Josephine."

"I will. Too bad you have to work. But, Pat, do me a favor." *Here it comes.* "Before you go back to the office. Get some food, maybe a coffee."

"I hear you, but I'm fine. Tab is closed."

"Fair enough. I'll talk to you soon."

"Bye, Billy boy."

Pat stumbled off the bench and took to his glass. The conversation had brought him back toward sober thoughts he didn't want. *One more with Reilly and kaput.* One more, if you didn't count doubles, which Pat didn't. He didn't need to be lurching around with Bill, who would ask, then get, the MS story, and ruin dinner feeling sorry for him and asking a bunch of fallback questions.

Where are you with Dan's college fund? What's in the bank, and what's left on the house? What is Anne going to do? Pat stared down at his lap and stretched each leg. They both felt fine now, limber even. Pat swizzled and swallowed. *What you can't feel can't hurt you, right?* Pat raised his head and peered at the liquor bottles in their rows. Reilly had one eye on him, the other on the cable channel for Yonkers. Harness racing and one cigarette after the next. *Riles is, what, five years younger than me?* Pat looked down the bar at the regulars. *Every single one on the downhill. Christ.*

Pat paid his tab and threw a ten-dollar tip on the bar. Reilly deserved more, but he had to keep a few bills for the hotel and the airport taxi. *Okay, time to depart.* He was on the first flight out of LGA tomorrow.

"Thanks, Riles, good to see you."

"My pleasure—one last cover of the ice?"

"Sure, but then I'm off to the Russian front."

Reilly poured him a half to a whole. "Can I get you a taxi, Pat?"

"I'm good—hotel is down the street." Pat shot the last drink down like medicine. "You're a good citizen."

His legs were cooperating for the moment, and Pat hit Third Avenue with slow, smooth steps. Pink and orange light snuck between the cracks of the midtown canyon, and Pat looked to his watch. *Seven thirty? Jesus, it's so late all of a sudden.* He kept steady toward Forty-Second Street, trying not to brood. *Why cancel on Bill? It would have been fine, could have hashed things out.* But he couldn't take that look of pity, and Bill would try to disguise it and be calm and sympathetic, and that was worse.

Annoyed, Pat threw up his hand in a gesture that looked like he was talking to himself. He half-realized this, if no one else did, and scanned the crowds rushing toward the trains. He developed a theory as he looked at face after face—*Everyone lost right there, just behind their eyes, everyone in their own world.*

Pat walked west on Forty-Second Street, his limp returning. *Left, right, shuffle, come on, left.* He returned to thinking about the passersby ducking through traffic. *All of them alone up here.*

This time he muttered "up here" aloud and raised a spastic left hand to his temple. *Everyone up here in their own heads, unaware of what's going on around them.* Pat looked to the chevron at the top of the Chrysler Building, an indifferent beacon, the office lights blazing below. *And I'm the only one who notices this. It's because I'm sick. I'm sick, but I can see it.* He picked up his pace as best he could and continued on. He needed to eat but kept thinking he was on to something. Some truth about people, the city, and himself. He reached the northeast corner of the public library and looked up at the marble columns streaked with soot. *Here's something they built. Something built by men who saw past the rush and left their mark. They were here and they laid their temples out in stone.*

Pat kept walking toward the lights of Times Square. *Eat and go to bed.* But he had other things in mind. One or two more drinks and the glow might return. Or maybe it would be better than the glow, it would be a clear nothing. He would see this dirty city for all it truly had become. He reached a corner and stood under the unnatural gleam of a giant Panasonic sign. *There's Lindy's—go in quick and get a sandwich. Nah, not hungry.* He continued west, unnerved by all the commuters, the swarm toward the Port Authority, that toilet bowl that flushed buses under the Hudson. Pat took a breath and kept moving. The old limestone buildings, the Times, the Paramount, entombed in neon billboards, the present soldered onto the molars of the past. It was stupid to go farther west— *All peep shows and muggers*—so he turned north and thought about HoJo or maybe Nedick's. But those places, this whole area, were infested with crazies. The traffic coursed down Broadway, like blood cells feeding a tumor, and he cut back onto Forty-Fourth Street. It was still there. Tir na Nog. A ridiculous run-down dive, like a splinter stuck between office towers. Pat couldn't remember whom he used to meet there, but what bar in midtown didn't cast a dim recollection now?

Tir na Nog—*It might have been Hannegan's back then*—was near empty, sunk in uremic light. Pat almost backed out but was soon on a stool facing bottles in front of a mirror. On the TV the local weather guy was pointing to a satellite shot of a tropical depression forming southeast of the Dominican Republic. It was forecast to become the fastest-moving hurricane since the Yankee Clipper in 1938. Pat wanted a Bushmills, but the bartender looked like a Fenian, so he ordered a Tullamore, and drank a toast to the storms of his youth.

○ ○ ○

"HOLD IT STEADY."

Pat's mother, Hannah, chewed on two box nails while trying to hammer the one between her fingers and thumb. Galloping past the Jersey shore, the storm was still south of the Bronx and the city, and they were boarding up the windows to the Malone grocery on the corner of 135th Street and Willis Avenue. Each swing of the hammer summoned Hannah's anger and annoyance. Pat's father had been missing since ten in the morning. "Off to the bank" was the excuse, but the bank, the whole neighborhood, was now shuttered, with no sign of Jack.

One last drive of the nail and Pat let go of the board now fastened in place. He watched his mother tap each nail for insurance.

"All right, Paddy boy—if we blow away, we tried." A wild, raw breeze tunneled down Willis Avenue. The skies were slate gray and wind picked. The pressure was dropping and the air felt heavy, almost tropical. "Let's board the door and we're done."

"Is the hurricane gonna break the windows?"

"I don't think so, love. I'm more worried about after the storm.

People go nuts, Paddy, for no reason. And the police will have their hands full." Hannah had said enough to scare the child and stepped back. "Now, don't worry, nothing bad's gonna happen. Just a little protection from something blowing in and to keep the crazies moving past."

They boarded the glass in the door, and Pat followed his mother back inside the grocery. She threw the dead bolt, but Jack had a key. They gathered candles and Tommy, the guard cat, who had already hunkered down behind the baking soda and was in no mood to be disturbed. He scratched and hissed at Hannah, but she ignored this and carried him up the stairwell.

"Knock it off, Tom-cat. Paddy, check the back door."

Pat had done so twice, and he did again. He peered through the beveled glass above the knob and worried about the small chicken coop in the back. His mother had three hens, Aoife, Oona, and Grainne, and when last he checked they appeared content to sleep through the storm. The wind hollered at the back door, and Pat ran up the stairs to the hallway. He knew his way through the darkness to the apartment door. The Malones lived in a railroad flat above the grocery. One Seventy-Three Willis Avenue had been built after the Tenement Acts, but that didn't stop the four-story walk-up from falling down around them. Hannah was filling pitchers of water from the tub. Their faucets weren't on a pump— his father, Jack, had yelled at her about this—but she hoarded water all the same.

"All right, Paddy, all we're missing is this storm." Hannah stacked the pitchers on the ledge by the tub and poked her head toward the window by the fire escape. "Maybe it will jog."

"Where's Dad?"

"The Lord loves every last-minute fool." Hannah shook her head, arguing this point with herself. "He'll be here. A little late to help, but don't worry. He'll be here before the bad stuff passes through."

Pat's bedroom lay off a foul-smelling air shaft hidden behind a slim, smeared window. He checked his contraband—comics, candles, and caramels—and lay down on his bed listening to the wind whistle overhead. Hannah ferried back and forth, muttering prayers and curses, and finally retreated to the kitchen to start dinner. *Better to light the gas now and boil everything. Before it gets bad. And before this man shows up in God knows what state of lunacy.*

An uneasy hour passed, and the apartment darkened as the long, swift bands of the storm swiped at the city. Here it came now, and with it, coughing on the landing and a turn of the key. Jack Malone barged in.

"Hannah? Paddy? Where is everyone?" The door creaked open a second time. "Katie, bar the door, for Christ's sake. This wind. Family, we have company."

Hannah and Pat appeared in the hallway, and there was Jack, stooped, wheezing, with a sailor of the British navy standing behind him.

"There they are. Hannah, this is Tom Donovan. Paddy, come meet your long-lost cousin. His ship is in, and I found him as they were closing down Feely's for this blow." Jack still hadn't caught his breath as he missed the hook with his cap. "Come in, come in. Before we gust away. Nowhere to go during this feckin storm."

The two of them wafted into the living room on fumes of booze and tobacco ash. Hannah kept her distance and glared from down the dark hallway.

"Pat, shake Petty Officer Donovan's hand. He's in His Majesty's Navy. Family from Cork, like us—what ship did you say you were on?"

"The *Halcyon*." Donovan grabbed Pat's hand with his big clammy palm and lurched toward him. He was a sailor all right. Blue jean collar, bell-bottoms tucked into once-white wool socks, and the dark trimmed cap. Just like on a box of Cracker Jacks, except his cheeks were more red with booze than windburn from the North Atlantic. "Hey, little man, whaddya say? You a Yankees fan?"

"Dodgers."

Donovan, the son of a Liverpool Corkman, had clearly run through all his American baseball knowledge and screwed up his face. "Dodgers? What the hell is that, Jackie?"

"Ah, don't worry about the boy. He's a real con artist. Come sit and take it off." They parked on ends of the couch as the wind shook the windows. "This storm ain't so bad. Wouldn't want to be in City Island right now. Tide coming in high." Jack started feeling his pockets for his smokes and something else. He sprang back up. "It'll jog in a couple of hours. But they closed down the El, and our man here—did I tell ya his family is from Carrigaline?—can't get back to the city. Now, my old man worked for the Donovans, who did the pottery, you know, the eggcups with those little shamrocks on 'em, my mother loved those eggcups from Carrigaline. Hannah, do we still have those eggcups? I also need a couple of jars."

"Jack, calm down and sit down," Hannah yelled from the kitchen.

"Ah, this nervous woman, Tommy, I tell ya, no fun. My old man worked with a Frankie Donovan." He turned toward Pat with his crooked drinking smile. "And now that's Tommy's grand-uncle. How's that for a small world? Practically kin."

Jack pulled a bottle of Seagram's from the pocket of his work pants and slipped into the kitchen, leaving Pat to stare at the blood-eyed not-so-able seaman on the couch, who sat there in a bloated stupor, staring back. Hannah hissed threats at Jack in the kitchen, and thirty seconds later, Jack yelled, "Enough!" and stalked back into the living room. He went over to the sideboard and brought out two Carrigaline eggcups, into which he poured shots of whiskey.

Jack coughed and cleared his chest, then lifted his eggcup to Tommy's. "May the devil never make a ladder of your backbone."

Jack quaffed it and then fell into the grooves of his green leather wingback, his eyes unfocused and rolled up toward the rattling of rain at the windows.

"This hurricane ain't much. Over before they realize you're gone, Tom."

"No worries." Donovan belched. "I'm taking my leave. They won't miss me." Pat didn't quite know what to make of that and wondered what the punishment was for desertion. *Firing squad?* He was not opposed.

"Here's one more. Mud in your eye." Jack slapped the eggcup on the end table like he was betting the house with it. "I'll tell you, when I was over there they never had a good count of us. They kept better track of the bullets than the boys. For damn sure." Jack was about to revisit some dark trenches of memory as Seaman Donovan belted another eggcup of Seagram's and stroked his throat as it went down. He was shifting his boots on the floor, not sure what to make of this storm or his port in it, when suddenly the couch poked him hard and sharp in his ass. The sailor jumped up.

"Ah, sorry, mate, the damn cat. His name is Tommy too. Hannah, why didn't you leave this foul beast locked in the store?" As Donovan rubbed his rear end, Jack stuck his head down at his feet to take a look, then laughed like a devil who had planned it all along. "Pat, son, grab the feckin cat out from under there."

Pat squeezed by the sailor, who almost fell into the coffee table. Ignoring all of this, Hannah came into the room, took up the eggcups and replaced them with mule mugs, and returned to the kitchen entirely fed up. Pat crouched down and found Tommy jammed under the coils of the couch, hissing, ears pinned back. He looked up at his father, who was wheezing with laughter.

"He won't come out."

"It's not up to him, now, is it?" Jack poured another round in the mugs. "Come on, Pat, take him by his scruff and yank him out of there."

The rain pelted the windows like shrapnel. Pat took another look at Tommy the cat and with eye contact tried to make it clear it was him and he meant no harm. Pat reached in, and that's when Tommy bit him.

It was no warning bite—with the storm, his dislocation, and the dark boots of the drunk stranger, the cat was terrified. His fang sank right into Pat's middle finger. Pat twitched, and then Tommy grabbed with his claw and brought the boy's hand closer. Before pain could even bloom across the boy's face, the cat had finished his attack and bolted along the baseboard. Pat yelped in shock and pulled his hand back out, his wrist raked and scratched, his finger pulsing with dark blood.

"Goddamn it." Jack threw back his whiskey and stood, inspecting his son's finger. "Now what have you done, Pat? Jesus. He mangled ya good. Go put it under the sink."

Hannah dashed into the room. "For the love of God . . ."

Pat stood there, his finger shaking and dripping with blood. He wasn't going to cry. The sailor took his arm and raised it. "Keep it above your heart," he said in an annoyed, flat voice.

"That's it! I'm getting rid of that fuckin' cat. It's gone mad."

"Stop it, Jack." Hannah brought a tea towel to Pat's finger, and they headed toward the bathroom. "Your horseshit antics caused this."

These words set off the dark fury in the man, and Jack charged into the bedroom, retrieving a pillowcase. Jack came back down the hallway, growling: "Where is it? I'm gonna drown him in the fuckin' river."

Through tear-blurred eyes, Pat witnessed this from the bathroom. "No, Da. It was my fault," he cried weakly, and Hannah held him. The wind wailed.

"Tom, hold the bag while I get this piece-of-shit cat. Where is it?"

The sailor held open the pillowcase as he slumped all fluthered back down on the couch. "Take it easy, Jackie."

"Where is it?" And then Jack Malone spied the tail behind the radiator. He snatched Tommy by his back legs and into the pillowcase he went, tufts of calico swirling across the living room. Hannah ran cold water over Pat's cut. It was a small but deep puncture, and it began to pulse with pain. Taking the pillowcase back from Donovan, Jack started on a coughing fit that ended with a long gulp of whiskey straight from the bottle. He was cruelly calm. "Once a cat bites, it can't be trusted. It's gone mad." He looked down as the cat clenched and clawed from inside the pillowcase. "Let's go."

"In the middle of this?" Donovan slurred. "Are you gone in the head?"

Hannah reached into the cabinet for the iodine. Pat could only hear the helpless, terrified Tommy growling from the other room. "It's not your fault, Paddy," his mother whispered.

"Fine, you're fuckin' useless too." Jack hacked hard and swallowed his sputum, his anger beyond the pale. "Fuckin' cat does fuck-all. Rat shit strewn all over the fuckin' store."

Jack Malone lurched to the door with Tommy the cat howling for his life. Down and out of the building he went. Through gale-force winds Jack reeled his way toward the Willis Avenue Bridge to drown the animal in the boiling brown chop of the Harlem River.

Hannah locked Pat and herself in the bathroom, where they wept with the rain. The deserter Donovan passed out on the couch. Hannah found herself between despair and desperation—half wishing that her brutal husband would throw himself off the bridge too. Paddy sat on the toilet as the iodine burned into his cut. He looked up at his mother, heartbroken, washing all the blood away.

"Paddy, what in Christ's name are we going to do? He's sick. He's sick, and I don't know what to do."

○ ○ ○

PAT SHOOK HIS HEAD AS HE FINISHED HIS SECOND WHISKEY. AT THIS point he was maintaining a dull, drunken hum. *Who was it who said the only relief from mental anguish is physical pain? Not true at all.* Pat knew the two compounded. Say what else, but Pat as an actuary understood a lot of the likelihoods of the universe. Could there be surprises? Flukes? *Sure.* He scanned a *Daily News* sitting on the stool next to him. *Some senator running for president plagiarized in law school. No one cares. It's like that story in the Dallas papers where the minister tried to kill his wife. Strangled her in the driveway. He'll get away with it. The senator too.* But over the long run, the anomalies flattened and vanished. Follow the arrow of time, and every variable recedes to its limit—once assets become liabilities. Pat ordered a fresh—*Let's call it third and final*—whiskey and studied it. All the unseen motion in that glass, and over time the ice melts, the glass breaks, the bar rots, the building's mortar cracks, the street sheared by the schist of the island, and it all folds back into the dark, unbearable heat of a planet that winks out after its star decays.

Pat was comfortable around numbers and probabilities, having learned them early on the ledgers of his father's corner grocery. During the Depression and then the war, everyone in St. Jerome's parish was on the pad until payday. Even then bookkeeping was a form of risk assessment—*Mrs. Reeves owes $6.35, but Mr. Reeves was at the door of Feely's bar, so good luck with that.* During tough times, Pat learned that most people pay, are honest and proud, and you spent 90 percent of your time chasing the other 10 percent who are not.

His father, Jack, was a Corkman who fought in World War I to gain citizenship. He enlisted with the Fighting Sixty-Ninth, heralded by Joyce Kilmer and made famous by Jimmy Cagney. Gassed badly at Lunéville, John Malone compounded his terrible respiration with smoking, and then drank to overcome the wheezing. He died when Pat was fourteen, leaving him and his mother with the store and little else. Hannah sent Pat to Cardinal Hayes, where he aced the math exams under the Christian Brothers, which led to a scholarship from Fordham. He majored in statistics, which his uncle Dermot, a sandhog, counseled was a ticket for creating bullshit rather than shoveling it.

After Hannah sold the grocery, Pat held more hard-labor jobs in high school and college than he cared to remember. But with that, along with the veteran pension, they got by. He graduated from Rose Hill and landed an entry-level spot in payroll for American Airlines. Then years of night school, again at Fordham, for actuarial science and a JD. He worked his way up the back office, married Anne, moved them to Fordham Hill, and got Hannah out of the South Bronx and into a postwar on Kappock Street in Riverdale. She died of a coronary the winter before Anne became pregnant with Dan.

Pat looked up at the bar mirror and rubbed the stubble on his cheek, flushed from this new stint of drinking. *At the end of the day,* Pat believed, *the average man, the best he can do is not be a burden.* He had a disease, like many, and he had his vices, yes, but an hour or two at the bar was not going to upset the mortality tables of the AMR Corporation.

Okay, one more.

"You all right there, buddy?"

"What now?" Pat snapped out of his reverie.

"You okay? You're kind of hunched over there mumbling to yourself."

"Sorry, bad day."

"No problem, but I think we're done here."

Pat had a thought to argue and then groped for his wallet. "That's fine. Sorry."

"Just disturbing the peace a little."

"Blessed are the peacemakers, for theirs is the kingdom of heaven."

"Excuse me?"

Pat blinked—*Besides entropy, that's the answer, right?* "Nothing. Just the second coming. That would be the only other way this ends."

The bartender was having none of it. "Okay, chief. Time to go."

"I'm going." Pat stood up with this resolute courage that it all made sense now. "My father—"

"All right, professor, out of here . . ." The bartender started to come around the side of the bar.

"I'm leaving. Take it easy. Okay, wait."

But a meaty paw was already locked on his arm above the elbow. Out of dark habit, Pat reached for his drink—*Still a couple good belts left in that glass*—but he was pulled away from it, and the glass went crashing to the floor. The other patrons went silent and watched. A bit of slow motion and blur followed as Pat was returned to Forty-Fourth Street.

"Did I pay you?" he asked, upset at himself.

"You did. Now go home, chief."

"Did I tip you?"

"Sure you did." And the bartender disappeared back through the door.

"See you in the funny papers." *That's that.* Pat mimed the raising of a fedora and stumbled back toward Times Square. *Fine then, time to stop drinking. Time to head to the Marriott for a few hours of shut-eye before the flight back.* He looked down at his Timex. *Eleven twenty-five!* He'd forgotten to call Anne. *Shit. Where did the time go? Time indefinite. Have a disease. A chronic sclerosis of the body. Have to be up soon. Such an idiot. Sleep it off on the plane. Then shave and a coffee and ready for the lion's den.*

Pat walked as straight a line as possible across Times Square. With a half-lidded eye he registered the statue of Father Duffy, the chaplain to his father's regiment in World War I. All Jack Malone would ever say: *The hero priest. Busy converting the heathens before the army buried them. A good man for the cloth. He kept up hope when there should have been none.*

Pat then swiveled around to give his regards to George Cohan. So here Pat was, at the crossroads—the pulsing, sclerotic heart of the city. And here were these two statues, monuments to his father's generation. The priest and the patsy, fitting tributes to the Irish American. *Sure, boyo, we likes to fight and pray and warble out a tune for our spuds.* Pat felt sick—hungry but too tired, too nauseous, to eat. *This is sloppy and stupid, just like fucking Jack Malone. Forget him, forget all your troubles come on get happy. Get ready for the judgment day. Calm down, stop spinning. Remember Father Arnall at Hayes: "Cease to be whirled about." Marcus Aurelius. Don't puke. Reel it in. Don't get sick.*

And so, utterly exhausted, Pat crossed Broadway muttering to himself, "My mother thanks you, my father thanks you, and I thank you." He reached the revolving door for the Marriott, poured himself into his hotel bed, arose before dawn still drunk, grabbed a fetid taxi, and hurtled toward the dark wheel of the terminal at LGA.

Broken, battered, and headed back toward Dallas, now home.

ANNE MALONE LOOKED UP FROM HER COPY OF *THE THORN BIRDS* AS Courtney McDermott coughed in her sleep; stirred, then settled; and returned to slow, uneasy snoring. Sitting beside her in the girl's bedroom, Anne studied Courtney for a brief moment—her blond hair combed and curled like out of a fairy tale. Outside the window, a mockingbird trilled and flitted along the branches of a mimosa tree. It was late afternoon, and Courtney's cheek, then her forehead, twitched. She was deep in dreams.

Anne was part of a rotation of St. Rita's mothers who were helping the McDermott family care for their daughter. Courtney should have started college that fall, but in her senior year at Ursuline she had gone to Padre Island for spring break with her girlfriends. How much drinking or drugs were involved was unclear, but on the ride back to Dallas Courtney was at the wheel. Highway 77 out of Harlingen. No one wearing seat belts. The two other girls in the car—one in the passenger seat and one in the back—were killed on impact when the car swerved into the guardrail. Courtney was thrown from the car and hit her head on the ground. The paramedics brought her back, but she had already lain on the road losing blood and oxygen to her brain for seventeen minutes. That was over six months ago. She was now in a coma, and everyone was hoping against hope for Courtney to wake up.

Anne mouthed a quick Hail Mary and returned to Father Ralph de Bricassart talking Meggie through her first period.

"You're only doing what all women do, Meggie. Once a month for several days you'll pass blood . . . Do you know what 'mature' means?"

"Of course, Father! I read! It means grown up."

Meggie *is no Jane Eyre,* Anne thought, *but with these men in her life . . .*

"The bleeding is a part of the cycle of procreation. In the days before the Fall, it is said Eve didn't menstruate . . . But when Adam and Eve fell, God punished the woman more than He did the man, because it was really her fault they fell."

Anne spat a muted "bleh." She liked the wry humor of Andrew Greeley better. Anne looked up from the book and watched the Saturday afternoon light ease across the far wall and dapple down the girl's vanity. The mockingbird had left the brown pods of the mimosa, and the room was silent. Anne stood and moved closer toward Courtney's bed. Anne closed her eyes and listened to the girl breathe. *Wake up, dear. I'm praying for you.* When she opened her eyes, she half expected Courtney to open hers; it almost felt as if the poor girl had heard her. That there was an answer to her prayers.

o o o

A HALF HOUR LATER, COURTNEY'S MOTHER, VERA, RETURNED FROM shopping and chauffeuring her youngest, Brian, to soccer, and her middle, Jessica, to dance team. Anne noticed Vera had a tough time coming into the bedroom right away, and so she kissed Courtney on her forehead and came down the hall to the kitchen. Like anyone stuck in the full undertow of grief, Vera was exhausted. Anne felt awful for her, and from a cruel, disconsolate part of her mind she heard: *You can't let a girl run off like that, she was too young.* She wasn't trying to think like that, but she couldn't help herself. Now she stood there listening to Vera go on about the doctors and what her husband, Raymond, thought, and the whole time feeling worse and worse for being judgmental. *Christ, how as a parent could you forgive yourself?* But she smiled and hugged Vera, and they walked out of the house together to the curb and Anne's car, and smiled and hugged again. Vera was lost in it, and in a different way, so was Anne. *How can anyone handle any of this?* She was relieved to close the silver door to her Mercury Zephyr but felt a terrible despair for what was ostensibly a good deed. *Mysterious ways*, Anne mulled, and then realized that wasn't even a line from the Bible. She needed to clear her head. It was a quarter to five, and she was just down the street from St. Monica's. If she hurried, she could make evening Mass.

○ ○ ○

St. Monica's had a much prettier church than the Malones' parish, St. Rita's, which had the feel of a converted gym. St. Monica's was a version of Texas midcentury modern that actually worked: built in the round with white plaster archways and floor-to-ceiling stained glass and a rose window raised to an oculus above a mosaic altar tessellated with a pale pink Ascension. A minute before five, Anne settled into a back pew on the far left of the altar near the organ and knelt to pray.

Growing up in Sts. Peter and Paul Parish in the South Bronx, Anne had her faith inculcated in the normal severe and thetic manner. And while bridled by uncertainty—and a suspicion she was overlooked and underestimated—she became a novice with the Sisters of Charity after graduating from Cathedral High School. Her mother, Mary, was pleased and proud, but her father, Billy Mulligan, wanting grandsons, brooded with dissent.

Anne frowned as she saw Father Ronald B. Timmerman pacing in the narthex. A diocesan priest in his late thirties, Timmerman was now pastor for Monica's. She had heard him speak before to a volunteer retreat group at Montserrat up near Lake Dallas, and was left unimpressed. *He was certainly sure of himself,* Anne thought. He also drove a black Corvette. *Which is wrong for all sorts of reasons, even if he didn't take a vow of poverty.* He had a holier-than-thou routine she objected to—prostrating before the cross, creepily groping the Gospel with his eyes closed and kissing it, his long . . . solemn . . . pauses . . . between . . . prayers. He was overly pious—*Like some sort of Pharisee.*

At Cathedral, Anne had been a star student, and her mentor, Sister Elizabeth, had not-so-subtly pushed her into vocation. During discernment Anne had doubts but was told all do, that was normal, and so she sheared her long brown hair and took the habit. The convent was on the campus of Mount St. Vincent's, and the order would send her to college to become a teacher. Those classes were the only inflection of the twentieth century on her daily life. The residence required upkeep, endless chores. Seniority bullied, and the novices were quite literally indentured. Mopping and waxing the dark hallways, weeding the prayer garden, polishing the shrines to Our Lady and Elizabeth Seton, and of course long afternoons peeling, chopping, mixing, boiling, stewing, and serving meals after vespers. She was bone-tired, with little time for prayer or study, and it was unclear how any of this brought her closer to God. She didn't mind the discipline, but there was a devious architecture of rules designed just to catch mistakes, to bludgeon the ego before the order, and what did that have to do with the life of Mary?

Timmerman appeared on the altar, and the Mass began. He sped through the opening prayers and through the Liturgy of the Word, the gospel from Matthew 21:

"A man had two sons. He went and said to the first, 'My
boy, go and work in the vineyard today.'

"He answered, 'I will not go,' but afterwards thought better of it and went.

"The man then went and said the same thing to the second, who answered, 'Certainly, sir,' but did not go.

"Which of the two did the father's will?" They said, "The
first." Jesus said to them, "In truth I tell you, tax collectors
and prostitutes are making their way into the kingdom of
God before you."

This is the word of the Lord.

The homily that followed confirmed all of Anne's suspicions.
This priest is running for messiah of North Dallas. As he began, Timmerman gripped the lectern and stuck up his chin, peering in-
tently over the sparse attendance. *So theatric, like Charlton Heston
from the set of Mount Sinai.*

"When I was in seminary, we studied this passage with an old
priest, Father Fontenot, who had spent many years of his life at a
parish called St. Maurice's near Storyville, the famous red-light
ward of New Orleans. Father Fontenot had endless St. Mo stories
from his years there. His faithful were the gamblers, the loan
sharks, the bums, the druggies, the prostitutes, and their pimps—
all of these folks would show up for his evening Mass at St.
Maurice's.

"And Father Fontenot thought nothing of it: because as the
Gospel tells us Jesus ministered most to the sinners in this world.
And so what this parable touches on, and what Father Fontenot
saw in real life, is that good-intentioned hypocrisy of those who
practice faith as a get-out-of-jail-free card for their sins. A lot of
Father Fontenot's stories involved Nellie Flower, an infamous
madam of her day. Nellie knew and liked the young Father

Fontenot, and she would insist that all of her girls go to him once a week . . . for confession."

Timmerman cocked an eyebrow and looked out at the first set of pews in front of him. A couple chuckles filled his pause. With this mild encouragement, he went forth.

"Now, Father Fontenot was not a prurient man who got into details, but let's just say he became quite familiar with how precisely these women tabulated their sins."

A few more laughs—and Timmerman grinned. Anne was unamused. *This is what he thinks of us: sinners counting sins.*

"And in the Gospel there are many women of ill repute that Jesus tries to save. These women come to Him, but our Lord does not judge them. Instead He offers a new covenant with God based on forgiveness."

Anne bit her upper lip. *And women are known for only one thing, huh, Father?*

"And what Jesus is careful to remind us about is that there is good in people of all stations, even the women of the oldest profession. And we as a Christian society believe in this idea. Think about all the movies that feature the hooker with the heart of gold. Take for instance *Gone With the Wind*—my mother's favorite novel. There's the character of Belle Watling, who runs the brothel and covers for Rhett when he is accused of killing the Yankee soldiers. She saves his life with her alibi, but the scandalized women of Atlanta won't speak to her."

Oh yes, if only this Church treated women like it were the nineteenth century . . .

"And whether it's Atlanta during the Civil War or in Judea two thousand years ago or a house of ill repute on Rampart Street, there are women, sinners though they are, who show faith and are more likely than the second son of the vineyard owner to enter into the kingdom of heaven . . ."

At this point Anne had tuned out, and she stared down at the cover of the missalette, which depicted the Deposition, Jesus's descent from the cross and lamentation. It was by an old Italian master, and Anne counted the three Marys there—the Mother of God, Mary Salome, and Mary Magdalene. Anne sucked on her cheek. *Even here. When all the men are gone, when a mother's son is dead and deserted. Even here they have to make their point: don't forget what women really are.*

Timmerman droned on for a few more minutes, and when he was finished, he returned to his chair, where he sat for another unnecessarily long pause. *What in God's name is he meditating about now?* Anne wondered. Finally Timmerman stood up, the organ bellowed, the basket came, and then the gifts. Anne left right after communion, her obligation fulfilled.

○ ○ ○

Taking Merrell Road, Anne drove home, past the Episcopal School of Dallas and then winding down Rosser, shooting across six lanes at Royal, past the field of high-tension power lines, to the turn at Northaven Park. Her thoughts spiraled back again to her novitiate, her frustrations and loneliness. She had written to Sister Elizabeth, who tried to root her on: life as a bride of Christ only got better; her faith would awaken, deepen.

And then prayers were answered and Anne was assigned to Father Sacramoni's daily Mass. Vincent Sacramoni had been born in Jersey City and taken his orders with the Christian Brothers at De La Salle. He was a handsome man in his thirties, with a shock of early gray hair; his summers pastoring on the Jersey shore had kept him tan and healthy. He was also chaplain to all the teams at Manhattan College and was often seen on the quad trying to corral some boys into following him to the basketball courts.

Anne obeyed the speak-only-when-spoken-to order, but Father

Sacramoni had plenty to say while getting ready for Mass. They argued Yankees/Dodgers and Harriman/Stevenson in equal measure, and each afternoon, Anne found herself rushing to chapel earlier, preparing for Mass quicker, and leaving as much time as possible in that cramped sacristy for this chatty priest. Father Sacramoni heard confession for all the sisters at Mount St. Vincent's. He could recognize the sound of Anne's voice through the screen, so she stuck to a rehearsed list of venial sins about concentrating on prayer and heeding the sisters. Father Sacramoni would chuckle slightly and then ask in his clipped, rhotic accent: "Is that all, dear? If so, I'll put you up for sainthood."

"That's all I can think of, Father."

"No impure thoughts?" he asked casually. Anne, kneeling, leaned back in the confessional.

"I'm sure I've had some, Father, but to recall them . . ."

"You're right, Anne, don't dwell there. For penance I want you to . . ."

And at that brief suggestion, the impure thoughts came and Anne couldn't help but dwell there.

On Palm Sunday, she sensed Father Sacramoni's move coming when she was turned around in that dark, cool sacristy. He was supposed to be getting dressed, but there was his hand on her back, the other at her hip.

"Listen," he said softly.

Anne went blank. She moved away from him, but not so fast. A nervous smile became a kiss.

o o o

THE SOCCER FIELDS WERE EMPTY AS ANNE DROVE OVER THE DRAIN-age creek that connected this neighborhood with her own. Almost six thirty, and she'd be walking in on two hungry Malones. She sped down Cox Lane, determined not to stop at Tom Thumb for dinner. *Something quick. Hot dogs for Dan and what for Pat?* Pulling onto Crown Shore, she was overcome with déjà vu. Whether it was Timmerman's droning hocus-pocus or the repeated pattern of ranch houses, Anne wasn't sure, but she came up the driveway in a shimmer of recall. *This is your house, now turn off the car.* So very familiar, like every thought and movement prescribed. *This is where you are the mother and the wife. And that's all that you have to say for yourself. That's not going to change.* She got out of the car. *Even if you got a new house, you would still just be in a driveway somewhere, looking at a house that is yours and not yours. You don't own this. Pat's name is on the mortgage.*

And then the déjà vu, bland as it was, slipped away. She went inside. *My house. My living room. My dining room, where I put down my purse and my keys.* She looked around. *My cabinet, my hutch, my glassware.* It was like her ruminations were trying to reconcile how the past had brought her here, and the more she thought about these things, the more alien she felt. It all seemed so unnecessary now. Just the accretion of a thousand pieces of crap that didn't matter but nonetheless clung to Anne's static ball of unresolvable self-doubt, worry, and regret. *Forget it. Stop. Stop rehashing it.*

She couldn't help but recall then the stern, beady expression on the face of her mother superior, Sister Angeline, when Anne came clean about Father Sacramoni. In the past year, the community had lost one novice to pregnancy, another for breaking curfew, smoking grass, and Lord knew what other kinds of carrying on. Sister Angeline was not about to lose a third. She had to come down hard. So she nodded impatiently and stretched her fat fingers across the desk as Anne tried to couch things in such a way that no one would get upset or hurt.

"Father Sacramoni is a handsome man, is he not?" Sister Angeline interrupted.

Anne took a panicked breath.

"And you are attracted to Father Sacramoni, correct?"

"No, Mother Superior, it's not—"

"But you like working in that sacristy, no?"

"I serve as best I can."

"And you have had thoughts of him like that, have you not?"

Anne couldn't even conceive of this reaction. She shook her head frantically, but lying about it didn't matter.

"You must conduct yourself as a sister of this order at all times. Do not smile and flirt. Do not ask him questions or talk more than necessary. Never turn your back to him. Don't you see? All of these things are a way of giving him permission. You can't lead him on. And you must cleanse yourself of thoughts about him. Is that clear?"

"*He* touched *me*. I didn't—"

Sister Angeline opened a drawer and pulled out a piece of brown leather.

"You have to be mindful, Anne, that the body is a corruption of the spirit. That you haven't developed control over your body in a way that will not bring notice to it." She stood menacingly. "It's good that you came to me this early."

"Sister Angeline—"

"We have to control ourselves. Otherwise we abandon the Lord, and this"—she pointed at her own buxomness and paunch—"will do the work of sin. Please kneel before the desk." She raised her hand, coiling one end of the leather strop around her palm. With tears streaming down, Anne could think of nothing to say.

o o o

ANNE GATHERED THE MAIL THAT HAD BEEN PITCHED THROUGH THE slot in the front door. Below the normal crap and coupons, there was a letter from the city addressed to Ann Malone. *My name misspelled, the other not really my name.* It was a summons.

Jury duty. *Christic.*

"Moooooooom . . ."

No hello, no how are you. Just Dan doll eyed in front of the computer in his room yelling out.

"What's for dinner?"

The way Dan whined the question, Anne refused to reply.

Jury duty. I hope it's for some defeated housewife who turned on her unfeeling husband and child.

And with that sad joke of a thought, the déjà vu kicked in once more. As she checked the pantry for hot dog buns, the whole pattern was set in motion again—the sound of the TV from the den, Pat's shake of the ice in his glass, and Anne's immediate thought: how long had he been at that, drinking alone? That worry followed by the next, and it was overwhelming, and she couldn't step out of it.

Anne put on a pot of water, and as she waited for the water to boil, she relived that long gray bus ride back to the South Bronx. Her mother and Sister Elizabeth were in the parlor, drinking tea, waiting for her. Anne had little to say. She didn't mention Father Sacramoni or Sister Angeline.

"What's there to be confused about?" her mother scolded.

"Give it time, dear. It isn't how we stumble, it's how we regain the path," Sister Elizabeth offered.

She couldn't face their disappointment and escaped to the bedroom she shared with her sister Cathy. She removed her habit, dropped onto the bed, and prayed for forgiveness. In the evening, her father came home, his work boots clomping down the hall.

"Annie dearest, what are we gonna—"

"I'm sorry, Da."

"There's no shame in it." He sat at the end of the bed.

"They made me hate it all. God, Mass—"

"Don't blaspheme, now."

"I'm so tired."

"To hell with them, Anne girl." And there was her father's wry smile.

In the Irish immigrant tradition, they ate meat and potatoes and no one spoke about it. Days became weeks, and Anne's mother shrugged off her discontent. Anne applied to Fordham for the fall. She studied literature, the poems of Herbert and Hopkins her favorites. She met Pat Malone on a blind date during the '66 transit strike. They cruised out to City Island for crab boil. She made the first move that night. They married after graduation. Anne earned her teaching license and had her baptism by fire at Teddy Roosevelt High School on East Fordham Road. The young Mrs. Malone became a fine teacher. Sister Elizabeth referred her to job after job teaching in the parochial schools, sometimes for better money than she was making under Shanker's new deal, but she balked and demurred. When Pat finished law school, she went on to Hunter for a master's in counseling. Anne never stopped going to church, that was a clear sin, but her faith wandered. She studied Freud and Jung, Schopenhauer and Nietzsche. Each poked at the veil in search of something, and the discovery was what she relished about being a teacher, even if it was with a class of clownish kids. The rules of grammar might never take, but her kids would occasionally express a truth or two in shambolic proto-essays about a brother serving in Indochina, an *abuela* in the hills outside San Juan. She had to be strict, in a constant holler, and was set back by simple tasks like collecting textbooks or getting names onto papers. But each year she battled and attained small victories of concentration. By graduation, her kids returned the favor with quarts of perfume and hilarious costume jewelry bought at Alexander's. The wounds of Sister Angeline slowly scarred over, and Anne applied for the PhD program in psychology at Fordham. She scored well on Miller Analogies (catharsis : emotion :: absolution : guilt) and was accepted.

Anne was brought out of her reverie by the sound of Dan

tapping away at the computer keyboard, his game a bunch of annoying digital chirps. The pot was failing to boil. She made herself a vodka cran before starting on the rest of the dinner.

○ ○ ○

LATER THAT NIGHT, ONE VODKA CRAN HAD BECOME THREE. DAN WENT to bed shortly after nine, and Pat had farted his way to the back room to watch the Saturday evening movie. Anne dug around in the clandestine recesses of her purse and found a crumpled pack of Benson & Hedges. She had pretty much quit smoking, and during the week, when everything was on a timetable, she was fine. But there was something about the unbounded arc of the weekend that led to nic fits.

Anne's first semester at Fordham as a doctoral candidate was daunting. Psychology being taught at a Catholic university was heretical to begin with, and Anne was well aware of the irony that in another century the Jebbies would have tried her as a witch. She was also the only woman in the program, but it was run by a younger lay faculty and very much up to speed. In the fall of 1968, as the teachers' strike dragged on, she enrolled in "A History of Behaviors."

That's when Anne first noticed Ronan Carroll. Dark Norman Irish features and an unruly brown beard and brown eyes. He wore a tweed jacket and an unironed oxford that left little doubt he was a bachelor. As the professor dragged them through trauma and apoplexy, repression and phobia, Carroll scribbled on long legal pads, apparently writing down everything said verbatim. At the hour break, they met at the coffee machine.

Carroll rummaged for change. "Why do I bother? It's like they're pumping the East River through this thing." Anne smiled and said nothing.

A week later, they exited Dealy Hall together. Carroll leaned in with a stage whisper. "Is it me or did the good Professor Robbins develop a facial tic while describing what causes them?"

"I saw that." Anne pointed down at his notepad. "You don't miss much."

"Shorthand. I learned it in college when I was going to be the next Jimmy Breslin."

"You wrote for the newspaper?"

Carroll stuffed the notepad into a satchel already crammed with papers and folders. "Not really. I got sidetracked."

Anne raised an unsure eyebrow.

"I thought I was going to be a priest."

o o o

ANNE TOOK THE GARBAGE OUT TO THE ALLEY, AND HIDDEN FROM THE house behind the termite-ridden back fence, she dragged on a smoke. She peered down the alley at the back of the Schraeders' house. She liked that family—the husband a deacon at Rita's, the wife not above her station—German, reliable. Unlike the Callahans. Their backyard was a calamity—the aboveground pool an eyesore, the rotting cedar-shake cabana and deck quadrupling its hideousness. At least the Peñas next door had the decency to sink their pool into the ground. But their latest attempt to grow palms and banana trees—well, it just wasn't going to happen, and Anne stood there in the light autumn chill considering the brown and yellow husks of the banana leaves and palm fronds. They looked like dried tobacco and *Christ* she had to quit smoking for good. She heard her father's voice in her head—*Stop this nonsense, Annie*—stubbed out the butt, and kicked it into the drainage line of the alley. She stood there alone, a little cold, contemplating a waning moonrise above a dead banana tree. She walked back toward the porch light and the patio. Granted, she was a little drunk and therefore prone to stare into the void. At this tired hour, her operating valence could be sad and inert, a lot like her father.

○ ○ ○

OVER PROPER TEA AT THE STUDENT CENTER, RONAN CARROLL TOLD Anne he had been a Jesuit scholastic for three years and how he came to flee Ireland.

"My father wrote me off. My mother still speaks to me."

"Do you have siblings?"

"An older brother—he's a butcher, like my da. And an older sister who yielded a passel of nieces and nephews. I was the runt, the princeling, so they put me through the books, but honestly"— Carroll lowered his shoulders, still trying to parse it—"I never heard the call."

"That's not your fault."

"Yes, but the disappointment was too much for them. I became a sinner."

"We all are," Anne said quietly, and sipped tea, keeping her own failing to herself.

He offered her a ride. Anne protested, the bus was fine, then agreed. Carroll drove a dilapidated Chrysler Imperial.

"The junkyard paid me to take it off their hands." He winked. "Be ready to push, Mrs. Malone."

The car barely made it across Fordham Road. Chugging along, the two of them diagnosed the faculty members of the department, each borderline in their own way.

"So how's it going as the only woman in this loony bin?"

"Kind of like the Church. A lot of men with ideas, ignoring the women."

They passed under the IRT at Jerome Avenue. "So where am I taking you?"

"Fordham Hill."

"Classy."

"We just moved. I grew up in Melrose."

"What does your husband do?"

"He works for an airline."

"Jet-setters." Carroll nodded his head in an impressed fashion. In addition to having a barely functioning car, Carroll couldn't operate the clutch. They lurched onto Sedgwick Avenue.

"Listen, if you ever need a ride to campus—"

"I'll call a cab." Anne put her hand on his arm as Carroll chose a lane. Horns blared from all sides.

"I must admit I learned to drive last summer. In Kinsale, we tend to ride around on goats . . . or my uncle Finbar."

The Imperial growled up the incline to the Fordham Hill oval. "Last stop, Mrs. Malone."

"Thank you, sir."

"Listen, Anne, Erikson is speaking at Columbia on Thursday night. I was going to go."

Anne had a foot out the door of the car. "What's the lecture about?"

"Identity crisis."

o o o

ANNE RETURNED TO THE DEN AND PLUNKED DOWN IN ONE OF THE burnt-orange chairs she had brought down from the Bronx and had reupholstered. She wanted another drink but had to keep a semisober eye on Pat. *I've picked too many fights with him lately.* The man was sick, and she felt terrible about it. But when she saw him stumble around the house every evening, all she had was anger. *You could have left this. No. You* should *have left this.*

For distraction she cracked open *The Thorn Birds* again to find Meggie plagued by brutish men. *Oh, Meggie, where are you going to now, girl?* Anne skimmed ahead, reading the dialogue to follow plot—a trick that got her through Dickens in school. *Okay, look out:* Father Ralph, now Archbishop de Bricassart, was back in Drogheda.

"In a sense Ralph was like God; everything began and ended with him . . ."

Pull it together, Meggie. Anne jumped ahead a few pages, her annoyance growing. Now she was on Matlock Island with Reverend Richard Chamberlain lurking around.

"Before she could reach the veranda . . ."

Anne looked out at the concrete patio of her house. Verandas caused a lot of adultery.

". . . he caught her, the impetus of her flight spinning her round against him, so hard he staggered . . ."

Anne sat up. *Here we go . . .*

"Up slid her arms around his neck, his across her back, spasmed; he bent his head, groped with his mouth for hers, found it . . . He could feel her yet he did not feel her . . . never again would he not know the up-thrusts of breasts and belly and buttocks."

Anne fidgeted in her burnt-orange sofa chair, and for a few seconds she was able to turn off the part of her brain that realized this writing made getting laid sound like a butcher watching aerobics. Anne thought of Ronan and the afternoon she drove up to the College of New Rochelle. He had gone back to the cloth. Not as a Jesuit; Diocesan. They walked down to that park to be alone. Through the tree line, which opened up to a rocky shore and blue skies over the Long Island Sound.

"Because at last he understood that what he had aimed to be was not a man . . . I can never be God; it was a delusion, that life in search of godhead . . ."

Anne tossed the book on the end table and moved toward her purse and the B & Hs. Instead she retrieved a square of gum from a yellow box of Chiclets. *These goddamn priests. All fragile, fallen angels.*

She couldn't read, she couldn't drink, she couldn't think about him, and so—and who knows how this plan came to her—she went to the laundry closet and pulled out the phone book. She found the number for St. Monica's.

"A church named for a woman who just sat 'round weeping for her son Augustine, the big Church father," Anne muttered to the washer and dryer. "Always kowtowing, venerating the venerated, that's your role, Monica."

She dialed the main number for the church, figuring the call would bounce to the rectory. She hadn't checked the clock in the kitchen, but it was past nine and closer to ten. *Borderline too late.*

"Hello?"

"Yes, is Father Timmerman there?"

"This is he."

Anne felt like hanging up then and there. She had already jammed the line for someone on their deathbed who needed last rites. *No, keep your nerve.*

"Listen, Father, I was at Mass this evening, and I have to take issue with your homily."

"Who is this?"

Arrogant from the get-go, Anne thought. Before embellishing her complaint, Anne craned her neck to check that neither Pat nor Dan was lurking in the kitchen.

"Father, that's not important. What's important is that your homily, quite frankly, was offensive."

"Listen, ma'am, unless you can tell me—"

"No, Father, this isn't about me, it's about what *you* said this evening."

"It's rather late." His tone was trying to wrap up and conclude. "If you want to come to my office and discuss this in person . . ."

Anne nervously stretched the tangles in the phone cord. *Here we go . . .*

"Father, do you think of all women as prostitutes?"

"Excuse me?"

"Maybe because you are celibate you don't understand us, but the least you can do, Father"—Anne coughed, her throat dry from the cigarette and the rush of excitement—"the least you can do for half your congregation is treat them with respect."

"I always treat women in my ministry—"

"Then stop telling stories about how we are all sinners," Anne said, her voice rising. "We're not all whores put on this earth to wash your feet with our goddamn hair."

Okay, that was a little aggressive, Anne realized. And there was a pause as Timmerman considered hanging up. He exhaled heavily and switched ears with the receiver.

"That was not the point of the story," he said in a grim tone.

"I can hardly blame you." Anne accidentally snapped her Chiclet with her tongue and spat it out into the dregs of her vodka cran. "The Church has always been this way. Women are either held up to this impossible standard, this Madonna, this perfect, docile, weeping figure of complete subservience. Or we're held in the same company as the whore with the heart of gold. Iniquitous, feeble women with the lone hope of our Savior. I hope you agree there's more to women than that."

"Of course there's more to it—"

"We're all born of women, right? All raised by women?"

"Ma'am, it's late, and I'm not going to argue this for the sake of arguing."

"Please, Father, you're not a bishop yet. Sorry if I don't kiss your ring." Anne tried to convince herself that this was what Thomas More would say to rebuke Wolsey or insult Cromwell. "But I think you're afraid of women and that's why you deride them."

"I'm hanging up."

"The worst thing that happened to our Lord was he had twelve *men* for followers!"

"Good night, and please don't ever—"

"I'm sorry, Father, I'm not trying to be rude," Anne interrupted. That wasn't true, but she wasn't finished. "We're not the
enemy, Father. We're the mothers of this Church and all its sons."

"Thank you for your call. I will pray for you."

"And I am praying for all our clergy to realize the respect
women deserve."

"No one is disagreeing with you. You are arguing with yourself."

"So you agree I'm right? I'm not even coming with the hard
stuff, Father. That if God made us equal, women should be allowed to be priests."

"Ma'am . . ." Timmerman sounded tired, Anne thought.

"Focus your homilies on something besides this whole blame-
your-spare-rib routine."

"Good night."

"Good night. Remember: we're not all whores, Father—"

And he was gone. Anne Malone placed the pink Southwestern
Bell Trimline receiver back in its cradle, like closing a plastic oys-
ter. She stood and walked to the screen door and flicked on the back
porch light, scattering a few crickets. She forced a self-satisfied
smile and looked out on a veranda that was still a concrete slab
patio.

MR. OGLESBY MARCHED INTO HIS CLASSROOM. THUMPER, A LONG, narrow dowel, painted gray, with a rabbit's foot chained to one end, marked his strides. He pulled his green-bottle-colored copy of *Lord of the Flies* from his army knapsack, found a nib of chalk, and wrote out the following line from Golding:

"'Fancy thinking the Beast was something you could hunt and kill!'"

The bell rang, and Oglesby was about to start when a yell went up from the senior courtyard. Everyone turned to the windows as a blur of khaki pants—a doofy-looking freshman with curly blond hair and clear aviator glasses—sprinted by. It was the annual rabbit chase—when a freshman tried to cross the senior courtyard on a dare. He had made it past the benches, hooked around two half-stoned seniors, did a taunting Bugs Bunny soft-shoe in front of the chapel, and lit out for his escape route—the back door to the cafeteria kitchen.

But there was a problem. The back door was locked. The freshman looked through the glass pane desperately. There was no one there to pop the door open. Betrayed by his accomplice, he turned and surrendered as seniors from each end of the breezeway poured into the courtyard. The vigilantes came out of nowhere, including the entire varsity o-line, their numbers, in the seventies, stretched across XXL game-day jerseys. The sophomores pressed to the windows to watch.

Sticky shook his head. "Dead meat."

"Almost made it," Dan replied, rooting for the underdog.

"Swirlie?" Rick asked. "Or wind sprints in tighty-whiteys?"

The seniors grabbed the freshman by the arms and legs and carried him out of the courtyard and toward the locker rooms. A freshman health class from down the courtyard cheered his attempt, and the hostage raised a defiant fist.

"Definitely swirlies," Sticky decided.

Oglesby thwacked Thumper on the teacher's desk. "Gentlemen, the short, exciting life of that freshman is now over. Return to your seats."

They settled in, and Oglesby began prowling back and forth across the front of the classroom, Thumper poking and pinging off the floor, the chalkboard, the radiator, and the first row of sophomores. He turned and put a death grip on Rob's shoulder and smiled.

"So what is the main problem the boys face on the island?"

Rob's shyness kicked in, and he chinned into his button-down collar for an answer. "Mmm, food? Shelter?"

"Perhaps at first, but what do they fear?"

"The Beast," Philip Humphrey spat out. "They fear the pig as a monster."

Dan half raised his hand but then put it back down, afraid to be called on. Oglesby saw the hesitation and pounced.

"Mr. Ma-lone"—Oglesby said his name slowly, like the spider to the fly—"care to contribute?"

Dan seized with regret. "No, sir, I'm good."

"Are you good with a failing grade for participation in my class?"

Jesus . . . Dan brought it back to what Oglesby had written on the board. "Their main problem is each other."

Oglesby took two steps closer to Dan, a menacing Socratic scrutiny. "Go on, Malone."

"It's fear of the unknown, but it's really a fear that they

manufacture in order to manipulate each other. And that leads to their other problem, which, frankly, is stupidity. It takes Ralph way too long to realize that Jack has turned the other kids against him."

"Okay, so Ralph is naïve. But why do they plot against him?"

"It's the savage part of our nature, an animal quality—it's amoral, capable of evil."

Dan was wading into the deep end now, unsure what Oglesby wanted and partially bullshitting.

"What's the difference between amorality and immorality, Mr. Malone?"

"Awareness. Intent . . ." Dan's thoughts scrambled for the answer that decoded the book—and his teacher. "And society. You take away society, and this amoral animal instinct takes over."

Oglesby was shaking his head in disagreement. "Do you need to take away society? There are murders every day in the city of Dallas. Too many. Mr. Malone is missing the point . . ."

Ouch. Dan thought he had cracked it.

"A point which you need to understand about this book, gentlemen, because the dynamic that governs *Lord of the Flies* is one of the keys to understanding this class, and"—Oglesby dropped his teaser—"winning the Game."

"Uh-oh," Sticky muttered. He had heard about the Game from his older brother.

"What did Dennis tell you about the Game, Mr. O'Donnell?"

"He said it was . . ." Sticky wasn't sure how to translate his brother's pants-crapping warnings. "He said it was a lot of our grade."

"Indeed. Twenty-five percent for the second semester will be determined by the outcome of the Game."

The Game was a central mystery to Oglesby's honors English and a wellspring of rumors and riddles for the panicked sophomores. Mere mention of the Game to Oglesby alums from previous classes produced a good-luck-with-that head shake and some cryptic comment along the lines of "The harder you try, the more likely you're to fail" or "Pay attention, you have to figure out how it's rigged."

"So is the Beast good or bad?" Oglesby asked, setting them back on track.

"Both," blurted Dan—he was figuring out how to unpack these trick questions. Maybe. "The Beast is us, part of our nature, it's good and bad."

"Are you certain about that, Mr. Malone?"

"Eh . . . yes."

A few of the sophomores laughed, and the teacher grinned— they were either onto a major philosophical truth or had missed the point of the book entirely. Oglesby didn't let on which way he thought the discussion was going but capped the discussion there and returned journals.

When Oglesby came to Dan's desk he plunked his journal down on his desk with no hitch for regard or comment. Dan leafed through to the final piece he had done on "Shadows and Tall Trees." He had tried to find a connection between the chapter in *Flies* and the U2 song of the same title, but he was straining. Dan had ended by quoting the best part of the song:

Do you feel in me anything redeeming?
Any worthwhile feeling?

He thought it through, or had tried at least. Did that mean anything—or was it just another jumble of human nature? He turned the page to Oglesby's comment:

You're taking your point for granted. Show, don't tell.

"Gentlemen, with the exception of Mr. Humphrey, who did a song-by-song exegesis of *The Wall*, these journals are quite unremarkable."

Humphrey raised his arms in a moronic concert salute. "Floyd rules!".

"Mr. Roger Waters thanks you. Remember, gentlemen, rule number fourteen: writing is revising. Don't just fill the blankness of the paper with pen marks—think. Then write. Then think again. Then revise. Remember, *revise* is re-vision, re-seeing the argument through the writing process.

"Gentlemen, writing means using your brain. Writing is a muscle—you must train it, and each time you do it gets bigger and better."

The sophomores looked on blankly. Oglesby dropped Thumper on the floor in a bit of rehearsed pique and exasperation. He grabbed his own lapels and scowled.

"And so let me put the challenges of this class before you now. There is the Game, which we will discuss in due time. But there's another trial some of you will undertake this year."

Oglesby went to the blackboard and wrote the same word twice.

Rattus rattus.

"What is this? Mr. Indovina?"

"Does it mean 'write and write' in Latin?"

"No. *Rattus rattus* is the common rat. The average black and gray rat is no more than six inches long. Nothing special about *Rattus ratti*. They live, they breed, they die. Now . . ." Oglesby returned to the board.

Rattus norvegicus.

"There's another kind of rat. It's a brown rat. It's bigger, a foot long at times—some in the subways of New York and London grow to the size of cats. The brown rat, the Norwegian rat, is smarter—all lab rats are descendants of the Norwegian rat. It adapts to everywhere. It's fiercer, it's more resilient. It will gnaw through a metal trash can if it has to. It is smart enough to figure out any maze, and it communicates with other rats by ultrasound, chirping like a bat or a dolphin. The Norwegian rat is special. Exceptional."

Oglesby reached into his bag and pulled out a foot-long brown rat with red beady eyes. He held it up, pendulum-like, by the tail. And then he threw it down the middle aisle between Flanagan and Deangelis, who took no chances and scurried out of their chairs. Okay, it was fake, but it looked pretty lifelike.

"And that's what this class is about—this is honors English. I want to know who is exceptional and who is content creeping by. In the coming weeks I want to find out: Are any of you Norwegian rats? Can any of you understand literature and write about it at a high level? Who will work hard and be ready for the Game? Can you do more than survive and crawl along like a common *Rattus rattus*? Can you adapt and thrive like a Norwegian rat? Who among you is smart enough to do that?"

The bell for class change rang, and Oglesby picked up the plastic rat and dropped it onto the teacher's desk. Dan looked down at his journal. A pulse beat in his brain, then his chest. He was lost in a maze of thought when suddenly a path cleared. The challenge was before him: *Show, don't tell, how smart you are. Show Oglesby. Write something inspired. Write who you want to be.*

And Dan Malone wanted to be a *Rattus norvegicus* very badly.

o o o

YEARS LATER, IN A DIFFERENT CENTURY, THEY WOULD CALL THE Jesuit/W. T. White rivalry the Battle for the Saddle, but in the late eighties, it was just the kind of classic private-versus-public-school matchup that exaggerated the narcissism of small differences. While it was really two middle-class versions of Dallas squaring off, the cultural divide felt like Notre Dame versus Alabama. On the football field, Jesuit was well coached and ran a disciplined (read: boring, predictable) offense, while White made the wishbone seem downright improvisational and had a knack for producing stars you couldn't possibly stop. That year's phenom was Calvin Murray, the younger brother of Kevin Murray, an all-American quarterback at A&M who had beaten Bo Jackson and Auburn in the Cotton Bowl two years before.

The Jesuit Rangers had a solid backfield of Judd Deuterman and Randy Holliday. Thunder and lightning, sort of. The Rangers were led by Gary Pasqua, who was a phlegmatic, God-fearing, hard-to-read Italian Landry and had coached the team for as long as anyone could remember. For practices he sported those legendary polyester Bike nut-hugger shorts that rode up on every coach's beer gut. But on Friday night, he wore gray slacks, cleats, and a Jesuit blue and gold windbreaker. He walked the sideline as if it were the deck of the HMS *Victory*—imperious, commanding, unfazed by good or bad fortune on the field, and barely noticing his team or assistant coaches, who gave him a five-yard halo of solitude that he only occasionally broke to grab a flanker by the collar of his pads to relay a call and shove him off to the huddle.

o o o

"YOU READY, NUMBER ONE SON?" PAT MALONE CALLED FROM THE driveway as he turned over the engine for his pea-green '70 Mercury Cougar.

"Yup." Dan slammed the front door of the house, silencing his mother's Talmudic instructions for check-in and curfew. He carried a can of 7-Up that he was slowly sipping and had pilfered three airplane bottles of vodka from his father's endless collection traveling non-rev for American. In the hutch in the den, the Malones had a whole air force of every type of booze and liqueur— even a mini Galliano that spired above the rest.

"Where is this game? Up by that field house on Spring Valley?"

"Yup."

Home field for W. T. White was Loos Stadium—whether to pronounce it "loose" or "lows" no one was quite sure.

"Am I picking you up after, or are you taking the IRT back?"

"What?" For the most part, Dan liked his father's corny teasing. "I'll get a ride home."

"Okay, try to avoid vans of Libyan terrorists."

"Check."

Pat backed them out of the driveway and flipped open the hidden headlights on the Cougar's black grille. "Danny boy, question. How's swim team? How are your frogmen shaping up?"

"Fall workouts don't start until two weeks from now."

"Ah. Right." Pat felt bad about how oblivious he was to his son's school calendar. "How's the Society of Jesus treating you? Any good classes?"

"Not really." It was a tired reply, Dan staring out the side window.

"Well . . . keep working hard."

"I am."

"Good." He turned onto Marsh, north over the LBJ overpass. Pat sensed Dan had more to say, but there was a long-running, unspoken father-son understanding to keep the long-running, unspoken father-son understanding.

"What are they going to do about your Cowboys, son?"

"I don't know. Danny White's gonna play. Are these games even going to count?"

"Yeah, these owners are a bunch of hard-asses. Scab football is no good. We shouldn't even be tuning in on Sundays. Never cross a picket line to steal a man's livelihood. Always be on the side of the workingman." Pat thought of his role at American and swallowed dry. "Can you do that for me, Danny boy?"

"Uh . . . sure."

"Your father and Mr. Hoffa thank you." Pat smiled, then Dan chuckled.

"Whatever, Dad."

They held quiet the rest of the trip, content and left alone together.

As Pat pulled into the drop-off for the stadium parking lot, his left leg twitched, and he stopped short, the front tires screeching for a hot second. Nobody noticed, but it broke the high school rule of not drawing unnecessary attention to oneself. Mortified, Dan smacked the dashboard and gave his father a what-the-hell glare.

"Sorry. Leg fell asleep there for a second."

Dan took a deep breath, caught himself and his 7-Up, which had thankfully not spilled. "It's okay. Just run over the kids from White, not Jesuit."

"Roger that."

"Thanks for the ride."

"Be good, bub, or at least not too bad," Pat said, but Dan was already out of the car and not looking back.

Pat watched Dan disappear into the crowd of teenagers. There was a certain civility in his son that put Pat at ease. He was fully a young man, who could do great things, and as Pat shook out the tingling in his leg, he said a quick prayer that his son would be healthy and do all the things he'd never had the chance to.

o o o

DAN FLASHED HIS STUDENT ID AT THE GATE AND WALTZED UNMOLESTED past two Addison police officers. He then scooted around the student section and ducked into the toilets. In the stall he poured the airplane bottles of vodka into the can. He took a sip and almost gagged but managed to swallow, which was followed by a burn in his throat and a shudder down his back. Dan studied the graffiti on the stall door as he took another sip.

A guilty remembrance of his father twitched in his mind, but he let that go.

It was Dan's small, dark rebellion.

It was also his coping method for watching the Jesuit Rangers get their ass kicked. Dan climbed the stairs into the bleachers. The cheerleaders went into a routine on the track between the crowd and the sideline, where Father Payne, the team chaplain, had the varsity all on one knee in prayer. Dan walked past as the defensive captain, Brad Stonecipher, capped off a Hail Mary.

"Our Lady, Queen of Victory."

And the whole team replied: "Pray for us."

The prayer was more than called for. Dan spotted Cady Bloom in the rear of the cheerleader formation. *Entirely too cute with her blue and gold pom-poms, short pleated skirt, and, well* . . . Chesty but not giving it away like White's Caballeras and Baby Bulls—two competing dance teams of tasseled and sequined cowgirls.

Dan stared at Cady for the long moment he walked past, baffled and crushed as a senior male cheerleader—some redheaded doofus named Embry Martindale—grabbed Cady's ass and hoisted her into the late-evening Texas sky. Dan took a sip of 7-Up and sucked his teeth in panic. *Damn it. I need a plan to get this girl's attention before some mouth-breathing jock moves in.*

The sun in the west was a drop of burning gold that slid nearer and nearer the sill of the world as the national anthem was played. Loos Stadium was underlit; the distant stanchions of floodlights cast shadows on both sides of the field. Dan found his buddies in the nosebleeds where the bleachers met the flightpath for Addison Airport. This was the crew's go-to hangout spot, where they could judge the action from a sarcastic distance.

"Let's go Rangers!" Rick yelled in Dan's face as he came up the steps. "Get jacked up, Malone!"

"I'm totally pumped." Dan drew an invisible six-shooter, just like the Jesuit mascot, Sam the Ranger, then pressed it against his temple and pulled the trigger.

Rob nodded to Dan's can in hand. "Whatcha got there?"

"Carbonated lemon-lime soda, Mr. McGhee."

"I can smell the booze from here. Where'd you get that?" Rob asked while mimicking the cheerleaders' semaphore routine.

"I grabbed this out of your mama's fridge."

"Hilarious, Malone, what's in there?"

"Nothing."

Sticky shook his head. "You are a fuckin' idiot—how did they not catch you with that?"

"I have a system—and I'm not a suspicious criminal like you."

Stick made a move at Dan to lift him and throw him over the bleachers, but Dan danced away in time.

The Rangers received the kickoff. The sophomores did have one player—one of their own—to root for. For the first time in the forward-pass era Coach Pasqua was starting a sophomore at quarterback. A cheer went up as number 16, Mike Goldenbaum, jogged into the huddle.

Here we go, Rangers, here we go.

First snap. Guard pulled and Holliday burst through the trap before the White linebackers could fill it. Twelve yards and a shoestring tackle by the weak safety.

"Let's go—run it down their goddamn throats."

"Same option right. They're cheating on it."

And despite that, the sophomore QB took it right, faked the pitch to Holliday in the flat, juked the outside linebacker, and was into the secondary. He crossed midfield in a blink.

"Go, G-bomb! Fuckin' go!"

The forty, the thirty, and the safety had an angle. The twenty. The safety drew in, and Goldenbaum stiff-armed him to the ground. The cornerback trailing the play tried to drag him out of bounds, but Goldenbaum high-stepped out of the tackle, stumbled at the ten, but kept his feet moving. Touchdown Rangers. The Ranger band fired up the fight song.

We sing hurrah for the blue and gold . . .

"Goddamn Goldenbaum. That was ridiculous." Rob pumped his fist as the extra point tumbled over the bar. "If we can run like this, we will blow them off the field."

○   ○   ○

WAY TO JINX IT, McGHEE. THE LONGHORNS GOT THE BALL ON A touchback, and the Calvin Murray show began. First play: a rollout with a twenty-yard bullet to his tight end. Second play: shotgun, keeper running at half speed, and fifteen yards, before stepping out of bounds. Third play: drop back, pump fake, freezing the secondary as the slot receiver ran a deep fade. From the far point in the horn of the midfield logo Calvin aired it out and hit the receiver five yards deep in the end zone. In stride. Touchdown. Forty-five yards on the stat sheet, the throw more like sixty yards in the air.

"Holy shit."

The White stands went loco. The Longhorn band played the *Dr. Who* theme—the horns super raw and brassy, the drums like a war taunt.

The rout was on. By halftime it was 35 to 7, and the Calvin show had put up two hundred yards rushing and two hundred yards passing. Dan was pretty sure that it wasn't until a Longhorns option run in the second quarter that went for five yards that the Ranger defense had even *touched* Calvin Murray.

By the start of the third quarter, Rob was the last of the crew standing, out of some protective instinct, but it was time to go—time to head toward Sticky's car, smoke a cigarette, and get the fuck out of Dodge. Dan, tipsy and tripping down the steps, took a passing glance at Cady Bloom. She had checked out of the game long ago and stood with her pom-poms on her hips, sharing sheepish sideways looks of embarrassment with Embry Martindale.

What little Dan could read into that gored him with jealousy. *Christ, how do I get her to notice me without dorking out? Come on, just man up and talk to her. It's easy. She knows you. No doubt she'll say yes to a date. No way, ugh, no way . . .*

Dan followed his crew out to Sticky's car. The bleachers may have been segregated, but the parking lot was a gauntlet of kids from White talking shit.

"Good thing the Jebbies taught you guys how to take it up the ass."

"Jesus Mary and Murray! We blew your fuckin' doors off!"

Even Dan was not inebriated enough to think a rebuttal was a good idea. But Rob McGhee, however sober, was still chewing on the loss and went into what could only be called "Bad Rob mode."

"Bunch of fuckin' dipshits."

That drew the attention of half of the White victory tailgate.

"You morons did an amazing job of sitting on your asses while a bunch of boys bussed in from South Dallas . . ."

Oh Christ. Now, Rob was the humble son of a minister, and Bad Rob was not evil, just sudden, and all that stuff that the good Lord had bottled up, well . . . it was now on tap. Dan watched Sticky and Rick take off through the parking lot—*We are not owning this.*

". . . run around a field. Well, if that makes you think you're better than us, congratulations, I'll see you later when you're delivering my goddamn pizza. You know what your average White player gets on the SAT? Fuckin' drool."

"You better fuckin' watch it."

Dan was waiting for a beer bottle or something to come flying at their heads, but strangely, Bad Rob was so blustery and ridiculous that his bullshit just drew laughter.

"Look at preppie boy all pissed off."

Bigmouth Bad Rob was strangely psyched to be mistaken for an upper-class douchebag; he was wearing his blue Izod, his dock shorts with Sperry Top-Siders—all of this amounted to a vaguely cocky *Risky Business* look.

Some White meathead jumped down from a trailer bed, cutting

Rob off from his escape route past a conversion van. Out of some hopeless fraternity—most likely to pick up punched-out teeth from the parking lot—Dan turned and tried to man up next to Rob.

"Jesuit snotheads." Here came a good ole boy with a wad of smokeless, hair slicked back like Max Headroom, Billy Idol earring. *Yup, this guy went to asshole training camp.* "Look at the fuckin' scoreboard."

"Whoa, Cooter, take it easy. Is this your girlfriend here . . . ?"

There was a teased-up and denimed blonde snapping gum over his shoulder. Max Headroom popped Rob in the chest, but he was uncorked and couldn't help himself.

"Or is that your sister and you left your girlfriend back in your barn?"

Before that could register, Dan yanked Rob by the arm and pulled him away from the scrum.

"Come here, dickhead . . ." Max swiped at Rob's collar, trying to grab him.

Rob took off in a full sprint, and Dan didn't need to be told to hustle—the two of them ducking through the crowd and across lines of cars until the White guys had lost interest in pursuit. They found Sticky's car, and the crew reunited at the far end of the lot, hanging under a drooping, tangled bois d'arc.

Dan put a hand on Rob's shoulder, catching his breath. "I have to give you credit—that was suicidal but impressive."

"Fuckin' public school Neanderthals." Bad Rob was feeling it for sure.

"Hey, Danny Malone!"

Dan turned to find Emma Wesselman wandering over. He wasn't much of a fan of the burnt-orange Longhorn colors, but Emma looked cute in a polo shirt for Longhorns girls basketball. She had grown out the curls in her brown hair and still had freckles from her summer tan.

"What's up, buttercup?" Dan immediately blenched at the nickname and felt the scrutiny of his Jesuit crew. *Play it cool.*

"Nothing, I was just hanging out watching your buddy there talk his way into an ass kicking. Then I saw you."

Emma and Dan had gone to grade school at St. Rita's together. They lived two blocks away from each other and for years had hung out, off and on. Emma wasn't a tomboy, but she was better than half the boys, including Dan, at basketball, soccer, you name it. Junior high brought different camps and cliques, and Dan and Emma drew apart to avoid teasing and ostracism. But they liked each other enough, and Emma had asked Dan to Sadie Hawkins freshman year. That night, he almost went in for the kiss, but Dan felt pressured and backed off. And then he didn't call. And Emma didn't know what to do and kind of gave up on him. He had known her like a sister for a long time, and it seemed weird to fool around or to even think about going together. But he was also used to making excuses, because the truth was: he'd blown it.

"Yeah, that could have gone wrong so many ways."

"How are things? I never see you now."

Emma said it very matter-of-factly, like the girl jock that she was. Not inappropriate, but Dan grimaced at the material she was inadvertently giving his crew to clown him with.

"Yeah, sorry about that. I guess I'm just going to school. Selling drugs to children. Normal stuff."

"Have you been drinking? You're all flushed."

Oh boy, now she sounded like his mother. And no matter how much Emma cared or was allowed to be personal with him, Dan was getting embarrassed.

"Well I *was* drinking. But can you blame me? Your Horns are killing us in there."

Everything was coming out wrong. Or just off and nervous. Across the parking lot, a car stereo was blaring "Boys Don't Cry," and the music jangled along as Dan's awkwardness grew and grew.

"How's school?"

"Sucks moderately."

Sensing things had stalled, Rick called over to Dan, "Dude, I think we're heading out."

Dan felt bad. Emma was a good girl. Not quite looking her in the eye, he started in: "So listen . . ." He had things to say. *Say you'll call her. She wants you to call her.* But he chickened out again. "I gotta go."

"All right, Danny. I'll see you around." Emma didn't waste any more time on him and was practically shaking her head as she turned back to a couple of her girlfriends from the basketball team. *Game over.*

Dan's shoulders brunted down as he watched her walk away. *Real smooth, Joe Camel. Buzzed or sober, you sure have a way with the ladies.* Emma looked good coming and going.

Rick smirked. "I think she wanted you to ask her out."

"I know."

But it was too late. He had already picked his tribe. And so Dan and his crew piled into Sticky's car and drove off into the Dallas night.

Room 120, Canisius Hallway, *in media res.*

Oglesby's class had turned to the unknown arts of Joyce's *Portrait*. Grimacing, the English teacher tapped the glands of his neck, contemplating whether to stick with his lesson plan of epiphanies, stream of consciousness, and free indirect speech. He gazed across the dark, fierce faces of the sophomores and decided that wouldn't reach them today. *What idea or ambition would draw them out?* he asked himself. He turned toward the window and the gray curtain of the morning. He bounced the white wood of Ashplant against the tight pile of the blue carpet. In this way, he summoned his lecture.

"Gentlemen, who do we have to thank for this book?"

They gazed at him blankly as Oglesby coiled around some deeper circle of thought. Rob McGhee raised his hand.

"Well, there's Joyce. But are you looking for some larger answer? Like the Jesuits . . ."

Chin sunk in his fist on top of Ashplant, Oglesby didn't acknowledge the response. "Did you know that Joyce tried to destroy this book? Here's another portrait of the artist: He was struggling. And he received a letter from a publisher saying that they couldn't print *Dubliners* because it was considered libelous. That means damaging and false to a person's reputation. In this case, the British king, and Ireland was still part of his kingdom. So Joyce's confidence was shot. He was living in a self-imposed exile, slightly depressed, slightly paranoid, always broke, and fighting with his wife, Nora, who told him to quit writing."

Oglesby broke out of his pensive stance and went roving down the main aisle of the classroom.

"And so he was arguing with his wife about all of this and he just snapped and yelled: 'All right, I'll give up writing.' And he stuck the manuscript for *Portrait* into the burning stove."

Oglesby frowned as he considered the snoutish face of Jay Blaylock. He returned to the teacher's desk to collect his thumb-blackened copy of *Portrait*, which he held up for emphasis.

"But fortunately his sister Eileen was there, and she snatched the pages out of the stove. She rescued this book. And later, when Joyce came to his senses, he realized what he had almost lost, and what he couldn't have rewritten, and thanked his sister.

"The point, gentlemen, is that this is hard stuff. Truly great artists must suffer to create. The hardest, most honest writing is a product of fear, anxiety, and paranoia that, when it works, we call genius. And who knows what would have happened to Joyce if this book had burned? Does he give up? Does he go on to write anything else?

"So think about that as you try to understand a writer. Think about their fears and doubts. Realize Joyce, for all his staggering knowledge, didn't know what to make of his own life half the time. Just because the type is fixed to the page doesn't make the author superhuman. And consider the matter of seconds between a finished book and a pile of ashes. Now, let me collect your journals."

Dan reached into his backpack and dug around. *Shit.* At his locker he had the journal in his hand. *So stupid.* A sudden woven anger overtook him, and he threw his bag to the ground.

"Mr. Malone, is there a problem?"

"I left my journal in my locker."

"What's rule number four, Mr. Malone?"

"'Your journal is your life-force.' I'm sorry, sir, I just—"

"Don't apologize, Mr. Malone, just come prepared."

"I did the assignment, can I go get it from my locker?"

Oglesby reached Dan's desk and tugged at his tie menacingly. "Mr. Malone, why does your soul lust after its own destruction? Bring your journal to my office at the end of the day with a bonus entry."

"Ha, hosed." Cameron Coleman sniggered.

Dan shook his head, gravely accepting his fate. "What's the topic?"

"Rule number two: organization is the key to high school."

More mocking laughter from the rest of the class. As he let go of the noose of Dan's tie, Oglesby changed his mind.

"Actually, life rafts."

"Life rafts?"

The period bell tolled.

"One hundred words on life rafts. You're floating along in here, Mr. Malone, doing enough to survive. It's time for you to figure out what this class means and what your involvement in life is going to be. See you after ninth period."

Dan pinballed out of the room and down the hallway to his next class. He had done the writing, and this unforced error aggravated him. He now had to carve out time for another journal entry—*So long, lunch and free period*. But that wasn't half as painful as the realization: *Maybe Oglesby's right. I need to act smarter. Like a Norwegian rat.*

o o o

LATER THAT AFTERNOON, JIMMY WHALEN WAS MISSING FROM THE assignment meeting for *The Roundup*. A chunky senior with a Bono mullet, Whalen thought being editor of the school paper was a career catapult toward *60 Minutes*. He was as serious as the hole in the ozone, and when *The Bear Facts*, the Ursuline paper, had gotten the scoop on how their greenskeeper was burning leaves illegally, Whalen had stomped into *The Roundup* office and pinned the article to the whiteboard.

"This is the type of story we need to be going after!"

Okay, Ben Bradlee, got it.

But Whalen had not shown up that afternoon—in fact, the top two-thirds of the masthead, all the junior and senior editors, were missing. Instead, five minutes late, Father Walter Argerlich came waddling in with the layout boards of the latest issue of *The Roundup*. Father Argerlich was new to Jesuit Dallas, having come from Strake in Houston by way of German South Texas parishes. He had been appointed moderator of the paper because he was an amateur photographer and knew how to run the darkroom. Part irate Goldwater, part pudgy LBJ, he wore thick black horn-rimmed glasses, and his receding hairline was blotted with what looked like black shoe polish.

The priest threw the boards onto the teacher's desk, put his hands on his hips, and caught his breath. Dan and the other freshman and sophomore cub reporters took seats as the priest composed himself.

"Well, I just came from the principal's office. And the bad news to report is that *The Roundup* will not be publishing an October issue. As a result Mr. Whalen and his editorial staff have decided to resign in protest."

Argerlich held up the front folio and showed the large red X Father Dallanach had run through Whalen's page one story. The headline: BAD FLOW DAY.

At the last dance held at Jesuit CP, the girls' toilets had clogged with sanitary napkins, which caused a backup in the entire plumbing system that Brother Finnegan had snaked and run the discharge into the creek behind the school. What set the front office off entirely was that this was the first they were hearing about it—and Whalen had interviewed some tool in the Dallas EPA office about raw sewage contaminants and E. coli levels. The story might result in a city investigation of the school and a fine. All this caused by menstruation at an all-boys Catholic high school.

Argerlich rocked on the balls of his feet, his hands folded across his beach-ball gut.

"Mr. Whalen made a critical error by not running this story past me, and now we are missing our out-to-printer date. The question before us today, gentlemen, is what are we going to do moving forward?"

Dan had no clue. He was a junior arts reporter, which meant that he had written two short pieces—one was a profile of Rob and Sticky's band 23 Years, which broke up before press time, so the story was pulled, and the other was a "human interest" profile of the octogenarian Father Callery, who threw pots and Eucharistic chalices in the school's art studio despite arthritic hands.

"For the time being Father Dallanach and I will be closely supervising the publishing of *The Roundup*." Argerlich was normally clipped and humorless, but you could tell he had been read the Ignatian riot act. "First order of business, we need to elect a masthead for the next issue."

Dan scanned the half-moon of sophomores and freshmen. George Tsimboukis (a Greek kid from East Dallas who liked to write about varsity wrestling) and Rick were there for the sports page, as was Sticky, who wrote funny slice-of-life for the campus page. Dan didn't really know any of the freshman reporters, and the only true pantload in the group was Teddy Boudreaux, who shared all his sophomore honors classes. Boudreaux was a smug and tubby know-it-all, a self-entitled band geek (he played the piccolo, for Christ's sake) who was just crying out to be wedgied, swirlied, or wet-willied. Boudreaux, however, was nephew to Jim McKenna, an alum who ran the presses and was the biggest advertiser in *The Roundup*. Father Argerlich didn't really know Dan Malone, but he knew who Jim McKenna was and the deal he gave on printing. He grinned at Teddy.

"Okay, nominations for editor in chief . . ."

And without hesitation, a freshman pigeon nominated Boudreaux. A smile grew from his potato-shaped head. Sticky let out a low whistle. The sophomores were all thinking the same—*if Boudreaux runs the paper, it is gonna suck.* Dan rolled his eyes at Rick, who then whispered to Tsimboukis. Stick tipped forward in his desk chair and joined their caucus. In a heartbeat, Stick raised his hand.

"I'd like to nominate Danny Malone."

Dan flushed with confusion. The sophomores around him—Kevin Veedon and Memo da Silva—were nodding in agreement. He then looked up at Father Argerlich, who was trying to disguise his pissiness. After Jimmy Whalen had gone all gonzo, he wanted Boudreaux as his toady.

"Okay, I'm not sure we have a quorum to make this a vote." He was trying to stall until Boudreaux could pack the photo desk with more of his band dweebs.

Rick stabbed at the air with the pencil he had been chewing on. "But you asked for nominees!"

"Fine. Mr. Malone, do you accept the nomination?"

Dan didn't know what to do, but he thought of Oglesby's rebuke. *Step up and figure out your involvement. You want to work on your writing? Well, here you go.*

"Yes, I accept."

Stick stuck out his tongue at Teddy Boudreaux, who looked like someone farted in his face. Still, the vote would be close—Boudreaux had the freshmen, Malone the sophomores.

The mirthless Father Argerlich looked like he was ready to lie down in traffic on the Dallas North Tollway. "Those for Mr. Boudreaux . . ."

Trying not to make a show of it, Boudreaux raised his own hand, which brought hisses from the other sophomores. His delegation of freshman minions voted with him. Argerlich started his count while Tsimboukis grabbed two froshes by their necks and death-pinched them into lowering their hands. This miraculously went unseen by Argerlich.

"Seven for Mr. Boudreaux. Those for Mr. Malone?"

The sophomores, minus Teddy Boudreaux, raised their hands. But it was not enough. Tsimboukis turned back to the freshmen he was bullying. Some illegal, disturbing Greco-Roman hold on their genitals was threatened, and their hands went up.

"Five, six, seven for Mr. Malone."

"Dan, raise your hand!" Stick yelled.

Stunned by this turn of events, Dan slowly raised his hand.

"Eight votes for Mr. Malone. Fine." Teddy Boudreaux tried to complain about freshman voter suppression, but Stick talked over him.

"That's it, eight to seven for Malone. Right, Father?"

"Well, yes, I suppose it is the wisdom of this conclave that Mr. Malone is the editor in chief. Since it's such a close vote, I think it's only fair that Ted Boudreaux be appointed managing editor."

Dan nodded to Father Argerlich and then looked over at Boudreaux, whose face was scalded, mortified. Stick, Rick, and Tsimboukis were all grinning like jack-o'-lanterns and plotting their next move. They went on to nominate the rest of the masthead, and the sophomores ran the ticket like Tammany bosses. Boudreaux stomped out before they could brainstorm article ideas for the next issue. At the end of the period, Argerlich dropped the censored issue of *The Roundup* on Dan's desk.

"Congratulations, Mr. Malone—I think the term 'poisoned chalice' might be appropriate at this moment."

"Sorry?"

"Just a joke, Mr. Editor—it's up to you now."

○ ○ ○

AFTER THE DISMISSAL BELL, DAN MADE HIS WAY DOWN THE LONG
hall that held the counseling wing. In addition to being an honors English teacher, Oglesby was the senior counselor in charge
of college placement. Dan poked his head around the corner into
Oglesby's office; he was returning calls to nervous parents of
seniors. He waved in Dan, who plunked down in a low-slung
creamsicle-colored lounge chair. By the doorway was an oversized
umbrella stand that housed all of Oglesby's teaching sticks, most
of them hewn in shop and gifted by acolytes from sophomore
classes past. Above the stand was a framed postcard that read:
"The beatings will continue until morale improves." Oglesby sat
behind a credenza desk in a padded pleather office chair that
creaked and pinged like a shot transmission when he leaned back.
Above his desk were diplomas for a bachelor's in English from UT
and a master's in counseling from the University of Dallas. And
one more framed dictum—two words in large gothic type: CURA
PERSONALIS.

Oglesby hung up the phone and, without making eye contact
with Dan, put out his hand. Dan reached into his bag and pulled
out the yellow spiral notebook that was his journal.

"Did you complete the extra assignment, Mr. Malone?"

"I did."

Oglesby flipped to the last entry. "This is it . . . 'The Raft of
Life'?"

"Yes, sir."

Oglesby started to read aloud: "'The Raft of Life . . .'"

Humanity is on its raft. The raft is on an endless ocean.
From his present dissatisfaction man reasons that there
was a catastrophic wreck in the past, before which he was
happy in some Edenic existence. Man also believes that

somewhere ahead lies a promised shore, a land of peace. But at present man is miserably in passage.

"Hmm . . ." Oglesby handed the journal back to Dan, shaking his head with apparent disappointment. "I was afraid of this."

Dan seized up. "Sir, I promise you I did all the assignments before class today."

"That's not the problem, Mr. Malone." Oglesby tried to rub the tiredness out of his face with both hands. He threw himself back in the creaky chair. "The problem is that you have the talent to be the best writer in the class."

"Oh."

"This piece is good. When did you write this?"

"Free period . . . and in Father Payne's theology."

Oglesby reached forward and drummed on the coffee mug on his desk. "Mr. Malone, why are you here?"

"At Jesuit?"

"Sure."

"To learn."

"Besides the obvious." With a wide, deep gaze, Oglesby corralled Dan's attention and bore down on him. "Think. Why are you here?"

"Because the Earth cooled at a moderate distance from the sun, and of all the orders of mammals, primates evolved from tails and knuckle dragging to bipedal locomotion and opposable thumbs."

"That's a better answer, but don't miss my point, Mr. Malone—you have it." Oglesby leaned forward and tapped his finger on Dan's journal. "Your ability to think while you write. Your retention for story and detail. These are important skills. This essay—this is you. It's smart, it's a little dark, and it's not sure where it's going. So, Mr. Malone: why are you here?"

No one had ever challenged him in this way. Without knowing what to say, he spoke.

"I'm here to become a Norwegian rat."

"Good. Then come to my class prepared. Being a Norwegian rat is not just answering the questions you know the answers to. You have to gnaw out of your cage, Malone. You have to show me more writing like this. Are you ready to work?" Oglesby creaked back in his chair, casting just enough doubt on Dan to spur him.

"Yes, sir."

"I'm going to give you another assignment. This is not a punishment. Think of it as a training exercise."

Oglesby launched out of his chair toward his bookshelves. He pulled down what looked like a gray textbook.

"Do you know who Bob Dylan is?"

"Uh . . ."

"That's okay. That's ideal, actually." Oglesby then riffled through his army backpack and produced a tape. "A former student of mine—he goes to Plan II at Texas now—made this mix of his favorite Dylan songs. Take the tape and this book."

Dan looked down at the cover, squiggles of graffiti over a photostat of Dylan. *LYRICS 1962–1985.*

"I want you to listen to the tape. Study the lyrics. Write about them. Tell me what you think. Mr. Malone, prove to me that you are ready for this. Prove to me you're a candidate for Norwegian rat. Try to answer the question that everyone—Dylan, Joyce—the question they all ask: why are we here?" Oglesby turned to his desk and let out a dramatic sigh of resignation. "Now get lost. I have parents coming in who have phenomenological certainty that their precious offspring must attend Duke University despite his mediocre grades and SATs and a hokey essay about baseball and life throwing him curveballs."

Dan got up and walked to the door.

"Oh, and, Mr. Malone—congratulations on becoming the editor of *The Roundup.* I've been dealing with upperclassman complaints about Father Argerlich all day. I'm glad you stepped up."

"Yes, sir. Thank you."

Oglesby smiled and waved him off. "Now don't screw it up."

Dan strode out of the counseling wing, down the main hall, and through the front doors with AMDG engraved into their handles. He found himself walking past the driveway half-searching for his mother's silver Zephyr in the pickup lane. The skies had cleared, and he noticed the golden traces of the sun stretching across the football fields and the small hillock that ran down to Inwood Road. He stood there holding in his hands his journal, the Dylan tape, and the songbook. Though no one seemed to notice him, Dan Malone felt a spark within. The trees that lined the school parking lot stirred and whispered in the late-afternoon breeze, and Dan felt a sudden awareness, a shimmering sense of discovery, that his journal, the newspaper, music, writing, reading, it was all connected with some hidden purpose. *I will become a Norwegian rat. I can do this.*

The hour when he would take part in the life of the world seemed to be drawing closer, and Dan wanted to think and write and listen to his heart and find out what it felt.

THERE WAS A PLAN TO SNAKE A MAN WITHOUT COLLARBONES DOWN the well. As the silver Zephyr sputtered through rush-hour traffic, Anne Malone listened to KRLD about the rescue efforts for baby Jessica. It was a Friday morning, and Anne had dropped Dan off at school an hour early so she could report for jury duty. Refusing the mix-master madness of Texas highways, she niggled her way along Inwood and Preston Roads toward the downtown Dallas skyline. *A man without collarbones?* That seemed awfully desperate—a resignation to the fact that they couldn't drill down in time. *But how could that be? It's in the middle of oil country.* Anne turned off the radio in despair. *Three days now. Somehow the child is still alive.*

Eventually she found her way through Dealey Plaza, past the Old Red Courthouse, past the spot where history veered, down through the Commerce Street underpass. After a half mile of highway no-man's-land, Anne turned into a parking garage attached to the hulking brown backside of the Frank Crowley Courts Building.

Parking ticket, elevator down, cheerless atrium, elevator up, gray terrazzo floor, beige hallways, and Anne arrived at the jury assembly room. She turned in her summons and took her seat on a long pew of blond wood. The jury pool was an accurate census sample of Dallas County—one half white retirees, civil servants, and housewives, the other half black, Mexican, Central American, and the working poor. A short video narrated by channel five's Chip Moody gave a Disney history of the jury system, from casting stones in ancient Greece to the Puritans' trials by drowning. A mention of the Magna Carta, sprinkle in the Bill of Rights, cut to trumpet flourish with mustangs running free across the plains of West Texas.

Quickly a bailiff, a scrawny woman with gold-rimmed glasses and prematurely gray hair, read off a roster of names. Anne hadn't even cracked her Frank O'Connor short stories when they called her to jury room D.

She sat there with thirty other prospective jurors while a different bailiff, a muscular bowling ball of a sergeant, passed out a questionnaire. *Name; date of birth; can you see, hear, and command English; ever done this before; tell us when and what happened; did you reach a verdict*—the normal stuff—but then on the second-to-last page Anne was struck by this paragraph:

> Because this case has received extensive publicity many, if not all, of you will have heard and/or read something about this case from the media. It is vitally important that you truthfully answer the following questions . . .

Anne turned to the last page.

> Do you know—or have you had any interaction with— Reverend Standing Raleigh or his wife, Margaret Raleigh?

Holy moly. This is the Raleigh trial. Anne knew Peggy Raleigh taught at Ursuline and tried to remember if they had met in person. She couldn't recall anything and answered: "Yes, I know of her and her husband, but have never interacted."

> Do you know that Reverend Raleigh has been charged with the attempted murder of his wife, Margaret?

Have you ever been a member of Reverend Raleigh's congregation at First United Methodist?

The following attorneys and court officers will be involved with the case, mark an X next to the name of anyone you have encountered in a legal proceeding . . .

Anne turned in her questionnaire and stared with disbelief at the jerky red second hand of the government clock. *It isn't even ten in the morning*, Anne realized, *but things are moving with a purpose*.

After all the questionnaires were collected, the bailiff let the jury pool pass around sections of the *Morning News*. And there Anne found it—B5 in the Metro section—*"Jury Selection to Begin in Raleigh Trial . . . the former pastor accused of strangling his thirty-eight-year-old wife in the garage of their Lake Highlands home, leaving her in a coma . . . Raleigh, arrested on July 14, has pleaded not guilty."*

The muscle-bound bailiff returned, and everyone stood and shuffled through a short hallway to the courtroom. Anne and the rest of the jury pool were seated in the gallery before the court of Judge Gideon Barefoot Samuels. The judge presided before his bench, to the right the two prosecutors, to the left two defense attorneys and the Reverend Raleigh, looking away with hunted eyes.

Judge Barefoot Sam gave the nod that everyone could be seated, and his clerk passed him the jury cards and a leather-backed selection grid with slips for twelve cards. The wizened judge had sandy blond hair and a punched-in pug face framed by look-over reading glasses. He smiled past the brim of a "Judges Rule!" coffee mug at the prospective jurors and began in a gentle Texas drawl:

"All right. We're ready to go. Good morning. The next case we're selecting a jury for—let me make sure I don't have any . . ." The judge looked down at his clerk's notes on the cards. "This case will not be scheduled for the twenty-sixth, so that shouldn't be a problem. This one will start on November second or the ninth, so we're okay.

"This is cause number six two oh dash seven one three six—I've had no request to shuffle so we're going to proceed. Folks, please sit in the jury box in the order we call you. If you move around, you'll confuse the attorneys and me, so please pay attention to the order in which you are called. This is cause number six two oh dash seven one three six, *State of Texas versus Standing Raleigh*. Reverend Raleigh is charged with the offense of attempted homicide. Mr. Whiteside, please stand up. Thank you. He is representing Reverend Raleigh . . ."

Haynes Whiteside pressed down his pink silk tie and turned to the gallery. "Good morning, everyone. This is my associate, Mr. Graybill."

Judge Sam continued. "And, Mr. Blackburn, who is a representative of Dallas district attorney Mr. Wade. Mr. Blackburn is going to be lead prosecutor. Sitting over here with him is Mr. Blackburn's compadre Miss Silverstone. And I guess she's riding shotgun, right, on this one?"

Douglas Blackburn stood with Miss Sutton Silverstone. They wore complementary gray suits. "Yes, Your Honor."

"All right. Those are your main legal participants. Have any of the prospective jurors in this room met or at any time dealt with any of the attorneys in this case?"

An older man lifted his raisined hand and in clipped English claimed to have done yard work for one of the attorneys.

"Which one, amigo?" Judge Sam gestured back and forth.

The man pointed at Mr. Whiteside.

"I take his word for it, Your Honor."

Judge Sam had the clerk pull the card for Mr. Morales and sent him back to the jury pool. "Okay, anybody else cutting grass or sold Girl Scout cookies to Mr. Whiteside, myself, or any of the attorneys? Or Reverend Raleigh and his family? No? Going once, going twice. Mr. Greenfield will now call your names in order.

Please take a seat in the jury box as directed by our bailiff, Sergeant Redman."

Five names in, the clerk read aloud "Anne Malone," and she moved from the gallery to the end of the first row of the jury box. A dozen and six alternates were seated. Mr. Whiteside took the grid from Judge Samuels and brought it over to Mr. Graybill, who had pulled the relevant questionnaires. After a long minute of consultation, Mr. Whiteside turned to the jury box.

"Mr. Garcia, it says here you work for the post office, is that right, sir?"

"Ms. Klais, you read the *Times Herald* every day?"

"Mr. Hovey. Is it Darnell Hovey? I got that right? You've had a prior incident with the Dallas PD?"

Whiteside used four of his strikes on the first call. Two black men and two black women were sent out of the courtroom, and the jury was reseated. The clerk, Greenfield, passed the questionnaires to Graybill. Anne sat perpendicular to Raleigh in the courtroom, looking straight ahead at him. He was balding in the tonsure pattern of a Trappist. He seemed frail, with large, melancholy eyes, the fires out, his lips ever so slightly tremulous. Anne sensed that his lawyers told him to avoid eye contact during the empaneling. *I can't even imagine what this must be like*, Anne thought, *to sit in this same room, unable to even look at the people who will decide your fate.*

Whiteside passed the grid to Blackburn, who approached the jury box.

"Good morning, I just have a few questions for all of you. Mr. Raleigh is on trial for attempted murder. The Texas penal code defines that as a second-degree felony with a punishment of up to twenty years. Does anyone here have a problem with that? Just raise your hand if you don't think that's an appropriate sentence."

No hands.

"Thank you. In this case, it is my job, the state's job, to prove to you that Mr. Raleigh had the intent to kill his wife, Margaret Raleigh. There is going to be medical evidence regarding Mrs. Raleigh that's rather grisly in nature. Anyone here have a problem with that?"

A woman behind Anne raised her hand and asked if there was anything related to rape or of a sexual nature.

"No, ma'am. Mrs. Raleigh was strangled by her attacker."

Anne watched the reverend. Not a flinch.

Mr. Blackburn went on to define reasonable doubt, intent to kill, some other basic notions of what he hoped the jury would understand. He then glanced down to the grid and picked at the cards.

"So this is the voir dire. Anyone know what that means?"

"To speak the truth." Anne couldn't help herself on legal trivia.

"Thank you, Mrs. . . . Malone. What is your occupation?"

Here we go, he'll try to get rid of me. "I'm a teacher."

"Where are you currently employed?"

"St. Rita's Catholic School . . . part-time." Anne was high on the sub list for all grades.

"And, Mrs. Malone, did you know about this case before your jury summons?"

"Yes, sir."

"How did you know about it?"

"From TV and the papers."

"And did you read or see anything that you feel would prohibit you from judging the evidence of this case in a fair manner and at the instructions of the court?"

"I don't think so."

"You don't think so?"

Anne looked up at Blackburn. Dark, dissecting eyes, pomaded gray hair, and Churchill scowl and jowls. *Trying to figure it out, huh? Culturally Catholic, but probably politically liberal like most teachers.* He seemed to glower at her, and suddenly the matter at hand being life-or-death registered with Anne.

"I can be impartial."

Mr. Blackburn stepped back and asked everyone.

"Everyone on the same page as Mrs. Malone's answer? Mr. . . . Caruthers, can you be impartial?"

"Yes, sir."

"Ms. Mirlo, do you know what Mr. Raleigh does for a living?"

"He's a minister."

"That's correct. He's a man of the cloth. Does anyone in this jury box have a problem sitting in judgment of an ordained minister?"

Three people raised their hands. Anne did not. *Why do I feel like we're the ones on trial right now?* Blackburn looked down at the grid and then over at Miss Silverstone to make sure she noted it.

"Thank you for your honesty. Mr. Raleigh is a representative of his church. A man of God. A Christian. Right? We can say that even though this is a government courthouse. Right, Your Honor?"

"He is a Christian, Mr. Blackburn." The judge didn't even look up from some paperwork in front of him.

"And so Mr. Raleigh has spent a lifetime preaching Christian values. Now, some of us, most of us, I would take it, believe those values too. Values like 'judge not, lest ye be judged.' Or 'he without sin, cast the first stone.' Or 'to forgive is divine.'"

Judge Samuels looked up. "Would you like to submit the New Testament as part of the record, Mr. Blackburn? Find your point."

He's a good judge. Doesn't allow the dramatic, and in control without having to constantly prove it.

"Yes, Your Honor, my point is that we are asking all of you whether you can believe that a man like Standing Raleigh, who professes the Christian faith, whether he can be guilty of a vicious crime and you can sit in judgment of him based on the evidence and judicial process put forth by the state of Texas as well as by

Miss Silverstone and myself. Mrs. Malone, are you one hundred percent okay with that burden the law is placing on you?"

"Yes. I'm okay." *Doesn't matter what I say. I've proven that I'm not easily led. I bet he strikes me.*

"If Standing Raleigh were a Roman Catholic priest, would you be able to say the same?"

"Yes." She didn't like Blackburn's papist undertones. *That's Dallas for you.* She recalled driving past Dealey Plaza that morning. *They killed the first Irish, first Catholic, president. No sign. No memorial. Like they had gotten away with it.*

"No problem with judging a man separate from his vocation to God? That a man who took holy vows could commit such a horrible sin? That a man everyone thinks is a good, honorable person could possibly transform into a very bad person?"

Anne Malone leaned forward on her seat. If it were only as simple as wearing a white hat or a Roman collar. She wasn't sure what to make of the pastor, who now bowed his head in penitential pose. She gripped her purse and sniffed, considering the questions put forth. *I suppose I know as much about a lapse from Christianity as anyone in this courtroom.*

"We are all capable of change."

"Thank you, Mrs. Malone." And with that answer Anne had found her way onto the jury for Standing Raleigh.

o o o

BLACKBURN KNOCKED OUT THE THREE JURORS WHO HAD RAISED their hands and gave the grid back to Whiteside. They took turns huddling and whispering before and after every question, and this took time. Anne figured out that Mr. Graybill was a jury consultant who was speed-reading the questionnaires and feeding suggestions to Whiteside. When the defense took away two more black women from the jury, Blackburn made a reverse Batson challenge, which seemed to give Judge Samuels indigestion. A long sidebar ensued with all four lawyers involved and Greenfield holding the jury grid like a cue card for them all to read from.

Anne mulled her answers to the voir dire. *Judge not.* The truth was she knew more about Standing Raleigh than had been revealed by Blackburn's interrogation. *Matthew 7, but then the Lord also warns of false prophets as wolves in sheep's clothing.* Anne had heard stories about the hotshot young minister. He was a bit of a local celebrity—a somewhat more liberal alternative to the dour, dispensational W. A. Criswell, who had shepherded First Baptist since the Normandy landings. First United was a mother church for Dallas and Methodism. Its pulpit was a feeder for bishops and a training spot for the best and brightest out of SMU's Perkins School of Theology.

But there was a lot of pressure that came with Raleigh's prestige. And his "controversial" support of equal rights for women and minorities, his opposition to capital punishment, his general yuppie tolerance, did not go over well with everyone in his congregation. This past Lent, he had received death threats. *"CHRIST WILL RISE BUT YOU'RE GOING DOWN."* For Easter, Raleigh wore a bulletproof jacket under his vestments.

In the congregation on that Sunday of Sundays, seated next to her own bodyguard, was Peggy Raleigh. In many of the usual ways she was the smile-plastered pastor's wife who raised their children, five-year-old Preston and two-year-old Claire. Peggy taught music part-time at Ursuline, even though working at a Catholic girls' school didn't score her any points with the congregants at First United, many of whom already found her a bit meek and withdrawn. While the outgoing Reverend Raleigh was always up to ten things at once for his flock, Peggy was quiet, remote, a gracious wallflower.

Also at Easter services was Lucy Goodfellow, the daughter of Bishop Wesley Goodfellow, whom Raleigh had replaced as pastor of First United. A woman with a lot of mascara and frosted hair, and a lot of rumors.

Raleigh's sermon that day was debunking *The Passover Plot*—a book and later a movie that claimed that Jesus, with the help of His disciples, had staged the passion and crucifixion and faked His death to become a false messiah.

Two days after Easter, Peggy Raleigh would be found strangled in the driveway of her home.

O O O

BY EARLY AFTERNOON, BOTH SIDES HAD AGREED ON A JURY OF TWELVE with three alternates. Judge Sam seemed satisfied and stood. The attorneys rose with him.

"All right, this is our group then. Thank you all for being forthcoming during the voir dire. I was very impressed, and so were the attorneys in this courtroom. Let me remind you of two things. One, shake off any jitters you have about serving on a criminal trial. All I ask is that you listen to the facts presented. This will be a difficult case at times, with lots of information, but I'm here to make it easier for you to understand."

The judge pulled at something under his robe, and the darkness around him shifted.

"Second, this case is going to get attention. TV reporters, newspaper people. They will be lurking around the courtroom, and they know better than to approach you all directly, but do not discuss the proceedings in any way, shape, or fashion until instructed to deliberate. Don't tell your boss the details of the case. Don't talk to the press. Don't tell your wife or husband what you think about this witness or that one. Just to be safe, don't whisper anything to your dog while he's doing his business."

A break of much-needed laughter. *Pat will be a bear about all of this.* Anne noticed Raleigh sat there sullen, lost in a stare.

Judge Sam looked over at his clerk's calendar. "We will begin this case two weeks from Monday, November second. Please report to the jury room at eight thirty a.m. sharp. Officer Redman will now explain where to go and how to access the building. The great state of Texas thanks you for your service."

The gavel dropped, and Anne was ushered through the back of the courtroom, was shown where to report, was given her pass for the Crowley building, and had her parking validated. Down and out of the courthouse, then up again, past the charcoal concrete pillars and ramps of the parking lot. She found her way to the dull silver Zephyr as the bright afternoon sun peered and poked into the umbral garage.

Anne had trouble admitting it to herself, but she was perversely thrilled by her jury selection. The morbid Reverend Raleigh fascinated her. *Those hands on his lap, hands that probably strangled his wife.* Anne tried to imagine it—*The look in his eyes when he does this. Is this the last thing Peggy sees? And what if she wakes up? What if they find him guilty, but she says he didn't do it? What good is our judgment then?*

She turned the radio back on, and the stringer in Midland was reporting about the parallel drilling operation and the dangers of a cave-in. Rescuers had dropped a microphone down the well and had heard the baby cry, but now there was less noise and the baby was sleeping, or at least they thought they heard breathing. No one was sure. There was too much acoustic interference from the drilling.

Anne let out a wounded breath. *Three days of this. The poor mother, like Mary when she left Him in the Temple. He was missing three days.* Anne now rethought what she took as gospel. *How do you lose Him of all people?* It was a sorrow of Mary, but it sounded suspiciously like neglect. Nonetheless Anne susurrated a quick Our Father and seven Hail Marys for baby Jessica. As she neared the house, Anne paused her prayers on a strange thought of faith and doubt. *What do we really believe when we suffer?* The child was hope both lost and found, and three days was a long time to be both alive and dead.

o o o

THAT AFTERNOON, DAN CAME THROUGH THE DOOR, WORDLESS AND reeking of cigarettes, and tramped down the hallway to his room, slamming the door. A few minutes later, Bob Dylan came jangling through the stereo. *That boy, always shutting me out.* Anne blinked and sighed and then crushed the head of iceberg lettuce against the cutting board, loosening its heart, which she extracted like a Mohawk. She then gutted a tomato—Dan didn't like the goo and its seeds—and pared it over the lettuce. She unsealed the box of Pepperidge Farm seasoned croutons and out tumbled the perfect white cubes of mummified bread. She shook the sediment of salad dressing into tornadic suspension and anointed the greens.

She turned on the five-o'clock local news. Clarice Tinsley was narrating hour fifty-five of the rescue operation. The parallel hole had been drilled, and now they had to dig a two-foot tunnel between the well and the hole. Carefully. The baby was quiet, but they were pumping oxygen down the well. The baby was singing to herself. Anne whispered another Hail Mary as she salted butterball potatoes in a Corning casserole. Those went in over the glowing Nichrome coils of the electric oven, and the pork chops came out of the Deepfreeze and into the microwave to slowly turn and thaw. Applesauce, farting out of the jar. And a bag of Birds Eye mixed vegetables brought to a boil.

Smacking her hip with a wooden spoon, Anne stood in front of the thirteen-inch Trinitron as the broadcast cut to Dan Rather. The drilling couldn't break into the well right on top of the baby. They had to go deeper and come up to her. *I should call Dan out to watch this,* Anne thought. *He has no idea what's going on out there.* The man in the hole was lying on his stomach, trying to poke through with a jackhammer. With all the noise, the baby was crying again. Faintly. They were getting close, and now the news hour ended but the coverage kept going. The sun had set in Dallas, and in Midland it was growing dark.

Wordless, reeking of booze, Pat Malone came through the door at six thirty and offered a tired smile before heading to the bedroom to change. He was limping badly. Anne made him a vodka and Seven, and herself one too. She placed them on coasters in the den in the hopes they could talk before the pork chops went into the pan.

She popped the foil seal from a can of Planters and poured two fingers' worth of peanuts into a small snack bowl that had been pilfered from an American Airlines first-class cabin.

Pat came out in blue sweatpants and the same work shirt. He was holding his glasses to read the paper but watched the small TV in the kitchen for a moment as the local news reporters carried on about the rescue. He muttered something about digging a hole to China and staggered into the den. *The Irish trifecta,* Anne dismayed, *drinking too much, miserable at work, and sick to top it off.*

"Do you want me to put that on in here?" He meant the bigger TV in the den.

"What?"

"The news. The baby rescue."

"No, it's okay."

Pat perched at the edge of the burnt-orange chair in the den and picked up his drink, the coaster at first stuck to the sweat on the glass, then falling off with a rattle onto the end table. A shower sprayed the backyard as the clouds rolled up like cotton bales in the western sky.

Anne swooped into the den and sat across from him. "Jack Hurley is coming to town on Monday."

Anne's brother-in-law was an FBI agent. "Welcome, Eliot Ness," Pat mumbled, took a long sip, and scooped peanuts. "Is he coming to the house?"

"For dinner and to see us. Yes."

"Wonderful. Where's Dan?"

"Barricaded in his room."

Pat ruminated on a handful of peanuts and took another swig. "How much did you put in this?"

Trying to wean him, she lied. "It's strong." It was half soda. "So I had jury duty today."

"Oh. How are the criminals and the clients they represent?" Pat chuckled to himself.

"I got picked."

"Christ. I told you to say you were religious. Picked for what?"

"The Standing Raleigh case."

"The minister who choked his wife?"

"Allegedly."

"That's going to trial? I thought he confessed or something."

"He was there in the courtroom."

"Good Lord." Pat finished his drink in a gulp and hobbled to the kitchen to make another. "How long is this circus going to be?"

"They didn't say."

"How did you let yourself get picked?"

"I didn't volunteer. They called my name."

"Everything I've read makes him out to be guilty as sin."

"I'm not supposed to discuss it with anyone."

"Jesus. This could take weeks. Were there reporters there?"

Just give me one ounce of support, Anne prayed, *please.* "They let us out the back way. But yes. The TV trucks were parked out front."

"Crazy. Do you even have time for this? They have alternates, you know. Who's gonna pick Dan up from school?"

Pat poured Smirnoff over ice. He opened the fridge, pretending to get the 7-Up, then lurched back into the den. "What kind of questions did they ask?"

"There was a questionnaire and a basic voir dire. They asked me if people can change."

Annoyed, Pat stared out at the rainwater ponding on the back patio. He took a drink. "They most certainly cannot."

○ ○ ○

DINNER WAS PLATED AND THE TV WAS SUPPOSED TO GO OFF, BUT DAN Rather was still on the air and the screen was split between him and a live feed of the well in Midland. A bunch of rig jockeys in gimme caps had sent a basket down the well to the operator in the tunnel.

"Looks like they're getting closer," Pat mumbled through a crunch of croutons. Anne dusted her salad in pepper. Lost in tired thoughts, Dan chewed and breathed through his nose. It was just after seven thirty now. Anne looked down at the salad, the pork chop, the potatoes and vegetables. It was all cooked right, but she was completely miserable about it and her worries laid siege. *This baby, lost in darkness.* She struggled to take a bite.

"Your mother is going to be on a jury. Did she tell you that?"

"No." Dan made the briefest of eye contact with Anne.

"It's a murder trial for that Methodist minister in the Park Cities. Don't tell anyone though—we should keep it quiet."

Dan shrugged. "How will you know if he's guilty?"

"It looks like he's pretty guilty. I just can't believe you got picked."

"Pat . . ."

"Sorry."

Anne watched Dan wolf down his food. "They present evidence, and then the jury decides. I'm part of the decision."

"This is CBS News live coverage of the scene in Midland, Texas. Dan Rather with Bruce Hall. We eagerly and anxiously await the next development."

"Oh." Dan scrutinized the tomatoes in his salad.

"It's a big responsibility."

"His lawyer is going to make him out like he's running for Jesus. Or that he has . . ." Pat circled his ear with a fork. "Problems. Watch."

"We shouldn't discuss it." *Alive or dead. Guilty or innocent. Settle down.*

"I'm not trying to argue. I'm just saying that if not him, who—"

"Stop . . ."

"Did he do it, Mom? Do you think he did it?"

"I don't know yet, Dan."

"Yes, Bruce?"

"Dan, it looks like they are getting ready to bring something up the hole. I can't tell. They are tightening the slack on the cable."

"Why doesn't the judge decide?"

Pat stabbed at his pork and ran it through applesauce. "Who is the judge?"

"This is still a very dangerous procedure as you bring up this child . . . This has been an exhausting fifty-eight hours."

Anne turned away from them. "Wait . . . quiet."

"And here she comes!"

And then the baby was there on the TV. Her head and fragile body tied to a spine board. Her eyes were open. Not frightened. Aware.

"Live and direct from Midland, Texas, Jessica McClure is up. She is alive. What a fighter."

And Anne pushed away from the table and began to weep. Her husband and son looked at each other, astonished, as she ran down the hall to the bedroom, sobbing.

LIKE THE CRUSADERS' FORTRESS IN ACRE, THE AMERICAN OFFICES ON the east concourse of Love Field were a besieged relic from the airline wars of the 1970s. Back then, Love Field was the gateway to Dallas, but American, Delta, and Braniff didn't want to contend with the peanut fares of scrappy upstarts the likes of Southwest and Texas Air. So with the help of future House Speaker Jim Wright, the big carriers made two moves. First, they transformed eighteen thousand acres of pasture west of the city into an international airport the size of Manhattan: DFW. Second, they lobbied the FAA and prevailed in limiting Love Field traffic to Texas and bordering states. Keep that pissant Herb Kelleher in his chicken coop, shuttling *abuelas* to El Paso and college kids to Harlingen. This was the gospel according to Bob Crandall.

Still, American maintained skeleton operations out of Love Field—a couple of gates for regional flights at the end of Braniff's now-defunct Terminal of the Future and a handful of offices. It was a rubber room for a slew of HR challenges—from senior management with pending litigation against the company, to reservationists who were deaf or had customer Tourette's, to mechanics suspected of workman's comp fraud—and Pat Malone was the lucky AMR executive who made the semiannual visit to this island of misfit toys.

Sitting in Gene Petzinger's office, Pat looked down at the

operations roster and shook his head. *How has it escaped this long? The cuts are coming. One more downturn and good night.* Pat smiled at Gene, who did not smile back.

"What's the news out of Irving?" Gene asked.

"You're not missing any Disney parades. Our fearless leader continues to march us forward."

Picking at a dust mote on the desk blotter, Gene tried not to grimace at the mention of Bob Crandall, the man who had exiled him to this post. Gene was officially the Love Field operations manager, but Pat noticed the calendar hadn't been turned since September. It was a Potemkin office, they both knew, and both didn't really care. *Why does the Pharaoh Crandall keep all of this on life support?* Pat shivered. *There but for the grace of God go I . . .*

"You guys geared up for the holidays?" Gene asked.

Pat flicked at the garnet in his Fordham class ring and stretched out his stiff left leg. "They say they are. Fuel is cheap. Ridership up. But when is it enough?"

"Never enough."

"What's the latest news on Love Airline?"

"Southwest's still running cattle cars to Lubbock and the like. Nineteen-dollar weekend fares. No seat assignments."

"No class."

"Exactly. Like a Greyhound bus."

"They're a knockoff. Loehmann's; we're Macy's."

"Come again?"

Pat blinked and realized Gene was a native. "Sorry, we're Dillard's. They're . . . uh . . . whatever the hell . . . Kmart."

"Roger that. They put butts in those seats though. Every flight to Hobby goes full."

Pat nodded. "True, but their whole plane goes for what we get out of two seats in first class. And they make their pilots clean the cabin."

"Ten-minute turnarounds. They squeeze every penny out of those 737s."

Pat didn't have the heart to go into the Sabre reports that made clear what a moribund toehold the Love Field operation had become. *I could have written this up from Irving. If folks want to fly Kelleher's cheapo airline, so be it. I've just got to hold on, make it another five years to get Dan through school.* Pat stood—behind Gene was a picture of LBJ taking the oath next to a despairing Jackie. *MS or not, I can still make five years and retire early on disability.* Pat then looked out the tinted windows of the office at runway 13L, smeared black with skid marks, and wondered where Air Force One had been parked during that dreadful moment. Pat noticed a 727 with a government tail number taxiing to the private hangar.

"Who's that?"

"Let me see." Gene checked the tower manifest. "Chairman of the Fed coming to town. Greenspan."

"Great name for the guy in charge of all the money."

Gene stayed wearily well mannered. "I appreciate the visit, Pat."

"Well, it's on my way home."

What good is a company that always casts off its own people? Pat shook Gene's hand and kept this futile thought to himself. He didn't give a shit about Love Field. No one did. And he wasn't headed home or back to AMR this afternoon. He was headed to the bar.

o o o

HAPPY LANDINGS WAS THE LAST REMAINING DIVE BAR ON THIS stretch of Lemmon Avenue near Love Field. It catered to the airport crowd and wasn't full of overflow from the drug motels and peep shows on Harry Hines Boulevard. The bar was A/C permafrosted and dark—well suited to the afternoon drinker. Pat strolled in around two p.m. and no one looked up. George Strait leaked out of a distant speaker, and a white fluorescent gloom fell over the pool table, the rest of the bar lit by neon signs and slivers of reality peeking under purple curtains. A few model airplanes hanging in approach over the corners of the bar were all that was left of the go-go seventies, when Happy Landings had been the unofficial departure lounge for all the fresh, young air geishas and cabin jockeys to points hot tubbed and coked out. Pat parked under a B-25 replica with the shark's mouth bristling across the nose. He hunkered down on a black pleather stool across from two old Braniff girls who looked laid over for good.

"Chicken Little kind of day?" It was the owner and bartender, Steve Miller. Not *that* Steve Miller, just a good ole boy in a striped off-blue cowboy shirt and jeans belted by a big-ass buckle made of two silver arrows. The one pointed up read: THE MAN; the one pointing down decreed: THE LEGEND.

"Work sucks, but I'm working on it."

"Work is for jerks. One and one?"

Out came a Miller Lite and a Jameson on the rocks. Pat shuddered as he took a long pull of whiskey through the red swizzle straw. That first sip painted all the corners as it ran down his throat into the pit of an empty stomach.

"What do you say, Pat?" Steve Miller put a foot of ostrich leather up on his beer fridge.

"Got my wife's dumb-ass brother-in-law in town."

"Aw shit. The not quite family."

"Exactly. And he's a fuckin' Fed."

"Based around here?"

"No, DC now."

"What branch of the Fed?"

"G-man." Pat pulled on the Miller Lite and swallowed a burp. "Don't ask me how that happened—can't find his ass with two hands."

Steve Miller cackled and refilled both tall and small. The first of several rounds as Pat read the paper and got lost in his cups, so it was some time before Pat looked up at CNN, playing on the corner TV. The volume was turned down—but there was a reporter on the NYSE floor and something coming across the crawl.

"What's going on?"

"Sky is falling." Steve Miller was working on a crossword and didn't look up. "Market crashed today."

"You're kidding."

"Nope. Dow Jones in the toilet."

"How bad?"

"Last I saw, it was down four hundred points. More than Black Thursday."

"Shit." Pat reached into his jacket, looking for his beeper. He patted down all his pockets. "Let me settle up with you."

Pat threw money on the bar and hustled out to his Cougar. He found the beeper on the passenger seat. The office had tried him four times. *Fuck.* Pat walked to the 7-Eleven at the end of the strip mall and threw a quarter in the pay phone. He had had two beers and four whiskies, but he shook off the buzz. He called Shapiro, director of personnel and his immediate boss.

"Les, just got your page."

"Where the fuck are you, Malone? I called Love Field and Gene said you were out of there two hours ago."

"Sorry, I left his office but was still on site—wanted to go through the personnel files without getting him all in a twist."

"Market tanked and people are freaking out."

"Want me to come back?"

"Nah, no good now. The market just closed. You might have missed the start of the next Depression. We're down seventeen percent. Not as bad as United, down twenty-two percent. I think we survived the day, but it was a bloodbath. IBM down twenty-three percent, US Steel close to forty, Kodak gutted."

"Shit." The Malones owned both IBM and Kodak stock.

"Where the fuck are you? They think it's going to be worse than '29. They had to stop trading on half the blue chips."

"Unbelievable."

"The phones are ringing off the hook—the pension fund took a major hit, and if tomorrow is like this, we're gonna have problems. I can't have you going MIA, Malone."

"I swear to you . . ." An eighteen-wheeler on Lemmon roared by. "I didn't get the page until now."

There was an uncomfortable pause. *Shapiro knows.* "Where are you, Pat?"

"I pulled over at a 7-Eleven on my way home." *Shit. He isn't buying this. Think, Malone.*

"I paged you four times. We're lucky Crandall hasn't called for all hands on deck. Probably too busy planning chapter eleven."

"Listen, Les . . ." Pat's left leg buckled as he shifted his weight. "I didn't want to say anything, but after Love Field I went to Medical City. I had an appointment with the neurologist about the MS, and I left the beeper in the car."

"Right, okay, sorry, Pat."

"It's no excuse. I'm the one who's sorry."

"Christ, Pat, now I feel bad. It's just that we're bailing water over here. Everyone thinks this might take us under."

"Understood. You sure I shouldn't come back to Irving?"

"Don't bother, seriously." Les sounded like he was about to cry. "Go home and stuff cash in the mattress. That's about all we got left to do."

The call ended, and Pat threw up next to the pay phone.

o o o

A BLACK CROWN VIC SAT IN THE DRIVEWAY AS PAT PULLED UP ON Crown Shore. Jack Hurley already making himself at home. Pat parked, hiccupped through a series of calming breaths, and tried to stretch out his legs so as not to limp. He walked in the door to a "There he is," which instantly negated all his self-soothing and brought back his brown mood. It was six o'clock, neither early nor late, but Pat was still half-drunk enough to be ornery.

Special Agent Hurley was perched on a sofa in the formal living room—the Malone museum of furniture that no one, except honored guests and heads of state, ever sat in. Leaning into the back of a chair, Pat reached across and shook his wife's brother-in-law's hand. The good news was he was slightly fatter and balder. Hurley put down the Manhattan Anne had made him on a cork coaster and tried to grind Pat's knuckles with his grip.

"Paddy boy. How's life in the boondocks?" Jack was wearing a blazer and dark trousers, a blue shirt with white collar and cuffs, suspenders, and an empty shoulder holster that Pat was certain was all for show. Jack loosened his vise. "When are you guys coming back to civilization? You're a long way from St. Jerome's, pal."

Pat grinned like an idiot at this—*How has no one shot this guy yet?*—and then scanned the house. Anne was working on some sort of barbecue chicken in the kitchen. Dan sat quietly on the far chair in the living room, chewing through potato chips and French onion dip while keeping Agent Hurley company. Jack took off his jacket and returned to sprawling over the good sofa. Built like an ox, Jack had played right tackle for Frank Leahy at South Bend, which he reminded people of every five goddamn minutes.

"Paddy, I haven't been down this way since we came to whip those boys at Southern Methodist. Played them at the Cotton Bowl. Had to clear the cattle off the field before the game." Jack slapped at Dan's knee to punctuate his corniness.

"Nice to see you, Jackie," Pat said. "You good on drinks?"

Jack rattled his ice. "I won't lie: this could use a sequel. Look how big your son has gotten—Danny boy, where are you going to go to college?"

Dan shrugged. "Notre Dame, I guess."

"There you go! Good answer, Dan the man." Jack then rolled up his sleeve to show Dan his tattoo of Clashmore Mike, the Irish terrier that had been the ND mascot before the leprechaun.

Annoyed, Pat put down his briefcase in the hall and shuffled toward the alcohol. "He's still just a sophomore."

As Jack made the terrier bark on his twitching forearm, Dan blurted, "I also like Princeton."

Jack fell back as if concussed. "That Protestant school? Jesus, Patrick—talk to your boy."

"Stop, Jackie," Anne called out from the kitchen. "Nothing wrong with the Ivy League."

"I work for Princeton grads, Annie. It's a first-class school, full of goo-goos who have no clue what's going on out there."

"Well it was good enough for Einstein . . . ," Dan offered.

"Yeah, Jack." Pat cracked an ice tray over two cocktail glasses. "And Bill Bradley!"

"I can tell I've lost you people to the heathens out here." Jackie rolled away Clashmore Mike but left his cuff undone. "Cheers, Paddy," he said, accepting the fresh Manhattan Pat handed him. "The house looks good."

Even Jack's benign compliments sounded like slights to Pat as he returned to sitting on the uncomfortable living room furniture.

"What brings you to town?"

Jack's eyes went wide like Sergeant Schultz's, and he replied, "I vill tell you nothing!" Followed by a big honking laugh, like a seal or a walrus. *Jesus.* "Seriously, I'm part of a task force. These S & Ls, Paddy . . ."

"We got out a year ago."

"Good. Stay away from it. Let me tell you, after today with the market, they're all going belly-up. Bunch of crooks pretending to be George Bailey."

Pat felt nauseous again thinking about the market. *Bourbon on top of scotch isn't helping either.* "Yeah, we went to withdraw a ninety-day CD at Vernon and Anne practically had to sit in for it."

"Good for you, Annie. That guy at Vernon is in hock so deep we can't even count it." Jack turned to Dan, who was sipping ginger ale. "Danny boy, neither a borrower nor a lender be. Right, buddy?"

Another barking laugh. Anne put out more potato chips, along with a wine-stained cheese spread and Wheatsworth crackers. Pat studied the miniature machete that came with the cheese plate. *Fucking hors d'oeuvres as the economy goes belly-up.*

"Anne girl, what do you say? Still teaching?"

"Trying to. A little at Dan's old grade school. How's my sister?"

"She's good. Getting a bit of that arthritis your mother had. Pat, I noticed you're limping around. What happened to you?"

The Malones shared quick glances, and Pat took the lead. "Sore from jogging. I think this knee is going on me."

Dan took his father's lie for granted. It was understood that they didn't tell people he was sick. *Nobody's business,* his father declared, *not even family.* His father had told him about the MS, but that was about all Dan knew. *If he's not that sick,* Dan mulled, *why does he hide it from people? Why does he hide it from me?*

"Getting old, folks." Jack shook his head as he took another big gulp of his Manhattan. "Age is supposed to bring wisdom, but I think in my case it came alone. How's everything at American, Pat?"

"We survived the day."

"Crazy business, airlines." Jack Hurley had lots of opinions based on what no one else knew. "I told you when you came out of Fordham to go the government route."

"You did." Pat was getting annoyed again. *Five more years—AMR might not last five more weeks.*

"I'm going to just grill these inside," Anne called out from the kitchen. "By the time we get the hibachi going outside, it'll be too dark. What did they say at work about the market?"

Pat guzzled the last of his Manhattan. *Keep it civilized.*

"I was out at Love Field all day. When I called in, people were panicked about pensions. It looks like aviation didn't get the worst of it."

Jack ran his fat fingers across his scalp. "My buddies over at Treasury knew this was coming six months ago. Told me to get out, which I did, thank you, Jesus."

"It'll bounce back." Pat looked over at Dan, who registered no concern, other than about which Ruffles chip to eat next.

"It's all going down the toilet. Your carrier might make it through the week, but when folks are down forty percent off their nest egg and don't have money to vacation with—you'll feel it by Christmas, that's for sure. There's only one employer that never has a downturn."

Jesus Christ, someone please knock this guy off his high horse. But Pat was too drunk and tired to debate him. "Uncle Sam?"

"Law enforcement." Jack joined Dan at the potato chip bowl. "Crime never goes out of business, Danny boy. You always have bad guys. I tried to tell your dad this years ago—tried to get him in at the FTC or IRS. Unlike the airlines, once they regulate, they ain't gonna deregulate. Listen to me now, Einstein, before you run off to Princeton."

"Want another, Agent Hurley?" Pat asked.

"Sure, Dean Martin, I'll join you for a small one." Jack snorted and gave an in-cahoots wink to Dan, who forced a smile.

Pat pretended not to stumble to the kitchen. *One more and I'll be on the level.*

"Want me to throw that chicken on the grill?"

"I told you I was going to use the broiler." Anne gave him the enough-already look.

"Just trying to help," Pat muttered to himself, refilled two low-balls with bourbon and ice, and sulked back to the living room. His leg was not cooperating and he braced himself against the armrest of the chair as he sat down, knocking the doily cover to the floor. He picked it up and realized that he hadn't sat in this chair since it was in his mother's house. *No one is going to hire a fifty-five-year-old actuary. We're going to have debt. And then we're going to have nothing.* Pat drank and thought of that old rat-hole apartment on Willis Avenue, missing some story Jack was telling Dan about Colombian drug gangs. Anne fluttered in.

"Dinner in about ten minutes. I don't know about this chicken. Apologies in advance. So how are John and Ryan?"

Jack futzed with the cheese and crackers. "John's doing well. Does crew every morning on the Potomac in addition to football. Just got him an old jalopy to drive to Paul the Sixth and back."

"Is he a junior?" Pat asked.

"Senior. Come on, Paddy, keep up, he's two years ahead of Danny."

"Right, and Ryan?"

"He's good." Jack's enthusiasm for this line of questioning was noticeably shot. "Runs up my phone bill like he's my daughter."

Anne frowned and hoped her nephews weren't as uncouth as their father.

"Okay, this chicken will be ready soon. Dan, bring the plates in. Let's sit at the table. Can you put the leaf in, Pat?"

They all moved into the adjacent dining room. Pulling the table apart and putting the leaf in was a gigantic pain in the ass. The table had been severely crippled in the moving van from the Bronx, and even though they had taken it to be leveled and refinished, it was never the same. Pat tried to align the dowels with the holes but was an eighth of an inch off. His leg was throbbing, and he wanted nothing more than to burn this table—a wedding gift from Anne's father—in the backyard. He looked at Dan, who, like a canary to his father's moods, was getting nervous as Pat's anger grew.

"Here, Dad, I got it."

"Wait, watch your fingers, Dan."

"Need some help there, Pat?" Jack was perusing old family pictures that Anne had framed and put out by the Waterford cabinet.

"It's like trying to dock a goddamn space capsule."

"I got it, Dad."

"Wait."

"Ow!"

Pat stumbled back from the table. He had pinched Dan's finger in between the table and the leaf. Dan sucked air through his teeth and shook his hand.

"Shit. I'm sorry, son. My fault."

"You weren't listening to me."

"Oh, Danny boy, did I get you?"

"It hurts."

"I'm so sorry. Go run some cold water on it. Is it bleeding?"

"No. God!"

Dan stormed off to the bathroom.

"I'm sorry, kiddo." *Why didn't we just buy new furniture when we moved down?* Pat was driving himself mad, and that realization only made it worse. *Goddamn insane. Cost the same as shipping all this crap down.*

Anne, who had missed the incident, yelled out, "Don't go far, Dan—dinner will be on the table in two minutes."

"Teenagers, like chickens without heads." Jack chuckled to himself. "What's Dan into these days? Playing any pigskin?"

Pat took a big swig of bourbon. "He's on the swim team."

"That's good. Did I tell you John set the record for TDs in Fairfax County?"

"Amazing."

"Yeah, as a junior. He's a little small for the big state schools. But the coach at Holy Cross loves him."

Pat straightened out a dinner cloth over the table. "Not BC? I'm sure they're looking for the next Flutie." He started pulling out knives and forks from the silver drawer. *All this useless shit we kept.* He stood back from the table. *Why did we put the leaf in? It's only the four of us. Fucking hell. Well, a few more inches of distance from this asshole.*

"Listen, Pat, speaking of college, there's something I want to bring up with Anne. I could use your help on it."

Pat finished his drink and put out the plates. *Time to switch back to vodka.*

Jack leaned against the back of the sofa, his gut hanging out of his suspenders. "First off, Cat and I are so grateful for how you took care of Mary."

"Uh-huh." Pat set the table. Mary was Anne's mother, who lived with them for her last year. He was half-listening and trying to figure out if he could have another . . . "Anne, should we have wine with this dinner or something?"

"I think we're okay," she yelled back from the kitchen. "Does Jack want wine? I'm not sure we have any."

"I'm fine. Listen, Pat . . ."

Dan came out of the bathroom and plopped in a chair at the dining room table.

"You okay, buddy?" Pat asked.

"I'll live."

"Sorry about that. This table is a pain in the—"

"So here's the thing, Pat. She had about ten thousand dollars. Half of that went to the doctors and the funeral. And the other half she wanted donated to the Church."

"That's right."

"Have you given that money to Tolentine?"

"You have to ask Anne. I don't think so. I don't know."

"Well it would be a big help to us if Cat and I got that half for John's and Ryan's college."

Pretending not to hear, Pat looked at Jack. "I'm going to open some wine. It's been a rough day."

"If you could help me talk to Annie about this."

"You can talk to Anne all you want, Jack. But it's not her mother's wishes."

"Half that money should be coming to us, Pat. You know that's fair."

"Half after we paid for everything, right? So half of what's left?"

"We helped her with the rent at University Avenue."

"That's the first I'm hearing about that."

"Well, it's true."

"Dinner's ready." Anne walked into the dining room and set down a tray of half-charred chicken smeared Indian red with barbecue sauce. She disappeared back into the kitchen for the sides.

Pat sat at the head of the table. The sight of the chicken brought on a new wave of weariness. "So how much do you want? What's the get here?"

Jack realized he had kicked a hornet's nest and backed off. "C'mon, Pat, this is not some king's ransom."

Anne came in with potatoes and coleslaw and sat down. Pat popped up from the table. *Ransom sounds about right.* "I'm opening wine."

"We don't have any." Anne inspected the chicken for doneness.

"Fine, just need a glass of water then." Never mind there was already one on the table in front of him. Pat went to the kitchen, hobbled into the pantry, and snuck a big, burning gulp of vodka. He then stumbled back into the dining room, kicked his own chair out to sit back down, and rubbed his bloodshot eyes. Anne, Dan, and Jack pretended not to notice any of this.

"So go ahead, Jack, ask her."

"Let's just eat." Jack smiled at Dan. "Danny, your father says you're swimming. What's your best stroke?"

But Pat was past the point of safe return. "Go ahead, Agent Hurley. Go ahead and ask my wife what you wanted to ask her."

"Let it go, Pat."

Anne put down the serving spoon. She realized they had forgotten to say grace in front of company. "What are we talking about?"

"It's nothing, Anne." Jack tried to wave it away with his fork. "Let's just eat."

"He wants what's left of your mother's money."

Anne looked at Pat. *He's shitfaced. And now my sister is going to hear about it.* That upset her more than anything. "Okay, I'll talk to Catherine," she said quietly.

"Thank you, Anne."

"Good." Pat stabbed the chicken with his fork. "And tell J. Edgar fucking Hoover to pay for your fucking kids' education."

Jack stood up and whispered an apology to Anne and Dan. He put on his jacket and walked out the door to his black government car.

Dan lost his appetite. He sucked on his pinched finger. *It was that stupid table. That set him off.* His father served him a potato like nothing had happened. Unable to process his fear of his father, it channeled into fury at his mother. *Her fucking dinner, her idea to sit at this table. She started this shit.* He ran back to his room.

Anne shook her head and returned to the kitchen. Seconds later she was crying.

Slashing and biting through the tasteless chicken, Pat Malone sat alone at the head of his table. When he heard his wife crying, he stopped chewing and blinked slowly. Then he threw his plate across the room, missing the Waterford cabinet, the chicken landing on the beige carpet with hardly a sound.

And so he sat there. Burning down the house in his thoughts.

"THE AMAZING THING, GENTLEMEN, ABOUT SCHLIEFFEN'S PLAN IS
that it almost worked."

Mr. Robert Donahue, sophomore history teacher, stood before
his whiteboards like an old master before the gesso on the *cappella* wall, furiously scribbling a quick map of the Low Countries
in blue marker.

"The German advance was like a gate, and it had to swing with
precision, following Schlieffen's command 'Let the last man on
the right brush the channel with his sleeve.'"

Donahue had been at Jesuit for eleven years and was considered by many the toughest teacher in the school. Any word written or spoken could appear in a test question, and Dan approached
the class with an on-your-toes boot-camp panic.

"But Schlieffen died in 1913, a year before the war, and the
German general staff didn't quite execute the plan according to
his design. Always fearing the unknown millions of troops the
czar might throw at them, they took two divisions from the west
to bolster the east. Then they spared the right, up here by Belgium, to strengthen the middle. And perhaps the biggest mistake is that this army turned in too soon, exposing its flank to
Paris."

After drawing the arrow for von Kluck's blunder, Donahue

shook his head. "Remember—all of this is based on train schedules and planned with minute-by-minute detail, down to the number of axles that would pass over a given bridge within a given time."

Donahue scratched his nicotine-stained mustache. He had round, rimless glasses and looked like a distempered, gray-badger version of Teddy Roosevelt, running on coffee and low-tar Camels. Dan could smell his skunked breath from the third row.

"Von Moltke, the chief of the German attack, expected to conclude the west by the thirty-ninth day of the war, and then the real threat—the Russian front—required this huge transfer of troops and materiel starting on day forty.

"This was what the Germans feared, having to fight a war on two fronts. Schlieffen on his deathbed told them, keep this right wing strong. But they hedged, and then the armies didn't quite meet up properly to encircle Paris. Which sets up the Battle of the Marne and a crazy last-ditch effort where the French commandeer every last taxi in Paris to race six thousand troops to the line. This miraculously thwarts the German advance and throws Schlieffen's timetable out the window.

"So, gentlemen, as von Moltke feared: 'No plan survives first contact with the enemy.'" Donahue turned to his sophomore class and placed a brown boot up on his desk. He had been a marine in Vietnam, which no one dared ask him about, and was still an active drill sergeant in the National Guard: talking and shouting were equal registers of discourse. "How this war started, how this all came to pass, is the result of a long chain of dominoes that we've been looking at in the century following Napoléon. The delicate balance of power established at the Congress of Vienna is thrown off by the assassination of Ferdinand and the goddamn Serbians' acceding to all but one demand in the ultimatum! Old alliances become entanglements. The British don't send enough support to the French, who, trying for a quick strike, ran right into the

German war machine. The Russians are ridiculously slow to mobilize, but their backward country is impossible to invade because their trains run on an antiquated gauge."

Stepping to the right of the whiteboard, Donahue retracted the great-powers map, which was mounted on spring rollers. All of Europe snapped up to the ceiling.

"This is how the First World War begins; millions die and Europe changes forever. So, my question to you and to General Schlieffen: Is war won by strategy or luck? Is history written by the design of rational nation-state actors, or is this all happening by accident? And, Mr. Flanagan, if you flick that pen one more time and drop it, you will disappear quicker than the Russian Second Army."

"Heil Hitler," Flanagan muttered, just a touch too loud.

Donahue placed the cap on his blue marker very slowly. "Excuse me, son?"

Flanagan sank into his seat. "Nothing."

"Stand up!"

Donahue's command was like the crack of a volcano. A terrified Flanagan stood.

"To the back of the class."

"For what?"

Donahue's face was bright red, full bull moose. "Mr. Flanagan, my class time is too short for your nonsense. *Back of the room! Now!*"

"Sir, I don't think—"

"That's right, keep talking," Donahue growled. "Make this easier for me and worse for you."

"Fine." Flanagan shuffled to the back of the room. No one dared make eye contact with him or Donahue. *Jesus Christ,* Dan thought, *Flanagan's triggered a Nam flashback.*

"You know what I see?" Donahue was barking so loud, the windows shook. "Know what the Führer thinks?"

Silence.

"I asked you a question, Mr. Flanagan. You know what I see?"

"No, sir."

Donahue stepped into Flanagan. They were inches apart. "A disrespectful little shit."

The sophomores stared straight ahead at the whiteboards. Dan was straining his side-eye to witness the massacre behind him. *Donahue might destroy Flanagan in order to save him.* Flanagan's chin was trembling. He gulped a breath. Donahue moved in even closer.

"Are you going to cry now? What kind of a wiseass are you? You waste my time as a student, and when you want to act like a joker, you can't pull that off either."

"I'm sorry."

Dan felt like crying for Flanagan, and Sticky gave him a "holy shit" look. *How could we have possibly lost the Vietnam War?* Dan wondered.

"No apology necessary, Mr. Flanagan. I feel sorry for you. You are a first-class fuckup, and for the rest of the year, you will speak only when spoken to. You will not like me, but you will respect me, and you will learn. How tall are you, Flanagan?"

Flanagan wiped his nose in his sleeve, head bowed to the carpet. "Five foot four, sir."

Donahue uncapped his blue marker, made a histrionic display of ballparking Flanagan's height from the floor, and then drew a small circle on a poster of the Magna Carta. "Put your nose right here, Mr. Flanagan."

Flanagan stepped to the poster and put his nose in the circle. It was two inches taller than nostril level, just enough to raise his chin and tip his toes in discomfort.

"If your nose comes out of that circle before the end of the period, you will be writing a twenty-page book report this weekend on *All Quiet on the Western Front*." Donahue marched to the front of the class, a kick in his step, the fury turned off like a light switch. "Gentlemen, we were talking about the best-laid plans of the First World War . . ."

And in the Catholic school tradition of "punish one, teach many," no one spoke out of turn in Donahue's class for the remainder of the year.

o o o

FROM THERE IT WAS A FRIDAY OF ATTRITION. DAN WENT FROM CLASS to class gaining work and worry for the weekend. His editorship of *The Roundup* was careening toward the wandering rocks. The deadline for all stories for the November issue was that morning, but when he checked the mailbox at the newspaper office, not a single reporter had filed. Polishing the lens of his Pentax, Father Argerlich shrugged. As Dan sat in Oglesby's class trying to focus on *The Old Man and the Sea*, he felt *salao*, the worst form of unlucky.

Oglesby stalked around the classroom as he went on about parataxis and iceberg theories of narrative. He sliced the air with Euclid, a former metal curtain rod that had been segmented with white notches. Dan tried to focus on Santiago, but all he could think was: *The old man was a Yankees fan, so life wasn't that bad, right?*

"Gentlemen, turn to the last two pages. Mr. Dowlearn, tell us what happens."

"The old man is resting. The boy is attending to him."

"And what about after that, Mr. McGhee?" Oglesby tapped the metal leg of Rob's desk. "Focus us on the last two scenes."

"There are tourists. They are looking down at the water and they see the bones of the fish. Its skeleton."

"Correct. And what then?"

"And they ask the waiter what happened."

"And what does he tell them?"

"That the sharks had eaten the marlin."

"And do the tourists accept that?"

Liam Plimmer's hand shot up. "No, they don't. They think the waiter is saying it's a shark's skeleton, not a marlin's."

"Exactly." Oglesby planted Euclid in the carpet. "They think it's a shark carcass and don't understand what happened to the old man and the marlin. So the question is: Why did Hemingway include this? Why did he essentially end the book on this conversation? Mr. Torkel?"

"It's a way of saying: all that for what?"

"Yes, but what's the bigger point?"

Dan raised his hand. "That no one can understand the old man's suffering or why."

"Okay. And so?"

"And so, even after being told the story of the old man, we don't know the *real* story. We know he endures, that he suffers, but no one *really* knows why this all happened. We still don't get it. Even the old man doesn't get it."

"That's correct. Sophomores, as Hemingway says, this story is all about what a man can do and what a man endures. And what does it mean to endure?" Oglesby flipped to a dog-eared page. "*'The thousand times that he had proved it meant nothing. Now the old man was proving it again. Each time was a new time and he never thought about the past when he was doing it.'* Every time it's a new telling, and every time, Hemingway realized, doesn't quite tell it completely, or come close to explaining why we must suffer and endure. Very good. All right, gentlemen, time to turn in your journals."

Dan winced. Sticky turned around for him to pass his journal forward. Dan shook his head, then, seized with regret, reached into his backpack. He had his journal with him; he just couldn't bring himself to turn it in.

This predicament had started the night his father made Uncle Jack storm out on dinner. Miserable and overheated, Dan holed up in his room, turned on "Bob Dylan's 115th Dream," and just wrote. The journal assignment was "1001 Things to Do with a White Elephant" and Dan let a furious, sad, and absurd part of his brain take over. After preambling about all the things he thought were possible white elephants—the *Spruce Goose*, Superman's Fortress of Solitude—he actually began writing out one thousand things to do.

#154 Tear Saran wrap with only one hand.
#155 Speak pig Latin to a Latin pig.
#156 Shut the doors to the palace of wisdom behind us.

And as Dan sat propped up on bed pillows, he kept writing every thought that came into his head. As Dylan jangled on about Captain Arab, with visions of desolate rows and sad-eyed ladies, and forgetting about today until tomorrow, something took over, and what he was writing wasn't coming in drips of thought but was *flowing*, and flowing fast.

#467 Steal Philoctetes's bow and leave him some Lotrimin foot spray.
#468 Go from catatonic to paranoid.
#469 Quit licking wounds and feed the dogs of Asclepius Alpo.

Dan started scribbling in his journal faster and faster. His hand cramped somewhere in the six hundreds but he kept going, the flow flowing, the Dylan tape popping at the end of each side, which Dan stretched across the mattress to flip. Around eleven p.m., he heard the footsteps of his father and his mother going to bed in separate rooms.

#832 Tell the truth when things are not fine.

#833 Leave this harbor of bad feelings.

#834 Accept when your father's sick and your mother's depressed.

#835 Don't despair. Don't suffer.

His hand throbbing, Dan stopped there. *Don't suffer.* Wiping away the tears, he went to bed.

Back in class, Sticky stopped chewing on his pen and popped Dan in the shoulder. "Dude, turn in the journal."

Dan pulled his hand from his bag. "I can't. I didn't finish."

Oglesby collected the notebooks but did not count them, and Dan was unsure if he noticed that his journal was missing. The bell rang, and Oglesby raised his hand to hold the sophomores in their seats for one last admonition.

"Gentlemen, Norwegian rat season is upon us. The first election is going to be soon, and before you know it, we will also be preparing for the Game. Prove to me that you are not just enduring, you are excelling. To paraphrase Papa Hemingway, rule twenty-two: keep your head clear and suffer like a rat. If you understand this lesson, you will be prepared for this class, the strategies the Game requires, and whatever challenge comes next."

Panicked and nearly in tears, Dan packed up quick and rushed from Oglesby's classroom, convinced he was now definitely and finally *salao.*

o o o

WHEN SCHOOL FINALLY LET OUT, DAN WENT HOME WITH RICK, WHO lived in a far northern kingdom known as Plano. Spanish for "really fucking flat," Plano was Dallas with even less of a strategy. In 1987, back before Plano was fully turnpiked and terraformed, half the land was still undeveloped, but the grid was filling in, and one hundred thousand people had arrived. To find Rick's house, imagine a beige brick, brown-shingled housing development, in the middle of empty prairie, curbs cut within sight of the pastures of Southfork Ranch. Welcome to the Colonnade of the Bowling Green Meadow Estates, a.k.a. the Colon Bowl.

Rick and Dan hitched a ride with Chad Gilchrist, another Plano kid, and discovered *Master of Puppets* to be a very wearying album for driving to the end of civilization. Eventually Chad dropped them off on Castlemere Drive. Rick Sr. was standing in his empty three-car garage smoking a cigar.

"Son, welcome home. Who is this you brought with you? A new recruit to our cult? Perfect. Take him back to the tabernacle and prepare for the sacrifice."

A trip to the cigar store punched the ticket for Richard Lee Dowlearn Sr. to be in a good mood. Rick Sr. was a true born Texan who grew up in all parts of the Dallas hinterlands, from Denton to Duncanville. He went to SMU until drinking got him kicked out. He then hunted and hoboed, jockeyed rigs in the Gulf, made a couple of runs to the border, and lived like an outlaw until it was time to make amends. He had been sober for a good long while, until of course he wasn't, but that was not a concern of late—the cigar store was part of his AA routine.

Rick and Dan went in through the garage. The house was as big as any in Preston Hollow, a long scalene run of ranch that triangled back on itself to accommodate a white dye pool and an untrampled green lawn guarded by willows and cottonwoods that divided the property from the sixteenth green of a golf course. The house smelled like paint and drywall and felt to Dan like part of an elaborate movie set put up moments ago to convince him Plano really existed.

As the boys walked through the laundry room, they were greeted by a clattering of nails and dog tags. Ruby and Ozzie, sister and brother wire fox terriers, ran toward Rick growling and gurgling with happiness. They then spotted Dan and circled him while barking in piercing pizzicato squeaks.

"Shut the fuck up, Ruby. Get down, Ozzie."

"Ozzie" was short for "Oswald." Ruby and Oswald. Dan froze as Ozzie snuffled him for wolf scents. *Clear.*

"Boy howdy. The men of Jesuit return. Hi, Danny, what do you say?"

Standing at the kitchen island was Rick's mother, Margaret, who waited for a peck on the cheek from her son. With wizened Scotch-Irish features, she looked a little like Loretta Lynn.

"You guys hungry? I've got chips and dip."

Sitting at the far counter, grazing on her own separate stockpile of chips and dip, was Melissa, Rick's sister, dressed in the yellow oxford and green tartan skirt for St. Paul the Apostle. The Dowlearns were easygoing Methodists who you might have thought had outkicked the coverage of good public schools this far up in Plano, but the truth was you couldn't matriculate with more than a week of unexcused absences in the Plano ISD, and Rick was going to miss much more than that with his fledgling acting career. When he got cast as Spalding Gray's son, Larry Culver, in *True Stories*, Rick enrolled in parochial school. He took the role, which amounted to a surreal dinner scene where he played tic-tac-toe with zucchini slices and Triscuits as Spalding Gray gave David Byrne a lecture on the coming disintegration of the modern workplace while punctuating his point with a cooked lobster. To this day, no one is sure what the hell is going on in that scene, but Rick got a closing credit, and St. Paul's gave the Dowlearns a good sibling discount on tuition, so Missy went too.

"Missy girl, come help me with the laundry. And if you give me that face we can add ironing to it. Also, we have to sweep that garage."

"Mooooommmm . . ." Missy was a world-class whiner.

"There's enough leaves in there that if Daddy flicks one hot ash from those foul cigars, he will send this house up quicker than Farrah Fawcett." Mrs. Dowlearn pulled the bag of tortilla chips away from her. "Come on, darling. Dan, can you believe these lazy children I have to live with?"

There was a productivity to the Dowlearns that was tireless—equal parts Protestant work ethic and an AA component of keeping busy for Rick Sr.'s sake. Dan, whose mother waited on him hand and foot, realized he was lazy. Home life for the Dowlearn children was a never-ending punch list of chores—Rick had to walk the dogs, skim the pool, take out the trash, everything short of building a barn and prime-coating it. Embarrassed not to be doing anything, Dan went around the back of the house and held the ladder while Rick cleared leaves from the roof gutters.

"Sorry, almost done with all this shit."

"No worries."

"Son . . ."

Rick Sr. peeked around the corner from the garage.

"Last thing tonight and then you and your compadre can hightail it. The pump on the Jacuzzi is throttling."

"In or out?"

"I think when it's sucking in, it's not catching a full drink."

"Okay." Rick dropped a giant wad of leaves below him.

"I think that valve is stuck again. Here, Dan, my lad, carry this toolbox for him."

Rick came down off the ladder and headed around to the hot tub. Dan lugged the big Black and Decker metal chest of tools and followed him across the patio to a greenhouse that looked out over the pool. Through glass doors was a hot tub covered with a white float like a giant marshmallow on top of cocoa. Rick pulled the side panel back and studied the pump. Dan crouched behind him, pretending to understand what he was looking at. As a summertime lifeguard at Glen Cove Swim Club, he was familiar with pool equipment, but this was a different level of mechanical understanding—one the previous Malone generation, who spent their lives hectoring undermotivated supers in the Bronx and at the mercies of various scamming repairmen, had not attained. Rick Sr. had taught his son to be handy, to tinker, and Dan—who could break a dipstick checking the oil on a car—admired that.

Rick popped the intake valve back into place. "Okay, go through that door into my dad's office, and when I tell you, throw the bottom breaker on the left."

Dan went into the small study and found the circuit box.

"Now," Rick yelled.

Dan hit it, and the hot tub roiled to life. Dan glanced around Rick Sr.'s office, which was a boring bunch of carpet books and paperwork. Then he turned and found the gun cabinet.

"Whoa."

It was a SWAT team's locker of firepower—rifles, pistols, shotguns, you name it. And a nice wooden cabinet too, like the kind his mother put all the Waterford in. On the wall adjacent there was a poster billowing with an angelic grouping of clouds.

God grant me the serenity to accept the things I cannot change, the firepower to change the things I can, and the wisdom to bury the bodies.

Rick came into the office, his freckled forehead sweating from the decathlon of chores. Dan stared at the cabinet.

"What do you hunt? The German army?"

"Deer and quail, depending where we go."

"Have the animals ever shot back?"

"If guns kill people, cars make them drive drunk. God-given rights, Malone." Rick was smart enough to spout his father's wisdom with only a half-serious measure. The pump on the hot tub made a labored gargle, and they both moved back into the greenhouse.

"Well, I'm coming to your house when the Russians attack. What are the dogs doing?"

Across the hallway in the dining room, Ruby and Ozzie were pacing in circles under the chairs.

"Yeah, they do that. I guess they like how it rubs their backs."

Dan watched them for a few loops. It was like a prison yard routine. *Stressed out, goddamn dogs,* Dan thought. Then just as their patrol couldn't get any more comical, Ruby ran into a chair leg and backed up traffic. This didn't sit right with Ozzie, who nipped at Ruby's dogleg left, and soon the two were wrestling and fighting.

"Knock it off, idiots." Rick went back into the waterworks. Dan watched the two terriers wrestle. Rick ran the pump in reverse, which created a high-pitched squeal, in turn setting off Ozzie and Ruby. In a split second, wrestling had escalated into a fight to the death.

"Uh, Rick . . ."

"What?" He couldn't hear anything over the pump, so Dan tapped his shoulder.

"Your dogs are trying to kill each other."

Ozzie and Ruby had each other by the throat. Rick turned off the hot tub.

"Ozzie, Ruby, no!"

But it was too late; they were locked in, and Ruby had scratched Ozzie, and the smell of blood drove them mad. Rick tried to put his hand in to grab a collar and almost lost it as the two terriers became one vicious ball of fight. Dan had horrified flashes of the Jack London he had read in junior high.

"Jesus Christ."

Ruby whined as Ozzie got ahold of her by the neck and clamped down. Tufts of dog hair went flying. The two dogs pulled each other into the hallway.

"Dad!"

Rick Sr. appeared, followed by his wife and daughter.

"Good Lord."

"The noise from the pump made them go apeshit."

Dan stepped back as the dogs continued to murder each other. Rick Sr. had a copy of *Texas Monthly* in his hand. He rolled it up.

"Son, get a collar."

"They almost took a finger when I tried that."

"Well, Ruby is going to lose if we don't separate them. Missy, go get the travel kennel. I'm going to throw one of these dogs in there."

And then Rick Jr. and Rick Sr. each took a dog by its collar. But it was no use. Ozzie was clenched on Ruby, and despite how they pulled he wouldn't let go. The Dowlearn men yanked and even raised the two terriers up off the ground. Ozzie's snarls grew more deranged, Ruby whimpered and rattled. Rick Sr. raised up the *Texas Monthly* and started whaling on Ozzie's snout. Nothing. Missy screamed as the dogs left a trail of blood along the hallway carpet. Rick's mom was yelling ten different things to do at both Ricks. After a dozen gigantic blows with the magazine, Rick Sr. gave up.

Dan thought of the gun cabinet in Rick Sr.'s office. *Are these people crazy enough . . .*

Just then Ozzie let go for the briefest of seconds, and Rick Jr. pulled Ruby away and ran off with her to the garage. Rick Sr. dunked Ozzie into the kennel as the dog went ballistic, scratching and snapping at his hands.

Rick Sr. kneeled down next to the kennel, exhausted. "Well, hell's bells. Goddamn dogs. So goddamn high-strung." He studied the cover photo of Henry Cisneros on his *Texas Monthly*, now spattered with blood. He started to chuckle and smiled with a touch of pride.

"Did you see that grip Ozzie had? Dan here looked like he was ready to shoot them both, I tell you what."

And as they began to clean up this Plano crime scene, the Dowlearns all started laughing.

The color returned to Dan's face. *Huh, Mom is right. These native Texans are certifiable.*

All he could think to do was laugh with them.

○ ○ ○

DINNER WITH THE DOWLEARNS INCLUDED MORE CHIPS AND DIP AND takeout from Herrera's, which was the normal *tia*'s special of tortilla soup and greasy enchiladas. Then around eight p.m., Beppe Ravioli, a classmate and fellow Planoite, picked up Rick and Dan in his mom's Tercel. In spite of his delicious-Stouffer's-frozen-dinner name, Beppe was a fairly cool dude with a joker face and a butt cut, who always had soft-pack smokes he stole from his dad. All three boys lit up as they got on the tollway heading south. The plan was to meet the rest of the gang at Josh Barlow's house in Highland Park. Mama and Papa Bear Barlow were out of town, and Josh had invited over half of North Dallas.

As sophomores, the boys were low on the social totem pole— better to be neither seen nor heard by upperclassmen while sneaking turns at the keg. Rick, mindful of living in his father's house, would not dare drink but was amused by Dan's attempts to lush it up when they went out. Instead Rick chased girls. And he even caught a couple, which brought with it a new set of problems.

The boys pulled up on Versailles Avenue. (All the streets in the Park Cities bespoke the hoity-toity—Bordeaux Avenue, Harvard Avenue, Beverly Drive, Not Your Country Club Court, and so on.) They could hear the party from five doors down, and as they walked up the Barlows' driveway to the thumping music, Rick looked unsure.

"Only a matter of time before the cops come."

He was right—the party was borderline bonkers, and way too loud for uptight Highland Park. From the front door they went through a living room obscured in a fat cloud of pot smoke and headed toward a sunken den with long green leather sectionals. That was where Rick ran into girl number one, Jane.

"Hey, baby, *que pasa*?" Rick smiled, unsurprised, playing it cool as a Cusack. Jane Osbaldeston was a dark-redhead with a smooth porcelain face that reminded Dan of the Oil of Olay lady on the box that sat by his mother's sink. Jane was all A's and honor roll but hated going to Ursuline and always dragged Rick downtown to meet up with her bummed-out Arts Magnet friends to enjoy collective melancholy. She also worked the lotions counter at Marshall Field's in the Galleria, another symbol of her worldliness, and was so over everything about high school, except Rick Dowlearn, who had her pretty twisted.

Barely able to shout over the blare of Whitesnake, Jane frowned and reported: "Welcome to moron central. Maura ditched me to go upstairs with the heavy drug addicts." She down-talked in a reverse Valley Girl accent.

"Did you work tonight with Maura? You poor thing." Rick was a natural at teasing and flirting. He had Jane half draped over him with just one line.

Time to leave these lovebirds, Dan thought. He found a possibly used red Solo cup, which he washed out in the kitchen sink, and concocted a vodka and flat, warm Pepsi. *Not great.* The party was packed, and he had to swim through a bunch of assholes standing around with not a whole lot to do. As he bumped his way by, he ran into Lili, Rick's girl number two.

Lili Villeneuve was a French foreign exchange student at Ursuline. Beautiful, dark features, pouty lips, a short angled braid pulled into a sideways ponytail like Demi Moore's in *One Crazy Summer.*

"Oh, Dan-ee." Her accent was thick as a milkshake *chocolat.* "Have you seen Rick?" *Reek.*

"I think I saw him out front. He might have been leaving."

"*D'accord.* If you see him, tell him to find me. Okay, Dan-ee?"

"Sure thing." She didn't seem like she was going to hunt for Rick herself. Which thankfully bought Dan time to warn him.

"*Merci.*" Lili shot him a kittenish smile. And then Dan realized. *She's playing you, and probably playing him. The French have a word for this . . . yup, she's a croquette.* Dan took another sour gulp of Pepsi and vodka and tried to wade back through the crowd to warn *Reek*.

Just then, Josh Barlow's psycho younger brother, Jayson, threw a long string of Black Cats near the fridge, which exploded close enough for Dan to feel the sparks on his ankles.

"Jesus Christ!" Dan turned and ducked through the sliding door to the backyard. Jayson thought this was the funniest thing ever, but it was soon trumped when senior linebacker and all-district dipshit Trevor Kowalski streaked. He came running around from the front of the house, hurdling the gate buck naked in a modified Fosbury. He rolled onto the grass and then ran straight at a gaggle of girls. The flock dispersed screaming, and Trevor raised his arm in victory like the happiest caveman rapist of the Pleistocene. He smacked a fleeing damsel on the ass and got a punch in the neck in return.

"Someone throw me a towel."

"Kowalski, it's not really cold outside," his teammate Jamie Allred yelled, tipping his beer can toward his southern hemisphere to accentuate the point. But that was just bullshit teasing. As everyone gave the naked guy a wide berth, Dan found himself standing next to his old friend Emma Wesselman.

"Hey, Dan."

"Hi, Emma."

Their eyes met, mortified in their mutual realization—Trevor had a *huge* dick, and he knew it as he went into Attic poses to "Sledgehammer."

"Uzfuck, bring that shit over here." Putt Uzbug, another Mensa member of the class of 1988, held a bottle rocket, which he gave to Trevor. Then Trevor bent down into a three-point stance. His hand—and the rocket—slid behind his back.

"Light that bitch."

Seconds later, Trevor Kowalski shot a bottle rocket out of his ass. Everyone howled with laughter as he patted out the shower of sparks that had landed on his hind side.

"Unbelievable." Emma shook her head. "Now it's a party."

"Yeah, Caligula here almost set fire to his taint." Dan stared down at his red Solo cup. Emma was not a drinker.

"Crazy to see you here."

Emma—*Again, not a surprise*—looked good. Her hair teased in cute tortoiseshell barrettes, wet lip gloss, a careful smile.

"I know, private school party."

"No, I didn't mean—"

"Rich kids, Highland Park douchebags . . ."

"Stop, I wasn't saying that."

"What are you saying, Dan Malone?"

"I don't know." Dan felt this sudden surge of honesty. "Listen, I should apologize to you."

"What? Why?"

"Emma, I just wish . . ."

And as Dan was about to pour out his Song of Songs to Emma Wesselman, Brady Bennison, the hotshot varsity wideout, came running out onto the patio.

"Cops are here! Everyone get the fuck out of Dodge!"

o o o

AND SO THE ADOLESCENT FIRE DRILL BEGAN. FOLKS THREW THEIR cups to the ground, and there was a surge toward the back gate. Emma ran into the house, and Dan was about to follow her when he heard the squawk of a cop siren and froze. Within seconds, a squad car had pulled into the alley. The Highland Park police, like those in any tony neighborhood, were particularly fascistic in their peacekeeping duties. A cop entered the backyard and first came across fellow sophomore Jason deMarini, who, to Dan's surprise, was not doing anything wrong, and screamed at him to get on his knees, hands high.

That set off a panic, and those left in the backyard scooted into the house to hide. But there were a couple of cops inside too, clearing out the kitchen. Dan had edged into the shadows of the backyard below a lone droopy pine. The backyard Gestapo kept yelling at people to get on their knees. *Is this asshole actually going to arrest people?* Dan started to freak out. He couldn't get arrested, for two reasons. The first was these were just bullshit circumstances—he wasn't even tipsy. The second was that he was more afraid of his mother than the Highland Park police department. He snuck behind the pine tree as the cop knocked wine coolers off tables and continued to harass the partygoers, shining his flashlight into various dilated pupils.

"You know who called us, folks? Everyone. The whole goddamn neighborhood complained. Ladies and gentlemen, we're officially done here." The cop grabbed some drunk wiseass—*Yep, that's Tim Hebert from honors bio*—by the collar. "Have something to say about that? Try me. All of you are in a shit-ton of trouble."

The cop turned away, and Dan hitched himself over the fence. As he swung his leg over the top, a spotlight fell on him.

"You! Get down!"

Dan swung his other leg around and fell into a row of hedges. He sprinted across the neighbor's yard, the thick St. Augustine grass a strange and beautiful blue in the moonlight. He had seconds before a cop tried to cut him off in the alley. As luck would have it, the next fence over was chain link and only five feet high, and Dan hurdled it quick on both ends, putting him three houses down. He heard the squad car begin its crawl down the alley. The next fence was twelve feet high and it was facing in, with no good crossbeams to make purchase on. Dan scanned the far end of the chain link. The house across the alley didn't have a fence at all and was an open run to the next street over.

The cop car was rolling down the alley, its searchlight cast on the yard adjacent to the Barlows'. Dan scooted toward the chain link, hopped it in a loud jangle, and made his break for it, darting across the alley in front of the cop car. The spotlight followed, and he was now in a dead sprint as the cruiser pulled up behind him. He booked it around the side of the house, almost tripping on the knotted roots of an unpruned peach tree growing sideways and south.

Around the corner, Dan veered left and stayed low as he scurried across several front lawns. There was a streetlight at the end of the block, which he avoided as he cut across. He looked over his shoulder—there was no spotlight following him yet. He kept running, hugging the hedges of the fancy houses and looking for another cut-through. *Another block or two and I'll be clear.*

And just then, the patrol car came roaring around the corner, full cherries lit. Dan ducked into the nearest side yard and hopped another fence. He wanted to hunker down, but something was moving in the backyard. Footsteps—no, it was something rushing toward him, huffing, panting.

Shit.

It was a dog, but not just any dog—a fucking red-eyed Rottweiler was on its hump careening straight toward him. Dan froze. The beast had him cornered. *I'm so dead.* The dog launched itself at Dan, who at the last second rolled to the side. The dog went flying and let out a bloodcurdling yelp as it slammed jaws-first into the fence. Dan took off across the yard as the dog shook off its concussion and growled. Now it was really riled. Dan sprinted ten steps and—*Goddamn it*—he almost went straight into a pool, which he tightroped and tiptoed around. The demon dog was back on his tail, barking. The patio lights went on, which were sure to draw the cops' attention. He hopped the next fence in two adrenalined steps and flew over onto the canvas cover of a Mercedes coupe. The car alarm went off, the Rottweiler howling while trying to hurdle the fence, and all the lights in the house went on. All Dan needed to make more noise was a spoon and a pot to bang on. The cops pulled up to the driveway of the house, and Dan rolled off the car and ran down the alley, back against the direction they were coming. Four doors down he found another yard without a fence and kept going, cutting over again and again until he was five or six blocks away. There he found a big ball of maiden grass and he rolled behind it, nearly hyperventilating, nearly vomiting. He wiped what felt like slobber from the dog off his face. It was that close.

A long, still moment passed. There were no flashlights following and no cop car in pursuit. It was just him, panting in the ornamental grasses like an exhausted springbok on the veldt. He retched up the few sips of vodka that he had downed. Another quiet minute under the moonlight, and still no cops, no cars, and no idea where he was.

Dan tried to fix his inner compass. He had run south from the Barlows'. *So that means that Preston Road is still on my left, the tollway on my right.* Calling his mom for a ride home would defeat the entire purpose of successfully winning a manhunt with the Highland Park police department. He was a fugitive from justice now. He decided to turn around, get to Preston, and start north. *Maybe go back to the Barlow house?* But that felt like exactly what the cops were waiting for him to do.

After ten minutes of walking he made it to the corner of Preston and Lorraine, where he stared across the six lanes as the occasional car sheered past. There were no taxis and no buses that late. Hitchhiking was just asking to become a dire urban legend. It was coming up on midnight, and he was supposed to spend the night at Rick's.

Crap.

Dan had no choice but to start walking home. He had escaped the worst trouble—getting caught drinking by the police—and could make up some story for his mother. *We got separated at a party. Rick left me stranded because of some girl.* He could work on that hard-luck tale as he tried to make it through North Dallas without getting killed or arrested. He trudged along Preston, the next block to a stoplight taking forever. He considered how Oglesby would rate his escape. *Norwegian rat caliber? I doubt he'd be impressed with Trevor Kowalski shooting fireworks out of his ass. And now I'm lost out here. More suffering, more* salao. *Big-time* salao. The gate for the country club came up across the street. *Goddamn rich assholes and their asshole police force.* He reached the light for Mockingbird.

As he waited for the light to change, a red Toyota pulled up to the intersection. The car looked familiar, but the windows were tinted, and Dan didn't want to invite eye contact.

And then the window rolled down. It was Rick.

"Jesus Christ, Malone."

"Oh thank God."

Dan climbed into the car. Beppe Ravioli was driving, and they had picked up Sticky, who looked at Dan like he was dealing crack.

"Holy shit, Malone—what happened to you?"

"The cops came, and I ran."

"Why?"

"They were arresting people. How did you guys not get busted?"

"We just stood there while they took all the booze and then made everyone leave the house."

"Oh."

"But they were chasing someone. They had three cruisers pull up and then started searching."

"Oh."

Sticky was about to have a cow. "Was that for you, Malone?"

"Maybe."

"You moron, why did you run?" Beppe snickered.

"I thought . . ."

Rick started to laugh. "More importantly, how did you escape the entire goddamn Highland Park police department?"

"I'm just that good."

"We went to IHOP and were about to give up on you, but Rick said we should make one last pass by the Barlows' in case you came back."

"Well, you found me."

"You're an idiot." Sticky looked out the window in disbelief.

Rick turned and offered Dan a high five. "Seriously, how the fuck did you pull that off?"

"Thanks for coming back for me." Dan slapped Rick's palm. "You two can go fuck yourselves."

"Fuckin'-a, Malone." Rick smiled and shook his head. "I can't believe you made it!"

The light changed, and Beppe made the turn onto Preston for the long drive back to Plano. And with that, Dan sat back and let Rick herald the legend of his escape from the law.

"Officer Bodel"—Douglas Blackburn stepped toward the witness stand—"can you describe the scene upon your arrival at the Raleigh residence?"

The Dallas police officer consulted his incident log and recited the following: "We responded to an emergency dispatch at eleven forty-three p.m., and arrived at 9324 Credo Drive at eleven fifty-two p.m. The paramedics from Fire and Rescue were already on location. We proceeded around to the alleyway behind the residence and parked at the end of the driveway. The garage door was half raised, and within the garage the medics were attending to Mrs. Raleigh."

"Was the light on in the garage?"

"No, sir."

"Then how could you see all of this?"

"Reverend Raleigh's car was still parked in the driveway; the headlights were on."

"Okay, and as you approached the garage, what did you see?"

"Mrs. Raleigh was lying on the ground."

"Did you notice signs of a struggle?"

"No, the garage and the house were tidy."

"Would you say someone had cleaned up?"

"Objection, Your Honor."

"Withdrawn. What was the state of Margaret Raleigh at this point?"

Juror number six, Anne Malone, perked up at this latest volley. She scrutinized the district attorney, who was almost too cool and composed. With the defense attorney Haynes Whiteside ready to pounce at the slightest, Douglas Blackburn took the quick rebuke in stride. In fact, he had already scored the point without needing the cop's testimony as to whether the crime scene looked too clean. *No struggle could mean she knew the attacker,* Anne speculated, *and let him get close.*

"Mrs. Raleigh was not breathing. She was unconscious. Her face was swollen, her neck covered in a series of red welts. The way she was lying on the ground, her head angled from her body, indicated that her neck had been broken."

"Was there a belt or a rope, or anything in the garage by which Peggy Raleigh could have choked herself?"

"No, sir. Not that we came across."

His hands. He had to be close. Very close.

"During the time you were at the Credo Drive residence, how long did the paramedics work on Mrs. Raleigh?"

"I would say ten minutes before they took her away in the ambulance."

"And in that ten minutes, what was Reverend Raleigh doing?"

"He paced back and forth between the house and the garage."

"Did he hold his wife's hand?"

"No."

"Did he kneel next to her?"

"No."

"Did he whisper a prayer in her ear?"

"No."

"Did he touch her? Stroke her hair or her arm?"

"No, he stayed clear. He said nothing and did nothing."

"Thank you, Officer."

○ ○ ○

DAY ONE OF THE STANDING RALEIGH TRIAL. AFTER JURY SELECTION
there had been a series of delays. Whiteside had asked for more
time to prepare, and that sparked rumors in the papers (which
Anne was not supposed to read but did anyway). The first was that
Raleigh was going to confess. But the case was too high-profile
for the district attorney to offer a plea deal. The second story—no
doubt started by Whiteside—was the DPD were looking into another suspect.

Both of these juristic rabbit holes kept moving the start of the
trial back until it landed on that Friday. That morning the jury had
heard opening statements. Blackburn was heavy-handed and
Miltonic—Reverend Raleigh had fallen like Lucifer himself. Whiteside was more nuanced, Anne thought, admitting Raleigh was a
man of frailties and sins, but that didn't make him evil or capable
of attempted murder. *Benefit of the doubt. Be aware of your own bias*,
she reminded herself. *Judge the facts, not the history of the Christian
church and its clergy.*

After lunch, the prosecution presented the medical evidence,
and Anne's stoic approach crumbled. The chief examiner described in detail how grisly it was to strangle Mrs. Raleigh and how
hypoxia to her brain had led to her current comatose state. It was
completely abominable, and Anne kept sneaking looks at Standing
Raleigh but couldn't get a read on him. He sat there emotionless
through it all. He wore a very expensive tailored blue suit with a
pocket square, his thinning sandstone-gray hair perfectly combed.
Inscrutable. Distant. And well coached, Anne surmised.

○ ○ ○

"YOUR HONOR, I'D LIKE TO CALL DETECTIVE HUME TO THE STAND."
Detective James Hume had a shaved bald head like Mr. Clean.

He wore a gray pinstripe suit and a silver silk tie, the knot hanging below a collar cheater. With a lineman frame filled out over years on the force, he was still imposing as the hard soles of his black boots announced each step across the courtroom floor. Blackburn gave Hume an assuring nod and began.

"Detective, can you tell the court how long you've been a member of the Dallas Police Department?"

"Eighteen years."

"And how long have you been an investigative officer?"

"Five years."

"Detective, when did you first meet Reverend Raleigh?"

"The morning of April twenty-second at the intensive care unit of Presbyterian Hospital."

"Walk us through that first encounter with the defendant."

"I arrived at the hospital room for Margaret Raleigh at eight a.m. I instructed our DPD photographer to take pictures of her injuries. I introduced myself to Reverend Raleigh and asked if it was all right that we conduct an interview."

"Was Reverend Raleigh alone?"

"No, he was accompanied by Bishop Goodfellow."

"That would be Mr. Wesley Goodfellow?"

"Yes, sir."

"How would you characterize Reverend Raleigh that morning?"

"He was exhausted."

"Was he reluctant to speak with you?"

"No, he was eager to talk to me."

At this point Raleigh's adrenaline must have worn off, Anne gathered, *and he wants to know what they know—or suspect.*

"To talk about what?"

"To help find the person who attacked his wife. My first question was if he had any idea who could have done this, and at this point Bishop Goodfellow produced a packet of letters."

"What was the nature of these letters?"

"They were a series of death threats against Reverend Raleigh."

"And Bishop Goodfellow produced these letters as evidence to you that someone was out to get the reverend."

"That's correct."

"Did any of the letters specify an attack against the Raleigh family?"

"They implied that something bad would happen to Raleigh, but there was no specific threat against his wife or children."

"Were these letters handwritten or typed?"

"They were typed."

"And were you able to trace where these letters came from?"

"Yes. They matched a typewriter at First United."

Bingo.

"A typewriter in the offices of Reverend Raleigh's own church?"

"Yes."

Blackburn wheeled around and faced the jury to let the moment land. There was a slight commotion among the press in the gallery as Blackburn returned to his witness. Judge Sam peered warily, wordlessly warning Blackburn that this was not to become more theatric than needed.

Anne was unsure what to make of the death threats. *If this is premeditation, it's poorly conceived. Then again, the letters don't exactly tell us when he decided to do the deed.*

If, if he did, she corrected herself. *The letters are cover for something all right, but he may never have thought to go through with it. Something about that night pushed him over.*

"Detective Hume, when you interviewed Reverend Raleigh that morning, did you discuss the reverend's whereabouts the night prior?"

"Yes, sir."

"Please walk us through that evening of April twenty-first."

"Okay, according to what Reverend Raleigh told me in that first interview, he came home that evening at six thirty p.m. He drove his car into the back driveway, where he found Mrs. Raleigh working on the garage door latch with Palmolive."

"Why was she doing that?"

To destroy evidence. Convenient.

"According to Reverend Raleigh, because the latch had been sticking."

"Did the Raleighs have a security system for their home on Credo Drive?"

"Yes, sir—recently installed as a precaution against the threats Reverend Raleigh was receiving at the church."

"And was the garage covered by this alarm system?"

"No, sir."

"Okay, so how long was Reverend Raleigh at home that evening?"

"No more than an hour. He told me that he did not eat dinner at the house but talked with his wife and shared a glass of wine with her. He then left for the Bridwell Library at SMU to work on a sermon."

"And so it's now about seven thirty in the evening. Did Reverend Raleigh go to the library?"

"No, he was in his car."

"How do you know that?"

"He made a call from his car phone."

"Who did he call?"

"Lucy Goodfellow."

That answer caused more than a commotion. Lucy Goodfellow was the bishop's daughter. Judge Barefoot Sam slapped his gavel on its pink granite block.

"Folks in the gallery, we can do this with or without you," he said.

Anne looked over at the press, none of whom were paying attention to the judge. *They have their scoop now . . .* Anne noticed Standing Raleigh glance over his shoulder with a slight frown. *This is all too strangely scripted and postured*, Anne thought.

"So from the records of the car phone," Blackburn said, cantering back and forth in front of the witness stand, "when did the reverend place this call?"

"Seven thirty-two p.m."

"And then where did he go?"

"To Lucy Goodfellow's apartment."

Several members of the press picked up and started moving toward the exit. Still time to make the evening news.

"Did Reverend Raleigh tell you this in your interview—the one you conducted at the hospital?"

"No. He said he was at the SMU library. Then later, after we received the phone records and interviewed Miss Goodfellow, he verified it."

"So he lied about it the first time?"

"Objection," Whiteside said calmly—he knew this was coming.

"Sustained."

Blackburn rephrased. "In the presence of her father, did the defendant admit to going over to Lucy Goodfellow's house the night of his wife's attempted murder?"

"No. That came later."

"After you caught him in a lie."

"Objection."

"Sustained." The judge grimaced in the middle of a sip of coffee. "Counselor, please move on."

The prosecutor is too gung-ho on the mistress, and the defense is almost playing possum, Anne realized. *It offers a motive, but Raleigh couldn't have been stupid enough to think there was a world where he runs off with her.*

"And when you confronted Reverend Raleigh with the evidence that he had called Miss Goodfellow and that in her affidavit she admitted he came over, what did he say happened?"

"He said he went to her apartment to borrow relaxation tapes."

"Relaxation tapes?" A few chortles of laughter followed Blackburn on this. Judge Sam eagle-eyed the gallery, ready to throw out the next person who made a peep.

"Yes, sir."

"And how long was he at Miss Goodfellow's apartment?"

"Forty minutes."

"And just to be clear, how far is Miss Goodfellow's apartment from SMU and the Raleigh residence?"

"They're all within about five miles of each other, less than fifteen minutes driving."

"So now it's past eight p.m. that evening, correct?"

"Yes, sir."

"And then where did he go?"

"To Bridwell Library."

"And how did you verify that?"

"A librarian there"—Hume checked his notes—"Ms. Janice Singleton, saw Reverend Raleigh sometime after eight p.m. Also a call was placed from a pay phone in the library to the Raleigh residence at eight thirty."

"Did Reverend Raleigh confirm he placed that call?"

"Yes. He said he spoke to his wife and told her to put the children to bed before he got home."

Suspicious. He's setting it up.

"How long did Reverend Raleigh say he stayed at the library?"

"For the next three hours, until close to midnight."

"Did that prove to be the case as you investigated his whereabouts that evening?"

"No." Hume rocked back in his chair.

"How do you know that?"

"Reverend Raleigh purchased gas with a credit card at a Texaco station on Greenville Avenue at eight fifty-three p.m. that night."

"Did he purchase anything else at the gas station?"

"Yes, a pint bottle of vodka."

Anne cringed as she thought about the empties of Smirnoff she had pulled out from under the seat of Pat's Cougar these past few years.

"Detective, did you interview a Mr. Javier Esparza?"

"Yes. He was one of the two paramedics who attended to Mrs. Raleigh."

"What did Mr. Esparza tell you about Reverend Raleigh?"

"That when he arrived at Credo Drive, the reverend was visibly intoxicated and he could smell alcohol on his breath."

"Okay, so at eight fifty-three the defendant is at the Texaco. Where does he go after that?"

"I don't know."

"You don't know?"

"Reverend Raleigh claims to have been at the library at SMU the entire night, but I can't place him there past eight thirty."

"So from eight fifty-three p.m. until he places the 911 call, at"—Blackburn checks his notes—"eleven forty-three p.m., you don't know where he is?"

"Well, he's within the vicinity of his vehicle because he made two calls from the car phone."

"Who did he call?"

"He called his house and left messages."

"Your Honor, I would like to play for the jury exhibit number twelve, the first message recovered from the Raleigh answering machine."

"Proceed." Judge Sam nodded at his clerk, Mr. Greenfield, who set up the audio player while Ms. Silverstone, Blackburn's assistant prosecutor, produced a poster. It was a transcript of the message, which played on a speaker.

"I don't have my watch on, but it's about nine thirty or nine forty-five. If you want to, go ahead and lock the garage door, and I'll park out front."

"Detective Hume, what time do the phone records put this call at?"

"Eleven twenty-four p.m."

"So almost two hours later than the defendant states on the message. Is that correct, sir?"

"Yes."

"And by the way, looking at the car phone records for the month of April '87, there are eight instances of Reverend Raleigh calling the number 787-1111. What is that number?"

"That number gives out the time and temperature."

"And why did Reverend Raleigh call that number so much?"

"Objection." Whiteside was growing a little testier.

"Withdrawn. Is it safe to conclude he was calling to find out the time from his car phone?"

"Or the temperature," Hume half-joked, "but yes."

"In your questioning of Reverend Raleigh, did you ask him if he wore a watch?"

"We did ask, and he did not wear a watch."

"So when he says in the message 'I don't have my watch on'—that's because Reverend Raleigh doesn't wear one, is that correct?"

"Yes, sir."

"And did Standing Raleigh park out front?"

"No, sir."

"He parked in the driveway in the back where the garage is, right?"

"Yes."

"The garage door, which Reverend Raleigh claimed Mrs. Raleigh was, earlier that evening, trying to grease with dish soap. Did you examine the lock on the garage door, Detective?"

"Yes."

"And was it broken or stuck?"

"No, the garage door and the lock were in working order."

Anne's imagination went wild with that key detail. *He came into the house first. She left the alarm off for him to come home. He lured her out to the garage . . .*

"And did you swipe the door, its handle, and the garage for fingerprints?"

"Yes."

"And did you find any prints other than members of the Raleigh family?"

"No."

"Anything else strange about the garage that you found in your investigation?"

"Well, there was no lightbulb in the overhead light."

He lures her there. Away from the sleeping children. The car still running so it's noisy enough.

"No lightbulb? So someone had removed it before the attack?"

"Objection, speculation."

"Withdrawn. So the garage would have been pitch-black the night of the attack because the lightbulb was missing from the socket. Is that true, Detective?"

"Yes."

Anne reversed course with a dozen silent postulations. *He didn't go into the house. He hid. He lay in wait in the garage for her to lock it.*

"Your Honor, I'd like to introduce exhibit number thirteen."

The poster board was swapped out, and the second message was played.

"Hey, you're probably asleep, but I'm on my way home."

"When did Reverend Raleigh leave this message?"

"Eleven twenty-nine p.m."

"So that is left just minutes before he actually came home and called the police."

"Yes."

Covering his tracks. Poorly.

"Your Honor, can we play exhibit number twenty-two?"

Anne glimpsed Raleigh again—stone-faced, holding a pen and legal pad but not writing. They listened to the call he made to the police dispatcher.

"Uh, I just came into the house, and my wife . . . Somebody has done something to her."

Anne tried to detect the tone of Raleigh's voice through the static of the tape. *No panic. Too vague. Too distant.* The dispatcher asks:

"Has she been assaulted?"

And Raleigh's reply:

"I don't know, she's foaming at the mouth or something."

The call ended, and Blackburn waited a long, silent moment as everyone imagined Peggy Raleigh convulsing in that driveway. Blackburn reviewed his notes to make sure he had walked the detective through everything he needed.

"So from eight fifty-three p.m. to eleven forty-three p.m., do you know where Reverend Raleigh was?"

Detective Hume uncrossed his legs. *He's careful. And fairly precise on the timeline.* Anne felt he was credible. *Rehearsed, but credible.*

"I don't know."

"Thank you. No further questions."

○ ○ ○

ANNE AND THE REST OF THE JURORS WERE LED OUT BY THE BAILIFF TO the jury room to collect their things and head home for the day. After grabbing her purse and copy of the novel *Cal*, Anne lingered in the hallway behind the courtroom, waiting for the women's room to open up.

A lot of testimony for day one, she thought, and hard not to prejudge any of it. So many sketchy moves. Why leave your family alone all night if you were getting death threats? Why had he pulled into the back when he said he would park in the front? On the message, he sent his wife out of the house to lock the garage. He sent her out there—into the dark—where it wasn't safe or covered by the security system.

But Anne understood why he might lie about that. Carrying on with the bishop's daughter. That would make page one. She had to stay even-keeled. All of this two days after Easter with two children in the house. Christ almighty.

Anne finally got her turn in the bathroom. The light was cosmetic-counter bright, and she studied herself in the mirror. A fat Roman nose with a dark brown freckle that annoyed her. Straw bleached hair held together in a bun with curls at her cheeks. Her tea-stained teeth. The light, the mirror, they magnified the flaws. She looked closer at her skin. Her pores giant, a stipple of dark pinpoints. She had lousy skin. Always freckling, keratoasting in the Texas sun, and sagging into a turkey neck. Like her mother. Too fair, too thin. Like her father. Something unfamiliar descended over everything in the bathroom—the light, the mirror, her face.

Anne came out of the bathroom to an empty hallway. She looked down the corridor in both directions but couldn't remember which way to turn. Her gut led her left, but she soon realized she was heading the wrong way, back toward the courtroom. Past the door to the judge's chambers, and then through a service exit, she popped out into the waiting area in front of the court. She spied the main elevator bank, and rather than turn around and walk all the way back, she pushed the button and got on the next car.

As the doors were about to close, the hand of a bailiff held the door back and onto the elevator came Haynes Whiteside and Standing Raleigh.

The bailiff spoke into a walkie-talkie: "Coming down, car four."

Anne moved to the back of the elevator and tried to disappear behind the shoulder of the bailiff. As the doors closed, everyone stood facing forward, turned away from Anne. Everyone except Reverend Raleigh. In the corner of her eye, Anne sensed he was off to the side, facing her. She glanced over, and their eyes met. In that half second, he just returned the look blankly. Then a moment later, he realized who she was and why he knew her face. And in that recognition he tried to compose himself like he was back in the courtroom—he went stone-faced again. Anne dropped her chin but could still see him. And there were his hands. Fingers folded together at his waist. Waiting, praying, holding each other. *Those very hands.* She looked back up at Reverend Raleigh, and their eyes met again. He offered a thin smile and the benevolent look of a pastor. Calm, innocent, a disciple.

Anne's heart was pounding. She looked away once more but could feel Raleigh staring at her. His hands moved to his sides.

The doors opened onto the main floor. A bevy of bailiffs had cordoned off the path to the steps of the courthouse. Whiteside whispered, "Okay, do not pass go. Straight ahead to the car." Reverend Raleigh and his lawyers stepped off the elevator, heading right toward the press gauntlet waiting for them behind the glass double doors.

Anne watched this spectacle unfold for two seconds before the elevator sealed shut again and she descended another level into the shadows of the parking garage.

THAT SAME FRIDAY MARKED DANIEL PATRICK MALONE'S FIFTEENTH birthday. And at precisely 6:57 a.m., just before dawn broke on the ides, Dan was dropped into the gloom of the Hockaday parking lot for swim practice.

The plans to build a pool on the Jesuit campus were slated for some time in the twenty-first century. Until then, practice was held at Hockaday, a girls' prep and boarding school that was even more stuck-up and posh than Ursuline. The Jesuit swim team was thoroughly second-rate, but the Rangers were building it back, and Dan was one of the many good, but not great, sophomores looking to drop time, qualify for state, and letter.

But none of that mattered as everyone dawdled on deck, adjusting goggles, some stretching, most still snoozing. The Hockaday pool looked as frigid and as appealing as the North Atlantic. Dan cursed the calm, hyaline skin of the pool, then kicked Rick, who was passed out in his Ranger hoodie. Dan scanned the windows for any cute Hockaday girls going by, but goddamn, it was too early for this shit.

At 7:07, just as the swimmers began to hope that practice might be scratched, Coach Chris Moyle came careening through the glass double doors. He was the son of the original Coach Moyle, who was the Landry and Lombardi of Jesuit swimming, with several state titles notched on the wall of the Ranger locker room. And Chris suffered all the unfair expectations of a coach's son, along with a severe case of who-gives-a-shit. Now, at thirty-three, with court dates for custody and alimony arrangements, the not-so-young Coach Moyle was nowhere near cutting it. For his day job, he was a "technician and inventory manager" for Dolphin Pool Supply but also bartended at the Fridays off Stemmons, which often turned into long nights chasing tail across West Dallas.

"Everyone in the water by the top of the clock." Coach Moyle steadied himself as he slapped the surface with a lane line. "Let's go. We are what we repeatedly do."

Even when sweating one out, Moyle was the Trevi Fountain of coaching aphorisms—ranging from the thoughtful ("If it doesn't challenge you, it doesn't change you") to the cryptic and quasi-Zen ("Don't wait for it, swim for it") to the tautological and banal ("Float, don't sink," "This is a lesson in the competition of life").

"Last one in can warm up with four hundred fly. Let's go, gentlemen. The later we start, the more pain I put on it."

Dan stripped off his sweats down to his blue Speedo, plunged into the deep end, and sank to the bottom of this blue world, letting the chilly chlorination wake him. Dan was the lead on lane three, which was respectable and on the cusp of varsity, which occupied the first two lanes. In pole position was Drew Radcliffe, their freshman sensation. Drew lived between lane markers from an early age and had that delphine build—shoulders like a linebacker, with a narrow waist and giant paddles for feet. He already held Ranger records for everything breaststroke and IM, and was ranked number five U18 in the state of Texas. He was just thirteen.

"We're doing four one hundred pulls in IM order. On fly I want to see strong rotation, but more important"—Moyle stroked his ribs past his diaphragm like he had indigestion—"I want to see this push here, that's what starts the next stroke, that's what moves

your ass through the water. Okay on the twenty. Lane one, wake
up, pay attention, ready, go."

Dan pushed off with Rick behind him. Dan wasn't fast, but he
could swim all day and was the only sophomore with a negative
split in the five hundred free—which made him a glutton for punishment. As soon as all lanes were off, Coach Moyle disappeared
out to his truck, probably for an eye-opener. After the first one
hundred IM, he was spied smoking in the fire lane of the parking
lot, then using the pay phone in the foyer of the natatorium. After
the second IM, senior Ron Fenatacci, who was a bit husky and had
the unfortunate nickname of Don Fatuccini, pulled Drew back
from lapping the rest of the team and then held the lead swimmers on the other lanes.

"Stop, he's not counting. Just say we did the four hundred."

Moyle's sixth sense kicked in, and he hung up the phone, pulled
the elastic around his Kappa track pants, adjusted himself, and
came out onto the deck.

"That was fast, Rangers. You guys did the whole four hundred?"

"Yes, sir, Coach."

"Shut up, Fatuccini—I know when you're lying." Moyle didn't
really seem to care as he rubbed bloodshot eyes. "Get off the
blocks. We're doing one-four locos. And I'm timing it. Shit, where's
my stopwatch?" Coach Moyle reached into his back pocket and
skidded along the wet tiles. "Goddamn it, first group at the top. I
want to see sprinting and then solid turnover. And if we don't do it
right . . ."

There was a banging against the double pane of floor-to-ceiling
windows, and the boys popped up in their lanes like curious mer-
men, pulling goggles back to see. The pounding was followed by a
muted "Chriiiisss." And standing there on the other side of the
glass wall of the Hockaday pool was Coach Moyle's "date" from the
previous evening.

"Chriiiisss, what the hell?"

Coach Moyle rubbed the gray oysters below his eyes and scratched his stubble before finally yelling out, "Lacy, go back to the fuckin' truck."

The boys stared. "Lacy" was something. Daisy Dukes, an ample bikini décolletage decamping from her cut-off T-shirt. A Heather Locklear bird's nest of blond, now cattywampus from being slept on in the back of a Dodge Ram. She was barefoot and had bangles on both arms, with hoop earrings and long pink nails. She stepped away from the glass and saluted with two middle fingers.

Dan and Rick looked at each other.

". . ."

". . ."

Lacy smacked the window again. "You left me in the truck, dickhead!"

"I called a taxi. Go back to the truck and *wait*!"

With glassy-eyed oblivion, the hungover swim coach turned back to the starting blocks.

"Rangers, I want your heads in the goddamn water! First group, ready go."

To his credit, the half-drunk Coach Moyle continued to run a hard-ass practice while ignoring the Harry Hines hooker he had left stranded in front of the Hockaday School for Girls.

o o o

"Eyes up here. Follow me. Is Mr. Blaylock alive? Someone check his pulse." Oglesby slammed Diviner, a pale yellow teaching stick that branched into a Y at its top, against the radiator. Jay Blaylock, who had been moved to the front of the class in the hopes of finding a cure for his narcolepsy, smacked the drool off his cheek. Oglesby rolled his eyes. "So what's this book about?"

"Holden Caulfield."

"Minus five for stating the obvious, Mr. Blaylock. Rule number three: think before you speak. Gentlemen, I'm getting impatient. We can just take vocabulary quizzes if we don't get this discussion on track. What is this book really about? What's the essential theme?"

"Being a teenager and how much it sucks," Sticky offered.

"That's a better answer. And why does it suck, Mr. Deangelis?"

"Because life is unfair, sir." Deangelis smiled as he parroted a favorite Oglesby rule.

"Okay, let me ask it this way . . . is Holden crazy?"

"The world drives him crazy," Rick shot back.

"How so?"

"According to him it's full of phonies."

"Good. Gentlemen, I have a handout today." Oglesby pulled a folder from his army bag. "Take one, pass it down.

"Okay, trivia question to steal the five points I'm taking off Mr. Blaylock's next paper. When Holden leaves to visit his teacher, Old Spencer, where is his house?"

At this point, half of the honors English class shrugged and the other half turned to Dan to see if he knew. Dan studied the handout in front of him and without looking up said, "He lived on Anthony Wayne Avenue."

"Correct, five points to Malone. And who is Anthony Wayne? Did anyone bother to look it up?"

Silence. No one had.

"Rule number five. Reading is close reading, gentlemen. *The Catcher in the Rye* was published on July 16, 1951, by Little, Brown. On July 16, 1779, one hundred seventy-two years earlier, Continental Army general Anthony Wayne attacked what was thought to be an impregnable British position in the palisades of Stony Point, New York. The attack was successful, and the victory so unexpected and brazen that it earned the general the nickname *Mad* Anthony Wayne. Honors sophomores, look at this list of phrases on the handout. All of them come from Holden."

The Xerox, typed on Oglesby's Selectric, read as follows:

```
kills me . . . I'm not too crazy . . . you have
to be a madman . . . chuckling like a madman . . .
serious as hell . . . mad about history . . . it
drives me crazy . . . it makes me so depressed I go
crazy . . . I wasn't too crazy about him . . . it
drove him mad . . . you're nuts I swear to
God . . . he was madly in love with himself . . .
they're crazy about themselves . . . like you're
dying to do them a favor . . . it was still coming
down like a madman . . . it looked pretty as
hell . . . he was mad about himself . . . smoking
like a madman . . . say no or I'll drop dead . . .
I almost wished I was dead . . . I damn near broke
my crazy neck . . . I was probably the only normal
bastard in the whole place . . . I apologized like a
madman . . . Girls can drive you crazy . . . old
Marty was murder . . . the girls nearly committed
suicide . . . that killed me . . . if you want to
say stay alive, you have to say that stuff . . .
I felt like jumping out the window . . . if you
think I was dying to see him, you're crazy . . .
that was cutting her throat over her too . . .
I didn't break my neck looking for him . . . I swear
to God I'm a madman . . .
```

"So what does this tell us about Mr. Caulfield?" Oglesby flicked his nose with his knuckle and twirled Diviner across his chest. "Anyone besides Malone? Fine, go ahead."

Dan sat up from his normal slouch. "Holden isn't sure if he's crazy or if the world is crazy and driving him crazy, and the whole time he's thinking about killing himself."

Rick let out a short whistle. "Jesus, Malone, you're killing *me*."

Oglesby nodded. "Correct. His language throughout the book betrays this. This is the problem the modern-day hero faces. They question the value of the heroic act itself. And if the answer is that action doesn't matter, then self-negation, suicide, is an alternative. Next year in Mrs. Felice's class, you'll read *Hamlet,* and this is the central question. What's a sane response to an insane world?"

"But what if Holden is crazy and the world is not?" Rob offered.

"Then he's unreliable as a narrator, no? But he admits it. This"—Oglesby waved the handout—"is not just Holden talking in slang. He's not sure."

"So Holden is just acting crazy?" Teddy Boudreaux asked like he needed a safe answer for the test.

"You tell me." Oglesby smiled. "What's the difference between acting crazy and being crazy? If he kills himself, is that a sane reaction? Are all the people in mental hospitals somehow sane?"

Rick bit his lip, trying to follow through. "Okay, that's the worst case. Holden is crazy and may give up. To him the world is crazy, or at least that's how he sees it, feels it."

"Good, or what else? What's really the worst case?" Oglesby swiped his stick across the front row of seats. "Malone knows. Anyone else? Mr. Malone, tell us what's the worst-case scenario."

"It's not either/or. Life is a contradiction. Both Holden and the world are crazy."

"Right. See how when we read the text closely we can parse this? Remember: the hero always has a personal flaw *and* an antagonistic universe to overcome. This will be a core question you must address in the Game—is there a way to build a society that can accept a hero like Holden, and that Holden can, in turn, live with? And more importantly, do we want that to be the case? Is the hero's fate to find contentment or to fight on?"

Oglesby glanced up at the classroom clock—ten minutes left in the period. "All right, gentlemen, it's time. We have enough grades from the first and second quarters to have our possible fall induction of the first three candidates for Norwegian rat."

Rob shot Dan a knowing look. *You've got this, dude.*

"Our first Norwegian rat nominee, with a grade average just below the human body temperature of ninety-eight point five, is Mr. Ethan Tsao. Please come to the front of the class."

"Of course," Sticky muttered. This was no surprise. Tsao was straight A's in every subject. He was a silent assassin, rarely spoke in class, always scribbling notes with a bored, tired expression. *More machine than man,* Dan thought.

"Our second nominee, Teddy Boudreaux, with a grade point average of ninety-six point two."

A few jeers for the smarty pants, led by Sticky's "*Boo*-dreaux."

"The third and final slot was very close. Mr. Malone . . ."

Dan half-rose from his seat. Oglesby held him back with Diviner. *Not so fast.* He turned to his grade book, finding his line of marks for Malone.

"So let's add in the five points you earned today. Also, when it came to the assignment '1001 Things to Do with a White Elephant,' only Malone endured to write a thousand entries."

"You are such a nerd," Sticky side-mouthed.

Dan had torn out the page from the eight hundreds about his family and finished his list. He'd tried to convince himself that he didn't want the comments to boomerang back to his father or mother, but the truth was he wasn't ready to write about those feelings and wasn't sure when he ever would be. That said, he felt Oglesby's "but" coming a mile away.

"But . . ." Oglesby turned away from Dan and slowly directed his stick at another sophomore. "Mr. Gilchrist has the same ninety-four point eight average. And his journal was not a week late. Which means this comes down to our latest vocab quiz."

Oglesby pulled a folder from his pack and found Chad's and Dan's tests to compare. Dan sat back at his desk and watched. And waited. And then finally Oglesby raised his eyes and looked at Dan, only to shake his head with a sad smile.

Oh no.

"Mr. Malone, what does 'indolent' mean?"

Shit. "Lazy."

"And 'insolent'?"

"Rude."

Oglesby grimaced. "You got them backward on the quiz, I'm afraid. Which means your average will drop below Mr. Gilchrist's, who is our third nominee. Mr. Gilchrist, please come forward."

"Oh, that sucks, Malone," Flanagan cackled.

Dan's face flushed, and his insides heaved themselves up into his chest. *How did I fuck that up?* Dan wanted to protest. Gilchrist took a victory lap to the front of the room, patted on the back by Rick and others. A rictus of anger flashed across Dan's face as he slouched back in his chair. He was about to crumble, but through his misery there was a tiny stoic voice in the back of his mind that told him Oglesby might be testing him. *The path of the Norwegian rat is never easy. This too is a trial.* As this trawled through Dan's thoughts, Oglesby turned to his backpack and pulled a copy of *Ficciones* and three rubber brown rats from his backpack, placing them out on the teacher's desk like trophies. Dan's heart ached at the sight of them.

Oglesby raised Diviner in Excalibur fashion. "To attain the order of *Rattus norvegicus*, you must undergo a mental trial. Gentlemen, are you ready?"

They all nodded as he began the incantation.

"Then repeat after me." He held up the Borges and turned to the following cite. "'*To think, analyze and invent . . .*'"

"'*To think, analyze and invent . . .*'"

"'*. . . are not anomalous acts, but the normal respiration of the intelligence. To glorify the occasional fulfillment of this function, to treasure ancient thoughts of others, to remember with incredulous amazement* *that the doctor universalis thought, is to confess our languor or barbarism.'"*

Dan sat there—too sick with himself to pay attention. *I did all this extra shit and it's still not good enough. That goddamn white elephant list. This is such bullshit.*

As the three boys repeated the oath, Oglesby set the book to the side and crossed them with Diviner. *"'Every man should be capable of all ideas, and I believe that in the future I will be.'"*

Teddy Boudreaux furtively reached for one of the rubber rats. Oglesby slammed his stick down on the desk.

"Just a minute. You must each answer a final close-reading question. Let's start with the first candidate-elect. Mr. Tsao, what are the names of the twin boys in *Lord of the Flies*?"

Tsao looked down at the blue carpet. He really did try to keep the lowest profile possible, an ultra-shy kid with big, owl-rimmed glasses. His face blistered with shame. He didn't have it. Teddy Boudreaux did.

"Simon and—"

"Incorrect."

"Samneric! Samneric!" Teddy blurted, and again reached for the rat, and again Oglesby brought Diviner down.

"Now for your question, Mr. Boudreaux."

"Ha." Sticky laughed, "Psych! You suck, Boo-dreaux."

"Second question for the second candidate. Who built the Trojan horse?"

"Oh come on." Sticky threw up his hands. "I know that."

"Congratulations, Mr. O'Donnell. You can write a five-hundred-word essay on it."

Dan broke out of his ignominy, sensing the trap. Teddy Boudreaux had a big smile on his face. He was falling for it.

"Odysseus!" Boudreaux pumped his fist.

"Incorrect."

The class gasped. Boudreaux's chin dropped like a guillotine.

Oglesby moved on quickly. "Mr. Gilchrist, do you know the answer? Who, according to Homer, built the Trojan horse?"

"Menelaus?"

"Incorrect."

Oglesby swept the rubber rats back into his bag.

"There will be no induction today. Mr. Malone . . ."

"Epeius," Dan replied, sad and calm. The small voice in his head, which, come to think of it, sounded like his father, offered this: *No crocodile tears. Don't let him see you hurting. Don't let him know that he's gotten to you.*

"Thank you, Mr. Malone. A Norwegian rat is smarter than the mousetrap; he can outthink the maze. Perhaps next time, gentlemen. Class dismissed."

Oglesby ignored Dan as the class packed up and exited. There was a small part of him that suspected Oglesby had set up this trial to push him further, but then the bell rang, and Dan couldn't help but get caught up on the miserable fact of how he blew this on his birthday.

○ ○ ○

LATER THAT AFTERNOON, THE BIRTHDAY BOY WAITED OUTSIDE THE principal's office with the layout boards for the chronically late November edition of *The Roundup*. After ninth-period dismissal announcements, the door opened and Father Paul Dallanach waved him in.

The office was unlike any at Jesuit, cocooned with purple curtains, the fluorescents abandoned for a low brass reading lamp; its inhabitant priest enchambered by lots of wood, books, and bottles. Father Dallanach mumbled something over his shoulder and offered a seat to Dan. He then stopped at the bottle of Cutty Sark, which he clinked against his crystal tumbler. The carriage clock housed in dark cherry read 3:50 p.m.

Father Dallanach fell back into his chair with mock exhaustion. Another school week realized and rendered. Dallanach carried himself with a Chevy Chase aloofness that was both fickle and endearing. Scarecrow skinny, he rarely wore the collar, but instead dressed in navy blue pinstripe suits. One wall of the office bore a roll of parchments from Harvard, Weston, and the University of San Francisco. He was an academic first—an educator, not a teacher—and a priest somewhere further down on the list.

"So, Mr. Malone, let's see what's been happening within the arcadian confines of our fair campus." He smirked and then pulled a red marker out of the desk drawer. Dan wasn't that worried, as Father Argerlich would have vetoed anything within a Ranger mile of controversy from the pages.

"Hmmm, is this an editorial about the NFL players' strike?" Dallanach tipped his chin into the tumbler while holding the big poster-board layouts smeared stiff with wax and black leading tape. "Didn't that end a month ago?"

"Yeah, we're a little behind on our copy flow."

"I'll say." Father Dallanach tapped his heart, looking for the soft pack in his chest pocket. "That's fine. As long as you haven't turned this thing into the *Daily Worker* we should be all right. Oh, so Mr. Tsimboukis concludes that the strike hurt the fans the most. That's a little safe, no? Look at all this sports bull. This is a school, you know. Where's the art page?"

Dallanach scanned the rest of the layouts. Dan didn't think he was reading the articles as much as proving the point he was the principal and publisher, but then he raised the red marker.

"Here, the wrestling coach, Hyman. I don't want him complaining about how Strake uses illegal holds. The principal there, Father Moran—Lord knows how he gets a copy of *our* school paper—loves to call and complain. That old goat has nothing better to do. Let's just change this quote . . ."

"But that's what he said, don't we have to—"

"Believe me, Coach Hyman doesn't remember." Dallanach knocked his skull. "A few too many thumps on the cantaloupe. Just make it say we hope to win, competition is the foundation of excellence, some crap like that, okay?"

Dan swallowed his concern and agreed. Dallanach handed the layouts back. "Otherwise approved. A little boring, and you need to do more campus life. Do you have anyone who can do that?"

"Not really." His staff was proving to be reliably unreliable.

"What about you? Oglesby told me you can write."

Dan's eyes hit the carpet in bashful reflex. "I guess I could."

"Listen, Mr. Malone, do you know why Mr. Whalen is no longer editor?"

"Uh . . ." The not-so-diplomatic answer was Father Argerlich thought he was a pain in the ass. "Not exactly."

"He surprised me." The priest flicked a long light-tar Benson & Hedges out of the pack. "You can print what you want, within rea- son, but I don't need city agencies shutting us down because they think this is Love Canal. If you have a good story, just tell me, and you, me, and Father Argerlich will figure out the way to tell it. You want to be critical of this school? By all means. Believe me, I know better than anyone that this place ain't perfect." Dallanach took another sip of whiskey and lit the cigarette. Friday vespers were well under way. "But just don't try to sneak some chicken- shit past me. Got it?"

"Got it—will bury the story about Father Argerlich being re- sponsible for the JFK assassination."

Dallanach chuckled and had that self-satisfied, half-lit glazed look, like he had performed a Jedi mind trick and now he and Mr. Malone were in cahoots. "*That* you can publish! I want to send that story to the provincial."

The priest then stood up and came around the desk. He gave

Dan a squeeze on the neck and then a push out the door. He squinted through the smoke and the drink and jabbed at the layouts under Dan's armpit.

"Just make this worth reading again. Be good, Mr. Malone, in all senses of the word."

○ ○ ○

DAN RAISED THE MEXICAN FLAG AT THEIR TABLE, SIGNALING THE waiter for a refill on Dr Pepper. For his birthday dinner, he had chosen Santa Anna's on Webb Chapel, which featured a giant mariachi riding a *caballo* on the roof. His mother, Anne, ate her soft taco platter (the Ponce de Leon) with a knife and fork, eyeing the refried beans and pico de gallo suspiciously. His father, Pat, was on his second Dewar's and molared his way through the gristle of his Cabeza de Vaca entrée. Dan had the chicken enchiladas (the de Soto platter) and wolfed down two baskets of chips and salsa.

It seemed everyone in Santa Anna's that night was celebrating life's minor victories, and the mariachis were busy serenading anniversaries, birthdays, and the like at each table. Their waiter told the band it was Dan's *cumpleaños*, but they misheard and sang something in Spanish to the tune of "He's a jolly good fellow" very loudly that went on for two verses longer than needed. When they were done, the Malones smiled uncomfortably, Pat thanked them, and Anne asked for some ice to water down her house red.

Dan was given a big IOU in terms of presents from his parents, who reminded him that if he wanted a car next year, he had to be good. So that left him with a Chess King sweater from his aunt Catherine, a horror show of blue and purple pastels. Earlier, in the parking lot of the restaurant, his father had palmed him a ten-dollar bill with a handshake.

In public, the Malones behaved like a reasonably happy (if

depleted) family, and while Dan knew his parents' tension wasn't related to him, a guilt pressed and folded in all the same. Finished with dinner, Pat swallowed the last of his scotch in one big gulp. He offered Dan a wordless happy-birthday pat on the head. Trying to dispel the silence, his mother smiled at him, which was truly unnerving. *Everybody in Hotel Malone is checked out*, Dan surmised, piling cheese, rice, and beans into one equanimous bite.

Pat asked one of the waiters (there were over a dozen buzzing around the tables, all dressed in black tuxedo vests) for another Dewar's, drawing a "Take it easy" from Anne and a reminder from Dan to raise the Mexican flag when he wanted to order something. Pat rattled the ice around his glass and watched the waiters and busboys falling all over each other.

"Mom, can we get sopapillas for dessert, please?"

"What are soapy peas?" Anne asked. She'd diligently eaten the ground beef out of her tacos and left everything else on the plate, which a busboy cleared the second she put down her fork.

"Mexican donuts. They're awesome." Anne nodded, and Dan raised the flag. The mariachis started singing "Cumpleaños Feliz" at another table for what felt like the hundredth time. And the Malones sat there with oncoming indigestion, waiting once again for the music to stop.

o o o

PAT MALONE PAID THE CHECK AND DROVE HIS FAMILY HOME. THE CAR reeked of free peppermints and taco grease. As he gunned the Cougar onto Forest Lane, Pat felt very tired and sour. A block later, he revved the car through a yellow light—*Right foot a little slow on the gas there*—and Anne sucked on her mint, annoyed. A left onto Marsh and two turns later, he brought the car down Crown Shore and up the driveway. It was a warm autumn night, the crickets protesting the dusk. The Malones went inside and deposited themselves in various rooms. Pat made himself a vodka and Seven and flopped down in the den. He turned on *The A-Team*—who were sneaking Joe Namath out of East Germany, God knows why—and turned the TV off again. He took a long sip of Smirnoff, his head buzzing like the waitstaff at Santa Anna's. Anne paced around the kitchen, finding ways to make noise, but with nothing to actually do, she finally shuffled into the den to sit across from Pat. To his surprise, he wasn't drinking alone tonight, as Anne placed her own Waterford cordial of Irish Mist and a pack of Rolaids on the end table.

"So, Pat, what do you have to say for yourself?"

"It's been a long day, love."

"Your son is a young man now."

"That he is."

"Put some music on or something."

His left leg was stiff again, and Pat limped, drink in hand, over to the stereo. The record player was entombed in a large wooden Zenith console they had brought down from the Bronx.

"What do you want to hear?"

"I don't know, the old songs are fine."

"That they are." Pat pulled out an album by the McNulty Family. *Irish Showboat*. Friday nights, his mother and father would listen on the radio. Pat plunged the needle, and then suddenly, a ship's foghorn bellowed out, followed by an accordion plunging over notes.

The ship will sail in half an hour to cross the broad Atlantic,
My friends are standing on the quay with grief and sorrow frantic . . .

The ship captain broke in:

"All ashore that's going ashore, all aboard that's going aboard. We are about to take a short pleasure cruise piloted by the McNulty Family. And as the brilliant green and gold craft steams up the bay, we hear . . ."

And the accordion riled up again, and Ma McNulty warbled "Hills of Glenswilly."

"That's good now," said Anne, sipping her Mist and patting the plush arm of the chair. Pat staggered into the kitchen to make himself another drink, which Anne ignored. Dan wandered into the den, hoping to watch TV before hitting the town with his crew, but instead found his mother cooing along to "Irish Soldier Boy."

"You'll win my boy don't fear,"
And with loving arms around his waist,
She tied his bandolier . . .

"Come, Dan, sit, you know these songs. Pat, play 'The Irish Rover,' he knows that one." His mother was smiling again—a facial contortion that made her son wary—and then added cheerfully: "That's the one where the dog drowns, remember?"

Dan rolled his eyes and huddled onto the couch. Bracing himself against the wall, Pat moved back toward the stereo and pulled the Clancy Brothers album from its sleeve.

"Here's this one, Danny boy, come on now . . ."

Dan blushed. Deep down, he knew and even liked the song, but he was no longer a child and an unabashed canary that would croon at Malone family drinking parties. But never mind—his father, face flush with wild life, burst forth:

In the year of our Lord eighteen hundred and six,
We set sail from the coal quay of Cork . . .

Anne started clapping in time, then stood, step-dancing as a goof and singing at her son.

There was Barney McGee from the banks of the Lee,
There was Hogan from County Tyrone,

There was Johnny McGurk, who was scared stiff of work,
And a chap from Westmeath named Malone.

"That's you, Danny *Malone!*" His father took a big gulp of his drink and crashed it onto the coaster on the end table. "Sing the next verse with me."

"You people are nuts, you know that?" Dan blurted as his mother let out a laugh, acknowledging that was true. They listened to the same songs, over and over, about how great Dublin and Donegal were, how terrible war and partition were, how they should have never crossed an ocean, leaving true love or green fields behind. In a thunderbolt of passion and coordination, Pat pulled Anne into his arms, like Gomez would grab Morticia on *The Addams Family*, and then twirled her free. Dan shrank into the couch, head in his hands, embarrassed by all of this. Pat and Anne fell into facing chairs, ready for the finale. "Here it comes!" Pat yelled, and they all sang together:

And the whale of a crew was reduced down to two,
'Twas meself and the captain's old dog.
Then the ship struck a rock, oh Lord what a shock,
And nearly tumbled over,
Turned nine times around,
Then the poor old dog was drowned.
I'm the last of the Irish Rover!

"Great stuff, Pat," Anne panted, and then, like she remembered that she was supposed to be worried and upset by everything in her life, abruptly returned to the kitchen. As Pat flipped through records, Dan slunk away to get ready to go out. That left Pat alone, drunk and humming "The Close of an Irish Day." He queued up the B-side of the Clancy Brothers and Tommy Makem live at Carnegie Hall, and realizing his family had abandoned him, Pat raised his ever-emptying glass all highfalutin, as if addressing the Al Smith dinner at the Waldorf: "To the British Empire, may she go down like this."

○ ○ ○

DAN SHOWERED, SHAVED (EVEN THOUGH HE DIDN'T NEED TO), AND changed into his going-out clothes: painfully bleached light blue jeans, yellow argyle socks, and a blue and gold rugby shirt. He made several passes through a cloud of Calvin Klein's Eternity, which Rick told him would de-panty any girl instantly. At eight p.m., he grabbed a pack of Marlboro Reds from their hiding spot behind the disk drive of his Commodore 64, slid on a pair of cordovan wing tips, and marched out to the curb for pickup by his crew. Four cigarettes into waiting—his mother kept peering out the window and Dan kept cupping the glow of the butt—the O'Donnell station wagon pulled around the bend on Crown Shore. Riding shotgun, Rick rolled down the window, the seltzer of some zydeco song off of *Graceland* burbling out.

"Hey, birthday boy, ready to hit it?"

Rob was AWOL—with his dad on some pastoral duty—so the backseat was empty as Dan slid in. Sticky checked his mirrors and rolled out. "Don't smoke back there. My mom had a shitfit about the ashes."

"Wasn't going to. Where we going?"

"Downtown." Rick turned down Paul Simon's ghosts and empty sockets.

"Meeting Jane, Tarzan?"

"I think so."

"I smell a bunch of arty assholes."

"First off, you are an arty asshole, Malone. Second, it's just going to be Jane, Maura, and another girlfriend. Maybe Winship and a couple others."

Tommy Winship was a sophomore transfer from Arts Magnet. He was witty and chummy, but Dan didn't trust it—or him. Part of this was jealousy at Tommy's social skills and sophistication, which Dan didn't have, but Tommy was *too* alternative, and there was a gag level of cattiness and poser ennui around that whole Magnet clique.

o o o

BEFORE ITS ENDLESS RIBBONS OF HIGHWAYS, DALLAS EXISTED because of the railroad, and Deep Ellum was the neighborhood closest to the central track. After the Civil War, bales of cotton came on those rails, along with free blacks who brought their work songs and spirituals and something that would become the blues. Blind Lemon, Lead Belly, Bessie, and the man who learned to play guitar from the devil, Robert Johnson, all passed through. After the Second World War, the railroads were replaced by highways and Deep Ellum was shunted and bypassed, its storefronts and factories vacated. The proper amount of urban decay to attract disaffected teenagers crawling out of suburban tract housing.

Dallas in 1987 was built on a lot of late-Reagan contradictions—mile after mile of strip malls, manicured lawns, and white-slated steeples—a bright shining Babylon of mirror-windowed office parks and big-box retail and prosperity cordoned carefully with blue laws and zoning. Sure, there were South African levels of apartheid, a top-five murder rate, and a river of greed as shallow as the Trinity, but God blessed us, and we were still winning—the NFC East, the Cold War, you name it. In short, plenty of materialistic asshattery to rage against.

And Deep Ellum was a teenage locus for this. An underground scene. Describing it, defining it, comparing it to Austin or Athens or wherever, would ruin its authenticity. The word "authenticity" ruins it. It was a blighted place with a bunch of self-aware, drug-addled kids trying to eke something out in a ten-block stretch of identity. The word "identity" also ruins it. This was before Generation X, before grunge or emo, before slackers, before irony became a de facto case of the fuck-its. Just the incandescence of adolescent rebellion in all its hits and misses. There were plenty of alt/boho kids, graffiti goths, acid phreaks, dropouts and runaways, cranked-up bikers, ink and piercing addicts more tatted and needled than Maori warriors, trustafarians, potheads, not so new wavers and chemical ravers, out and fabulous gays, grumpy lesbians, and even a few glam-and-glitter transvestites over at Club Clearview (a.k.a. Club Queerview). And post-punk Deep Ellum sure had a lot of punks hanging around—skate punks, head bangers and slam dancers, hardcore punks, death rockers, friendly skinheads and fascist skinheads, mascaraed droog types, self-conflicted preppie punks, and garden-variety Chelsea trad punks with Mohawks, combat boots, safety-pinned clothing, and ridiculous Texan oi accents.

The crew found a sketchy spot to park off Good Latimer. The boys got out and wandered down Elm Street, the main drag, past the tattoo parlor and the bikers eating quesadillas on picnic tables, past Easy Skankin', the ska spot on the corner of Crowdus, and then turning down onto Commerce and arriving at the patio for the Crescent City Café. Already parked at a prime center table with café au laits were Jane and Tommy, holding court with Maura, her friend Eileen, and Eileen's friend Brittany, and so on. Various arty kids with spikes, fades, and mushroom cuts thumbing through Chomsky readers and the *Dallas Observer* occupied the other spots on the patio. A huge Muppet of a man sat in the corner playing Leonard Cohen at a wrist-slitting cadence. The three boys tried to find seats, Sticky immediately ordered sopapillas (correction: beignets), everyone lit a cigarette, and the waitress brought fresh mugs of Community Coffee.

"Anything going on tonight?" Rick gave Jane the quick-awkward-boyfriend-kissing-girlfriend-in-front-of-his-dudes-like-we-always-do-this-right?

"Maura and I almost got mugged on our way here. Some insane, drugged-out homeless guy trying to sell us his dog." Jane shuddered with the perfect I'm-barely-over-it face.

"You know what I saw? Craziest thing . . ." Tommy put his hand to his chest. He was a bit ridiculous, but no one minded, it was part of his charm. "I was walking past here last week with Ashley"—Ashley was a boy from Magnet, and a douchey poser worth an eye roll—"and we saw a dog with a tattoo."

"Get the fuck out of here." Stick pretended to snort the powdered sugar heaped on his beignets.

"Swear on the baby Jesus."

"What was the tattoo?" Jane asked.

"'Bite me,'" Sticky offered.

"Just a paw print," Rick suggested. "or maybe a bone with angel wings."

"'Fido RIP,'" Sticky chimed in, now balancing a teaspoon on his nose.

"No, who is Fido's mom?" Jane thumped on the table. She almost had the joke.

"'Bitch'!" Tommy screamed. "That's right! It said, 'RIP Bitch'!"

Everyone died at that one. A DPD cruiser went screaming by, and Sweetums picked up the pace and sang "Police and Thieves" in zero-four time.

"So what are we doing, or is this it?" Dan asked. With $10 from his father, he was semi-flush for the first time in his limited history of going out.

"Anyone playing tonight?" Rick flicked a Zippo against his thigh. The clubs were all eighteen-and-older, which was why coffee shops like Crescent City were moth lights to the young and the restless.

Tommy sat up and ashed off his lavender Sobranie cigarette. "My friend Tristan can get us into Gypsy Tea Room."

"All of us?" Rick asked. "Who's playing?"

"I think it's the Reverend."

"Eh . . ." As in the Reverend Horton Heat. No one was really into punkabilly.

"When are the Smiths coming to Dallas?" Jane asked.

"Not until next year." Stick was practically an A&R man for all the bands they listened to.

"Boy afraid to put his hands on your mammary glands . . . ," Rick yodeled in a Morrissey falsetto, "because his cat might die . . ."

Dan started sniggering halfway through the impression, which was up there with Rick's herky-jerky Michael Stipe dancing. Down Commerce two jacked-up biker assholes pulled each other into the street. A scrum of denim, leather, and skeevy hog chicks with tassel jackets and poofy hair ensued. Everyone craned their necks to leer, missing the trio of Ursuline girls coming the other way.

"Reek!"

Dan heard her first. Or Rick was pretending to have gone deaf.

"Reek! Hallo!"

Lili, like a not-so-clueless *bébé agneau*, came bounding across the café patio. Her hair in a milkmaid braid, she was wearing a Jesus and Mary Chain T-shirt tied at her belly button and a swishy black tulle ballet skirt. She draped her arms over Rick and fell into his lap. Dan winced, afraid to look over at Jane.

"Reek, you didn't tell me that you were going here in the Deep End, no?"

Even Sticky couldn't laugh at the irony of that one. Lili brushed Rick's hair with the back of her hand and smiled at everyone at the table as if seeing them for the first time. Tommy caught Dan's eye and mouthed "holy shit" as they all turned to Jane.

"Uh, hello . . . ?"

Though they both went to Ursuline, Jane and Lili orbited in separate social systems. Each studied the other, eyebrows up, expecting the other to realize and recognize. Unable to crawl under the table, Dan witnessed the shock on the faces of Maura, then Eileen, then Brittany, and so on down the line. Lili, who was no dummy, noticed it too and leaned away from Rick. Jane's eyes narrowed, and she clutched at the edge of the table.

"Rick, what the hell?"

Rick squirmed, trying to peel Lili off his lap. "Listen . . . it ain't nothing like that . . ."

Jane buried her head in her hands, too smart to be talked down from this. "So full of shit."

Tommy put out an arm in support, but also possibly to restrain her. Her anger fought her humiliation. She couldn't bear to look up.

"After everything I've been through this year. After everything I told you."

"Jane, please. You don't understand."

Earlier, Rick had hinted to Dan in lowered tones that Jane had some unresolved shit with her father, who had left her and her mother. Something you tell your boyfriend because you know you have issues and you hope he won't compound them.

"Reek, what happens?" Lili, her defensive instincts kicking in, went back to playing naïve and lost in translation as Jane's little sorority all gave her the evil eye.

Jane grabbed her purse and then raised her head, trying to ward off tears. "Oh my God, Rick. You are so stupid. I am so stupid."

"Stop. Look . . ." Rick was stuck between uneasy poles of caring and playing it cool. There wasn't much he could say, but he stalled for time anyway. "Can we talk for one second?"

"This is so fucking embarrassing."

"Jane, please."

"Somehow I knew. I knew before fucking Marie Antoinette came over here and sat in your fucking lap."

"Tell me what I did. You are making a big deal—"

"Don't . . . just don't." Jane fished for a cigarette with trembling hands but gave up. "I have no emotions right now. I can't believe you . . ." And with that, she bolted out of her seat, bumping past the table, and in anger at that, punched at Rick, who dodged and took it in the neck.

"Whoa! Come on." Rick tried to play it off that she was "hysterical," but he was really frustrated he couldn't unfuck this. Jane raced away sobbing, followed by Maura and the other girls. After scrounging a few dollars for the tab, Tommy and the rest of his group lit out as well, leaving the Jesuit boys ready to regroup and rehash, except they were still plus one French croquette.

"Let her calm down," Sticky suggested.

"Yeah, no shit." Rick was rubbing the still-white welt on his neck.

Lili was unsure of her next move. In mere minutes, she had both won and lost. She wanted Rick's attention, but he was clearly in no mood. Her girlfriends—a clingy stoner chick named Dara Baird and Lili's host sister Delphine—were beckoning from the edge of the patio, wanting no part in this soap opera. So she stood there in a half twirl, waiting. Rick lit a new cigarette and shook his head.

"What am I going to do with you?" he asked.

"I didn't know, Reek."

"I think you did."

"Don't be cruel. You didn't tell me. I was just happy to see you."

"This is such bullshit." Rick scratched his scalp. "Why are you here, Lili?"

Lili took a step away, her hands moving to her hips. "Jane thinks I'm your slut on the side."

Sticky let out an uncomfortable laugh.

"This is not funny." Lili didn't have the words, and it angered her. Her foxy smile faded as it sank in—the girls would talk, and no one would defend her from the gossip, and this would set off a whole chain reaction that would ostracize her at Ursuline. Dan didn't know what you would call the pain she was feeling, but he was pretty sure the French had a word for it. She held out her hand (*Sharp*, Dan thought, *put it on Rick to make the call*), but Rick rebuffed her, and with that, the other girl in his life went running off into the night.

Rick gave Dan a fuck-me look, and Dan well knew he needed a friend, not a lecture.

"Jesus Christ, Dowlearn. Like sands through the hourglass over here."

Sticky eyed the chicory at the bottom of his mug. "I have to say, Rick. That was some major-league pussy trouble."

Rick chuckled. The mortification was slowly melting as the macho walls got rebuilt. The crew kept at it.

"Do you know the chances of Frenchie walking down this block on this night at this hour?" Stick was now finger-licking the powdered sugar. "That is unbelievable shit luck, *Reek*."

Rick slurped the dregs of his coffee. "I guess this means I'm a free agent again."

"Good luck, playboy." Dan patted him on the shoulder. "Might want to cool it with the Ursuline girls for a while . . ."

"Until the spring at least . . ."

"I was thinking the close of the decade."

o o o

THEY KEPT JAWING AND DRINKING COFFEE AND SMOKING AND DISSING chicks and cheering up Rick. At eleven thirty, the waitress brought the check, and the crew decided to prowl down Elm and

Main, hoping to see if something was happening. They slunk around, judging bouncers and doormen, all of them scoping IDs. There was nowhere to try to crash, and Dan was getting close to curfew. None of them wanted Anne Malone hectoring their parents after midnight with half-crazy panicked phone calls. But just as the crew was about to split, Dan spotted Cady Bloom and a flock of her friends flitter down July Alley. Seeing this girl on his birthday was kismet—the universe telling him to take action. Wired to the hilt on caffeine, Dan was determined to break through his shyness. *This is the gut-check moment in the made-for-TV movie that is your life, Dan Malone—don't chicken out.*

"Hey."

"Hey."

Cady still had on her pancake cheerleader makeup, which gave her raccoon eyes, but had changed into a polka-dot crop top and black jeans. And she was wearing patent leather red penny loafers. There was something about them that was the goddamn cutest thing Dan had ever seen.

"You heading to Dick Chaplain cotillion?" Dan called out.

It was a decent pull from seventh-grade memories. The two of them in church clothes with braces and sweaty palms struggling through Lindy and jitterbug lessons.

Cady giggled and stepped toward Dan. "Five six seven eight." Dan thought he was going to die. *Snappy on the comeback, and painfully adorable.*

"Where are you headed?" Cady asked.

"Home. Sticky's station wagon turns into a pumpkin soon."

"So does that make you Cinderella?"

"Oh, you're right. That doesn't work." *Idiot. Be cool.*

"We've gotta head out too."

"Cheerleading practice?" He was following Rick's advice: *Ask about their bullshit.*

"Well, we do need the practice." Cady fiddled with her hair and shifted her weight toward Dan. "Those girls are, like, really into cheer, but they are not as good as they think they are. Know what I mean? So over it. Did y'all get in anywhere?"

"Nah. Just hit the tattoo parlor with a bottle of tequila."

"Right. Maybe you can take me there sometime so I can drink you under the table."

"Like what's-her-name in *Raiders of the Lost Ark*?" *Too geeky? Shit!*

"Yeah, like if you want to lose!" She was swaying between flirting and teasing when Dan decided to take a shot at the end zone.

"So can I call you? You know, when you don't have to hang out with all the cool cheerleaders?"

"I don't know, Danny Malone. You might be more trouble than you're worth. Hanging out in Deep Ellum, smoking, tattooing."

Clever girl, putting me off just so. "I joined a biker gang, too."

"Bad boy, huh? What's your gang's name?"

"The Bugaloos."

"Intimidating."

"Ride or die. Can I call you?"

"Well . . ."

"C'mon, it's my birthday."

"Bullshit."

"I swear it's true. Scorpio. I love sunsets and long walks on the beach."

"Fine, call me."

Touchdown Cowboys. "Great. Gotta go rob a liquor store now."

"Remember the left-side pass." And Cady Lindy-hopped for two steps back to her girlfriends, her red loafers twinkling in the streetlight. Dan gave a smart little wave and tried not to fall over.

"Happy birthday, Dan," he whispered to himself.

THE DRINKS WERE GOING DOWN ANDANTE. PAT MALONE LIKED Bushmills on occasion for suffering, making him a traitor to his faith and ancestors. The Protestant whiskey wasn't syrupy and cloying like Jameson. A good bottle of Bushmills was like a contrail across the sky—a straight bite of apples and the barrel. A bad bottle was thin and medicinal, like furniture polish, herbal and anised. Today was a bad day but a good bottle, fresh and peppery, and each drink grace-noted him along, measure for measure, like a song without words.

Pat looked up at the gray pulsing light of the TV. An iceberg, twice the size of the state of Rhode Island, had broken away from Antarctica and was drifting into the ocean. Pat gulleted the last drops off the rocks and shoved the glass next to the $10 he had put on the bar. *Where am I again?* Uremic light, the Indian-red brick of the far wall—*Like a brick shithouse, this place*—yep, he was at Doll's on West Lovers. The bartender came over. A thick Mick with rosacea who made a face about pouring the Bushmills. *Kevin is his name. No, Kieran. No, Keith.*

"Another, Keith, if you don't mind."

"You got it."

Fresh ice was added, which Pat frowned at. The iceberg was impossibly massive. One hundred miles long, seven hundred fifty feet thick. The size of the country of Luxembourg. And Keith splashed out another double. Not skimpy though, which steadied Pat's mood. Keith placed it on a coaster for Shiner beer and pushed it back at Pat. The mass of an iceberg is 90 percent underneath the water. If the iceberg makes it into open seas it will create a huge navigational hazard. It could take years to melt, calving into a chain of ice islands, each silently prowling the austral currents.

Kevin returned to the other end of the bar and huddled over his crossword. *Shit, is his name Kevin? This is Doll's, right? It's definitely Doll's, but Doll is dead and now this Irish lug nut is running it.* Wherever he was, Pat was hot. The temperature outside had dropped down to something resembling fall, but Pat felt clammy. He took off his jacket, and there was the letter sticking out of the inside pocket. The letter Shapiro had handed him. Just one more drink, a few more measures, and he'd be settled in and could deal with the letter. *Besides, you know what it says. You know the package. You drew up the package.* Not yet though, a few more sips before he— *Goddamn it.* He was thinking about the letter now, and the glow was off. All that slow, deliberate drinking dashed on the rocks, and the song the whiskey played was now this mournful adagio, a somber horn against a dark void. All he wanted was a moment to regroup. But just like that, the taste of a good bottle had flattened into nothing but caraway and burn.

○ ○ ○

"LISTEN." LES SHAPIRO'S RIGHT HAND COMBED THROUGH A THINNING astronaut buzz cut, then landed on the envelope on his desk. "I asked you to meet with me because I have some important news I need to tell you."

Christ. Right out of the script from the manager's handbook that Pat had helped create. *Here it comes.* Panic drew over him like a white sheet.

"This is tough . . ." Shapiro searched for eye contact with Pat, who rubbed his aching leg. "As you well know, we're trimming across management, and, Pat, I fought to get you this."

"Thanks." Pat heard his mother's voice in his reply. *What's done is done. There is no point to arguing this now.* His shock hadn't yet turned to disbelief or anger.

Shapiro tented his fingers, leaving a fat thumb on the envelope. "It's so much more than industry standard, and with the cuts we're facing in the New Year, it's better to get this now than face a less certain future in terms of what the company can offer."

Pat stayed silent.

"It's a good deal . . ." Shapiro stuck to the script. The incentives: $18k up front and additional pension payments of $400 through the age of . . . Pat couldn't pay attention. He knew the package. But he was still falling. Shapiro pushed the main terms across the desk so he could see. They would extend health insurance for a full year.

The terrible irony was that Pat had proposed buyouts to Crandall as a magical way to chop payroll. With a grumpy wave Crandall had dismissed it and asked for alternatives. But the Pharaoh had an elephant's memory for cruel, penurious ideas. A 6 percent reduction of senior management, combined with layoffs, would result in a 10 percent payroll deduction, *while*—and this Pat had underlined in his report—*adding employees to the AMR workforce at the current 12 percent growth rate.*

And now Pat was starting to overcome the shock and question how he got hoisted on his own petard. If the airline was growing, then this must be about something else. *The MS? The drinking?* No, he had to save face: *These were just cuts across the board.* Pat was fifty-five—right where the senior actuary himself had drawn the line for buyouts to begin.

At that Pat did start paying attention to Shapiro. Let's not forget that getting rid of Pat made it easier for him to save his own neck. His jowls flushed red like he had been drinking. But Shapiro didn't drink. Didn't know how. *Not a hail fellow well met, Shapiro. You couldn't get close.* He wasn't a better manager than Pat. *He was just less risk, safer.*

Shapiro continued to stumble through the package. "Also there's a letter of recommendation from me and from Wallace . . ."

Bob Wallace, SVP of operations, and Crandall's Crandall. A miserly Scotsman, he had put the fear of God into Shapiro for years. Pat knew Wallace was all bark, but he could smell it on his now-former boss—that nervous dread of the salaryman. And Pat realized he was already outside the bubble. Shapiro was talking and talking and explaining a bunch of shit that didn't matter. And then he would tell Wallace that Pat took it hard, but he had coached him through it, managed it well. *Gold star, Shapiro. It's sad, but honestly: Pat Malone is a crippled drunk.*

"The economy wobbled this quarter, but I think next year you're going to find that you're back on your feet in no time."

Next year? Jesus, Christmas is coming. Fuck you, Bob Crandall. Twenty-seven goddamn years. I was here before you. Before deregulation, before you turned this place into a shit show.

"Really this could open up possibilities for you. You never know . . ."

Never tell an actuary what's possible. But Pat held his tongue, and Shapiro leaned forward in his seat, signaling that this was about over. The personnel folks had warned the managers: don't let them linger, don't give them time in the chair to think about it.

Pat went blank and bitter. He had stolen the buyout idea after he read about it in *Forbes*. DuPont had done it with their executives, Firestone too. Compensating job loss was an airline tradition going back to when they pushed Howard Hughes out at TWA. Back then it was called the golden parachute. And now Shapiro was standing up, and Pat stood up, and here it came—the golden handshake. But really, Pat wasn't that important an employee. As

Forbes would categorize the different levels, this was the golden boot.

o o o

PAT SIPPED, STILL THIRSTY, STILL TRYING TO CATCH UP TO SOME scherzo where drinking and thinking were reconciled. *Three months paid in full. Three months after twenty-seven years.* When Pat was little he read a story about Shackleton, how he survived on an iceberg for days, killer whales bobbing above the surface, auditing him with their tiny, evil eyes, and then ramming the ice floe, trying to break it apart and drop him in the water. Pat placed the letter in front of him on the bar but couldn't bear to open it. *Those killer whales knew exactly what they were doing.* He had to plan, and realized there was a plan for this: *You have savings, you have insurance.* But he didn't have luck. He had illness. He had a wife terrified they'd all end up in the poorhouse. He couldn't bear that all her pessimism would be proven right. All his work-related functions—company dinners Anne came along on—were now cast in a polar light of failure. She would pointlessly second-guess everything and wear him down. And wear herself down. And then remind him that Dan was going to college in two years.

Pat put the envelope back in his jacket and rolled up his sleeves. He'd inherited this dark little cloud of misfortune from his mother. Hannah was born under a tough star. So what did she do? *Work and worry.* And that's all Pat allowed himself to do. His father's store, the airline. *Work, work, work. And guess what, Mr. Malone: there's no luck in it. Work just creates more work. I should have been smarter. I should have seen this coming. Not everyone is unlucky. And yes, Keith, I'll have another.*

Pat sat up on his bar stool, and a blue line of pain wrenched his left leg. He almost fell off the stool but steadied himself. The involuntary spasms of his left side were happening more when he drank, but he would drink past it. An ominous flare-up of the MS before everything went dull again. He ordered another drink from Kevin—*Sorry, Keith*—and Pat slid another $10 on the bar. He had to be careful or he'd be calling a taxi. *Sip this one. Then maybe one more and that's it.* Pat dreaded the thought of going home. Into this anguish crept a warm female voice.

"*Hola.*"

Pat turned from the bar. She was brunette, pixie short but wearing heels with black jeans and a black bustier crop top. She was younger than Pat, but not by much, her skin no longer olive, more orange. She wore several gold chains, including one with a Guadalupe medal. She smiled.

"I'm Carmen."

"*Hola*, Carmen."

"You've been here before, no? We were talking? It's John, right?"

"Pat."

"Oh, sorry. It's good to see you, Pat. How are you?"

Pat had seen her in Doll's before. Maybe. He wasn't sure.

"I've been better, Carmen."

"I'm sorry, baby. Can you get him to come over?"

"Kevin. Sorry—Keith."

Pat bought her a whiskey *agrio*, and Carmen pulled up on the bar stool next to him. Keith and Carmen eyed each other knowingly, which Pat, punching his ticket for another Bushmills, didn't quite register.

"So what's wrong?" she purred.

"I don't know. A lot of things. Don't want to be here. Don't want to go home."

"Oh yeah?" She bit on a red swizzle and toyed with it. "Sounds like you're bored. I'm bored too. You bored, Pat?"

"This place could make you bored of being bored."

Carmen threw her head back and laughed. It was too much for

the joke and surprised Pat. By the time she had regrouped, she had put her hand on Pat's arm.

"You are funny. You live around here? You don't sound like a Texan."

"No, no Tejano." Something in Pat stirred as he looked down at her fake pink nails. Her smile, her slightly broken English, it all seemed gentle, just lonely and sad like him. *Everyone is this way deep down,* the whiskey told him.

"I'm from New York."

"Wow. New York. So are you traveling? Are you staying at a hotel?"

"No, I live in Dallas now."

"I see." Carmen swizzled a little closer. "So what do you do, Pat, so you're not bored?"

"Sadly, you're looking at it." Pat took a big pull off his whiskey. *Is this my fifth? Wait, are we counting doubles? No, five.* His new limit for driving and basic compos mentis. No mile a minute, no spins. Just warm and calm and dull.

"I like to drink too. Makes things . . ." She searched for a word. "Like, relaxed, cool."

And so they had another drink, and then another, and Pat found out a few things about Carmen. She was born in Mexico but had lived in Texas since she was a teenager. She had been married, but it didn't work out, and Pat nodded and sucked on his lip in sympathy. They both agreed on the weather, on sports—Carmen, like Pat, was a big baseball fan. In fact, everything Pat said or suggested found Carmen in agreement. They were very like-minded and very whiskey fueled. Carmen was from a different station in life, but Pat didn't mind. He crowed about how he knew a lot of Puerto Ricans in the Bronx, and Mexicans weren't much different. If anything he had an inebriate pride about how he had learned to walk with beggars and kings, and was Patricio

Malone, friend to the Latin race. And now Carmen's pink fingers were rubbing his shoulder.

"So listen, you're married . . ."

Pat thumbed at his ring finger as reality returned. The glow became a thin gray cloud. Carmen whispered through a slick smile.

"It's okay, I don't care. We're both adults, right?"

And Pat started to panic. His leg throbbed. He thought about Anne and the thousand questions she would have about the letter, and the package, and the extension of benefits, and for how long, and on and on, about this and that. *What did Shapiro say to you? What are we going to do now? Jesus Christ.* His head was spinning, and he had drunk three past where he promised himself to stop.

"Listen, baby, we should get out of here."

"Sorry, what?"

"We could go somewhere else. You know . . ." And then her lips came close to his ear and he couldn't make out what she was saying. Her words just echoed like the sea, and he could only focus on the smell of her perfume, and her cheek grazing his.

"Carmen, I can't."

"*No problema*, I just thought . . ."

"What?"

She sat back in a half pout. "You have sad eyes, Pat. I like you. And you like me, right? And I want to help you. Make you happy, right?"

Pat, drunk and unsure, fell for this. What she said seemed so clear and simple. And Pat wanted what was easy, warm. Her hand came back in a caress. Pat's head sank into his shoulders.

"What's wrong? Did I say something wrong?"

"No, you're right. I've been sad for a long time."

"I know, baby. It's okay."

Pat patted her hand and forced his face into a grin of assurance. She had smooth skin and huddled together with him, so Pat could look straight down her top and peek at her bra, red and frilled with roses.

"Listen, baby, let's go somewhere else. We don't need to be here, right?"

Pat sucked the last drops of whiskey out of the ice and nodded. He was entering a world below the one he normally lived in. "Where do you want to go? Can you drive?"

"I can't drive, but I'm around the corner. It's a nice place. Quiet. Private."

"Oh, how far?"

"Just one block behind here. We can walk. And plenty to drink, baby. Beer, liquor."

Pat checked his leg. *Completely numb,* which was good; he could make the walk slowly. Pat threw a final $10 on the bar, and that took care of things.

o o o

THEY EXITED TO THE OUTSIDE WORLD. THE CHILLY EVENING AIR FELT too deep, the parking lot somehow calcined and hyperreal, and this lacerated Pat's senses, sending him into a slight stumble. Carmen held his hand, and he steadied. A few doleful Irish ghosts pilgrimed past his mind. His parents, various Christian Brothers, an uncle or two. *No need for this, Pat,* they told him. *Like a bandit she lies in wait, and multiplies the unfaithful among men.* But then at the end of the pockmarked asphalt—on the corner of Lovers Lane, no less—he overruled them. *No one will know. We're all damned anyway.* Carmen's hand was at his back as they turned the corner toward her apartment building. At the door Carmen pulled out her key ring, which held a rabbit's foot dyed purple. Carmen pressed Pat's shirt and straightened his Brooks Brothers pinstripes, her hand sweeping his chest and down his arms, half propping him up, half hugging him. Pat barely noticed because he had justified this to himself as all well and good, and he wasn't stumbling along with some whore. As she popped the dead bolt, Pat did study Carmen in the streetlight—pancake makeup that now showed its brushwork, a few eyelashes clotted with mascara. The door swung open, and she swept them back into the darkness. Carmen took them three steps in and kicked off her heels, her dark red toes soaking into the burnt-orange shag carpet. The house smelled of a potpourri of adobo, incense, cigarettes, and Aqua Net hair spray. She turned toward Pat, and before his eyes could adjust to the dark she was kissing him and her lips tasted like whiskey sour and her fingers ran along the back of his neck and she took all the tension out there. Pat's hands came around her awkwardly, embracing her back like this was a movie kiss. And it was so strange because this was a stranger he was kissing, and he didn't know where to put his hands, but then lust finally kicked in and his fingers crept up to her chest.

"Oh, Pat, you're a bad boy, huh? I like it."

Carmen drew him farther into the cave of the apartment, and they kissed some more, and Pat was fine with that; he was nervous and needed a minute to remember how you made out with someone for the first time. As it got going, she pulled away, cooed, and went to get him a beer. He ignored the run-down, smoky, smelly apartment with dark feculent cloths draped over the blinds and a winking fluorescent light in a kitchen full of unwashed dishes and cruddy takeout containers. He was past everything that was sad and cheap about this. He teetered a little but tried to stand as still as was possible on his bad leg and against sloshing tides of booze in his bloodstream. Carmen returned with beer in a glass that Pat hadn't seen her pour.

"Time to get comfortable." She pointed up and down the line, at his shoes, his suit. "Do you want to take a shower first, baby?"

"What now?"

"Why don't we take a shower together, okay?" Her mien was

chorelike. And then Carmen started to strip down. There was the red bra, now matched with silky red panties, and she twirled toward him while taking off various threads of jewelry.

"What do you think?"

Pat chuckled and entered some soothing fantasy where his consort came toward him to take his shield and his sword, then undress and anoint him, and not because Pat was too besotted to get out of his own clothes. No, Pat was alligator hearted, in the full churn and rush of being ready for this. Carmen's hand undid his shirt buttons, the zipper to his trousers, and . . .

"Oh, Pat, so nice to meet you."

And when the clothes came off, she led him to the shower and stood him in the tub. The showerhead was on a cord, and she soaped him up. Bursting his priapic bubble, Pat imagined himself like a dog being hosed down. She stood outside the tub and just lathered him with baby shampoo and then teased his dick a little, and it smelled like talc and flowers, and when was the last time he got laid? That anyone besides Patrick Francis Malone had touched him there? She rinsed and toweled him off, and now he had to piss like a racehorse because of all the whiskey, and she positioned him over a trickling toilet made of blue porcelain.

"Come out when you're good." Her accent sounded more crude. Pat started to piss and realized that his wallet was still in his pants, which were in the other room, alone with her. But he wasn't worried. *Didn't seem like a thief, right?* And as Pat peed he took a look in the mirror at an old man with graying chest hair who was thin and bony from disease. He heard Carmen patter across the apartment and a door to the bedroom open. *Are you really going to fuck this strange woman?* All the whiskey in the world couldn't make this less surreal, and his alligator heart was really drunken panic that he was about to be beaten and robbed by her pimp hiding in a closet, and the desire drained out through his bladder.

And then Pat flushed and peeked out of the bathroom, naked at half-mast, and—he was not seeing double—there was another woman there.

She was a taller, more slender version of Carmen. She looked very young. Her jet-black hair fell past her satin black bra, almost to her black panties. Her face was long and oval, like a Madonna from an old painting, her skin a light color of wood stain.

"This is my girl Lupita. What do you think? She's nice, right?"

"*Muy linda.*" Pat's mouth was dry. The girl twisted into Carmen, trying to hide herself.

"You speak *español* now? *Bueno*, Pat. Listen, Lupita wants to join us. We can all have a good time together, no?"

"How old is she?"

"She's nineteen."

"Are you sure?"

"I should know. I'm her mother."

This stunned Pat, who was on some sort of receiving delay. He was a million miles out in orbit, as far from Shapiro's office or Doll's Bar as he could get. *Mother and daughter, huh? Well, that deserves a drink.* But before he could reach for his beer, Lupita approached him with a silent smile and put her hand there. She smelled like baby shampoo too, and her hand was soft, more gentle than her mother's, who earlier had milked him like a cow. The siren in the back of his mind wailed, but Pat ignored it and leaned into this young creature and her soft fondling. He touched her there, and this was what he wanted now. Both of them.

"That's good. She's nice, right? She go with you, then I go with you."

Pat stumbled back to the bedroom. Thin pink sheets, one limp pillow, more perfume and sanitary smells masking other odors. *A whore's bed that could be turned over quick.* He fell back onto the mattress. The girl slithered in between his legs and coiled into his chest. She unclasped her bra. They kissed as Carmen closed the door, and this girl looked at him with an expression that was neither here nor there, and again Pat thought of that pathetic distance between two people. *Even in this moment. Especially in this moment.* He took a deep breath and swung his hips into hers, his body seeking the concavity of hers, and she held him back and stroked him, and Pat buried himself in her hair and the nape of her neck. He tried to relax, but with all those drinks, he went soft, and Lupita looked up at him. His eyes rolled back into his head, and she tried again, more rubbing, her other hand brushing his chest, like she was applying a salve.

But Pat wasn't there anymore. He had blacked out. A noiseless iceberg drifting across a dark and empty sea.

RAIN DRUMMED DOWN ON THE WINDSHIELD OF THE SILVER MERCURY Zephyr as Anne Malone sat through a stale light, the screech and smear of the wipers keeping a bleary time. The hiccup in the wipers was a lot like the hitch in Pat's stride, Anne thought, which reminded her of a lot of other worrisome things. So she sat there sadly, considering her life in three-second smudges.

A December Monday morning coming down—*Pearl Harbor Day*—and Anne was on her way back from jury duty. She had reported at eight thirty a.m. to the jury break room. Nine a.m. passed, then ten a.m., and the bailiff came in to take orders for a coffee run but shrugged when asked what the delay was. Then at ten forty-five they were called to the courtroom. The lawyers Whiteside and Blackburn were standing in conference with Judge Barefoot Sam, who was hunched over, a dark blue Kentucky bow tie dangling from his neck. The bailiff and the stenographer were the only other people present—the court was empty, the gallery cleared. Anne immediately noticed that Standing Raleigh was missing. *Did they let him off? No, no way . . .*

Judge Sam did a quick tally of the jury, rubbed the rheum from one eye, and started in.

"Ladies and gentlemen, as you can see, we are missing our defendant this morning. His whereabouts are known: he is at Baylor Medical."

Blackburn returned to his table and started packing up his suitcase. Whiteside smiled wearily at the jury.

"Our trial is suspended until we know more about the medical condition of Reverend Raleigh and he is once again, in the judgment of this court, ready to stand trial."

Judge Sam leaned back in his chair, which accidentally knocked his gavel off its block. He did not bother to replace it there.

"Now, I know this is difficult to avoid, but I ask you not to talk to any media that has been malingering around this courtroom or the Crowley building. I ask that if you see or hear anything about this trial or Reverend Raleigh, whether it's TV, radio, or newspaper—please, turn the page, turn off that channel, stay off KRLD or WBAP for a while."

What a shit show. Anne had thought about reporting her encounter with Raleigh in the elevator, but the news of the morning made it seem so inconsequential.

"Seriously, folks, this is an unexpected hiatus in our efforts here, which this court"—the judge glowered at Whiteside—"will do its best not to turn into a lengthy delay. Sergeant Redman is going to check everyone's phone number and contact information, and we will keep you posted."

Judge Sam scowled with annoyance. *He's worried they're going to have to start over.* He stood and, in his long black robe, loomed wraithlike over the bench. "Thank you again for your service. I apologize for this interruption. And please remember: keep all aspects of this trial to yourself, do not discuss it, and if you do hear something about this trial in passing—*throw it out.* I know you will do your best to stay fair and impartial. Okay, thank you, folks, dismissed."

o o o

ANNE GOT BACK TO HER CAR AND IMMEDIATELY TURNED ON KRLD. IT was at the top of the news bulletin: Standing Raleigh had attempted to commit suicide. An empty prescription bottle had been found. Anne pulled out of the parking garage. The rain had started spitting down, and the scrum of cameramen and reporters scampered under the shallow overhang of the courthouse for cover. KRLD went on to report that today had been slated for the defense's final witness, Lucy Goodfellow, Raleigh's purported mistress, to come to the stand.

But now Raleigh was in the hospital. Unconscious but alive. Just like his wife.

The report ended with a sound-bite interview of a man who only would identify himself as a "servant of the Lord." Since day one of the trial he had stood in front of the Crowley building with a giant wooden cross wreathed with a crown of thorns. He was not alone, and the crowd of trial watchers had been growing steadily. Last week, Dallas police had moved them across Commerce Street.

"We pray for Peggy and for justice." The man had a thick Texas drawl. "And now, one thing is clear: Standing Raleigh is guilty as sin."

As crazy as this yahoo sounds, Anne shook her head, *I can't disagree.*

The rain kept slashing at the road, and Anne found herself once again siphoned along Lemmon Avenue as it ran east of Love Field. A puke-orange Southwest plane was taxiing in. *Goddamn airlines.* Over the course of the past week, Anne had put herself through all the stations of the cross that accompanied the news of what they were calling Pat's early retirement. He'd come home in the middle of the night, too drunk to explain. When he sobered up the next morning, she got some version of the story and felt the hollowing grief of someone whose fears had finally been realized.

After Pat told her, Anne didn't go volcanic. Instead she folded inward and started counting and saving money. She clipped more coupons. She lowered the thermostat and disputed the water bill. She moved the CDs to Forestwood National for a quarter-point-higher return. She started gluing Green Stamps in the S & H book and buying month-old Wonder bread at the Hostess Thrift Store off Webb Chapel. No more Smirnoff; they were relegated to Wolfschmidt in the plastic bottle, which the Goody Goody in Addison had for a dollar cheaper. She prayed rosary decades that nothing major would break. Like the wipers on the Zephyr, for example; she would endure a world of half-working things. They had until February before the severance ran out, and plenty of savings behind that, but she pauperized them within a week. She would send Dan down the alley to collect bottles and cans from neighbors' trash. She canceled the *Morning News* subscription but needed the coupons, so she would go on morning walks to steal papers from the driveways of folks on vacation. All of this frugality didn't make Anne, or anyone, feel better. It was just her response, her way of drawing a circle around what she could control. The real problems lay in shallow graves and on unseen trip wires, and so she would be driving on a rainy day, see the burnt-orange tailfin of the Southwest 737, and the tears would come.

The rain had sputtered to a stop as Anne pulled the car onto Crown Shore. It was just past noon, and the sun was creeping out of murky storm clouds. Pat's Cougar was parked at the top of the driveway, the garage door open. This was one of Anne's assignments for Pat—clear all the crap out of the garage, all the unopened boxes from the Bronx, and figure out what was worth selling. That was right, a garage sale in December. Pat promised to talk to the Peñas, the Phillipses, and the Callahans and try to get their part of the block to go in with them and place an ad in the *Greensheet*.

Anne helloed through the door. The house replied with silence. She dropped her purse on the kitchen table and made her way to the TV room in the back.

There was Pat laid out on the couch.

Her first thought was that he was dead, but then she heard the snoring. She stood over him and smelled a familiar sour odor. She reached under the cushion and pulled the empty fifth of vodka out from under his arm. She held the bottle by the neck and pictured breaking it over his head, the shards exploding over the pillows, his scalp blooming with blood. *It would ruin the couch*, Anne thought.

"Pat!"

No response.

"Pat!"

Out cold. She dropped the bottle on the floor in disgust and then shut the door to the TV room, sealing him off like the airlock on a submarine.

o o o

ANNE CHANGED OUT OF HER NICE JUROR NUMBER SIX CLOTHES AND put on Dan's outgrown St. Rita's sweats. It was lunchtime but she wasn't hungry, so she made tea and scratched margarine across an English muffin. Even with the door to the back room closed she could hear Pat's snoring, and she stared at the carriage driver on the Thomas' bag with his black whip and she felt her anger galloping along. *He's sick, and I can't even bring myself to pray for him.* She had to get out of that house.

Anne went out the front door and into the open maw of the garage to retrieve her gardening gloves and pail of tools. She dragged them around to the backyard and the small plot between the apricot trees and the forsythia where she kept her garden.

Since moving from the Bronx, the garden was her oft-foiled effort at being a Texan. This was her sixth attempt. She had started with the now-embarrassing rookie notion she could grow anything she wanted in the subtropical climate. First time around was something out of Exodus—the tomatoes became a Disney park for aphids, the cucumbers suffocated by leaf spot, and the rosebush caught witch's broom and blistered in the heat. The next season, she became obsessed with Texas perennials. This required a class at the arboretum and dozens of trips to Wolfe Nurseries. Pat started calling his wife Lady Bird when for two glorious weeks after the spring rain, the garden looked like a pasture blooming off I-35. The backyard exploded with an impressionist palette of bluebonnets, spire sage, snapdragons, pokeweed, four-nerve daisies, skullcaps, and purple obedient plant. But by Mother's Day it was already past peak, the heat kicked in, and the flowers broiled and browned by summer. Then Anne went in a minimal direction with a desert garden. She scraped off a half foot of topsoil and bought two hundred pounds of pea gravel, planted a sword yucca, a couple bearded cacti, and pipe vine. It was hard to tell what was soaking in through the pebbles and she overwatered, rotting this Sonoran tableau at its roots.

So she scaled back her ambitions and now as a veteran gardener she planted 80 percent things that would survive a nuclear holocaust—lots of bulbs, impatiens, milkweed, honeysuckle, caladiums, and lily grass. The other 20 percent were experiments—rock rose, basil and mint, and pink azaleas. The azaleas fell to gall and canker, but the garden held up well until frost, and everything grew like weeds, because frankly, that's what grew best.

In her attempts to earn her green thumb, Anne became a devoted listener to Neil Sperry's *Texas Gardening* radio show. Mr.

Sperry was a becalming presence on Saturday mornings in the Malone house. He had a voice like a soaker hose and took calls on KRLD for a couple of hours, gently assuring folks of the importance of the right fertilizers—boy, did he like fertilizer—and mulching the thin topsoils of white-rock Dallas. One time she even called in, and Dan listened on delay in the other room as Anne in North Dallas asked whether she should replant the little alien plantlets that were going apeshit on her hanging spider plant. It was really a BS question; she just felt a menopausal need to call Neil Sperry and tell him how much she liked his show.

Across the alley, the willow in the Schraeders' backyard shrugged like the coat of a mastodon. Out of it came a mourning cloak butterfly as big as Anne's hand, drifting across the yard, alighting on the forsythia, and then fluttering over to the shade and settling on the gas meter. Anne wrinkled her itching nose— she was allergic to all these plants but year after year pushed through—and scoured her face with the back of her gardening glove. She stepped toward the house and studied the butterfly, its brown wings fringed with pale corn-silk edges. *Of all the things that go into something so delicate . . .* As she drew nearer, the iridescent dots of blue glimmered as if they had been painted by hand. It was ridiculously Mesozoic in size as it laid out its wings flat against the silver pipe. It too looked annoyed in its attempts to overwinter, like its nymph driven mad by the gods. Anne studied its dark chocolate wings and could make out the thick fur on its thorax.

And in that moment, she thought of Ronan Carroll—their dinners downtown after lectures, their walks in Westchester where he held her close. Anne had all these things to say to him, to her husband. But then nothing. The early-afternoon sky was now a clear blue, the apricot trees in the backyard shimmering in the sun, the world bright and awake, indifferent to her disappointment. She stepped too close and up the butterfly went, floating on the breeze again and carried back to the willow tree.

And just then she felt a bite and looked down at her sandals. She had been standing less than a foot from a fire ant mound. She hopped back and felt another bright little pinch on her ankle. She pulled off her sandals and scanned below her knees for ants. Her ankle started to throb and a red welt was forming. Anne wanted to scream as she paced the yard barefoot as a savage, returning finally to the fire ant mound. The rain had flattened out its churn of earth and left it hidden under tendrils of Bermuda grass.

Goddamn it.

Anne marched into the house, put on sneakers, and pulled the twelve-quart stockpot out of the kitchen cabinet. She filled it to the lip with water and then set it on the biggest coil on the electric stove. *I should have seen this coming, all of it.* She stood there watching it, trying not to cry, the coil refusing to glow. *He was sick, and I knew it.* She scratched her ankle and went to the bathroom for calamine. It didn't help—she had itched it into a weeping rash— and she could hear Pat snoring again. She returned to the kitchen, the coil now a coke-fire orange, and stood over the pot.

Lord, I'm not ready for whatever fresh hell this is.

As she stood there, her face flushed, waiting and watching for a pot of water to boil, Anne thought of her father, whose temper and trigger she had inherited. At night, he would escape into his radio plays.

"The security of mankind is guaranteed by the balance of nature. The law of the jungle is implacable."

It had been five minutes, and the water was still cold to her touch. Anne had to be very quiet if she wanted to stay up and listen.

"You don't understand. These are army ants. An elemental force. An act of God. Ants, nothing but ants."

And Anne would stare at her father rapt in listening, a strange look in his eye, clouded and tired, and she made a wishful connection: *He's just like Leiningen versus the ants, stubbornness parading as resolution. Bless him or curse him for his anger and his fight. Despite the ants, despite everything, he won't give up. So what if you're driven mad by it?* Anne spotted bubbles forming on the sides of the pot. Like her father, she would endure.

"I always knew the ants would come."

A bubble floated to the top of the pot. She scratched her ankle again as it bled. She stood there sweating, upset at how long this was taking. She considered how much gas she had left in the can for the mower.

"They had me covered, and were devouring me. I couldn't die like that."

And finally, despite her vigil, the pot came to a boil. Anne slid open the screen door and put on oven mitts. She lifted the pot and carried it to the backyard. Her ankle itched fiercely.

Anne poured the boiling water over the dark hem of the mound. At first the water pooled at the top, scattering thousands, the ants pulling together in small rafts of survival. But the steady boiling cascade broke the surface tension and the mound became a red blanket of death. Still Anne poured slowly and carefully. As the gospel according to Neil Sperry had taught her, the water had to work down deep in order to scald the queen.

Dear Screwtape,

Great news, uncle—we've got him back. This junior
tempter just earned his horns as a series of
distractions I set in our prey's path led to him
breaking the Sabbath and cursing the day.

 First, I left a five dollar bill on the
ground in the parking lot of the diner where
our candidate has his weekend bacon and eggs.
This filled him with superstition that today
was a lucky day and the Enemy was shining down
on him. Your advice about focusing on his
fanaticism for the Redskins was heeded—he went
to the game instead of services—and working
with Scabtree, the devil that runs that
accursed Washington team . . .

Dan Malone paused and stared at the green hull of the Rem-
ington Quiet-Riter, his fingers poised like cat paws over the keys.
It was the day after Christmas, and he was trying to write Wormwood's reply as a journal entry—typing it up to paste in the
notebook like real correspondence. *The Screwtape Letters* was his

theology teacher Father Payne's recommendation; writing every day *(Rule number four: your journal is your life-force)* was Mr.
Oglesby's.

> Now tomorrow I will feed on the anguish and
> bewilderment of his hungover soul.

Dan stopped again and thought about this. *The tack is all wrong
here.* Whatever affection Wormwood has for his uncle, it never
overcomes his selfishness. Oglesby had warned him about this:
*Think like your antagonist, Malone. Negative capability is the key to
this class, it will be the key to the Game, and it is the key to unlocking
literature.* But Dan got lost in the double reversal: *What would they
teach a sophomore at the Tempters' Training College? How to create
enough distraction that you miss the point of life entirely?*

> I know he is a deplorable milksop who will
> want to apologize in the morning, but I'm
> planning a work crisis where our candidate has
> to figure out who to fire from the airplane
> factory.

Dan ripped the piece of typing paper from the carriage. *A draft
nonetheless.* Then another thought hit him, and he fed a new
sheet in.

> Idea: Write it from an angel's perspective,
> like Michael or Gabriel, intercepting the
> messages and decoding them, and then reporting
> on all of this Upstairs (to St. Peter??) . . .

Dan stood up and went to the window. The sky was a slate line
and held the quiet disappointment of the day after Christmas.

The lit-up reindeer on the Peñas' front lawn now seemed gaudy and gloomy. Dan put *The Freewheelin' Bob Dylan* in his Sanyo cassette player. He had found the tape in the Nice Price bin at Musicland and it felt like a sign. He fast-forwarded the A side to the seventh song. A response to Screwtape was fine, but he wanted to write something inspired. He grabbed his journal and pen with its chewed cap, and sat there on the edge of the bed waiting for this to happen.

The guitar starts with a strum, and then it's driving, looping, repeating—a basic Vedic circle of sound—and just as Dan gets used to it, there's a chord change and the song opens up and explodes.

I've stumbled on the side of twelve misty mountains,
I've walked and I've crawled on six crooked highways . . .

Dan listens closely. The verses haunt him, and he tries to wrap his head around each image. He pictures each democratic vista—the highways, the forests, the oceans, and the graveyard—the song cataloging and expanding at a dizzying rate. He thinks for a second—*the mouth of a graveyard*—and then scribbles in his journal: *Teeth crooked like an old cemetery.*

He can picture it, like a jack-o'-lantern, or his grandmother's lower jaw without dentures. *Okay, a line. Not bad.* He falls back into Dylan's incantations. Each line assaults him—*wild wolves, a highway of diamonds*—like the roar of a wave that could drown the whole Dan. It is intensely overwhelming and infuriatingly beautiful. Dan closes his eyes, soaring along with each line, his blue Scripto tapping manically.

How do you write like that? he wondered.

Dan opened his eyes and retrieved Robert Shelton's *No Direction Home* off his dresser and flipped to the chapter on *Freewheelin'*. He liked how ridiculously serious the biography was, calling Dylan Orpheus a lot, which seemed very serious indeed.

An apocalyptic vision in a series of grotesqueries foreshadowed by the Cuban missile crisis of 1962. It opens with a paraphrase of the classic ballad "Lord Randall."

Dan then pulled Helen Ferris's *Favorite Poems Old and New* off his shelf and scanned the index of titles. There was the anonymous ballad, and as he read, another chord was struck, and he picked up *The Catcher in the Rye* and flipped through until he found that Holden had to know that "Lord Randall my son" crap to pass English at the Whooton School. He moved back to the Ferris, studying the style. *You have to have two great opening lines, lines that swing the door open. A ballad is just like the blues.* The song was almost done again. Rewind and replay. He leapt back to the Shelton.

Lines etched in acid paint the ruins of war. A panorama of Spanish battle scenes comes to my mind, out of García Lorca's poetry, Picasso's tortured "Guernica."

There were no Lorca poems in the Ferris, but Dan found *Guernica* in his mother's copy of E. H. Gombrich's *Art and Illusion*. His focus darted from the cruel electric light to the nostrils of the horse to the horns of the bull, absorbing all the contortions, the soundless screams, the terrible misplaced eyes, the hard rain falling. Back to Shelton . . .

A thrust of imagery that owes a debt to García Lorca and Rimbaud . . . A landmark in topical, folk-based songwriting, here blooms the promised fruit of the 1950s poetry-jazz fusion of Ginsberg, Ferlinghetti, and Rexroth.

Dan turned to his journal and wrote down the names cited. The fallout from the song became a reading list. *I need to go to the library.* The tape for *Freewheelin'* stopped and popped. Dan looked at all the books now open and facing down on his bed. He had a lot of work to do, but there was a flow to it.

This is hard shit, but it's what you wanted. You wanted to be a Norwegian rat, he reminded himself. *Don't be afraid. Be open. Cut through your crap and write to the marrow. And read more. Read*

*everything. Read and write all the time. Talent is bullshit. Being an al-
ternative poser is bullshit. Being some antic Irish Catholic kid from New
York, Texas, wherever, is bullshit—they don't get you, because there's
nothing to get.*

I have to earn this, he chided himself, but it felt good, like an
ascetic scourging his will into mastery. *The only path for the Norwegian rat is suffering. And one of these keys—the song, the poems, the
biography, the painting—is going to spring the lock on my ideas.*

He had to keep going, he had to know more, but he also fiercely
felt the need to write and respond to all the clues. The last pieces
of this puzzle were sitting on his desk. Oglesby had also given
him Hawthorne's *Mosses from an Old Manse* to read over the break
as a supplement to *The Scarlet Letter.* There had to be some connection between Screwtape and Young Goodman Brown if Dan
just could reread them together. He picked up his journal . . .

> *Idea:*
> *Write a ballad about how the devil tricked everyone into argu-
> ing with themselves.*
> *Refrain:*
> *The devil came to me in a dark wood,*
> *Telling lies how he was misunderstood.*

The words were simple with bluesy timbre. He was picking the
right downshifting vowels for a cautious, moonlit duel with the
devil. Dan flipped the *Freewheelin'* tape, and "Don't Think Twice,
It's All Right" purred along. He was coming into the zone, vibrat-
ing with ideas, tameless and swift with thoughts and songs.

And then a hard knock, and his mother—having returned
from Porlock, no doubt—opened the door. Dan heaved a sigh with
his back to her.

"What?"

"Don't start with me. I've had enough already." Dressed in an off-white robe, she was loaded for bear. Christmas for the Malones had been Cold War tension turned proxy conflict turned quagmire. In Dan's mind, his mother had escalated things, and he allied with his father's failed attempts at pacification. It had started after Mass on Christmas morning with the opening of presents, of which there were few. They sat around the artificial tree, and Dan unwrapped a Hecht's box to reveal a red cable-knit cardigan—*Two sweaters in two months!*—from his aunt Catherine, which he liked in an ironic Mr. Rogers way. Anne's turn. Santa had gotten her a bottle of Chanel No. 5, which was most certainly her fragrance. The only problem was that she had gotten the same for her birthday in July. Pat sank into the sofa when reminded of this fact.

"A lifetime supply," Anne hissed. "Great. I'll be dead before I fucking run out."

It was eight in the morning, and Anne was performing Samuel Beckett's little-known adaptation of "The Gift of the Magi." Pat, who didn't want to think how lit he had been at the perfume counter at Dillard's, was quietly cueing Dan to open another present when his wife went exothermic, her ire spewing forth all at once:

"Why are you spending money we don't have?

"Do you ever think about someone besides yourself?

"Why can't you get your shit together, Pat?

"Why haven't you had a single interview or call about a new job?

"What are we going to do? Tell me. You sit around all day with time to think about it."

It was a miserable combination of below-the-belt punches. Pat tried to deflect and not take the bait.

"Calm down. I'm sorry."

Anne threw the Chanel No. 5 into Pat's lap, demanding he return it. Then she stormed around the tree picking up scraps of wrapping paper until she broke down crying. Dan escaped to his room, where he lurked until dinner listening to Dylan. His father retreated to the back room and pretended to care about the Sun Bowl while waiting for an early cocktail hour. At dinner, Pat told Anne again he was sorry, but that just set off another venomous litany. This time Anne was triggered by forgetting to take the bag out of the turkey before putting it in the oven, and it had been cooking all day, but the stupid thermometer hadn't popped, and when she skewered into the breast the juice didn't run clear, and it was a twelve-pound bird and still underdone, and *what a fucking waste of money*, and the oven was cycling off too much, which was the real problem, and that was another thing *we don't have the money to fix, and I forgot to make gravy, and the Brussels sprouts are a little burnt, and the stuffing dry, and the sweet potatoes the only goddamn thing that turned out, and sorry, folks, but no one helps, and I work like a dog and have to do everything, and it's not my fault, none of this is my goddamn fault.*

So that was Christmas—the three of them locked in on each other around the dinner table with nothing good to say. Now began day two of the siege. As his mother took a step into his bedroom, Dan shook his head and waved her off. It was obvious he wanted to be left alone, and that was when his mother was the most hectoring.

"Fine, I guess we'll all just sit in separate rooms and not talk to each other."

Good idea, Dan thought.

Anne was in a royal mood to pick a fight but instead caught herself.

"I'm sorry about yesterday. Your father can drive me crazy."

"Mom . . ."

"We both love you." Anne noticed the copy of *The Scarlet Letter* on Dan's desk, but it did not stop her; she was in martyr mode. "It's just hard with how things are now."

"Mom, stop. Just leave me alone."

"I'm trying to talk to you!"

"And I'm trying to work! Please just get out."

"Fine, you and your father. No one can talk to either of you."

"Go!"

"Stop yelling at me."

At this point, the coils in the pullout mattress in the back room creaked and popped. Pat had woken up. The truth was he had barely been asleep—his mind addled, his legs racing with uneasy, tired fits. He heard this carry-over argument between his wife and son and sat up.

Anne continued in a fake whisper. "Honest to God, Dan, no one can talk to you."

"Fine. Go away." He turned up the volume on Dylan.

"Don't tell me what to do."

The way she kept turning the argument around on him—this drove Dan nuts.

"Stop!"

"If you were just civil to me for once."

"Stop!"

Dan was trying to end the fight, but his mother just provoked and prolonged. A pressure inside his head and chest started to pulse.

Anne threw her hands in the air. "I don't know what I did to deserve this type of treatment!"

"*Get out!*" Dan screamed, and then swiped the books off his bed.

"Calm down." Anne took a step out of the room.

"*Get the fuck out!*"

Pat hobbled into the hallway. "Stop it! Dan, stop screaming."

Dan looked at his father in his light blue pajamas and saw how worn down and upset he was. And he just started crying.

"Please, just leave me alone. Please!"

"What is wrong with you?" Anne sneered.

"Leave him be." Pat put his hand on the doorknob and moved them both back into the hallway.

"Your answer to everything . . ." And the door shut on Dan's mother as she pivoted like a mongoose toward Pat, their bickering carrying down the hall.

Dan wiped his tears.

Dylan was bouncing through the bars on "Corrina" and a bird that sings, and *enough*—Dan popped the tape. He sat for a long minute trying to calm down, but he could hear nothing but the muffled, aggrieved inflections of his parents. He moved back to the desk and turned on his Commodore, staring at the blue field of the monitor as it booted. He didn't feel like reading or writing anymore.

o o o

THE REST OF THAT MORNING AND AFTERNOON DAN GAVE HIS MOTHER the silent treatment, but there was a problem: he had a date that night with Cady Bloom. Inspired by *Happy New Year, Charlie Brown!* and driven mad by holiday wish fulfillment, he had called her, and Cady said "sure" in a way that was a little underwhelming and hard not to read into. So now he was stuck, and before dinner he ignominiously asked his mother for a ride. He caught her in a reflux of guilt about the ruined Christmas, and she muttered something about getting out of this godforsaken house. A begrudged accord was struck; both sides had lost and left it at that.

It was a cold, clear Saturday night when Dan hopped out into the Chili's parking lot off Montfort Road. Cady Bloom was standing out front and gave him a small clandestine wave. She was cuter than Christmas—a holly-green argyle sweater with suede elbow patches, a crisp white oxford shirt, a gray skirt, and gray tights. Dan reached her, smiled, and hadn't thought about how he was going to greet her, and now this was painfully obvious.

"Hi. Sorry . . . well . . ."

The moment lingered for what felt like the rest of the Reagan administration, and just as Dan leaned to hug her, Cady turned and swung open the door to the restaurant.

"Sorry. Hi . . . well . . ."

They sat in a corner booth. In ladylike fashion, Cady spat her cud of Juicy Fruit into a Kleenex. They drank Dr Peppers from heavy frosted mugs and shared chips and queso while Rick Astley warbled "When I Fall in Love" from the bar area.

Cady chewed on her straw. "How was Christmas?"

"Really great, how about you?"

Cady had an Oscar-caliber eye roll. "Oh my God, like shoot me, my family is so crazy."

That set Cady on a rant about the Bloom clan, and Dan just soaked in every detail of this girl—her clear lacquered nails tapping the talavera tiles set into the table, her brown hair curling over pearl earrings, her dark eyes darting like wrens—and he was just happily lost and infatuated while pretending to follow something about Cady's racist grandmother from Corsicana. When she finally came up for air, Dan nodded vigorously, overselling his disbelief.

"Wow. Really?"

"I know, right? Ugh, so bizarre."

In the amber light of the booth, she seemed very kissable, even as she wolfed down queso. To her credit, Dan noticed, Cady didn't scoop, but dipped her chip daintily.

A coked-up waiter in suspenders sidled by. "How's this happy couple doing?"

They both blushed and giggled. Dan thought about ordering a cup of coffee to seem more worldly, but Cady asked for the check.

"The basketball game starts in an hour. We gotta get out of here."

"Right." Distracted by devising right and wrong moves, Dan had spaced on the Mavs game they were going to. "How are we getting down there?"

"Well . . ." Cady frowned and glanced over Dan's shoulder. "My brother is driving us. I apologize in advance. Todd, you ready to go?"

Dan turned around and there was Todd Bloom, Jesuit senior, scourge of the underclassmen, and one of the biggest pricks to ever come out of Preston Hollow. He bolted out of one of the back booths with his doofus sidekick, Lang Dudek, in tow. He gave Daniel a knowing feline smile.

Fuck.

○ ○ ○

TODD BLOOM DROVE LIKE A JACKASS DOWN THE DALLAS NORTH Tollway making stupid jokes about Cady and Dan feeling each other up in the darkness of the backseat of his Jeep Wrangler, which had no shocks and a canvas top that turned highway driving into the Iditarod. He even listened to music like a dick—knuckling the preset stations on his Pioneer stereo while mocking every song he heard as for fags. The upside was the more her brother embarrassed Cady, the better Dan seemed in contrast. They made their way downtown until hitting a traffic jam two blocks from Reunion Arena. The game was about to start, and Todd should have let them hop out, but instead he honked and screamed at his fellow late-arriving assholes. Finally the Jeep lurched into the Escher ramps of the parking garage and they found a spot with five minutes before tip. The four of them were rushing across Reunion Boulevard when Todd shot back onto the curb. Dan caught this in the corner of his eye and grabbed Cady by the arm, sure they were about to be hit by oncoming traffic.

The light was a stale yellow turning red with nothing crossing. Todd had done it just to fake them out. Lang cackled like a hyena.

"Made you look!"

Todd Bloom, ladies and gentlemen.

Running to the gate and tickets stubbed, they thankfully split up—Todd and his butthead buddy Lang took two in the section behind the Mavs' bench, and Cady and Dan had the mezzanine seats at half court. Both were primo spots in the arena—Cady's dad was on retainer for Trammell Crow—right in the fat-cat sections. They skipped up the escalator grille as a soprano sax player asphyxiated on Francis Scott Key for three eternal minutes, and scooched into row fifteen just as James Donaldson stepped in elbow to elbow against Hakeem Olajuwon. Cady and Dan looked at each other like they had just made the last train out of Paris, and it was whirlwind and romantic, and Dan almost kissed her there, but then Hakeem swatted the ball to Sleepy Floyd and the crowd settled down in mild disappointment, the game begun, the moment of anticipation gone with it.

o o o

With its football teams in decline and fall (Landry in act one of *Lear*, the NCAA salting the SMU campus), Dallas, for the first time, became a basketball town. With a Mark Aguirre–sized chip on their shoulder, the Mavericks were underrated and coming off two road wins, including an upset against Jordan in full demigod mode. James Donaldson played center like a cop who had seen it all; Sam Perkins was Kevin McHale on quaaludes, somnolent but productive; Derek Harper and Rolando Blackman were the sneaky best backcourt in the league. The bench was like a casting session for *Hoosiers* (Brad Davis, Steve Alford, Bill Wennington), possibly directed by Leni Riefenstahl (Detlef Schrempf and the Big Bratwurst: Uwe Blab). And the secret heat check: the prelapsarian Roy Tarpley as sixth man. Their head coach was John MacLeod, who registered on the Pat Malone scale of Catholic sports stars for having carried Bellarmine basketball sometime before the flood.

Hakeem's first shot rimmed out, Perkins rebounded, and Derek Harper brought the ball downcourt, his chin up like he had a nosebleed.

Cady whispered not so softly into Dan's ear: "I'm so sorry about my brother."

"Not your fault." Dan scanned the bench for Tarpley, who had his head draped in a towel like a Bedouin. "These are great seats."

"Yeah, I guess." Cady looked out over the court, feigning interest.

Dan realized he had a problem. Here was the best basketball team in the world not named Celtics or Lakers, and he'd be an idiot not to watch . . . but . . . he was on a date.

"I mean, it's great they're together . . ." Dan blurted the rest: "You know, away from your brother. Sitting together. Us . . ." *Shoot me now.*

"Totally." Cady smacked her gum, and it dawned on Dan that the Mavericks weren't the only ones who might have trouble scoring tonight.

Fifteen seconds into the possession Perkins waddled into the paint and Harper lobbed it in. Perkins posted Hakeem, double head-faked, and then flicked the jump hook. The shot went in with a foul for reaching in. The crowd erupted like it was the first three-point opportunity in the history of the franchise.

"Do you like basketball?" Cady asked brightly.

"I love it. I love Roy Tarpley."

"Does he play for the Mavs? Which one is he?"

"He's on the bench. He's coming in later."

"Is he not good enough to play?"

Oh boy. Then he looked down at Cady's clear manicured nails and her James Avery rings and her hands pressing the pleats in her skirt, and Dan missed Perkins's hitting the free throw. *Okay, I'm on a date until the second half.*

"So you think Roy Tarpley isn't any good? Are you saying you're better than him?" Dan popped his eyebrows to make sure she saw he was kidding. "Should we get you down to the floor?"

"Hey, I'm pretty good. I can shoot for baskets."

That was kind of cute. She pretended to know too little, he too much, and they flirted like this for the first quarter as the Mavs and Rockets collided.

"Here comes our boy Roy."

The crowd gave it up as Perkins high-fived his way to the bench. The whistle and the inbound and Tarpley was on Hakeem's hip.

Cady pulled her hair back over her neck. "You remember Julie Houlihan? She went to Rita's with us?"

Dan thought of himself lurking below the Ursuline balcony that night of the dance. "Yup."

"Well, Samantha Schimmel told her that she heard from Misti Ushio that Jasmine D'Errico did it with Trey Diller."

"Wait, Trey Miller, the senior?"

"Noooo! Trey Diller, the junior."

Growing up in Dallas, you ran into a fair share of Treys. But Trey Diller, class of 1988, was a Spicoli-style burnout, and Jasmine was the prissy empress of the homecoming court. This was total *Breakfast Club* territory.

"That can't be true."

"I know, so gross, right?"

"Well . . ." Dan was left to figure out the gross part as Tarpley stole the dump pass to Hakeem and then dribbled out into a fast break and rifled a no-look pass to Brad Davis for a corner three. Mavs rolling. The crowd tom-toms: *De-fense. De-fense.*

"I bet she has herpes now," Cady said in a very sad, resigned way. "Also I heard everyone is bailing on the winter formal because Caroline Mackenzie's parents are away and that's where the party is going to be."

"Wait, when is that?"

"January twenty-second."

Dan knew when it was. In fact he had been planning on asking Cady to go to the winter formal at the end of the night. "I can't even think about our school calendar right now, so depressing."

"Totally." And then Cady revealed her agenda. "So we should, like, meet up at Caroline's that night."

"Sure. That's cool."

"Cool."

So two dates now? That's sort of good. Time to do something gentlemanly to earn this. "Can I get you a hot dog?"

"A hot dog?" Cady shot him a startled look. "Gross."

"So two hot dogs then? Extra sauerkraut?"

"You're insane." Cady flicked her hair again. "I've got gum. I'm good." She pointed at the purple wad smooshed between her molars.

"Yeah, I'm good too." Dan was starving—somehow chips and queso had made him more hungry. In the blocks, Tarpley drove in for an over-the-head dunk as Hakeem wisely cleared out. The crowd roared, and Bill Fitch slapped his clipboard and called a time-out. Mavs up by six now.

"Such a good game!"

Cady didn't hear him as the crowd screamed even louder at the forced time-out. "You want to walk around a little?"

Sigh. "Sure, let's do it."

They meandered the halls of Reunion Arena, Dan dying at each rise and roar of the crowd—Tarpley was single-handedly dismantling the Houston space program. Dan bought some Blue Bell to share with Cady, and he watched her lips on spoonfuls of peaches and cream. He needed less distraction to plan strategy. He had a tentative date on the books, but he still needed to kiss her, and there was an unspoken shared terror that this was expected. But frankly the corridors of Reunion Arena were as romantic as a big beige urinal and not so conducive to Beatrice-Benedict repartee.

"Do you watch *L.A. Law?*"

"No, my parents watch *Cagney and Lacey.*"

"Oh. *L.A. Law* is like the best show ever."

"Sorry."

While they were both trying, Dan felt the swing in momentum, much like the Mavericks, who let the Rockets back into the game. Halftime came, and the crowds swarmed into the hallway. Time for a move, and Dan made one—he grabbed Cady's hand and pulled her up the ramp for their section. It wasn't exactly Burt Lancaster on the beach with Deborah Kerr, but when they got back to their seats Cady didn't let go of his hand.

Like good teams should, the Rockets and Mavs survived the third quarter, trading buckets, sizing each other up for crunch time. At the start of the fourth, Perkins picked up a cheap fifth foul and MacLeod put his hands through his gray perm in disgust. So here came Tarpley. The Rockets had been threatening to start a run, but Tarpley grabbed the board off a Hakeem baseline shot. He ripped it down and then kicked it out past half court to Aguirre, who backed in with his big butt and easy off the glass. Fitch took another time-out in disgust. Rockets down by five.

Dan smiled at Cady. They were still holding hands when "Shout" came on the speakers. The crowd stood up at the command of Otis Day's long tambourine rattle.

"Do you want to dance?" Dan yelled at Cady.

Say that you love me, say that you need me . . .

Cady's cheerleader training kicked in, and they shimmied together while the whole arena screamed "Shout" at the Rockets' bench.

Now wait a minute . . .

A few in the crowd yelled out *Yeah yeah* in response and Dan lip-synced into an empty Dr Pepper like Boon in the movie. Cady grinned but apparently hadn't seen it.

A little bit softer now . . .

Shots of the toga party on the Jumbotron. Dan held Cady's hands as they dipped into a crouch. The whole stadium was ready to pounce, and then . . .

A little bit louder now . . .

Cady and Dan swung back up together, and it was time to *SHOUT* again and everyone in the stadium forgot who they were—a few beers went flying, a few fights broke out, and a couple of people were having a good time.

Hey HEY hey HEY . . .

And the time-out ended and Derek Harper poked away the inbound and found Blackman on an ESP pass, who sank a long two. *Smooth.*

"Cady! Let's go . . ."

Two minutes left. Houston down by seven—*not over*—and fucking Todd Bloom was beckoning from the aisle.

"Come on!"

They couldn't argue over the crowd noise. Sleepy Floyd for the quick layup . . . blocked by Tarpley! Everyone went bananas. MacLeod kept him out there for crunch time, and Sam Perkins looked like he was okay with it, fanning the parquet with his towel like it was on fire.

"We're leaving your asses if you don't come now."

Fine. They shoved past everyone in their row and headed into the tunnel as Aguirre hit a dagger three and the arena detonated. Another time-out and cue "Celebration." But Todd Bloom had them scurrying like rats out the back gate. Dan grabbed Cady's hand again, trying to make the best of a bad exodus.

o o o

TODD BLOOM DUMPED DAN ON THE CURB OF CROWN SHORE DRIVE. There had been no chances for fireworks at the end of the date—which was kind of a relief—just a dull ride back to North Dallas with Lang Dudek picking his nose in the passenger seat. Nonetheless Cady had nuzzled into Dan and they shared sugary and assured smiles. *Safely on to the next date*, he thought.

Dan walked up the moonlit blue driveway, pulled the extra key from under a rock hidden in the Ligustrum, and crept in the door. It was past eleven, and the front of the house was dark and still. He turned down the hallway toward his room, noticing a light under the bathroom door. *Crap.* The problem with holding hands in the second half: no bathroom breaks, and he needed to go now. Dan got ready for bed, stripping to his boxers. He cued his Dylan tape to "Mr. Tambourine Man" and waited to hear the bathroom open up. A long minute went by. Dan checked the hallway. The door to his parents' bedroom was closed, but the back-room TV was on, muted. The couch had a bed pillow and sheet on it but wasn't pulled out. Another minute and the silence from the bathroom was broken by the sound of the toilet seat falling. Dan really had to go. He stepped to the bathroom door and knocked lightly.

"Dad?"

"Occupied." His father's voice sounded like he was gargling.

"I got to go, Dad."

"Is it just you, Dan?"

"Yes."

"Go to bed, honey," he slurred.

In a huff, Dan stomped off to the kitchen, took down his Willie Randolph Big Gulp cup, and peed in it. He threw it down the drain of the sink and rinsed the cup before stacking it in the dishwasher. He came back down the hallway. He still needed to brush his teeth and was thinking of knocking again when he heard a crash and a rattle. It sounded like the door to the shower.

"Dad?"

"I'm fine!"

"What happened?"

"Go to bed."

And Dan cracked open the door. His father was between the toilet and the tub, trying to pull himself off the floor. His left leg was pinned back at the knee. The shower door had been punched out of its track and dangled from the top rail. Dan moved toward his father as Pat's head lurched down into the toilet bowl and he vomited.

"Good God, Dad."

Pat retched again and again, hovering over the bowl and ignoring Dan for a long time. Eventually he looked up, his bloodshot eyes welling with tears, and motioned to Dan to help him up. But then he gagged again, and this time there was nothing but bile and spit. When he was done, he gasped for air and, with trembling hands, started to push himself off the floor.

"I'm sorry, Dan," Pat moaned. "I think it's the flu. I can't keep anything down."

Dan struggled to pick his father off the tiles. Pat tried to stand, but his legs were numb and he almost fell back into the tub. He braced himself against the sink and wiped his mouth with his sleeve.

"Should we call a doctor?"

"No. I'll be fine." The blood returned to Pat's legs, and the numbness started to tingle away. He took a step closer to the sink to wash his hands and face. He bent over and gulped water from the faucet. His skin was crawling and his head felt like it was bleeding from within, and just then Pat realized he had purged the booze out of his system.

Dan took a deep breath. "Can you walk?"

"I'm fine."

"You're not." Dan was trying to whisper and not wake his mother.

"Get out of my way."

Pat stepped out of the bathroom and then had to turn back and throw up in the sink. Nothing, just dry heaves now.

"Okay, that's all of it." He was shaking and red faced as he hobbled down the hallway. "Just need to lie down and die."

The joke didn't land, and Dan felt his heart drop. Pat's left foot snagged on the carpet, and he scraped by the door to the boiler closet. He grabbed the doorknob and made the last few careening steps down the hall. Dan went to the kitchen and brought the big ceramic mixing bowl and a glass of water to the back room. His father fell onto the couch and lay there exhausted, his head rolled back like he had broken his neck.

"Dad?"

"Just leave it. Thank you. I'm sorry."

"It's okay, Dad."

"Listen, Dan, one thing. Go to the garage and get me a bottle."

"No."

"Dan, please do this for me. I feel terrible . . ." Pat's face crimped into a sob that he tried to hold back. "I can't sleep with this flu, and I just need a drink to knock me out."

Dan took his father's water glass and went out the back-room closet through to the garage. In the dark he poured the water on the ground. Dan found the case of Wolfschmidt and cracked open a bottle, pouring three fingers. He came back into the house and presented the glass to his father.

"Here."

Pat had the spins, and he opened his eyes like he had been caught falling. Dan saw how frightened his father looked as he grabbed the glass. Then Pat stopped and remembered himself. He looked up.

"It's okay, Danny boy. Thank you. I'll be better in the morning."

Pat took a sip, and Dan watched as he regained himself. He thought about the Hawthorne story where they drink from the fountain of youth and the miserable brume of cares and sorrows and diseases lifts like a dream, only to curse the drinkers. Pat took another swallow, finishing the drink, and tried to sit up on the couch.

"Did you bring the bottle in?"

With a terrible anger, Dan left his father lying in the dark and returned to his own room.

PAT STOOD BEFORE THE STEAMED-UP MIRROR. HIS FACE WAS GRAY, minus his nose, which had turned bright red at the tip. *Can't shave.* He had acne and a staph infection on his chin that was irritated and wouldn't close, and his skin felt too raw, thin, and dried out. He combed his hair, his scalp riddled with dandruff and itching madly. He blotted the condensation off the mirror and looked into pink, rheumy eyes that ran dry and then too watery. A small sty was forming on the lid of his left eye. His left leg was bad this morning, *way too stiff,* like it had fallen out of its socket at the hip. The instep of his left foot was pulsing with something called plantar fasciitis. His neurologist had sent him to a podiatrist, pretty sure it wasn't part of the MS, and the foot doctor explained it to him by talking about the silver skin on a raw chicken. It wasn't just the foot; the sheathing of his heel, ankle, leg, and torso were all either too loose or too tight. *Strung out or worn away.* Pat leaned into the mirror, studying his dark, desiccated pores. He reached into the drawer for a Q-tip and dug at his ears, which were clogged with wax the color of soot that cracked like rocks on his eardrums. He brushed his teeth gingerly; his mouth was full of canker sores, and his tongue looked like it was smeared with white paint. *Too painful to Listerine.* He spat out the toothpaste—when he wasn't drooling and sucking spit into a swallow, his throat had a dry catch to it. He toweled himself off, his underarms and sides rashed from the starch in his shirts. He held the towel in a trembling hand with skinned knuckles. *Don't remember how I did that.* There had been too many falls lately. A wave of nausea crashed over him as he bent down to dry himself, his head like a weeble wobble that took forever to right itself. When he stooped over there was a sharp pinch in his gut. *Like my appendix is about to burst, or something, probably my liver. Feels untucked.* His stomach rumbled, but he had no appetite and for the past week had had watery, unpredictable bowel movements that would suddenly swell within him and result in panicked, hobbled dashes to the toilet before he lost control. Pat stood still to regain his balance, his hands flush against the sink to stop their shaking. Gripping things all the time to stop the tremors made him realize how weak he felt. He had just taken a lukewarm shower and his body temperature was unable to calibrate. *Sweating and shivering at the same time.* The towel slipped off, and he couldn't catch it before seeing all of himself in the smudges of the defogging mirror. *Can't remember the last time I got him up.* And when he tried he found himself holding his breath for so long he nearly passed out. So he just gave up, his thing limp, blue, and shriveled, his jock itching with the same staph infection from his chin, and he had to rub calamine through the crack of his ass, his taint, and the crevice between his leg and his gut. He tried to clear his head with a cleansing breath but came up hacking, a lingering bronchitis that wouldn't go away and produced dirty brown phlegm.

A lot of rot goes into an empire, Pat thought. What was exacerbated by MS was hard to reconcile, but the drinking was taking its toll. And Pat was determined to stop. This was his New Year's resolution. *Never again. God as my witness.* He was done.

Day one.

○ ○ ○

DAN MEANDERED INTO THE TV ROOM, WHERE PAT WAS SWEATING IT out just as Timmy Brown brought the kickoff back for the Irish. His father had a Willie Randolph Big Gulp cup of ice water and a smaller Mike Schmidt glass of ginger ale. Dan lay down in the gray gloom of the couch. Notre Dame was driving as the Heisman winner caught one for twenty-plus over the middle.

"There you go. Pride of Woodrow Wilson High School." Pat scratched his scalp and tried to relax his jimmy legs. "Do you know, Dan, who the other Heisman Trophy winner from Woodrow was?"

"I give up."

"Davey O'Brien. Played for TCU."

"Oh." As his father spoke, a picture of the leather-helmeted number 8 appeared on the TV.

"Played for the Eagles, but we won't hold that against him." Pat stretched out his left leg and tugged at the chair cushion. "And then he gave up football—retired and became an FBI agent. Like your uncle Jackie."

Pat let out a sigh of regret as they both thought back to that dinner. Notre Dame QB Terry Andrysiak found you-know-who on a drag route, and number 81 sprinted to the end zone. Touchdown Irish.

"Suck on that, Sherrill."

Dan was no fan of the Aggies, but he had more tolerance for what his father called "slick Southern sideliners" like Jackie Sherrill. Texas A&M, clad in their home maroon, answered with a field goal and then a touchdown soon after. The Cotton Bowl looked like a frigid quarry pit on TV. Dan wandered off to the kitchen.

I really should be going over the classifieds, Pat thought, *redrafting my résumé.*

The Irish were driving again when Andrysiak threw an interception in the Aggie end zone.

"Stupid Polack." Pat fished for a chunk of ice to chew. He had bugs crawling down his sleeves, but he shook those out. *Got to stay distracted and get over the hump here.*

Dan returned with a grilled cheese just as the game swung away from the Irish, and while he didn't recognize signs of withdrawal and detoxification, he did understand his father's sports universe—and the wheels coming off for Notre Dame in the Cotton Bowl did not obey the laws of that universe. Or if it did, there was a deeper causal sin that had yet to be discovered—like failing to recruit quarterbacks with good Irish names such as Jim Kelly and Steve Walsh. This was a very superstitious cosmos, with many ways to be relegated to a circle of hell (dance routine following a touchdown, taking on a called third strike, not boxing out properly), but with apologies to Aquinas and Alighieri, there was a great chain of being to whom Pat Malone rooted for . . .

CATHOLIC SPORTS HIERACHY, ACCORDING TO PATRICK FRANCIS MALONE . . .

Angels. Level One.
You're from the neighborhood.

Specifically, the Bronx. Any athlete from the Bronx was as tough as they come. The perfect example of this was Dolph Schayes. When invoked, he was immediately ascribed with the modifier: *who grew up on Jerome Avenue.*

Archangels. Level Two.
You're black but have an Irish-sounding name. This includes Jackie Robinson.

Pat Malone was not *ostensibly* a racist man. He would have been the first to admit that black people were better athletes and was happy to leave it at that. In fact, Pat was an early adopter of expanding the definition of "black Irish." So welcome aboard, Karl Malone, Desmond Howard, and Shaquille O'Neal. NB: This wasn't about slave names—and if you brought that up, get ready for the litany on eight hundred years of Hibernian oppression. Rather, have you overcome a sufficient level of misery that an Irishman would be *proud* to endure?

And so, QED, Jackie Robinson is an honorary black Irishman.

Ophanim. Level Three.
You are Italian and Pat Malone has to hand it to you.

Growing up in the Irish parishes of the South Bronx, Italians were an acceptable ethnic other that Pat Malone appreciated for all sorts of contrarian and convoluted reasons. Pat hated the Yankees but always had honorifics for Yogi and the DiMaggio brothers. *Did you see that chip by Mark Bavaro on Jim Jeffcoat? You have to hand it to him . . . Don Shula? Has that Italian kid Marino slinging it like Paul Hornung* (see level six).

Later in life, Pat professed more admiration for Latin baseball players as they replaced Italians in the big leagues. So everyone from Clemente to the Alou brothers retroactively became a credit to their people.

Pat grabbed the arms of his chair to keep from tremoring. Dan noticed his father's clamped-down posture—*It's the game, right? Not the MS?*—and started rooting for an Irish comeback, if only to put his father in a more relaxed mood. Instead, A&M orchestrated a long, disheartening drive. Touchdown Aggies.

"Just one series." Dan shoved a couple of Fritos into his grilled cheese for crunch. *If I ask about what's really wrong, he'll get mad.*

"We're letting these rednecks dupe us . . ."

"Sorry, Dad," Dan offered calmly, noticing his father frowning the same way Lou Holtz was on the Irish sideline.

Dominions. Level Four.
You are Irish.

Here the heredity laws were not very strict. Being Irish meant any part down to a dram. So Jack Dempsey, who was a quarter Irish, was the greatest Irish heavyweight, and by the Gaelic transitive property, the greatest heavyweight ever. The Mara family were the smartest owners in the NFL, followed by the Rooneys. Was Doug Flutie Irish? Didn't matter. He threw the ball to Gerard Phelan, a good Irish kid out of Archbishop Carroll.

The shamrock loophole: any part Irish also meant any team with one Irish player, allowing Pat to root for Protestant teams, or, in one extreme case, BYU, when Jim McMahon was their quarterback.

Virtues. Level Five.
You went to a Catholic school, preferably in the Big East.

In the Pat Malone sports empyrean, here was the consummate collection of holy ballers (Providence, Seton Hall, St. John's, Nova, Georgetown, BC), and the great Pat prophecy was someday Fordham would join them (*a.k.a. the Second Ascension*). And when Fordham was no great shakes in basketball (which was all of the time), St. John's became the crosstown team Pat rooted for. Lou Carnesecca, well, you had to hand it to him, and the McGuire brothers too (Johnnies, Irish, and from the neighborhood trinity). Everything about Big East basketball was born of gritty Catholic determination. Case in point: John Thompson, who went to a *different* Archbishop Carroll and took Providence to an NIT title with Ray Flynn, the most certainly Irish mayor of Boston.

Powers. Level Six.

You went to Notre Dame.

Despite all the fancy-pants golden boys at Hayes who went to South Bend—Regis Philbin, Pat's brother-in-law Jack Hurley—Notre Dame was officially consecrated the national Catholic team. Plus, they were the *Fighting* Irish.

Did you know that Art Donovan (from the neighborhood, Mount Saint Michael) went to Notre Dame for one semester before becoming a marine who fought at Iwo Jima? *Fighting* Irish.

Angelo Bertelli, you had to hand it to him: found out he won the Heisman by telegram while at Parris Island. *Fighting* Irish.

Paul Hornung: There was none greater. He could run like a deer/the wind/a world-class track star, had an arm like a howitzer/rifle/bazooka, and was a helluva kicker, literally to boot. He also served in the army. Because he was *Fighting* Irish.

Outcast angel

Goddamn Digger Phelps. As Satan was chief of the Powers in heaven, Goddamn Digger Phelps should have stayed at Fordham. If he hadn't left for South Bend, Goddamn Digger Phelps would have taken the Rams into the Big East, fulfilling the prophecy of the Second Ascension.

That afternoon in the Cotton Bowl the prayers of the Irish faithful went unanswered. The Notre Dame offense went doodlebug, curling into a ball and doing nothing. The A&M defense kept Tim Brown in check. He would not score the rest of the game. And before you knew it, the tally was 35 to 10 Aggies, and the Irish were dazed and downtrodden. Halfway through the fourth quarter, the Aggies lined up for the kickoff following their final touchdown. This was back in the days of Sherrill's Twelfth Man,

which meant the entire kickoff team was a bunch of walk-on ka-
mikazes who flew around the field trying to concuss the receiving team. On this last kickoff of the day, two of these knuckleheads
tackled Tim Brown and one grabbed his towel while the other
held him down. This drove Brown and Pat Malone crazy.

"Look at this, they're mugging the poor kid. Bunch of goddamn
yahoos."

Tim Brown got up from the pile and with a seven-yard head of
steam speared the towel thief in the back. Of course the refs saw
that and ejected the Heisman winner.

"Such bullshit. They were scalping him! This was premedi-
tated. What a disgrace."

"Calm down, Dad," Dan pleaded.

Pat realized he was sweating, shaking, and raving. He tried to
push deeper into his chair, sitting on his fists, and smiled sheep-
ishly at his son.

"Sorry, Danny boy, but did you see that? They literally robbed
the kid."

"I know, Dad. It's not fair, but that's football."

Thrones. Level Seven.
You went to a Catholic prep school, preferably Jesuit.

Long before recruiters were publishing their big boards in the
Sporting News, Pat Malone was scouring the Catholic prep school
system for the Next Great One. Extra points if you came through
the Jebbies. There was some hindsight regret and obsession behind this—if Pat had gone to Fordham Prep like Vincent Scully
the Blessed (levels one, four, and five), he would have been running American Airlines from a floor-through on Park Avenue—
but it was mostly ingrained Irish reverence for Jesuit institutions.

Did it matter that Fidel Castro went to a Jesuit high school? It
did to Pat Malone. Did you know the Cuban Missile Crisis could

have been prevented if the scouts had just brought Fidel up for a serious tryout? That's why he was anti-American—because the Washington Senators passed on him.

Classic example of the Next Great One: Chris Mullin, who came out of Power Memorial and Xaverian.

Cherubim. Level Eight.

You are not Catholic, but you are so good Pat Malone wishes you were.

This is just a catch-all for outstanding, first-ballot Captain America types: Bill Bradley, Sandy Koufax, Joe Frazier, Secretariat, Y. A. Tittle.

Seraphim. Level Nine.

They slayed the dragon.

Loyalty to one team per major sport is mainly an exercise in defeat. Even good teams, and Pat had his share—the Brooklyn Dodgers, the New York Football Giants—let you down 99 percent of the time. And so what you really root for, the second thing you check on the sports page in the morning, are the moments when your rival is vanquished from the field of play.

There are pure and blessed examples of this: Jesse Owens and Joe Louis defeated Nazis. Gil Hodges and Bill Mazeroski triumphed over the Yankees. Good Catholic coaches such as John McKay could beat evil secular teams like Alabama. These immaculate moments sustained the hope that the great chain of being was in order.

"Well there's no chance now."

The Irish had to throw the long ball, and on third and forever this mediocre kid out of Michigan heaved it down the line—*Where Tim Brown is supposed to be*—and was picked off again.

"Hail Mary same as a punt there," Dan offered, trying to take any sting out of it.

Pat felt light-headed, anemic, his throat scraped and raw. "Get me another cup of ice, kiddo."

"Sure, Dad. Want to watch the Fiesta Bowl?" Dan asked. *The only consolation for bad football: more football.*

"Sure." Pat realized his son was trying to soothe him. *Do this for the right reasons,* he reminded himself. "Did I ever tell you about the '41 Cotton Bowl Fordham lost to A&M? I mean, this was just after Lombardi, but still a great team, and those goddamn Aggies are offsides on the extra point—"

"And block it and Fordham loses thirteen–twelve." Dan finished the gospel, chapter and verse.

Pat smiled at his son. "Oh, so you were there?"

The Godhead.

And next to our Lord and Savior, at the hand of God, sitting on an austere cathedra of seven blocks of granite, was St. Vincent Thomas Lombardi.

Mr. Everything Fordham, and Giants coach, and, the way Pat Malone described it, St. Mark's in Sheepshead Bay was practically a parish in the Bronx. A former altar boy, just like Pat, Lombardi was a Knight of Columbus, and just like Pat, fourth degree. Lombardi was a winner because he was a good man, a good Catholic, and he possessed a type of integrity that Pat knew infallibly was something we were supposed to aspire to, protect, and pass on.

The rest of the day kept presenting new evidence that the universe would not bend to the laws and hierarchies of Pat Malone.

The defenders of the faith were in short supply as Florida football stormed the gates. After a doleful pork chop dinner, Pat hit the worst of his withdrawal as the Hurricanes bloodied the Sooners. He watched his son root for teams that were demon fast, obscenely celebrating every tackle and first down, and undeniably dominant.

Pat felt like hell and hobbled to the bathroom. He was no longer banned from the master bedroom, but he would be up all night with the fidgets and the sweats and the nausea, and he needed more ice, maybe something sweet, but he had no appetite, and maybe he should just have one drink to take the edge off. *One drink, like medicine, that's all, what's the harm in that?* It was a new year, and if he could just keep it to one drink a night, then he wouldn't have a problem and he wouldn't be in misery, and everything would be fine. *One stiff drink and that's it.*

[JANUARY 31]

A COLD AND EARLY SUNDAY, THE EVE OF ST. BRIDGET'S, AND ANNE Malone put on her fake lambskin gloves to go turn over the Zephyr. *Bridget, a woman who prayed for her beauty to be taken away so no one would marry her . . . God Almighty . . . the Irish mother of the Church, ladies and gentlemen.* Anne sighed, thinking of her own Irish mother and all her beyond-the-pale superstitions. Bridget's feast sat uneasily on a cross quarter day. Midway from solstice to equinox, half in, half out. On a day like this, Anne remembered her mother saying, to look at the shades of winter, it felt like you had caught something looking away from you.

The Zephyr stammered at ignition, the engine wheezing and retching before settling into something resembling internal combustion. Anne turned both defrosters on low—anything stronger would stall the car—and grabbed the scraper from the glove compartment. A cold snap had perfectly entombed the car's windows in a quarter inch of ice.

Anne's resolution to go to early Mass every day in the New Year was still holding. *St. Bridget, hear my prayer, and grant me the strength to break this goddamn ice off the windshield.* The scraping was taking such effort that Anne was now sweating under her coat and church clothes. Finally the iceberg calved and slid onto the hood. Anne paused before attempting the back windshield. It was then that she spied the paper at the edge of the Peñas' driveway. *Still visiting family in Illinois*, she thought, and in her helpful neighborly fashion, Anne reached down furtively to steal their paper and Sunday coupons and stash it inside the house when the headline caught her.

RALEIGH AWAKE IN HOSPITAL
POLICE, D.A. RELEASE SUICIDE NOTE

Anne pulled a glove off with her teeth and unfurled the front page of the *Dallas Morning News*.

Standing Raleigh had come out of his coma. He was confused but responsive. No word about when the trial would resume—Judge Samuels was unable to be reached for the story—but a quote from Henry Wade, the Dallas district attorney: "Reverend Raleigh must have his day in court and be held accountable. I will wait until kingdom come."

Anne followed the jump to the first page of Metro, and there was the note Raleigh had written before his suicide attempt:

> There is a demon inside my soul. My demon tries to lead me down paths I do not want to follow. My demon is working inside my soul again, filling me with despair and taking away my hope.

> All of my life people have seen me as strong. The truth is just the opposite. I am the weakest of the weak. People have seen me as good. The truth is just the opposite. I am the baddest of the bad. People have seen me as virtuous. The truth is just the opposite. I am the lowest of the low.

> Pray for Peggy, take care of my children, and forgive me the pain I inflict on so many. I have grown weak. God has remained strong. Therein lies your hope. I have none.

Anne stood there in the plume of exhaust as it billowed across the lawn.

The end of a new year. Same old shit.

○ ○ ○

THAT EVENING, ANNE AND DANIEL MALONE SHEERED ALONG North-west Highway, heading east into the dark streets of Lake Highlands. The rain was coming down in a thin sleet, and Anne was nervous that the roads were icing over. Her tension filled the cold air inside the car—the heat in the Zephyr was diverted entirely toward defrost. There was no room for chatting; Anne had to concentrate—on the lookout for patches of black ice and other unknown perils. That it was a gloomy winter evening in East Dallas, an unfamiliar part of town, added to her worry. Dan had the Mapsco on his lap and had already rerouted them once. Anne had been heading on Walnut Hill to Lake Highlands High School, but that wasn't where the swim meet was—they had to find the White Rock Natatorium, and they were a little lost. Dan raised the map into the glare from the headlights of the cars behind them. If they had just taken the LBJ, like he suggested, it was easy. But highway driving in these conditions was inconceivable to his mother, who clutched the steering wheel awkwardly at nine and six o'clock, afraid to go hand over hand in the turnoff for Garland Road. The only problem was there was no turnoff for Garland Road. Then a sign. CONSTRUCTION ON GARLAND ROAD. ALT ROUTE, JUPITER ROAD.

"I don't know where we are."

"It's okay, this will loop back."

"So take it?"

"Make a right." Dan looked up from the Mapsco, scanning the darkness for a street sign or landmark. "This is better, actually."

Back to anguished silence. Luckily they did loop back to

Garland Road and, after a couple more turns, were relieved to find the parking lot for the pool.

"What time does this end?" Anne asked over the crunch of tires on gravel mixed with sleet.

"Eight or nine, I guess."

"Are there bleachers inside?"

"I don't think so."

"Okay. I'll come back."

Anne was cold, but two hours of chlorinated air and the deafening echoes of cheering inside an indoor pool would drive her batshit.

"I'll come back at eight thirty—"

"Fine." Dan slammed the car door shut, which Anne read as haste with the icy rain coming down but was really conflicted teenage moodiness—he wanted her there and he didn't want her there, and he was annoyed at having both feelings.

Anne burrowed into the cold of her car, the headlights of the Zephyr illuminating a turned-over goalpost on a wintered soccer field. She picked up the Mapsco and found herself. *East Dallas, the undiscovered country.* There was shopping on Skillman—*Maybe a Tom Thumb to stroll the aisles and warm up in.* And then she remembered: *Lake Highlands. Their house is just off Audelia and Royal.* She found Credo Drive in the street index.

o o o

SLEET STIPPLED THE HOOD OF THE ZEPHYR BUT DID NOT STICK TO THE road. Anne drove toward the Raleigh house expecting some part of her would win the argument for turning away. *Judge Sam never said we couldn't. Just a quick drive by.* She knew the address from the trial, 9324 Credo Drive, and in minutes she was on their block, the look and layout of the houses here familiar from the nightly news. Credo Drive hooked and veered left, the roads in this part of town all curved like this, partly by design and partly inflected by the various creeks that fed White Rock Lake. Anne crawled along and then came to a stop two doors down. The house was a bleached oatmeal color, with a large sycamore swiping an umber roof. The windows were shaded, no light on the porch. The house was . . . *inoffensive* . . . and in the darkness could have been mistaken for a million other Dallas ranch houses. There were few cars on the block, and Anne was a little surprised not to find any police stationed there, but then again, it was too late, the house just a remnant. *Creepy quiet though.* She nudged the accelerator and drove around the bend until Credo Drive dead-ended into an unmarked road across from railroad tracks. She looked both ways through a sequence of sodium streetlights—no cars, no people, just more road. She felt a little nervous—*If I get caught out here, would that be grounds for a mistrial?* Standing Raleigh's suicide attempt and the long delay, now going on two months, counting the holidays, had probably caused that already. But it was those same jitters that spurred her to make a hard right and turn up the alleyway behind Credo Drive.

The car prowled along the dim alley shrouded by a thicket of leafless trees. She had counted the number of houses from the Raleighs' to the corner, *eight*, so she could backtrack like this. An animal darted across the path—it wasn't a pet but carried itself on its haunches like a raccoon or possum, its pink eyes refracting the headlights like dull crystals before it scuttered below a hole in a fence. Anne pulled up to the driveway in the back. The door to the garage was shut, lights out. The papers reported that Raleigh's kids had been staying with families from First United and had not returned since that awful night. *Nothing to see. The back of the house less revealing than the front.* Just the off-whiteness of the garage door and an asphalt drive oil-stained and cracked. Anne sat there, her foot on the brake, staring at that handle on the garage door. *Say for a minute it wasn't Raleigh. The alley is dark but too narrow to hunker down in and not be spotted from a passing car. If it was a neighbor, the fences on either side of the driveway offer no line of sight. Is there another perch to watch the house from?* Anne couldn't find it, and then realized if there were, that person could be watching her. Danger didn't feel imminent but rather as if it had moved through a while ago.

And so Anne sat there, focused on the driveway where the minister's wife had been strangled. Like Peggy, the house offered only silence. As close as Anne now was to the horror of this assault, it felt distant. *Strip away the scandal of this case, what's left? Something fierce and predatory,* she thought. *An ignorant animal attacking another in the dark.* She had to stop ruminating reasons to believe one theory or another. *Is he really wrestling with demons? Is there even such a thing?* There were plenty of blind alleys that offered no answers, and she had to stop crossing the line in terms of her own research of the case. She knew better, but she couldn't abide by the evidence presented only in the trial. The trip to Credo Drive was near intentional, as had been the visit to First United, two weeks before. She had sat in the empty winter light of the pews, gaining no insight. Now, in the cold, dark car, she parsed the suicide note. It stopped just short of admission. *Why not go for the full absolution? He had a guilty conscience but was too weak to free himself.*

After the trip to First United, Anne flashed her St. Rita educator's pass at the Perkins School of Theology and got her hands on back issues of the *United Methodist Reporter* to close-read Raleigh's sermons. Most were pablum—*Life is a journey from darkness to light . . . live in the moment . . . in marriage there is only giving*—but then she found a transcript of Raleigh's Easter sermon, the Sunday of the supposed death threats. He started with a synopsis of a book called *The Passover Plot.* It rang a faint bell. So Anne went into the Perkins stacks. BT 301.3.S36. Schonfield, Hugh. Nineteen sixty-five. A book about how Jesus orchestrated the crucifixion and resurrection, and the plot was to sell himself as a false messiah. *So Raleigh faked the threats to make himself seem persecuted and in danger,* Anne theorized. *This was* his *Passover Plot. So why be so obvious?* The best explanations here that Anne came up with: *He wanted to get caught, or was stupid enough to think himself cunning.*

Anne pulled away, down the dim alley, until it spat her out onto another side street of the subdivision. A sudden gust bansheed through the vents of the Zephyr, but the rain had stopped and the wipers were now chattering on the windshield. *Did he look right at Peggy that Sunday? Or his mistress?* Both were in the congregation that morning. Anne brooded on this sermon a lot. It was beyond suspicious, but every time she went over it, her understanding of Raleigh tangled.

Just more evidence that proves nothing

[FEBRUARY]

30-DAY CLINICAL TRIAL FOR
HYPOVITAMINOSIS CHOLECALCIFEROL
PATIENT DIARY, PATRICK FRANCIS MALONE

February 1
Taken with each meal per instructions, no noticeable effects.

February 2
Coffee tasted weird after morning dose, otherwise no effects.
Left leg sore, which is normal. Early spring predicted by large
rodent.

February 3
Nada. Patient, i.e. me, thinks he got the placebo.

February 4
No worse for wear. Did a phone check in with Dr. Landis. I
asked him if I had to fill out this diary and he said it was optional.
So here's the tally: Diet good, drinking moderate, exercise bike
20 minutes every morning. Three doses, stools soft past couple
of days, but Landis said that's a possible side effect. Leg feels okay
today. All of this comes and goes.

February 5
Three doses. Pretty sure these are sugar pills. I have MS. No
change there.

February 6
Three doses and no flare-ups in past two days. I feel good—I think. Just bored and unemployed.

February 7
Took one dose before communion this morning. Prescriptions for mortal and immortal life. Hedging bets all around.

February 8
I apologize to the folks at the MS Society for the most boring medical diary ever written.

February 9
On the advice of Dr. Landis, I went to an information expo the National MS Society held in Arlington. "You never know," he says, which is one of the many things doctors say off-handedly and don't realize how they sound. The expo was more for doctors and specialists, but there were others like me—"the diagnosed," as we were called a few times. Those of us there ran, or rather limped, the gamut. One guy was a body builder diagnosed in 1974 and there to proselytize some steroid drug. Aside from the Lou Ferrigno wannabe, there were also a lot of folks with aggressive cases, and that depressed the hell out of me. The wheelchair and walker brigade looking for some miracle cure.

It was held at the Howard Johnson's across the highway from a water park Dan used to like called Wet 'n Wild. The main ballroom was a sign up for various clinical trials, and this is what Landis recommended I check out. Everything under the sun . . . there was ballroom dancing and ballet, and one *Clockwork Orange* guy who wanted to monitor how much your eye moved back and forth for a year. I almost registered for water aerobics—but it was all the way down by Parkland and I'm not going to jackass that far—lots of exercise and yoga studies, one was even meditation with a Buddhist monk.

There was a line out the door for interferon, word having spread quick that it was the most promising trial, but it was already filled by the time the expo had started and people were just signing up for waiting lists. I stayed away from the experimental drugs. Who the hell knows with this stuff, and the side effects could be worse than the disease. One drug called bifuobinase listed loss of bowel control as a possibility. Great, sign me up.

Someone might go into a room like this and think: *Thank God they have so many people working on a cure for MS or trying to figure it out.* But after an hour of hobbling around and pretending to be curious, I was left with a very sad realization: They have no idea what causes or cures this illness. It's all shots in the dark.

And so this is my shot in the dark, this God forsaken trial where I'm taking heavy doses of vitamin D for thirty days. Truth be told, I signed up to keep my wife off my back, and it didn't have an age cutoff or sound like something Dr. Frankenstein would suggest.

February 10

Three doses and no change in symptoms or temperament. I've been going to the Park Forest library to job hunt. I read the want ads in the *Times Herald* and *Aviation Week*, but it's mostly to get away from the loving scrutiny of my wife. Today, I looked up vitamin D in the medical encyclopedia. It has a lot to do with calcium in your bones. My joints do feel like they're raw, arthritic, but Landis claims it's the nerves, not the bones.

I have no idea if I'm even taking vitamin D, but I read the instructions from the MS Society and checked with Landis—I'm allowed to drink, so I've set a two-drink limit on myself while undergoing this trial. Two drinks to prove the point. No more and no less. And to be honest, I think it's doing more good than the vitamin D. Two drinks is a balance I can live with. Moderation in all things.

February 11

Slightly nauseous before coffee and stiff getting around this morning. Otherwise right as rain.

Went to the copy shop and then sent out 100 letters to everyone I know—just a "hello and if you hear anything here's my résumé." Dan helped—licking stamps and envelopes. Such a good kid. Anyhow, shaking the tree.

February 12

You can feel my wife's mood from the other room, from the other side of the house. Worry, worry, worry. It's driving Dan and me crazy. To-do list: get a job, just to escape this woman's gravitational field.

No real changes. Three pills. Two with coffee, one with vodka and Seven.

February 13

Dilemma for V day tomorrow: get her flowers and get yelled at for wasting money on flowers, or just go with a card and come up short that way? I understand now why they named the holiday after a martyr. I should dragoon Dan into this—if it comes from both of us, A. Mulligan will like it.

February 14

My legs, knees, joints, plantar f all feel fine for the first time in weeks. Promising. Will stick with the three doses. Dan and I got the Mrs. a black forest cake from Tom Thumb—too much chocolate, but it averted another Valentine's Day massacre.

February 15

Two weeks in and this might be working.

February 16

My family hates me. Last night, I'm sitting in the den after dinner watching Bob Newhart run his inn in Vermont. I have two fingers of vodka left on my second drink but I'm lucid and everything's in evening susurrus. The phone rings. Anne answers and it's her sister. Now, my wife had a couple drinks too, and I can tell she's tired, so maybe that set her off. But it doesn't take but two minutes before she spirals into this full Cassandra routine. I can only hear her half of the conversation but I'm instantly annoyed because it's clear they spoke recently and she told her sister that I lost my job at American. The thought of Anne's jackass brother-in-law nodding gravely at that news started to burn me. Then he would say "to be expected" or some other self-righteous bullshit.

So I can hear all this coming in from the kitchen and my better half starts broadcasting this tale of woe about how we are running out of money, and she'll let Catherine know if they need a loan, but thank you, thank you for your prayers and your offers to help, and all this other horseshit like we're completely broke. She's making no sense and has this panicked, worked-up tone and is ignoring the fact that I'm ten feet away and can hear her throw out possibilities like having to send Dan to go live with the Hurleys because I'm at death's door. I turn off the TV and escape to the back room. But now I can't hear her and I'm just replaying the tape—why did she have to go and tell those assholes our business? Suddenly I'm so furious I find myself in the garage taking pops off a fifth of vodka and I'm just so fucking sick of it.

And so half an hour later she finds me shitfaced in the garage and starts screaming at me because I'm just proving her point now. I don't say a word. I'm too tired to argue. Sure, this is all my fault, just go with that and leave me alone. She starts sobbing and slamming doors and Dan peeks into the garage and sees we're back to square one and he starts slamming doors too and I'm fucking alone now.

February 17
Throbbing pain in my leg now. I took all my doses but feel like

crap. I drank way past the lighthouse last night. I woke up on the couch and Dan was off at school and Anne was out, and the house was empty and silent, and I just lay there like I was shipwrecked and washed up on the beach of a desert island.

A couple thoughts kept occurring to me. The first was: *Stop doing stupid shit.* The second was: *Is this it? Is this all there is?*

I think I have a problem with booze. One becomes too many too often. And maybe it's the MS but the hangovers and comebacks are torture and practically forcing me to go with hair of the dog. Something—my liver maybe—ain't right, and I drink like it's going out of style, and I'm always thirsty, always thinking about it, even though there's no pleasure in it anymore and there's seemingly no end to it.

When I drink, all I want to do is quit, and when I quit, all I want to do is drink.

February 18

Took doses, nothing bad or good to report—stiff and hobbled as usual. Since no one in the house is talking to me, I made a baloney sandwich for dinner and got good and drunk on the dregs of an old handle of Clan MacGregor, which, let me tell you, will burn a hole through your tartan. So I'm officially off my two drinks a night regimen and not sure I care—I feel like this has to run its course like it always does. That sounds like I have a fever, and that's funny because last night while gagging on shots of Clan MacGregor paint thinner I came across a body snatcher movie on channel 39. The old one from the 50s. And it's weird but that's what it's like now with the drinking. Like I'm contaminated, and it takes over and I become this different person. And I'm strangely removed from it, like it's no longer part of me, but then I wake up and I don't know what happened and start thinking about drinking again.

February 19

Ten o'clock news reports: American Eagle flight 3378,

scheduled domestic from Raleigh/Durham to Richmond, departed during low ceiling, low visibility, and night conditions. The aircraft ascended to about 300 feet but shortly thereafter crashed into a nearby reservoir. Both crew members and all ten passengers were killed.

I morbidly expected the phone to ring. I was the one who liaised with the NTSB. Instead I'm lying on this couch, imagining how the Pharaoh Crandall is taking all of this.

Fuck you, Bob. With your cigarette gloom, your snaggleteeth, your gnawed fingernails, your coffee breath, your frat row haircut. Fuck your operating profit. Fuck your 12,000-square-foot house with marble floors, an indoor swimming pool, a moat—a fucking moat—around the dinner table, and a pink toilet you flush by stepping on a button in the floor.

And to think of every spreadsheet I pulled and every hour of overtime I slaved for this bastard. Every marathon meeting that turned into the Spanish Inquisition. *Why was this plane six minutes late? Why four no-shows on this flight? Who the hell approved this yield on the Nashville routes?* And when the answers didn't present themselves, he would just bang on the table like a child. *This—*POUND—*is—*POUND—*simply—*POUND—*factually—*POUND—*wrong—*POUND POUND POUND. This one time, he throws his tantrum and tires himself out, so now he's chain-smoking and sitting there silently in his black suit, suffocating the room with his gray smoke, unable to look at us, just staring at the table in front of him, and ten fucking minutes go by this way before he snaps out of it, and out of nowhere, he starts lecturing us about how we shouldn't offer bereavement fares. *Like going into a department store and asking for a discount on a black dress because your relative died.* And then like some bloodless reaper, like Nero at his most dour and fatalistic, he stabs out the cigarette. *Nobody lives forever. We're all just ants on a marble.* Meeting over.

February 20

No side effects from the vitamin, but this has to be it for the booze. God help me—I've had enough. And what's the point now—by the time I drink enough to feel it, I make myself sick. No more. Enough.

February 21

Escaping the dreary purview of Anne "The Scowler" Mulligan, I went back to the library today. I looked up MS in the medical encyclopedia. No new information. Not hereditary, possibly environmental. To look at the South Bronx now you'd think I grew up in Beirut, but it wasn't that bad. We had milk and vitamin D. The sun occasionally shined on Willis Avenue.

Then I looked up dipsomania. A bad business. And I must admit, I have some of the maladies—drinking alone, drinking to forget, maintaining a level of comfort by drinking. So new plan: no alcohol except on the rarest of occasions. No drinking in bars, no stumbling around the house. If I get a new job: one celebratory Johnnie Black. If Dan gets a scholarship to Georgetown, make it a Chivas. Only drink with the good news, not the bad.

February 22

I have fever dreams when I come off the drink. Weird nightmares waking in cold sweats. Last night I dreamt of Anne's father in a dim corner booth of the old IRT, like the Greek riverman who you pay your token to get to the underworld. I pass him unnoticed, and then I'm down there on a platform somewhere in the Bronx. The punks have put out all the lights, and it smells God awful and the train is nowhere to be found. There's laughter and screams bouncing off the walls. When I look down the platform, the columns recede and I feel sick. And then the train comes and it's on fire, and I can feel the heat off it, and the doors open and there are Anne and Dan and I don't know what to do. Do I take them off the train? Do I get on? The car is molten hot and it's burning my eyes, and the two of them are just staring at me as the doors close, and I realize too late it's a purifying fire and I'm stuck in this dark and wretched place. And I wake up on that and there are all these birds chattering and twitching and carrying on outside the window but it's dark out, dawn an hour away still.

February 23

Haven't touched the sauce in four days, which is something. If I can make it a week, then a month, then we'll see.

Dan has been such a trooper. This morning he was reading the paper and he found an article in the business section about American opening their new HQ in Fort Worth. "If they're expanding, maybe you can get your old job back." It was said with such love and hope and I kissed him on the forehead and wanted to cry and now I'm completely crushed and empty inside.

February 24

Trying to turn this corner on the drinking, but I'm as fragile as an egg. I remember my mother sent my father to Father Mahon at St. Jerome's when it got bad and he came home having taken the pledge. Didn't really stick, but the memory of it spurred me to confession at Christ the King. I picked that parish for anonymity— the priests at Rita's and Monica's all know me. So I went into the booth and offered my confession and told the priest my big problem was the booze and I was praying for a cure. The priest had a very gentle voice and he absolved me and offered to meet in his office to talk about the drinking. Come after reconciliation, he said, so I said my penance and waited. I almost chickened out, but at the end of the hour I saw him come out from behind the screen and I gave him a few minutes and then followed his path out of the church to the parish offices. He met me straightaway, Father Thomas Meacham, Dallas Diocesan, and he offered me an iced tea and told me he was four years sober himself, which struck me funny—a surprise openness I wasn't ready for. He drilled me with questions about my drinking—when had I last drank, was I ever in the hospital for it, etc. I didn't tell him about the MS, or losing my job, and started walking it back on how big a problem the booze was. (Probably a sin of omission.)

He was very exacting—I almost wrote "sobering" there—as he listed options for me. The first suggestion was through the Church—a prayer and meditation retreat. A month at Montserrat to dry out, basically. This sounded a little too holy roller to me, and while becoming a monk had its advantages in the Dark Ages, I have a mortgage and tuition payments to make, so I need to stay on the job hunt. Then he mentioned outpatient therapy, which was offered at Medical City and elsewhere. This shocked me—the Church I grew up in was very anti–head shrinking—but again I didn't mention the MS and I was worried that this was a complication that could cross wires, and I'm sick and tired of doctors and treatments without cures.

And that brought him to AA, which he said was started by a Catholic and offered a lot of guidance and fellowship similar to the Church, but at this point I got off Father Meacham's train of thought. Like many a priest, he was used to hearing himself talk. A bit of a droner. On and on he went, and I noticed in the corner of his office a small painting behind a chalice that marked some anniversary. I peered at it closer and I could make out that it was St. Anthony. On the left side of the painting he was beset by demons, and on the right side he's casting one out from the house of a poor shepherd. And it occurred to me—back then they just called it the devil, and now we call it a disease. But it's being overwhelmed by temptation, and you can call it evil, but it lives in the person and it has to be purged, exorcised somehow. I thanked the good Father Meacham, who blessed me, and I left.

February 25
They say that depression comes with MS. Like overcast skies making it hard to focus.

February 26
Got my last check from American today. Severance severed. We are now running at a deficit. Probability of ultimate ruin equals one. Sent out another 50 résumés, now going past airline contacts into want ads and headhunters. This is getting hopeless.

February 27
Whiskey. The water of life. I've been good all week, and I can take it easy—there ain't anything hard about drinking. Just a taste, as the old man used to say. The old man had a problem but he didn't know. I at least know, so if I confine it and control it, I'm fine. I'm not hurting anyone. As long as I keep to myself it's fine. What's a life without whiskey? What is that worth? And what's the point of being miserable?

February 28
Can't stop. Can't think. This train has gone express somehow. Nothing left to do but drink. Drink one drink, then two, then a river, a lake, an ocean, it's all the same. The drinking makes me sick. The not drinking makes me sicker. Great job, Pat, you fucked up entirely.

February 29
I have to stop. Every night ends in tears. Anne and Dan won't speak to me. I'm all alone and it's my own goddamn fault. I did this to me. Fuck me. Just let me fucking die.

March 1
Last day, last pills. I stopped taking them five days ago but what the hell. My apologies to the MS Society, who will have to do without this bullshit.

Heard from Frank Borman's office at Eastern about a position. Wants to fly me down to Miami. So that happened. God help me. I have to go. I have no other leads. So I'll go. On a wing and a prayer. I'm sorry for all my bad behavior. I'm sorry for making a mess of things. I'm sorry for how sorry for myself I am. I'm sorry to my family and I'm sorry I got sick. And I'm sorry for how long and whiny this is. If I had more time, as they say, I would have written something shorter.

"Jesus Christ, McGhee, it's like you were born late. Are you waiting for your engraved invitation? Get on the goddamn bus."

Pacing the carpool lane of the Jesuit parking lot, Coach Moyle looked down at his clipboard without really reading it. He hiked his jeans and combed his mustache with his palm.

"So much for an early start. Gonna hit rush hour and pay for this all the way down 35."

"Sorry, Coach, Steve O'Donnell is ovulating in the locker room and I had to talk him through that."

It was a surprisingly lewd comment from the apprehensive preacher's son. Rob threw his duffel bag into the belly of the Ranger bus as Coach Moyle shook his head.

"O'Donnell's time of the month? Fantastic. Are all you ladies on the same cycle? We have to move with a goddamn purpose. Who's left in the locker room?"

The answer was the entire Jesuit swim team. Coach Moyle slapped the clipboard against his thigh and stomped off toward the doors to the athletic wing. As Moyle came into the school, Rick and Dan came out. He yelled at them for taking their sweet-tea time and ordered them onto the bus. The Ranger swim team was (slowly) gathering to drive to San Antonio for the TCIL state meet hosted by Central Catholic. The only good news about this: missing a day of school with an excused absence, and that State this year wasn't at Cathedral in El Paso, which was a drive that took longer than Lent. Rob nibbled at his fingernails, trying to figure out the best seat on an empty bus. The back of the Ranger bus was reserved for upperclassmen, too close to the front was like sitting in an octane exhaust cloud, and anything near the wheel well subjected you to a death rattle at the slightest pock in the road.

Dan plunked down across the aisle from Rick, three rows from the steering wheel. Rob slid behind them and pulled a bag of Funyuns from his backpack. "I'm going to sleep the whole way there." Which was something you said at the start of a pain-in-the-ass five-hour bus trip, but Rob's default setting was skittish and wired. He was nervous about State—Rob had joined the swim team as a diver. This was largely on a dare from Sticky, who, unlike Rob, actually had some ability. But to be honest, the Jesuit diving team was basically an excuse to keep the crew (Rick and Dan were the only real swimmers) hanging out together.

Rob popped the foil bag, and the front of the bus bloomed with the perfume of onion powder.

"Did you guys hear about Devin Osweiler?"

"*Qué pasó?*" Rick already had his nose in *Henry IV, Part 1,* pretending to be doing the English reading, while already heading into a nap. The sight of the Oglesby assignment made Dan glad he was ahead on his work: he had spent the previous weekend in a cubicle at Park Forest library listening to Caedmon recordings of the Henriad, living in each weary lilt of Gielgud's voice for hours.

"Eighth period with Quickly, and she's doing the whole female reproductive talk." Jan Quickly was the sophomore biology teacher—how in an all-boys school run by priests she got assigned this lesson in anatomy was a question worth asking. "Osweiler stands up and asks a question with a hard-on."

"Tented or . . . ?"

"Yup, Warner told me it was popping his khakis."

Rick snorted. "What was the question?"

"He pointed at it and started yelling, 'What do I do? *What do I do?*'"

"Did she jerk him off?" Rick asked in his best Rather/Brokaw fake newsman voice.

"Of course, and then straight to penance hall," Rob shot back.

Coach Moyle hopped up on the bus.

"Who we got here? Malone, Dowlearn, McGhee. Christ, where is everybody? It's going to be past midnight with the traffic. This is two sacks of uncut bullshit, I tell you what."

Over the next fifteen minutes, the dribs and drabs of the swim team poured onto the bus. Then the upperclassmen came loafing back from a Taco Bueno run. Coach Moyle screamed and made faces while stealing a few chips from Preston Sarder's nacho tray. Last to arrive: Drew Radcliffe, the team's superstar, for whom Coach Moyle practically broke out a pillow and bonbons.

"Drew, sit anywhere. McGhee, move out of his way. I'm coming back there."

Tortured by the smell of queso, Rick put down his Arden edition. "So who's driving this bus?"

A minute later Mr. Donahue stormed through the exit doors of the athletic wing. He had a giant army thermos of coffee and lit an unfiltered Camel. Somebody had the good sense to not let Coach Moyle be the lone chaperone on this trip, and it turned out Donahue's National Guard unit was drilling what to do when the Soviets crossed the Brazos, and so welcome aboard. Coach Moyle bummed a cigarette off him, and the two of them smoked in the well of the bus stairs while doing a head count. Then Donahue butted out and claimed the driver's seat with a dragon's breath of nicotine and coffee. He turned the engine over on the first try, which was some sort of miracle for this pilgrimage to San Antonio. Just as the doors closed, Sticky, who was wearing blue and gold sweats with his blazer, came wandering down the steps from the cafeteria. Donahue put the bus in gear.

"Let's give O'Donnell a scare." And he pulled out of the driveway toward Inwood.

Rob cracked the window the two inches it would go. "Run, Sticky, they're leaving your ass!"

The bus roared past the "Come on" flying out of O'Donnell's mouth as he stood on the curb for two seconds before he started running to catch up. Coach Moyle heehawed and backslapped Mr. Donahue, who watched Stick in the driver-side mirror.

"Man, is he slow. Run, white boy."

"Come on, Steve-o, you can do it!" Rob screamed. Everyone was dying. The bus was going five miles an hour and Sticky was barely pulling alongside the back tires.

"I think I'll take him out for a couple miles on the tollway."

"Fine by me." Moyle waved him over to the bus's door side. "Damn divers never get in shape."

Donahue gunned it one last time before reaching the turn for Inwood and popping the door open. Sticky climbed aboard completely winded from jogging fifty yards.

"So glad you could join us."

"Thanks, Coach, it's an honor." No matter the situation, Sticky sweated sarcasm.

"You know, O'Donnell"—Donahue checked traffic while taking a swig of coffee—"if you were an AEF doughboy and that late to the fight, you'd be SOL."

"What?" Sticky lay down in the aisle like he was dying.

"'Shit out of luck,' son. 'Shit out of luck.'"

o o o

As expected, the Ranger bus soon hit rush hour and the exits crept by for Duncanville, DeSoto, and Lancaster. Coach Moyle settled in a back row for a nap next to golden boy Drew Radcliffe. The sophomores kept to the front as Mr. Donahue gulped coffee and cursed traffic.

"What are you listening to, Rob?" Dan asked.

Rob stretched out over Dan like a cat. "The Eagle, but it's starting to go out of range. Did you bring food? Your mom always packs extra shit."

Dan did have a second lunch courtesy of Anne Malone catering, and he handed some Chips Ahoy! to Rob. Rob ripped the blue foil open but then stopped, looked up, and whispered grace. Dan crossed himself, mocking his friend.

"You're going to hell, Malone."

"Those cookies are cursed by the devil." Dan, admittedly, was trying to set off Bad Rob mode.

"Stop it."

"Do you really think there's a hell? Do you think God has nothing better to do than keep track of who is praying for cookies?"

"Not funny."

"What if you choked on the cookies?"

"Shut up."

"What if we die in a bus crash right now? Does the cookie prayer deliver your soul to heaven?"

"Look, can't hurt"—Rob put the cookies on the bus seat between them—"but let me say this . . ."

Dan took one and chewed obnoxiously. "What if these were really crappy sugar cookies? Same prayer? Better salvation for Oreos?"

And rather than activate Bad Rob, Dan got his smart and calm spiritual brother. "Hey, God is good, all the time."

Shocked by the simplicity of that and embarrassed at his teasing, Dan swallowed his cookie. Rob combed his hair behind his ear and scooched into the aisle. "Mr. Donahue, how long until we pull over for dinner?"

"When I hit something that looks like good eating, I'll give you the signal to go back and scrape it off the road." Donahue gave Rob a don't-fuck-with-me marine stare in the rearview, then softened. "We are an hour from Waco, then two hours to Austin. We have a shit-ton of miles to go."

Rob winked at Dan. "How much coffee have you drank today, sir?"

Donahue bit his lip in estimation. "I'd say this is my twelfth cup. But it's the office stuff, like drinking dirty water."

"You seem jumpy, sir."

"And you seem like a smart-ass, McGhee. Stop trying to trigger a Nam flashback where I drive us off the road."

As the traffic finally broke up, Rob and Dan crept into the stairwell at the front of the bus to secondhand Donahue's chain-smoking and reload him on coffee. Donahue was in full discourse mode, doing twenty solid minutes on Irish history (it was St. Patrick's Day), the Afrikaaners' claims to the veldt, a deep dive into the war of independence that Ho Chi Minh had been fighting, and the fact that short of "nukes and putting down blacktops in Hanoi" there was no way to win there, then a sudden veer into David Shipler's *Arab and Jew* to explain the intifada. By Waco, Dan needed a break from this caffeinated run of Facts on File and wandered to the back of the bus, where Stick was playing hearts with Lee Molfetta and a couple of upperclassmen. A big rig air-horned, and Coach Moyle bolted out of his nap.

"Lord Almighty." He scratched at his stubble and patted down his mustache. "Where the hell are we?" Coach Moyle stared out at the darkness of I-35 looking for a billboard or road sign. Then he started to sniff.

"Oh shit."

Moyle hopped out of his seat, half-waking Drew Radcliffe, who was passed out next to him. Moyle grabbed the gym bag below him. It was dripping.

"Goddamn."

"What's in there?" Stick asked.

"The motion lotion. I brought it for the shave-down."

Dan shook his head. *This trip keeps getting better.* He thought Moyle was joking about shaving their legs and chest for the state meet.

"Gotta have the motion lotion, Coach," growled one of the up-perclassmen lying down in the back rows of the bus.

"No shit. Tell you what, we'll stop at Eckerd's when we get down there and I'll make a new batch."

"What's in it?" Stick cracked the nearest window.

"That's a secret recipe, trademarked, Moyle Aquatic Supplies."

"It's lube and vodka, isn't it?" Lee Molfetta deadpanned, not looking up from trying to shoot the moon.

"More to it than that—there is a science to the motion lotion." Moyle pulled out the spray bottle from his bag. Yup, it was cracked and leaking. "Takes off the dead skin and makes you slick as a seal."

"What gives it that green color?" Dan asked.

"Well that's the horse urine."

His coach broke into a smile.

"Malone, hand me that plastic bag to throw this shit in. God-damn. Smells like a port-a-john back here now."

"When are we doing the shave-down, Coach?" Ron Fenatacci asked.

"Tonight if we ever fucking get there, or first thing tomorrow. I brought barber clippers. Look at Malone's face. Like he didn't sign up for this."

"Oh, Malone," Karl Amberson, junior asshole and backstroker, chimed in, "I'm taking off your eyebrows and gonna run those clippers down to your taint."

"Hey, Amberson," said Clayton Dieter, captain and balancer of the Force, "are you trying to make it sound like the gayest thing possible?"

"Is that a sign for Killeen? We're not even fucking near Austin and it's dark." Moyle shouted up to Donahue. "This thing go above thirty-five?"

"If we throw the freshmen off I can take it up to forty," Donahue barked back.

"Let's do that then." Moyle rolled his eyes. "Goddamn."

At this point Drew Radcliffe, who was still pretending to nap, let out a polysyllabic fart.

Moyle jumped two rows away. "Fucking disgusting."

"Want me to pour the motion lotion on him?" Fenatacci offered.

"Open the goddamn windows . . ." Moyle was both gagging and breaking into laughter. "I'm breathing your fucking bean burrito, Drew. Jesus."

○ ○ ○

It was past ten p.m. when the Ranger bus wheeled into Circle the Wagons Cafeteria on the outskirts of Bexar County. The Circle cafeteria, with its big orange neon sign braided and knotted like a lasso (the L in "Circle" was burned out), was run by a Jesuit alumnus, Gerry Tillotson, and his wife, Gail, who seemed to stay in business by the infrequent subsidy of Catholic sports teams visiting the San Antonio area. For a restaurant on the major arterial highway of the state of Texas, it attracted less transient business than the flypaper in the toilets. The dinner rush ended promptly at six fifteen p.m., so the Circle was usually long shuttered at this late hour, except for its weird funereal side lounge, which looked like a bar in a bowling alley. Mr. Donahue had pulled over in Round Rock to let Mr. Tillotson know they were running late, and he'd agreed to keep everything out on steam trays.

"Look." Rick pointed across I-35 at the candy-cane-striped A-frame of a Whataburger. "We can just hop over there, it will probably be faster—"

"Stow that crap, Dowlearn." Moyle was cranky hungry. They all were. "Just take your meal ticket and hand it to the cashier inside."

The boys were starving as the Tillotsons met them at the door, stacks of dinner plates under their arms.

"Now, this is a family establishment," Mr. Tillotson admonished, and then adjusted his browline glasses with a greasy thumb, "so I expect you all to comport yourselves like gentlemen. Not like your slapdick wrestling team, who should have been put out in a barn. Am I clear, boys?"

Without any assent or dissent from the team, Tillotson started handing out plates while Gail gave everyone a lobotomized smile and collected the buffet tickets. In went the boys to the dining room. To their credit, the Circle cafeteria had laid out a staggering spread, and it probably had all been edible around noon that day, when it was first cooked and trayed. At the front of the line were two heaping piles of Texas toast and biscuits, which was the old buffet trick of putting the bread first to hog room on the plate. All the boys fell for this, except Sticky, who nonchalantly pocketed a biscuit like it was a billfold. Fast-forward over the salad, which was barely chopped chunks of iceberg. Get past the taigas of broccoli and asparagus, forget the mucusy okra and something resembling succotash, and skip ahead to the station for the mains and sides. The choice was meatloaf surfing its own au jus, a sweaty pile of spaghetti, or fried chicken with an impossible nook-and-cranny mahogany breading burnished by the golden heat lamp. And then came mac and cheese by the yard, a *Close Encounters* amount of mashed potatoes, and two long porcelain boats in the shape of chuck wagons for glopping white and brown gravy. And as the boys' gang tackled the fried chicken, out came two piping trays of beef enchiladas and pork tamales. Amazing.

For the next hour, the Jesuit boys devoured this carousel of cuisine. Dan and Rob, whose diets had been apportioned their whole lives by their mothers, quickly regressed into a semiferal state of hoarding every morsel and went back multiple times. Under the aurora of the buffet, everything glistened and life was a banquet of possibilities. Rob watched Rick pile salt, Bac-Os, and enchilada sauce on his mashed potatoes and did the same. Dan cursed his stupidity at taking a fried chicken breast—*Way too much white meat to chew through*—when there were the superior crispy-skin ratios on the drumsticks and thighs. And then there was dessert, which was equally unlimited, and the boys made four or five trips to try everything. First was the giant carameled flan—a sucker's move, Dan realized; better to save room for the key lime squares and coconut cake and brownies and Blue Bell with hot fudge. On top of this were endless refills of Hawaiian Punch, Orange Crush, Big Red, and Dr Pepper, and maybe the fountain mix was a little off, and the ice machine made a lot of noise but very little ice, but that was okay, *you had all you could eat or drink,* and the gluttonous freedom of that kept Sticky and Rick scraping their plates into the trash when the Tillotsons weren't looking and heading back for more. At one point Dan looked over at Mr. Donahue, who was carefully inspecting his meatloaf. Moments later, his fork went down, next to a plate of uneaten food, as Dan stabbed at his beef enchilada, which induced an orange slick of grease to ooze forth.

The buffet pillaged and insulin levels rising, Coach Moyle stood to address the team.

"Gentlemen, first off, raise your cokes to the Tillotsons, who kept the kitchen open for us."

Sticky, bold and brave, tried to sneak off to the buffet for a third dessert.

"O'Donnell, get back in your chair. Guys, 'all you can eat' doesn't mean you have to eat it all. Okay . . ." Coach Moyle frowned at his Casio watch. It was almost eleven thirty, and qualifying heats started tomorrow at eight a.m. "Mr. Donahue is going to drive us over to the motel and we are doubled up on rooms, so the curfew is the minute you enter that room. We're running really late tonight, so everybody brush their teeth and hit the hay—lights-out midnight. No exceptions. Radcliffe, how much flan is that?"

"Fenatacci bet me—"

"Stop it. Stop eating flan to impress your boyfriend. You're a goddamn athlete, not a pet pig. Okay, gentlemen, starting now, let's cut the shit. I'm knocking on doors at six a.m. and we're coming back to the Circle for breakfast, but not to load up—nothing that slows us down in the water. Tomorrow is a big day. Tomorrow is when all the hard work pays off. Am I right, Rangers?"

"Yeah." Dan sniggered at Rob, who was nodding off into a half-eaten pile of chicken carcass.

"I said . . . right, Rangers?"

"Yeah!" It wasn't much better. It was way too late.

"Okay, thank you. I know we're all tired, but we've done all the work to get us here. These races are a celebration of the training. O'Donnell, put down the goddamn brownies, you've had enough. And no smuggling food out of here. This is not a final meal on death row, this is not the Last Supper."

Moyle belched through a breath and rubbed his stomach. "Okay, get some rest, focus on tomorrow. I know that was a long bus ride, but, gentlemen, I have a good feeling."

Moyle belched again but tried to disguise it. "Rangers, bring it in. We are going to kick their ass tomorrow! Am I right?"

"Yes!"

"You can do better than that. Are we going to swim hard? Let me hear you say it. Swim hard!"

"Swim hard!"

"C'mon, let me hear it. Central, Strake, Cathedral—these boys are going to eat our wakes. Are we going to *kick their asses*?"

"*Yeah!*"

"That's right, Rangers. Let's kick some ass. Let's go!" Moyle pumped his fist and stormed out of the restaurant.

○ ○ ○

"MY ASSHOLE MAY LITERALLY FALL OUT OF MY BUTT, COACH."

"Get on the bus, McGhee. And quit bellyaching, all of you."

The last twelve hours had been rough. Rob took two steps to climb onto the bus and then pushed Dan out of his way as he ran back into the motel looking for a free bathroom. Dan barely noticed. *That nasty, greasy enchilada on top of fried chicken, what was I thinking?* He hadn't slept and had been switching off between the sink and toilet with Rob all night.

"Where's O'Donnell and Dowlearn?"

Dan lowered himself gingerly onto a seat. "Bathroom."

"Molfetta?"

"Bathroom."

"Christ." Moyle steadied himself with a knee on the driver's seat. Dan lay down in his row. If he stayed very still he might make it back to Dallas. *How could there be anything left in my stomach to upset it?* he wondered. The night had been sheer intestinal hell. He missed his five hundred qualifier, but Dan was just one of a score of scratches that morning. Drew Radcliffe turned in the only good performance, winning the prelim for the one hundred breaststroke, then vomiting over the lane line. The gun went off for the two hundred IM with Rick still in the bathroom stalls. By midmorning the whole swim team was severely (and ironically) dehydrated. Rob, Sticky, and the other divers were all suffering from hurling bouts of reverse peristalsis. Moyle himself had to coach through the runs, and he couldn't cobble together a single bowel-continent relay team. The Rangers had to forfeit.

Donahue came onto the bus with a giant 7-Eleven coffee and two trash cans he had stolen from the motel. Moyle sipped a ginger ale and looked up at him. "You ever have this in the marines? Any suggestions?"

"Don't eat at the Circle cafeteria." The joke was met with

several groans. Donahue was the only one currently not in danger of shitting himself. "We now have two emergency toilets. Bucket number one is for upchuck and bucket number two for letting the dog out. Get everyone on the bus, I don't care how sick. All of them have to drink a ration of Imodium. No Pepto, it doesn't do anything once it's past the stomach."

Donahue started passing out eight-ounce bottles of Imodium. Dan reached up and grabbed one. "This stuff is plaster for your gut. It will stop the need for bombing the Oval Office. All right, let's try to get through this together."

An angry wet fart marked the end of Donahue's evacuation plan. The rest of the Ranger team limped onto the bus. Dan closed his eyes and sucked down the loperamide. *Tastes like peppermint lead paint.* Eventually he felt Sticky shove his feet away to collapse down next to him. He heard the bus door close and the engine belch to life. The air on the bus was a nauseating cloud of carburetor, motion lotion, Donahue's cigarettes, and the mint varnish of Imodium. Dan's stomach was a tight knot that felt every dip and acclivity of the interstate, and he dared not crawl out of the fetal position, praying: *Lord Almighty, merciful Christ, please don't make me have to go again.*

As Donahue drove the bus back north, they all lay still, trying not to resort to bucket one or two, desperate just to hold it, and hold it, and hold it some more.

PAT MALONE STOOD AT THE EDGE OF THE TARMAC STARING AT A DARK
bronze statue of Captain Eddie Rickenbacker. He had landed in
Miami twenty minutes ago and had taken a courtesy Jeep—
essentially a luggage cart—across the airport to the buildings and
hangars that comprised the headquarters for Eastern Airlines.
The Florida sun was shockingly bright and bleached out everything. He squinted in the whitewash glare of building 16, the corporate offices. There was Captain Rickenbacker, the flying ace and
founder, a hand in the air like he was saluting the Red Baron or
perhaps hailing a cab. Behind the statue were the marble columns, pediments, and sea nymphs of the Rickenbacker Fountain.
The fountain and its whirlpools, however, were dry and rusted at
the spouts, the water drained and the power cut off years earlier in
a cost-saving move.

For a minute, Pat stood on the griddle of the concrete tarmac
deciding what to do. He was fifteen minutes early for his interview
but worried about sweating through his suit. Like the fountain, he
was dry but still a bit clammy from withdrawal. So he moved inside building 16, the glass front doors giving way to a hemispheric
lobby with blue pearl granite floors, the walls sheathed in a tacky
orange wallpaper that had bubbled with the humidity, and a reception desk in the shape of an airfoil. Pat wandered to the left to
study the hanging route map, the blue and green peels of the Mer-
catored Americas with tiny lightbulbs dimly burning at the point

of each Eastern destination. Lima flickered like a dying star as Pat tried to take a minute and rehearse some interview answers. Eastern's labor costs were notoriously high. And the load factor, i.e., butts in seats, was not great on a lot of these routes to the Caribbean and points *sud*. Eastern was a big boy, but the littlest of the bigs, and the north–south frost-to-flowers routes made it a vacation airline with price-sensitive markets. Where American's corporate pride was driven by fleet size, passenger loads, and revenues, Eastern was a little more humble and looser in terms of its management and marketing—the official airline of Mickey Mouse. Their immediate threat was Charlie Bryan of the machinists' union, who was holding out for concessions when none could be offered. Pat was interviewing to be director of employee benefits— a step up in title even if he was downgrading from Cadillac to Chevy in terms of carrier.

After milling around near the map, Pat was not too early anymore and stepped toward the reception desk. His legs felt fine for once, and he was going to will his way through walking today. *Nail this interview and you could show up day one on crutches. Just get an offer. Keep your hands steady. Be confident. You ran a department three times this size. Do it for Daniel. Do it for Daniel's college bursar.*

Pat announced himself and was escorted to the ninth floor. Past screaming orange wallpaper again, up a cantilevered stairwell of poured concrete, through a series of doorways with Moorish cutouts like he was entering Rick's Café, he was eventually led to the reception area for the office of Colonel Frank Borman, chief executive officer, Eastern Airlines, and former pilot, Gemini and Apollo space programs.

o o o

PAT HAD NEVER MET AN ASTRONAUT BEFORE, BUT HE HAD HEARD stories about Borman—West Point, hard charging, not one for nuance. "Uncomplicated," which was offered as code for "ass-hole." Pat had considered all of this: *If America had to send someone to the moon, they wouldn't send an asshole, right? Or maybe it takes an asshole to get you there?*

The door swung open, and the former fighter pilot, still at his 168-pound flying weight, bounded out of the office.

"Pat?"

"Yes, sir. It's a pleasure—"

"Great to have you here. Come in, come in."

He had cut off Pat, but that was to be expected. Pat had heard through the rumor mill that Borman was near deaf. His old buddy at American Jack Crowdus claimed all the spacemen were hard of hearing from sitting on those Saturn Fives. But Doug Dorsey at Delta had told him that Borman busted his eardrums while dive-bombing with a head cold. *Uncomplicated.*

Pat walked a perfect line across the tangerine carpet into an office that had the aesthetic appeal of a shoe box wrapped in green vinyl. The intercom chirped, and a call came in. Borman frowned and asked Pat for thirty seconds.

"It's our friends in New York. Look around while I take this."

"New York" for Eastern meant Chase bank, a "Rockefeller and Rickenbacker" airline since they bought it outright from Alfred Sloan at GM. As Borman murmured into the phone, Pat wandered the perimeter of the office. There were three oil paintings of fighter planes streaking across the American West and photos of Borman's two sons, both square-headed blonds like him, both cadets at West Point in their parade uniforms. Then Pat came upon a large framed invitation:

YOU ARE CORDIALLY INVITED TO ATTEND

THE DEPARTURE OF THE

UNITED STATES SPACESHIP APOLLO 8

ON ITS VOYAGE AROUND THE MOON,

DEPARTING FROM LAUNCH COMPLEX 39 KENNEDY SPACE CENTER

WITH THE LAUNCH WINDOW COMMENCING AT

7 A.M. ON DECEMBER 21, 1968

To the right of the invitation was a portrait of Borman and his crew, Bill Anders and Jim Lovell, in their white nylon space suits, the famous shot of Earthrise from above the charcoal lunar desert, and the mission patch, which was a red figure eight looped around the Earth and the moon.

"Checking out my greatest hits over there, huh?" Borman hung up the phone.

"Just glad you made it back in one piece, sir."

Borman smiled, and Pat was unsure he had heard him. The colonel pointed at the next frame, which offered a schematic of Apollo 8. "You hear folks now saying how they put us there in a tin can, but let me tell you, the rocket and this command module were made out of five point six million parts. Even if NASA got ninety-nine point nine percent of everything right, that meant fifty-six hundred defects. When you think about the risk involved in that, we were very lucky. But more than lucky, we were good."

The nod to actuarial appreciation impressed Pat. "That's amazing to think about, sir."

Borman squared his shoulders and pointed at another photo. "So you're sitting on this rocket that's taller than the Statue of Liberty. You've got to get her up to twenty-four, twenty-five thousand miles per hour and travel two hundred thirty-nine thousand miles to the moon. The first stage gives you a hundred sixty million horsepower."

"Wow." Pat realized that for the facts and figures to be coming this quickly, they had to be part of some set piece Borman had recited countless times.

"And the moon is barreling along in its own orbit at twenty-three hundred miles an hour, so you have to aim in front of it to catch it."

"Did you have computers—"

"I was in charge of twenty-four instruments, forty event indicators, seventy-one lights, and five hundred sixty-six switches." Borman's recitation could not be interrupted. *Autopilot,* Pat thought. "And that's not including the actual controls to fly and doing some of that with four to five Gs of force coming down on you."

"I remember following your mission over the Christmas holiday. Did you—"

"It wasn't Eastern's first-class to the Bahamas. Oh no . . ."

Pat was now worried Borman was completely deaf and on some sort of broadcast mode. There was no indicator light for that.

"It was more like sightseeing in a Sherman tank. We had this one small window to look out and you couldn't see the moon on approach because of the sun's glare. But then we orbited the moon ten times and I was the first man to see with his own eyes the dark side of the moon."

"Unbelievable."

"Unbelievable we made it back." Borman chuckled. *So he is hearing me? Unclear.* Borman stretched out his arms, his hands falling on the imagined controls of the command module. "Once you escape Earth's gravity, it's very quiet. You fire a thruster and there's just the thump of the solenoids opening and closing. So it's noiseless and still, and then we got around to the dark side, and it's just sameness. And remember when you're behind the moon you lose the radio signal with Houston. So you're far away and it's this big battered expanse of nothing. Crater upon crater, hill upon dusty hill. So there I am like Columbus or Magellan, seeing this, and I'm thinking, *This is it?* There's nothing there. We go all that way, and then nothing."

Borman realized he was starting to drift off and turned back to Pat. "So they tell me you've put up with Bob Crandall since de-regulation."

"That's one way to put it."

"I like Bob, but he reminds me of my mother-in-law's terrier." Borman smiled and studied the Earthrise photograph again. "Always barking."

"Well, you always know where you stand with Mr. Crandall." Pat wasn't going to fall into the trap of bad-mouthing him. *This is the test to see if you're loyal.* "But he is a terrific leader and I'm proud of my time at American."

"These classes of kids come in from all across Miami to tour the planes, and they meet me, the astronaut, you know what the question I get most is?"

Pat smiled with confusion—the Irish call it a shit-eating grin—as he realized the interview had veered back to the moonshot.

"'How do you go to the bathroom in space?'" Frank Borman shook his head. "So I tell them all about the waste management protocols. For number one, we had this tube, and you roll on the condom, open the valve, and try to go—with your Johnson Space Center there connected to the vacuum and the void. And then you dump it and it freezes into droplets of ice that are iridescent in the sunlight. It's quite beautiful actually."

Pat could swear that Borman was almost floating off the ground in memory of pissing into space. "Now, number two is much trickier, and I should know. The first twenty-four hours of the Apollo mission I was sick as a dog. Could have been flu, but I now think it was my last meal on Earth, steak and eggs, was under-cooked. Lord knows, but I had diarrhea, and in a space suit that is just not going to work out for you. So NASA had come up with this flypaper thing for your rear end, and what a mess, and so that doesn't work, and now we're chasing it around with paper towels."

Borman told the story with utter seriousness, and Pat had no idea how to react to the fact that he had turned Apollo 8 into a flying shitcan.

"And Anders and Lovell are downplaying it—last thing we wanted was to stay in Earth orbit and scratch the mission."

All these astronaut stories—maybe Colonel Borman is trying to impress me and carry on as a way of getting me to come to Eastern.

"So that's the story I tell these kids. I went faster and farther than any human at that point." Borman shook his head and let go of the invisible controls. "And what I really needed was a commode."

"Did the Eastern stewardess at least offer you a blanket and a magazine?" Pat found himself yelling a little as he noticed the thread for Borman's hearing aid.

"Ha!" The joke landed, and Borman cracked a smile. "Yes, she worked the first leg, but because of union rules, we had to leave her on the moon."

"So who served drinks on the ride back?"

"I tell you, these labor issues could drive you to drink, but I'm a teetotaler now." Borman's tone was instantly stern. He turned away from his wall of fame toward the glass slab of his desk. Pat followed, waiting to take a seat. "You've probably heard about my wife, Susie, and her problems."

Pat shrugged. He noticed a plaque on Borman's desk: EX AEQUO ET BONO.

"Well, she had a problem with booze." Borman plopped down in his padded leather chair. "She was expected to appear to the public as the perfect wife married to the perfect husband who was a perfect astronaut with a perfect American family raising perfect children." Borman stared out the window at the gauzy Florida sky. "Mission impossible."

Pat scratched his palm, growing uneasy about why Borman was telling him this.

"She was crying for help, and I always put my mission and

flying first. I feel guilty about that, and when her drinking was out of control, I blamed myself. I wanted to help her, but the doctors told me it was Susan Borman, not Frank Borman, who had to change."

Frank looked straight at him. "Now, Pat, I've heard things."

Here it comes. Pat had worried so much about the MS that he was caught unprepared for this.

"Sir, let me stop you right there. I've been sober since before I left American." It was a lie, but it sounded right somehow. He had been trying that long at least.

"Good. You know I instituted a rehabilitation and counseling program at Eastern, but we're talking about a very stressful labor situation. And I need all hands on deck and I need to know my team is mission focused. I love my guys who work out there on the aircraft, but their union is run by a bunch of thugs. Animals, Pat. I'm getting death threats. I had to meet with the FBI. They told me to wear a bulletproof vest in public. Can you believe this? Instead I have this little guy." Borman kicked his leg up on the desk and rolled up the cuff of his pants to reveal a .38 Special holstered on his ankle. "That's why I need my director of employee benefits running on the straight and narrow. I'll be honest with you, Pat. If we don't bring these jerk bosses to heel, our board of directors will lose faith and panic. And then my ass is on the line. So I need men I can count on."

Pat felt certain the colonel would rather take live fire than negotiate. "It's not a problem you have to worry about."

"Thank you, Pat. I'm not worried about it. If we work together, I just want you to stay on the path, and if you need help with it, I'll be there."

"This all sounds good to me, and I appreciate your personal interest." Pat wasn't sure where he stood or what to say. *Did he just offer me the job? No, but close I think. Should I pledge sobriety?* Before he could find a way to elaborate, Borman stood up from the desk.

"I always used to say, don't think about the parachute, think about the controls. But I was young then and didn't know any better." Borman put out his hand to shake Pat's. "There's more to life than living."

○ ○ ○

AN HOUR LATER PAT WAS IN EASTERN BUSINESS CLASS HEADED BACK to Dallas. He hadn't closed the deal in the room, and any positive indications from Borman were scrapped by the head of HR telling him they had more candidates to interview, ending with the normal "We'll call you" bullshit. Pat played back the tape on his talk with Borman and sank into dejection. They never really discussed his work experience, just more detail about how you have to slow-roll a space capsule like it's on a barbecue spit so as to evenly spread the radiation against the hull, how Apollo 8 touched down into ten-foot swells in the Northern Pacific and Borman got seasick, how he had passed on Apollo 11 and why he didn't want to go back to the moon, *"Seen it, done it, knew what was in store for that crew . . ."* Pat left knowing more about lunar telemetry than he did about a job at Eastern. So he picked his sour grapes: *Everyone knows Eastern is a shit show, an airline on the ropes, and the colonel*—Pat still couldn't believe he was packing a pistol—*is going full Nixon on his enemies in the union. His days seem numbered.* Maybe that was too strong, but Pat got the distinct sense that Borman was a good but troubled man, who alternated between velvet glove and iron fist, between bended knee and thrusting chest, and that was very hard to read in a boss.

The airplane taxied from the gate, and Pat stared out the window at the shimmering runway, and beyond it, a grassy ditch filled with black puddles. Feeling underwater himself, Pat was suspicious of a place where rain collected rather than ran off. *Always smells like a storm is coming.* And then something caught his eye.

An alligator climbed onto the bank of the runway. It was at least five feet long, its scales dark and wet, and it slunk leisurely with its belly close to the ground until it was on dry grass.

"Can I get you something, sir?"

Pat looked at the blue face of his Timex like it mattered. He ordered a Johnnie Black double, rocks. If Borman had a spy on the plane, so be it.

The plane took off and gained altitude, and Pat sipped but strangely found himself not thirsty for it. He was sick of the taste, sick of chasing it. The plane leveled off, and Pat closed his eyes, imagining a rocket launch and that cauldron of white and yellow fire. *Borman was right; after the initial acceleration there is no sense of motion.* Pat opened his eyes and asked the stewardess to clear his drink. He looked out the Plexiglas oval and saw the Everglades below. Thick knots of vegetation, steam clumped over the canopy, thousands of roosting birds like white pinpoints on the map. To the distant south, a long brown smudge of fires burning. To the north, the afternoon storm clouds were churning in, the lightning glowing like flashbulbs under wads of cotton. *Always a storm coming.* The stewardess brought Pat a fresh drink—she had misunderstood. Pat knew they were moving, but he couldn't feel it. He looked at the drink and then back at this long green tangle until it gave way to the western shore and the gray, waveless waters of the gulf.

"YOUR HONOR, THE DEFENSE CALLS THE REVEREND STANDING Raleigh."

Anne Malone snuck a peppermint Life Saver from her pocketbook and studied Raleigh as he moved in tandem with his attorney toward the witness box. Raleigh looked down, unassuming, penitential. *The same well-practiced demeanor he used for Sunday services,* Anne thought. Haynes Whiteside laid a binder open on the lectern and adjusted the black foam tip of his microphone. Sergeant Redman administered the oath to the witness, and you could hear the shutters of a dozen cameras. Even though this moment for the media had been sanctioned by Judge Samuels, he erupted when it carried on too long.

"I will have this room cleared . . ."

Judge Sam pointed his gavel at the line of cameramen, who lowered their lenses. Then silence.

"Proceed, Mr. Whiteside."

The defense attorney shook off his annoyance. Having Raleigh testify was a huge gamble, and the judge had just aggravated the delicate tension. The bailiff brought Raleigh a fresh glass of water as Whiteside began.

"Reverend Raleigh, did you attack your wife?" Whiteside asked, calm as could be.

"No I didn't," he replied, rubbing his eyes but showing no

tears. Raleigh was wearing a dark blue suit, a starched white shirt with a forward point collar, and a red paisley tie. *Too flashy for a minister*, Anne thought, *anywhere except Dallas.*

"Do you know who did?"

"No, I don't." Raleigh's voice broke slightly.

It was the Friday after Easter. The trial had restarted two weeks before. The delays brought on by Raleigh's suicide attempt had been compounded by hearings about his mental health, his ability to take the stand, and an endless parade of motions and side contests that had put Judge Barefoot Sam in a very ornery mood. Many in the press thought for sure that he would declare a mistrial, but the defense was strangely keen on continuing. Whiteside had drawn a jury he liked, apparently, so no restart, and through juristic half steps and a procedural stubbornness, Judge Sam had kept this trial going as it entered its sixth month.

On their return to court, the defense had spent its first few days rehashing the testimony of Officer Bodel, Detective Hume, and all the other witnesses from the record. Then an FBI forensic specialist had explained the keystroke matches between the death-threat letters and the typewriter in the offices of Raleigh's church. That was followed by the DA's bombshell witness, Lucy Goodfellow.

Through tears, Miss Goodfellow confirmed her affair with Raleigh. He had visited her the night of Peggy's attack, but they had an argument, and she felt he was close to breaking up with her.

"He was angry we couldn't be together," she confessed, "but I'm sure Standing is not capable of violence of that kind."

Good Lord, she still thinks she can have him. She still wants him to leave his family for her. Lucy Goodfellow came off a little airheaded— *Self-deluded, but believable, and too naïve to be covering for him.* She was accounted for by a confiding call to her sister Libby, which was proven with a long-distance phone bill, as well as neighbors who put her car on the block and Lucy in her apartment that entire night. Her real purpose on the stand was to show Raleigh was a liar, an adulterer, and a hypocrite. Point made, but the supposed bombshell witness was ultimately a dud. *If anything,* Anne reasoned, *the fact that his mistress is a run-of-the-mill bimbo and not conniving enough almost plays in the reverend's favor.*

On Holy Thursday, almost a year since the supposed death threats against Raleigh had begun, District Attorney Blackburn had rested the people's case.

On Easter Monday, Haynes Whiteside had begun the defense with a parade of character witnesses for Raleigh. The *Times Herald* deemed it the "Raleigh Revival" as parishioners, church leaders, and everyone minus Raleigh's own mother told the jurors how great a pastor he was. This did not sway Anne. *Oblivious holy rollers,* she deemed them all. *Pharisees in the street.*

And now, on Bright Friday, the defense presented their last, key witness.

"When did you meet your wife, Reverend?"

"At SMU, we were both graduate students. I was studying theology, she was studying music. She was the best organist I ever heard play."

Anne's antennae tuned in on that. *Rehearsed.* It was in the manner of married couples who have pat answers about each other, but there was something else to Raleigh's reply—something throwaway that came off as inauthentic.

"She is the light of my life." Raleigh's voice cracked again.

Whiteside corralled Raleigh's recollection to the days leading up to the attack and the death threats he had received.

"The church had a pretty large file of unsigned letters, referring to me as a Negro lover, a communist, that I should keep my nose in the Bible and out of politics."

Raleigh then testified about the precautions taken as a result of this—primarily, the security alarm installed at the house. But the Raleighs weren't used to having it, he claimed, and Peggy didn't activate the alarm regularly. *Why didn't he take his family's security more seriously? And why hasn't anyone bothered to theorize who else could have done this?* Anne puzzled. She then noticed Raleigh's shoulders hunch in tension as Whiteside began talking about the night in question.

"I came home that night, I'd say around six thirty. Peggy was out in the garage trying to fix the latch on the garage door. It was sticking, and she was trying to loosen it with Palmolive."

Unbelievable.

"Then what happened?"

"We had a glass of wine, chatted about the kids, and I left."

Another lie.

"Where did you tell Peggy you were going?"

"Back to the library at SMU to work on my sermon."

"And where did you go?"

"I went to the apartment of Lucy Goodfellow."

"What was the nature of your relationship with Miss Goodfellow?"

Raleigh dropped his chin and bit his lip. "We were having an affair."

"Did you have sexual relations with Miss Goodfellow during this visit?"

"No, we had a fight."

The real fight was with Peggy about Lucy.

"How long did you stay at Miss Goodfellow's apartment?"

"Thirty minutes, I think."

That's not right, Anne thought. She couldn't remember exactly, but it was longer than that. *They are messing with the timeline. Compressing, distorting it.*

"Then did you go to the library?" Whiteside caught himself leading Raleigh. "Sorry, withdrawn, where did you go next?"

"To Bridwell Library."

"For how long?"

"About an hour."

"So you left Bridwell around eight thirty?"

"Correct."

"Where did you go then?"

"I went to the Texaco on Greenville to get gas." Raleigh tried to offer a faint chuckle. "And some alcohol."

"Any reason why you were drinking that night, Reverend?"

"The fight with Lucy had rattled me. I was trying to find courage in a bottle."

Courage is not the word I'd use.

"I had told Lucy that we couldn't see each other anymore. I told her it was wrong in the first place, and then with the death threats I was receiving, I felt we were being watched."

Trying to raise a bogeyman . . . the killer still at large—all this felt weak to Anne. And then a strange, sudden thought occurred to her: *Did Pat ever have suspicions of me? He knew who Ronan was, but what else did he know, or worse, suspect?* Anne sank into bitter realization. *My husband is oblivious, and in this I'm no better than Standing Raleigh.*

"So where did you go next?"

"I went back to Bridwell."

"Straight there?"

"Straight there."

"Did anyone see you there? Any of the library staff?"

"There was an attendant at the desk, but I can't say for sure."

Anne looked over at the prosecutor's table. Blackburn and his associate were conferring nervously.

"Why did you go back to the library?"

"I was finishing my sermon, and I was looking for a certain book. Which I left a note for."

"With the desk attendant?"

"No, I left the note on the desk of the research librarian."

"Your Honor, I would like to bring into evidence the note Reverend Raleigh wrote that night."

"Objection, Your Honor." Blackburn was turning all shades of pissed off. "We have no witness to this piece of evidence—"

Whiteside: "Judge, this note comes with an affidavit from—"

"Your Honor"—Blackburn started halfway around his table—"we cannot—"

Judge Sam raised his hand to halt him. "Mr. Whiteside, bring me the note and the affidavit."

After a minute of scrutinizing the note, the judge called the lead lawyers and their associates into a sidebar. Anne tried to read the body language, but the attorneys remained restrained and professional. *They don't have to fix the prosecutor's timeline,* Anne realized, *just punch holes in it.* Judge Samuels passed the note to his clerk. The lawyers returned to their stations.

"Defense is allowed to enter the exhibit into evidence."

"Thank you, Your Honor. Reverend Raleigh, who is the note addressed to?"

"Gail Greenough, the research librarian at Bridwell."

Anne understood now—there were two of them, the head librarian, who saw Raleigh leave at eight thirty, and the research librarian he left the note for. *That's why this was a surprise. The cops didn't interview the second librarian.*

"And what time and date is listed on this note?"

"April twenty-first, ten thirty p.m."

Anne noticed Blackburn shaking his head ever so slightly.

"So you were at the library until ten thirty?"

"Yes, I left shortly after that."

"And returned home?"

"No, sir. I went back to Lucy Goodfellow's apartment."

"Did you enter that apartment?"

"No, the lights were out. I wanted . . ." Raleigh trailed off and then restarted. "I wasn't leaving Peggy. I think this was an infatuation. I felt attracted to Lucy, but it wasn't love. I was acting out of lust."

"Were you living a lie?"

"Yes, I was."

"You betrayed your wife's trust, did you not?"

"That is correct. But I committed adultery, not murder."

This struck Anne as very rehearsed. *Too matter-of-fact. Too helpful in his own defense.*

"So how long were you outside Miss Goodfellow's house?"

"I'd say twenty minutes."

Convenient amount of time. The kids were asleep. I bet he was on Credo Drive.

"And did you knock on the door or try to call her?"

"No."

"Were you drinking?"

"Yes, sir."

"And then what?"

"Well, I called home. From the car phone."

Whiteside made a quarter turn to the jury. "We have heard that message for Peggy. In it, you claim it's about nine thirty or nine forty-five, correct?"

"Yes."

"But that wasn't the time, was it?"

"No, it was later."

"About two hours later?"

"Yes, I was lying to Peggy about the time"—he paused—"because I was creating an alibi to cover my attempt to see Lucy. I assumed my wife was asleep and she would hear these messages in the morning."

His carefully worded answers, Anne felt certain, all of his practiced testimony, was backfilled from what happened.

"Would that be true for the second message you left?"

"Yes, my guilty feelings made me give Peggy more information than she needed."

He's good, he believes his own bullshit.

"So, Reverend Raleigh, those guilty feelings you talk about. Would you say those feelings are overwhelming at times?"

"They are."

Whiteside shifted his weight. "And in the days and weeks after Peggy was attacked, did the guilt of having cheated on her and not being home at the time overwhelm you?"

"It did."

"When the police first came to you to talk about Peggy's attack, did you tell them about your relationship with Lucy Goodfellow?"

"No, I hid it. I lied."

"But then it became obvious that this trial was going to reveal your affair, correct?"

"It did, and that was so upsetting to me I tried to take my own life."

Raleigh looked up at the ceiling and blinked, then pulled at his tie like it was a noose. He was breaking, but Anne couldn't tell why exactly. *Seems more embarrassed than upset about his wife's near death.*

"Reverend Raleigh, you wrote a suicide note before that attempt. Is that right?"

"Yes, that was my moment of absolute and total despair."

The clerk produced a copy of the note and handed it to the bailiff, who walked it over to Raleigh.

"Can you explain this letter, Reverend Raleigh, particularly the part about the demon?"

"When I say this about the demon, I was talking about an inner restlessness that has been with me all my life. I didn't just have lust, I was unfaithful to Peggy."

Raleigh had tears rolling down his cheeks. Anne felt the tears were genuine, but not for Peggy. *They're for Standing Raleigh. He turned the note into a sermon, and the devil can cite scripture for his own purpose.*

"If I had been at home that night, this may not have happened. That's what I mean by the lowest of the low."

Raleigh threw his head in his hands and winced with pain as he stifled his sobs. Anne watched the white knuckles of the defense attorney relax and let go of the podium. *He believes the lies. Raleigh thinks he has everyone fooled, including himself.*

"Thank you, Your Honor, no further questions."

○ ○ ○

DOUGLAS BLACKBURN STRODE TOWARD THE WITNESS STAND WITH HIS legal pad and ballpoint tucked against his chest. As Raleigh composed himself, Blackburn gave the jury a wry smile. He wore a gray, stippled suit with a banana-yellow tie and waited for a signal from Judge Sam. Anne scanned the courtroom. The anticipation for the cross-examination was apocalyptic. *Bread and circus for these assholes.* Judge Sam looked up and behind at the giant Roman numerals on the clock. It was just past three p.m. Raleigh exhaled wearily and crumpled tissues up his sleeve. Judge Sam nodded, and Blackburn began.

"Dr. Raleigh, do you have anything you want to get off your chest?"

"Excuse me?"

"Anything you want to confess to, like you did in the suicide note?"

"Objection, Your Honor." Whiteside had barely sat down and he was rising up again.

"I said what I needed to say," Raleigh offered.

"Dr. Raleigh, is it true you saw Miss Goodfellow on the day you attempted suicide?"

"Yes. As I said, it was a moment of despair for me."

"So you met with your mistress—who you lied about to police investigators—as your wife lay in a coma in Presbyterian Hospital?"

Raleigh muttered assent at a barely audible level.

"Dr. Raleigh, the way I read this suicide note, it sounds like you're confessing to doing something very bad to Peggy Raleigh."

"I was ashamed and overwhelmed that I was not at home at the time someone tried to kill my wife."

Overwhelmed—there was that rehearsed word again, Anne realized. Blackburn continued.

"The night of the attack, you left a note for the research librarian at SMU, is that correct?"

"Yes."

"And is it typical for you to write the date and the time on your notes like this?"

"Yes, sometimes I do that."

"Even at ten thirty at night, when establishing the time doesn't really matter, unless, say, you were—"

Judge Sam raised his palm in the air, warning Blackburn.

"And this note—no one saw you leave it for the librarian?"

"I'm not sure. But I don't think so."

Blackburn smacked the lectern, the microphone amplifying his frustration. "Dr. Raleigh, this is very important, if you are planting an alibi with this note—"

"Objection, Your Honor."

"Counselor, knock it off." Judge Sam sat up and rested his chin on his knuckles, a number 2 pencil speared behind his index finger.

"Withdrawn. So no one saw you at the library at ten thirty?"

"Objection," Whiteside repeated.

"After you left the library the second time that night, unseen by anyone, including the desk attendant, you claim to have gone back to Lucy Goodfellow's house."

"Correct."

"But no one saw you there. And you said you were drinking, drinking and driving, actually. Is that correct?"

"I had been drinking, but I was not that intoxicated." Raleigh grimaced as he realized how bad that sounded out loud.

"Not too drunk to remember the exact time or how long you were curbside at Miss Goodfellow's apartment building?"

"No."

"I see, good memory then," Blackburn deadpanned. *Stop hamming it up*, Anne cautioned, but the looks of disbelief around the courtroom showed her that it was working.

"And then did you call your wife?"

"Yes, just after eleven."

"Right, at eleven twenty-four. To lie about the time, and lie about where you had been that night." Blackburn ventured back out from behind the lectern. "And so a lot about your alibi for your whereabouts was false that night, correct, Dr. Raleigh?"

Raleigh nodded. "I was lying to my wife about Lucy, yes."

"Dr. Raleigh, if you lied about that alibi then, why are we supposed to believe this alibi now?"

"Objection, uh . . ." Whiteside had nothing but exasperation.

"Sustained," Judge Sam said quietly. He let the point score. "Mr. Blackburn, move along."

Blackburn pivoted. "How often did you have sex with Miss Goodfellow?"

A yelp of shock came from the gallery. *The mistress is a red herring*, Anne thought. *Locate him at the crime scene.* Judge Sam gaveled for silence. Not nearly long enough for Raleigh, who was still caught off guard.

Whiteside shot up. "Your Honor . . ."

Blackburn talked over the objection. "Let me be more specific. The week prior to the attack, the week of Easter, the holiest week of the Christian calendar, how many times did you have sex with Miss Goodfellow?"

"Objection . . ."

"Overruled. The witness will answer."

"Twice."

"What was that, Reverend?" Blackburn cupped his ear. *Again, too much*, Anne thought. Blackburn had heard the *reverend*.

"Twice that week."

"You said that you were living a lie."

"Yes, I did."

"So how do we know when you're telling the truth?"

"Objection, Your Honor, the witness is under oath."

Blackburn pressed on. "Did you type the letters, the threats to your family?"

Now, that's a better line.

"No I did not."

"Now, can you describe to me the scene when you came home that night to Credo Drive?"

"Starting when?" Raleigh asked, irritated. *Blackburn's pinballing is wearing him down.*

"As you are coming up the driveway to your home, please."

"I put the car in park and opened the door. I saw half of Peggy's body in front, sticking out. So I jumped out of the car, and ran to her," he said haltingly. "And her face was red and purple and swollen. She was gurgling, there was something—foam, spit—coming out of the side of her mouth."

He sees this with his hands around her throat, Anne decided.

"Let me ask you one more time, Dr. Raleigh: anything you want to get off your chest?"

"No." Raleigh was shaking and began to cry.

Anne watched closely as the minister broke down again. She felt strangely distant. *Blackburn went for a confession, but he's also trying to get headlines and TV time. He went hard. Maybe too hard.* But Anne had heard and seen enough. She was ready to convict Raleigh right then and there.

"We pass the witness, Your Honor."

OGLESBY PASSED BACK THE ESSAY TESTS ON *To Kill a Mockingbird* with grim quietude. Once he had every paper returned—from Atherton to Winkleman—he let the sophomores read over his comments while retrieving his teaching stick Ptolemy, a blue and gold scepter with a shepherd's crook, from the well of the blackboard.

Dan leafed to the last page. He had done all right. A flat A with an "Interesting" next to his answer for what was really on trial in the book, and an "Excellent" by his explanation of all the bird names—the Finches, Tom Robinson—and how they related to the title. *Phew. Got all five names for Scout too.* He looked over the slumped shoulders of Cameron Coleman in front of him. A sea of red marks. *Ouch.*

"So now we turn to *Animal Farm* by Mr. Orwell. Everyone up on their reading? That is the case, right, Mr. Humphrey?"

"If you have no further follow-up questions, then yes, absolutely, sir."

Oglesby stamped the floor with Ptolemy. "Rule number sixteen: by failing to prepare, you are preparing to fail. Gentlemen, you are almost upperclassmen. Don't waste my time."

Oglesby wheeled around to the teacher's desk and picked up his copy of the Orwell.

"Mr. Dowlearn, what kind of a story is *Animal Farm*?"

"An allegory, sir."

"Good. An allegory about . . . ?"

Rob raised his hand like he was shooting a free throw. "The British Empire?"

"The Russian Revolution," Oglesby replied flatly. "I'm not giving anything away—if you had read the preface by Mr. Orwell, he tells you that."

Frustrated, Oglesby looked up from his paperback at the asbestos tiles in the ceiling. It was Friday, the golden afternoon streaming, tantalizing, through the blinds. Everyone was restless and semipresent. Right then, he tacked to a different course.

"You need to understand this book deeply, gentlemen, because *Animal Farm* is the key to winning the Game. And since we're clearly not ready to discuss *Animal Farm*, I'm going to explain the Game and assign roles."

He threw his Orwell paperback at his army bag and came to his signature position—chin resting on the back of two hands that lay on the top of his teaching stick. He had kicked the sophomores out of the horse latitudes of a Friday and gotten their attention.

"I'm sure you've heard a lot of rumors and scary talk about the Game. All true, no doubt, but the premise of the Game is simple: Scientists have discovered a panacea called the Blaireric. The Blaireric comes from a plant on the Blaireric Islands, and from it you can derive everything man needs. Endless power, endless wealth, and ultimately a potion for world peace."

"Question, sir?" Liam Plimmer was suffering major indigestion from grade insecurity.

"I didn't ask for questions, Mr. Plimmer. Put your hand down and listen. The Game will decide which form of government should be in charge of the Blaireric."

Oglesby reached back to the teacher's desk to retrieve his grade book. He opened to the class roster.

"Okay, first I have to assign heads of state. Mr. Dowlearn?"

"Yes, sir," Rick replied with a confidence that first pick was a good thing. It was not.

"You will now be King Richard. Your country will be run as a monarchy."

Rick stood up and feigned a courtly bow. "God save me."

"Settle down, my liege. Flanagan?"

"Yes?"

"Your Excellency Bishop Flanagan now—you are in charge of a country run by a theocracy."

The transformation into Richelieu was immediate as Flanagan grinned with delight at his perceived power. "What's my country called?"

"That's up to you."

"The Holy Empire of Flanagan?"

"If you think that name is going to impress the judges, then yes."

Plimmer was about to lose his mind. "Wait, who are the judges?"

"At this time, the identities of the tribunal are secret." Oglesby slammed the business end of Ptolemy on Plimmer's desk. No further questions.

"Mr. O'Donnell, you are now Comrade O'Donnell and in charge of a communist country."

"What?" Sticky tapped the metal cubby below his seat with a blue Bic. "That's the sucky one!"

"Talk to your proletariat about what sucks. Mr. Boudreaux?"

"Yes, sir," he replied meekly. Like Plimmer, Boudreaux was a gradehounding worrywart.

"You are philosopher-king of your own meritocracy. Everyone in your country is selected by their special abilities and skills. Mr. McGhee? Are you going to read Mr. Orwell and work hard as a head of state to argue for the Blaireric?"

"Sir, you can—"

"You are in charge of an oligarchy." Oglesby shook his head— Rob always had a wind-up and delivery, and he had to cut him off. "Do you know what an oligarchy is?"

Rob imagined a good answer but then safely retreated to: "No, sir."

"It's where power is held by a few elites. So let's call you Robber Baron McGhee, and you and the other captains of industry in your country—"

"Uh, sir . . . can I switch with Flanagan and do theocracy?"

Oglesby balked out of reflex but remembered Rob was a preacher's son.

"Mr. Flanagan, any objection?"

"Am I God in this theocracy? Or just like a Pope?"

"Whatever divinity you claim is up to you. You can be an ayatollah, a rabbi, a patriarch—just remember the judges have to be convinced that your holiness is next to godliness."

"Ayatollah, huh?" Flanagan was starting to get the delirious, glassy-eyed confidence of a cult leader.

"Come on, Flanagan, let me do the religious one." Rob riffled through his backpack until he found the remains of his half-eaten lunch. "I'll throw in some Little Debbie Nutty Bars."

"Deal."

Rob tossed the cellophaned wafers at Flanagan.

"Fine, McGhee is theocracy, Flanagan a nut-bar oligarchy."

"Sir, can I—?"

"No more trading." Oglesby swatted across the front row with Ptolemy like a roulette dealer waving off bets. "The final country must represent democracy. So let's see . . ."

Oglesby's mouth curled into a wry smile, and he looked to the back row. "Mr. Malone. Or should I say President Malone? You will head the democratic state in the Game."

"Thank you, sir." Dan swallowed his excitement. A disappointed groan came from the rest of the sophomores as Oglesby had clearly selected his favorites for heads of state. Malone especially. The Game felt rigged.

"Be careful what you pine for, gentlemen. In my seventeen years of teaching, the democracy has never won."

Oglesby gave Dan a cool, ominous look that suggested he rise to the occasion. Dan returned fire with a cocky scout's salute that disguised a cascade of internal panic. *Yup, I'm screwed.*

"The rest of you will be the Vox Populi and graded on your debate, which will factor into the vote made by the judges. So study Mr. Orwell's allegory well. Consider Atticus, Prince Hal, Daedalus, and all the other heroes we've encountered, and ponder how their words and deeds could help win you the Blaireric. The Game will happen April fifteenth, a week from today."

Dan felt the pressure coil in his shoulder blades. He knew what was on the line without Oglesby's saying it: *If I win the Game, I'm a Norwegian rat for sure.*

○ ○ ○

"WHY ARE ALL THE SIGNS IN . . ."

"Vietnamese?"

"Uh-huh."

"Welcome to East Richardson."

Steve O'Donnell made a turn off Campbell Road into a subdivision. It was Dan's first time visiting Sticky's house, and their plan was solid: a sleepover with little sleep—Sticky's mom would come home, everyone would go to bed, and then the boys would duck out for a little late-night action downtown. Rick had warned Dan that spending the night at Sticky's house was something special. As they pulled up, Sticky's littlest sister, Mary Kate, was sitting in the oil smudges of the driveway, spinning the working wheel of a broken upside-down tricycle. There were a lot of half possessions littered across the front lawn. MK was the youngest of six and the only girl. Sticky's oldest brother, Dennis, was gone for the weekend to a track meet in Houston. Since his parents' separation, Sticky's mother had been working as receptionist/reporter/copyeditor/ad sales manager/publisher for the *Echo*, Richardson's local paper, so all the O'Donnell kids were latchkey. After St. Paul's let out, the three middle boys—Connor and the twin eleven-year-olds, Brian and Brendan—roamed the creeks and strip malls of Little Saigon like wolf whelps. That MK was amusing herself, all right but unsupervised, meant the pack had made it home.

Stick sidled through the front door with a precipitous, checked-out weariness that made him seem like the man of the house. Nothing was on fire, but nothing was under control. School clothes, shoes, and book bags were strewn as if the front living room had been evacuated. At some point in the past, the kitchen had been raided for peanut butter and jelly, leaving jam trails and licked jars on the dining room table, along with a lice comb, literally called the Nitpicker. All of this mess weighed on Stick, who, finding his brothers in the back TV room wrestling over the gun for Duck Hunt, started barking orders at his siblings. Everyone was starving, and so Dan returned to the kitchen with Stick to help stack grilled cheese sandwiches for the toaster oven.

"When's your mom get home?"

"Six usually."

Dan knew better than to ask about Sticky's father, but his absence was the invisible elephant looming behind any O'Donnell family conversation. Two years prior, Mr. O'Donnell had moved out of the house, and was living with a "roommate" down in Oak Lawn. He had also left his job in flood insurance claims and become a flight attendant for Southwest.

MK pranced into the kitchen with her permanent runny nose. Sticky stanched it with a paper towel, and MK started rooting through drawers she could reach.

"What do you want?"

"Scissors."

"For what?"

"I'm gonna fix the tricycle."

"Not gonna happen, baby girl. Want some Honey Nut?"

Sticky pulled the cereal box out of the pantry and then ducked his head into the fridge.

"Dang, no milk, MK."

"That's okay, I need the scissors now. And a hammer too."

"Put that tricycle up in the garage. You want Honey Nut with water?"

"Naw," she replied with sweet disappointment.

Dan poured himself a glass of tap water. *Bleh.* It had a foul sulfur smell that the O'Donnells were used to and no longer noticed. A calico cat jumped up onto the kitchen counter. It was one of several felines loosely associated with the household.

"What's its name?"

"I just call it Asshole."

A loud thud sent Asshole scurrying, and the house rattled to the rafters. This was followed by three seconds of silence, then blood-curdling screams. Stick and Dan ran into the TV room.

"Connor, what the hell?" Stick hollered, his voice stern and reedy.

"It was Brian!"

Brendan was lying on the ground, crumpled in pain. His hands around his own neck.

Stick turned to the other twin. "What did you do?"

"I didn't do anything!"

Through tears came Brendan's police report. "He tried to choke me and then he suplexed me."

"Knock it off, all of you. Mom is going to be home in a minute, and she doesn't need your shit."

"My neck really hurts."

"You're fine, Brian, get up. The next person who starts wrestling, I'm throwing into a figure four."

Connor, who was an awkward, husky thirteen, wasn't buying it. "You're not Dennis, Stevie, you can't kick our asses. We'll gang up on you."

And then Sticky and Dan both smelled it—the grilled cheeses burning under the broiler. They ran back as brown smoke was just starting to waft out of the toaster oven.

"Fuck." Sticky pulled the rack out with a mitt and dropped it on the stovetop.

Dan felt terrible as Stick's mood slid from bad to worse. "Just black on the corners. You can still eat these," he offered.

"Too burnt. And they're all too picky. Goddamn it."

"Sorry."

As Sticky scraped the blackened lava flow of Kraft singles into the trash, MK came wailing back into the kitchen.

"Stevie, Stevie, I saw Daddy!"

"What?"

"He drove past the house. I saw him from the driveway."

"Are you sure?"

"Yes! He slowed down and waved at me."

"He's not supposed to be near the house," Sticky said darkly. "Are you absolutely sure?"

"Yes."

"You can't make this up, MK." He crouched down to look her in the eye. "We can't make things up."

"I'm not making it up!"

"Okay." Sticky turned to Dan, unsure what to believe. "That's creepy if it's true. But MK imagines a lot—"

"I'm not pretending this time!" MK started to fidget like she had to pee.

"Don't tell your brothers."

"Why not?"

"It will just upset them, and they'll tell Mom."

"Oh." But MK wanted to blab to the whole world, and Sticky knew it was useless to tell her otherwise. She wiped her nose with her fist. "Is Daddy coming back?"

"Christ." Sticky looked up to the shitty popcorn ceiling for an appeal. *Oh, baby girl.* Another wrestling move in the TV room shook the house. Everyone was hungry, and Sticky's mom was late getting home.

○ ○ ○

TIRED FROM HER MARATHON DAY IN COURT, ANNE INSPECTED THE skinless chicken breast rotating and thawing in the microwave. Dan was gone, and Pat had called semilucid with some sort of "car trouble" in Addison. *Lord knows with that man. I'm past the point where I want to know.* So Anne found herself with a rare evening home alone.

The pink cut of chicken looked less appealing with each turn. The water for the rice pilaf simmered in the pot on the stove. Anne reached into the pantry for one of the three dozen cans of Del Monte green beans she had bought on triple-coupon day at Tom Thumb for ten cents each (no limit per customer).

Her déjà vu returned and with it everything familiar and anxious. Her thoughts of the trial and her marriage churned together. *Guilty as sin, but watch, he'll walk.* Anne darkly considered her own options. Like Raleigh, she was searching for a way to pull free.

Is this it? This is how it's going to go?

She put the can back. She turned off the stove. She punched stop on the microwave. She riffled through her purse, looking for cigarettes. *Out.* She poured a drink. She checked the mark she'd notched on the bottle of Wolfschmidt. Anne let out a weary, saturated sigh. *No change. He's sneaking from somewhere else.* She dug through her purse again. *I know I have one left.* Instead she found her old address book. A bad idea came to her, and she thumbed through the names from long ago until she found the listing for . . . *her friend* . . . Father Ronan Carroll. She pulled out her MCI card, went to the phone in the den, and started dialing the dozen numbers it took to make a long-distance call.

Halfway through she hung up. *This is crazy. He is just a man. He'll let me down too.* A storm was rolling in—every night, high temperatures tangled with the wet Dallas spring, leading to thunderclouds and sudden downpours. Through the glass patio door, Anne watched the silent heat lightning with a sense of dread. She didn't know what to think about this priest, or any of the men in her life. *Dan will hate me for it. And Pat will become a drunk cripple with no one.* And so she sat and cried through unwelcome tears.

But if she couldn't leave, she could still see him, right? *Maybe Pat will get a job back in New York.* She could make her choice then. She picked up the phone and called the rectory. *He'll be back from evening Mass by now.* She just wanted to have an option. Someone to be possible for her. The phone rang and rang until finally a young scholastic with a thick Puerto Rican accent picked up.

"I'm trying to reach Father Ronan Carroll."

"May I ask who is calling?"

"Anne Mulligan." She wasn't sure why she used her maiden name.

"And this is regarding . . . ?"

"A personal matter." Her voice sounded disconnected, suspicious.

"One moment."

Anne cradled the receiver closer, trying to will herself through the call. She closed her eyes and prayed for him to pick up. *This is a dumb idea, Annie.* But she just wanted to hear his voice.

"Hello, this is Father Faherty." An older man.

"Yes, I'm trying to reach Father Carroll."

"May I ask what this is regarding?"

"I'm a friend and colleague from Fordham and I'd like to—"

"I see," he said, cutting her off—*This is the priest who hears Ronan's confession.* "Well, Father Carroll is not here anymore."

"Excuse me?"

"Father Carroll is no longer ministering the College of New Rochelle. He took a new assignment."

Anne sat back, unable to think.

"Do you know where I can reach him?"

"The Kakuma Mission."

"Where?"

"It's in Kenya, dear."

○ ○ ○

"HERE, GIVE ME THE PHONE." STICKY PULLED THE SNAGGLED extension cord from Dan and looked up a number in the St. Paul directory.

"The Budnips family. I can work with that." He dialed the number. "Hello, is Merrill Budnips there? . . . Good evening. Mr. Budnips, I'm Steve Austin calling from the Baskin-Robbins on Belt Line Road. We're running a fun little contest down here. If you can name all thirty-one of our flavors in under a minute—ah shit, he hung up."

Dan searched the parish directory. The two of them were sprawled across the floor and bunk beds in Stick's room, which he shared with Dennis. Stick had the lower bunk with *Peanuts* bedsheets that he pretended were his younger brothers', but Dan didn't really care. The rest of the room was clearly Dennis's: running trophies, a Cowboys calendar that made tight end Doug

Cosbie look like a sweaty gigolo, an acid-lettered poster of Tawny Kitaen, and a framed and signed green Adidas track jersey from John Treacy, the Irish Mudlark, who was Dennis's cross-country idol. The room smelled like Tinactin.

Dan took back the phone. "Let me try . . . oh, here's a good one. Barbara and Jeff Turdlinger."

"No way."

"Look, I'm not making it up."

Dan dialed the number and got Barbara's daughter, who—quickly checking the directory—was Marsha, sixth grade.

"Marsha, why the hell did you hang up on me? Excuse me? Excuse you! What kind of relationship is this where I just give and give and you just take and take?"

Sticky shoved his head into the Linus pillow on his bed to stifle howls of laughter. Dan smiled as Marsha tried to answer and calm him down.

"Marsha, don't act like you don't know who this is. Fine, I'm going to put Uncle Turd on."

Dan passed to Stick. He had a scratchy voice useful for prank calls.

"Marsha, why you treating Junebug like this? He knows about your flatulence and he's okay with it—ah, too much, she hung up." Sticky tapped the switchhook on the phone. "That was a good one. We should call Ursuline girls."

Stick fetched the white pages while Dan contemplated his next victim.

"Want to do the survey?" Stick suggested.

"That never works. Let's do 'leave a message for Lupe.'"

"Okay, I'm Gonzalez then."

Dan picked a number at random from the phone book and dialed.

"*Hola, me llamo Guillermo. Quien es? No habla español? No*

problemo. Is Lupe Gonzalez there? No. Okay, I need to leave a message . . . That's okay, you just tell Lupe I have his rooster. Okay? Don't worry about it. Just tell him I have his rooster and everything is *bueno. Comprende?*"

Dan hung up and handed the phone to Sticky. "Can we smoke in the backyard?"

"Nah, my sister might see us. She's asleep now, but she gets up a lot, creeps around."

Why am I so itchy for coffee and cigarettes? Dan wondered.

Stick had talked to his mom around eight. She was trying to close the edition but had to run to the printers in Addison and wouldn't be back until late. The plan to break out and raise hell had stalled. Stick's mom would call in a pizza delivery. *Put the brats to bed. Home by ten. Sorry, hon. Will make it up to you and Dan.*

"Steve-o, what are we going to do?"

"Tonight? I don't think—"

"No, I mean in life. What do you want to do when you grow up?"

"Probably become a porn star. I don't fucking know. What are you going to do?"

Dan was too shy to say for real. "Well, I don't want some boring-ass job, working at some company, killing myself like my dad, over what? To make money?"

"Yeah." Sticky nodded. "Screw that."

"I want to move back to New York, and read books, and figure shit out."

"You should become a writer. That's what Oglesby wants you to do." Stick said it point-blank, and it was gratifying for Dan to hear it from someone else.

"Maybe." Dan hesitated but couldn't say it, as if naming what a Norwegian rat trainee wants would jinx things.

"All I know"—Stick hit redial on the touch pad—"is we need to get the fuck out of here."

"*Hola, esto es Lupe.* Any messages? What do you mean wrong number? Who called? Guillermo? I told that cocksucker to stop screwing my chickens." And he hung up and giggled.

Dan propped his head on the corner of Stick's clean laundry pile. "We should have rented a movie or something before we came home."

"Yeah, sorry." Stick felt bad. They were stuck in the house and missing the rest of the crew cruising down to Deep Ellum.

"It's okay. Let's do the survey one. C'mon."

"I dare you to call Cady Bloom with the survey."

"Nope." *I can't talk to a girl in front of an audience, even if it's Sticky.*

"Don't be a chickenshit, Malone."

"Okay, wait, let me do a quick one to build up to it." Dan leafed through the pages of Southwestern Bell and picked a number.

"Hey, man, it's me, I got rid of the body. Now here's what I need you to do. Shit . . . didn't work."

"I'm looking up the Blooms." Sticky started flipping to the B's in Dallas proper.

"Stop, I'm not ready." *I need a distraction,* Dan thought. "Do you guys have like a liquor cabinet or anything?"

"Mom threw it all out when . . ." Stick didn't finish that thought but kept looking for the Blooms' number. "Here they are. They live on Joyce Way? Fancy schmancy Preston Hollow. I'm dialing."

"No!" But Dan was coming around on it. *It would be fun to prank her. Not the worst excuse to call.*

They wrestled for the phone, struggling quietly so as not to wake up the little bears in their beds in the next room. Stick eventually got his foot in perfect position for a groin shot. Dan called mercy before Stick racked him.

"Call your girlfriend, playboy."

"She's not my . . . I'm doing Chinese delivery instead."

"No, do the survey."

"Fine. Whatever."

Dan dialed, and Cady's mother answered with an East Texas cackle.

"Hello, is there a Cady Bloom present at your domicile?"

Somehow that brought the girl to the phone. *On second thought, this is the stupidest . . . too late.* Dan covered the receiver with a washcloth and used his best bored, bureaucratic voice.

"Uh, yes . . . good evening, Miss Bloom, I'm Noman Clature calling on behalf of the United Coalition for the Prevention of Tragedy and was wondering if you had a couple minutes this evening to discuss some issues important to all Americans."

"Who is this?"

"Yes, the coalition is a part of the Walter Mondale Achievement Institute. Let me ask you, Miss Bloomer, are you the person in your household who does the majority of the shopping?"

"Uh, no."

"Excellent, the next question is about baloney. How often do you use coupons when purchasing sandwich meats?"

"Who is this?"

Crap, I'm out of material. Dan's heart was half in it, and he couldn't think of anything.

"This is really a pro forma quid pro quo survey, ma'am, and we have just a few dozen more questions. Now, it's listed here in our research that your dog has cooties. Is that correct?"

"We don't have a dog."

"I see, so you're the one with the cooties?"

"Listen—"

"No need to explain, I appreciate your honesty, Miss Bloomquist, and I'm just going to move on quickly here. If you could answer yes or no to the following, we'll be done right quick. Who do you think would win in a fight between a gerbil and a hamster?"

"Uh-huh, okay, no . . ."

Yup, she's too smart for this, Dan realized, then dry laughed. "Everyone says the hamster, isn't that something?"

"Okay, whoever this is—"

"Miss Bloomingdale, just to sum up, our research here shows that you are single, spend too much on deli meats, and contracted herpes from a hamster. Is that correct?"

"Very funny, jackass."

And right then Dan hung up, a jumper cable of nervous thrills. Stick looked disappointed.

"She was on to you."

"Yeah. Survey only works with half-deaf old people. She's not gullible enough."

At that moment, the phone rang. Sticky and Dan freaked out.

"Could be your mom."

"That would be weird."

Sticky picked up on the second ring. "Hello, welcome to Arby's, home of the big beef in your mouth. This is Kyle, how can I make your day taste special?"

A moment of listening passed, and Sticky made an oh-shit face at Dan.

"Hang on, he's right here."

"Don't give me that!" Dan melted into a mortified jelly.

"It's Cady. She knows it was you."

"Shit." Sticky practically punched Dan in the nose as he shoved the receiver in his face.

"Hi, Cady! Ha ha. You got me."

She should be pretty cool about this, Dan thought. *I didn't take it too far . . .*

"Dan Malone, how dare you!"

"I'm sorry. How did you know?"

"I star sixty-nined the call. When that croaky O'Donnell kid picked up, I figured it was you."

"All in good fun."

"You're a dick. Don't you have anything better to do than bothering me?"

She's not that upset, Dan realized. *She's pretending too.* "Sorry, we're bored. Sticky and I are stuck at his house."

"You know my mother is going to ask me who called and you're going to get me in trouble."

"Sorry. Sticky made me do it."

Sticky punched Dan in the shoulder.

"Ow. He's really the mastermind of the whole thing."

"Well, you're going to have to make it up to me."

Dan heard giggling in the background. "What are you doing home on a Friday? Who's there with you?"

"Dan Malone, I can't believe you tried to prank-call me. I might never speak to you again."

"A little dramatic, no?"

"Now you have to take me to the Spring Cotillion."

"What?"

"I'm serious."

"That sounds serious."

"Come on—it's at Christ the King, and the girls have to ask the guys."

"Cady . . ."

"You need a tuxedo. You have a tux, right?"

More giggling in the background and Dan was conflicted. *This sounds like a bunch of Park Cities bullshit.* He wanted to see her, but a cotillion was as far from fun as you could get.

"How about I take you out on a proper—"

"Don't make me call your mother and turn you in for prank-calling me."

"Blackmail. Wow, Miss Bloom."

"So yes?"

"I've never heard of this dance, and I don't have a tux."

"You can rent one."

"Listen, Cady, how about—"

"Anne and Pat Malone, 3741 Crown Shore Drive, 286-1525. Is that the number I should call?"

"Okay." *Maybe we can go to Whataburger after the cotillion.*

"Okay what?"

"Okay, yes, I'll take you."

"Fine. So I guess goodbye then." Like a good saleswoman, Cady had closed the deal and knew to get off the call quick.

"Bye."

"Oh, and, Dan . . ."

"Yeah . . ."

"Gotcha back!"

Click.

Dan had fallen for it. Sticky just shook his head. Fallen hard.

THAT SAME FRIDAY AFTER EASTER, PAT MALONE LIMPED TOWARD THE Dugout, the baseball-themed bar of Dovie's restaurant. He had spent the morning jawing with some Jed Clampett at Addison Airport who was scaling up his operation of flying asshole oilmen around the Permian Basin. Not a bad idea, but Billy Bob Gulfstream didn't grasp what an actuary was, and what he really needed was a charter concierge to cater to and coddle his J.R. Ewing jet set.

The morning crapped out, Pat was nowhere in this job hunt—Borman's office had turned into a black box. Anne would give him grief for a restaurant bill, but Pat, in the logic of self-pity, deserved a lingering lunch. Dovie's was actually built out from a ranch house Audie Murphy had bought but—typical of North Dallas real estate—never lived in. The staff was setting up for a rehearsal dinner that night, so the dining room was closed and lunch served in the Dugout. The host offered Pat any table, so he made for a booth in the back, ordered a High Life, and unfolded the *Times Herald* want ads. Taking his first gulp off the beer mug, Pat realized that his booth was decorated with a picture of Don Larsen being tree-climbed by Yogi Bear after his perfect game.

Goddamn Yankees.

Ever the discomforted Dodgers fan, Pat moved to the bar. One beer became three in short order, and it was time to eat lunch—just past noon—but he wasn't ready. He had no appetite, just thirst. Unable to catch a buzz, Pat was tired of this. *And tired of being tired of this.* He sipped his beer and brooded.

And that's when Mickey Charles Mantle hobbled into the bar and perched two stools down from him.

"Howdy."

"Hi."

Holy Jesus. It took Pat a minute to make sure it was him, and he spotted that lopsided, bucktoothed grin as the Mick ordered a white wine, then changed it to a bourbon. But there was something Pat didn't recognize about the man until he stretched, the way he used to unlimber with a bat behind his back. Gone were the cut-from-marble muscles, the broad shoulders and fire-hydrant neck; instead he kind of plopped and sagged onto the bar stool. Pat tried not to stare. The Mick's hair was graying and thin, and he took out a pair of dime-store reading glasses that did nothing but magnify the road map of tiny broken blood vessels spread down the slope of his nose and etched around his once-hawklike eyes. He squinted through his specs at the lunch menu and kept looking around. *Uneasy alone*, Pat thought. The Mick hunkered over his double bourbon, and Pat pretended to read the paper. They were the only two in the Dugout.

"How'd the Yankees do?" the Mick asked.

"Off. In Milwaukee tonight."

"That's a win."

After an impatient five minutes of the Mick craning his neck to look at the front of the house, his lunch date walked in. Pat peeked over the sports page—it was the sportscaster, the one who had been the kicker for his goddamn Giants. His arrival relaxed the Mick and let him settle in. The sportscaster ordered a matching bourbon in his honey basso.

"Why the hell we ain't at the club?"

The Mick shot him a disappointed look. "Bunch of rich cocksuckers—can't get any peace to play holes."

The old kicker didn't buy it. "So they threw you out?"

"Oh yeah." The Mick smiled.

"What for?"

"Buck naked at the buffet."

"Jesus, kiddo." The sportscaster snorted. *Preston Trail Golf Club, all boys, just a couple veers up the tollway.*

"Fuck that place. I hold the club record. Twelve lost balls for nine holes."

The two of them started to drink and shoot the shit, and Pat tried not to be aggravated at the irony. Like a South Bronx Fabian waiting out an occupying enemy, he had suffered through the entire Wonder Boy campaign. For eighteen years he couldn't escape the Captain America idolatry. Pat pried himself from the bar to use the john. He had let go of the Dodgers, but the second-best thing that could still happen in the box scores was the Yankees losing. Pat's left leg tingled out of numbness and he hop-stepped past the bar. The Mick noticed.

"Bad knees, fella?"

"Bad everything," Pat muttered.

"I hear ya, I got near nothing holding this one together." He smacked what was left of his famous right knee. "Sore all the time. Like a real dull toothache."

Pat nodded as he got his feet working, and he shuffled off to the bathroom. He stood in the cool, damp stink of the porcelain and thought back to the '56 series and the Mick outrunning a drive by Hodges to left center. *Backhanded in Death Valley at full speed; it was a great fucking catch for a guy who played with bum knees. The wall was at four eighty in center then. Deep and lonesome. What no one remembers: the Duke made a better catch the inning before, diving in on a Yogi line drive. But no, it was the Mick's catch that kept Larsen's perfection going. The goddamn Mick.*

When Pat came back from the john he was finally ready to eat. *A burger. A club sandwich. Something.* Instead he found a bourbon neat by his beer.

"Compliments of the gentlemen."

Pat caught the eye of the Mick, who nodded like a shortstop at second to cover. Pat saluted and downed the shot. "To the Duke!"

"Oh shit." The Mick's aged face puckered as he elbowed off the prow of the bar. "I'm buying a drink for a Brooklyn bum?"

The DJ in the next room tested his speakers with the country station. The catgut fiddle of "Pissin' in the Wind" came jangling through as bourbon snuck its way into Pat's bravado.

"Actually grew up in the Bronx, near the stadium."

The Mick signaled for another round. "The Bronx, yeah, I spent my summers there. Hey, what was the name of that big building out past right? Corner of 161st?"

"The courthouse?"

"Yeah. You know, some asshole used to get up there with a big mirror and shine it in our eyes. It was a long ways off, but it was like lightning."

"That was me." Pat pushed aside the lunch menu and welcomed another shot of bourbon.

"I believe you." The Mick chuckled. "Well, here's to making it out of the Bronx."

Pat forgot to order lunch and kept at it with the beer and bourbon back. As they continued to get lubricated, he tried to leave the Mick alone but kept getting pulled into the gravity well of his stories. *Of all the famous ballplayers I had to run into.* Pat held his tongue as his thoughts went back. *Sure, the Mick and Willie were great, but don't forget: no one hit more home runs in the 1950s than the Duke.*

Just then a kid, a few years younger than Dan, and his mother came over from their table on the patio with the gleaming hide of a red-stitched Rawlings. The mother was a piece of work, tight jeans, fluorescent blue T-shirt, and a kind of Texas shandy tan that matched the yellow of the Mick's jaundiced skin. The Mick frowned at their interruption.

"Can I help you?"

The mom began her plea. "We are so sorry to bother you."

"No bother." He gave the mom a lupine grin and borrowed a pen to spell out his name in that famous Palmer-method signature. Finished, he rolled the ball down the bar at the kid.

"Thank you."

"You're lucky, kid, your mom has nice tits."

The country music station was playing some Bob Wills rag now. Pat watched the mother and child blush and laugh through the bad taste. And the Mick turned away. There was your evidence—*He's a cocksucker*—but Pat figured otherwise: his best defense was being offensive. *He's signed a million baseballs, and all they want is that stupid third-grader signature.*

"You know, I led the league six straight years in the crabs." The Mick continued his crude assault as he turned to Pat. "Did you know that? Major league record."

The sports announcer rattled the ice in his glass and set up the punch line. "Still hold it?"

"Still hold it! And my wife was second four times."

Mantle howled with laughter. And through all the drinking, Pat recognized this was and wasn't the Mick. This wasn't the Wonder Boy swinging with ballistic efficiency. *That guy is in a cemetery called Cooperstown. This guy acts like a hick and a drunk. And I'm a drunk.* And as his drunkenness coagulated around this sad realization, Pat was terrified of being sober. He had to get out of the Dugout. Away from the fading half-life of the Mick. Pat laid four fives on the bar and slid off his stool. His leg was completely stiff. The Mick jawed another line about shitty knees, but Pat wasn't listening. And some other Dovie's customers came over and the Mick was repeating the lost-golf-ball joke and then a new one about Steinbrenner giving Billy Martin a million-dollar contract—one dollar for a million years. *Goddamn Yankees.* As he passed by, the Mick caught Pat's glance with rat-red eyes.

"Adios, pardner."

The Mick had the hollow glare of someone looking for their own importance in the reflection of others. Pat's sole thought was to finish his drinking alone.

○ ○ ○

PAT PLUNKED DOWN IN THE PLEATHER STUFFINESS OF HIS MERCURY Cougar. Both legs were seizing up on him now. It was early afternoon, but the day was shot. *A couple hours until Anne and Dan are home.* He started the car and lurched out of the Dovie's lot. Traffic went screaming by, but Pat darted across Midway. This was it— *Just enough vodka to settle in and pass out for a nap and then I'm done. Last run to the liquor store and it's all over. Where is the liquor store? Goddamn Baptists with their blue laws.* Pat lefted onto Belt Line and went west, figuring Addison was dry to the county line. It was muggy as all get-out. *Too early for this summer hell.* Pat hit traffic on Belt Line and pumped his brakes a little too hard, screeching to a stop. *Take it easy. Just get to . . . what's the next town over? Carrollton? Carrollton's wet, just a few more blocks and there's got to be a liquor store near there. Does Belt Line cross that way? It does. No, wait. Fuck. Just head west until you hit something.*

Pat's hand slipped on the wheel and skidded the car into the center lane. *Stop it. Stop weaving. Go steady.* He could take Belt Line all the way out to the airport if he wanted. *Maybe drive out to AMR and piss on the hood of Crandall's blue Brougham.* Pat drove like he was heading somewhere, but this was where Dallas kind of trailed off into prairie. *Shouldn't have had that bourbon.* "Bourbon and blues," Pat said aloud to himself, and he sounded crazy. *Wait, shit . . . Carrollton is dry and Addison is wet. Or is it Farmers Branch?*

He had gone all this way for nothing. *Great job, Pat. What a fucking drunk, you can't even find the liquor store.*

Attempting some sort of sobering distraction, Pat turned on the radio. He crawled around the dial, somehow landing on an AM show-tune station, playing the original cast recording of *Carousel*. Christine Johnson as Aunt Nettie. *My mother's favorite. Those pipes.* Pat's left leg was quite numb now. His mind whirred over each song with a clarity only brought on by a long episode of drinking. And then the cast, the chorus, joined Nettie in a warm orchestral rise:

Tho' your dreams be tossed and blown
Walk on, walk on.

He thought of his parents, Jack and Hannah, their chins high, their silver songs. He pictured their store and looking out the windows at the end of a storm, the rain crossing from the Bronx into Queens, leaving a wind-picked sky above Willis Avenue.

Pat drifted along in this dark, deep memory as he was speeding toward the overpass for the Trinity River. Gathering in the wide open of the city limits was a menacing, dark column of thunderclouds. *Storm's coming. This evening for sure. Tossed and blown.* It would be another half mile in the wrong direction if he didn't U it immediately. Pat veered into the right lane to turn, and that's when he couldn't feel his leg or the brake pedal, and he panicked and jerked the car off the road, missing the retaining wall by inches.

The black mouth of the Cougar tore through weed trees, and then the car bucked over the berm by the road and dipped down until Pat finally found the brake. The car heaved into a ditch a few feet from the Elm Fork of the Trinity River. He braced himself against the dashboard and steering wheel, and the car stopped, the engine groaning over the rushes.

He was lucky not to have gone full-on into the river, and Pat, his head and heart swimming with adrenaline, the throbbing gone from his legs, looked out at the miserable brown flow of the Trinity and thought of lying on his childhood bed as the radio from the McGarritys' kitchen blared from across the air shaft. *Scully takes over the call from Allen. Top of the fifth, one out, Hodges drives it to left center. And somehow the Mick gets there. And Larsen is still perfect.*

All of Willis Avenue was listening, and he could hear the cheers and claps echoing down the shaft. And Pat realized, he didn't care. He just hated losing more than he ever wanted to win.

[APRIL 15]

Number seven, Donna Passerine, picked at the edge of the cheap and chipped wooden table with crimson nails, her head bowed as if in prayer, as she speculated to her fellow jury members.

"I'm pretty sure she confronted him that night about the affair."

"We don't know that," Dr. Mark Ferris replied. He was the foreman, juror number one. When the deliberations had started, he cheerily shared that he was a dentist and then made some canned drilling-down joke. Dr. Ferris was like a lot of chivalrous, prosperous Dallas men, and Anne was quick to detect undertones of chauvinism in his feints at being trustworthy.

Donna sensed it too and was struggling not to be timid. She was young, no more than thirty, but seemed a bit swollen, moon-faced, as she scratched olive skin at the elbow. She couldn't bring herself to look up. "What if he wanted to be with that girl and not his wife? What if Mrs. Raleigh threatened to reveal—"

"Well, miss, I tell you what, the road to confusion is lined with what-ifs." Ferris made a damping-down motion with his hands like he was trying to get a golf shot to lay up. "As Judge Sam told us, we have to deliberate on the evidence, not the morality. Let's stick to what we know for sure."

Another man confident and certain—there's something we all know for sure! Anne glanced at the sweep of the institutional clock. *Friday morning, coming up on eleven; I still have time to work on these people.* The closing arguments and conflicts on the court calendar had drawn out the last week of the trial. For the defense, Whiteside had stuck to the story of a fallen preacher thrown by temptation into a compromising situation. Blackburn appealed with pictures of Peggy Raleigh lying in Presbyterian. *Barely breathing,* Anne recalled, *fed through a tube, forced to wear a diaper, walled off, muted, the bruises to her neck still visible weeks, months, after her attack.*

"So what do we know?" Ferris counseled. "Margaret Raleigh was strangled in her garage."

"Maybe," Anne chirped.

"Excuse me?"

Anne scrounged for a Life Saver from her purse. "If we're sticking to what we know for sure, there's nothing in the evidence to suggest that he couldn't have come into the house first, strangled her in the kitchen, and then moved the body to the garage."

"But there was no evidence that he did that either." The dentist's mouth was somewhere between a smile and a snarl.

"You're absolutely right." Anne looked down. The next color on the Life Saver roll was green. *Bleh.* She suddenly felt the urge to smoke. "We don't know. Except in the 911 call he says he came into the house."

"Well that's where the phone is."

"Right, but he doesn't locate her body. It's possible he could have attacked her anywhere and then cleaned up the house and the garage. I guess it doesn't really matter. If we come to the conclusion that he strangled her, then—"

"I don't think we know if any of that is true."

"Right, that's my point. We don't know." Anne settled for the lime candy and lodged it against her gum. *I have to start making an actual case here.* "So what part of Standing Raleigh's story is true?

The part where he's lying in messages to his wife? Or the part where he's creating alibis and getting caught in his lies?"

"Completely agree." Dr. Ferris feigned like he was listening and not annoyed at Anne's derailing theories. "But let's settle what the law requires."

Anne realized she had to back off or she'd lose the ground she'd gained. *Bide your time. Don't be too pushy. Or too advocating. This isn't a PTA meeting in the Bronx.*

"Okay. So starting that evening. He gets home around six thirty. He sees Peggy."

"Then he goes and visits *her* . . ."

Tamara Robbins, number nine. Anne got the distinct impression that Tamara wanted a count for adultery for Standing Raleigh. Anne studied the women at the table—four of whom had wedding rings. *The cheating counts for something.*

Ferris's hand and smile went up. *Again with the golf etiquette.* "Before we get there, he sees his wife and children. And Peggy is trying to loosen the latch on the garage door."

"Correct." Mustache and mullet, Jim Keller, number two, nodded. He wanted things to hurry along and Anne figured he had his mind made up already. "Which would explain her coming out later—"

"And why there are no fingerprints," Anne interrupted. "Remember we only have his testimony claiming she was soaping up the latch."

"Mrs. Malone, I appreciate—"

"Right, we don't know," Pilar Golondrina, number twelve, echoed.

"It's convenient, that's all." Anne cracked down on the Life Saver with her molar. *I'm close. If I can get these women to dare with me . . .*

Ferris ignored them. "So after an hour he leaves and goes to Miss Goodfellow's apartment."

Anne stopped short of rolling her eyes. *None of this is in dispute.*

"Can I ask the room?" It was Dale Caruthers, number five, a bank manager from the Park Cities wearing a blue Valentino shirt with white cuffs. "Did y'all think she was covering his tracks?"

Anne wanted to blurt out how that didn't matter, but the question felt like bait. He was trying to agitate the women on the jury.

"This ain't about Miss Lucy." Carla Mirlo, number ten. She had the tired, saturnine frown of an older housekeeper. "It's about him and his lies."

"I felt like she was protecting him somehow," Mary Crane, number three—retiree, busybody—warbled.

"Like she was in love with him and she couldn't let it go?" Caruthers asked, egging her on.

Honestly—Anne threw a hand at her temple—*the mistress did it? That's your theory? It's a misdirection.* Anne had the women on this, so she didn't say anything. *Let Caruthers hang Raleigh on implausible love-triangle theories.*

The foreman dentist conceded the point. "I suspect there's more to that story."

Anne's eyes darted around the table. *Those two, Ferris and Caruthers, are in cahoots.*

"Let's keep retracing Raleigh's steps and see if we can all agree—"

But Anne didn't have the patience. "The important window is eight fifty-three to eleven forty-three." She pulled out her notebook. She had written out the timeline.

"Well, before we—"

"That's from the receipt at the Texaco to the 911 call," Anne interrupted. "So even if you believe the note he left for the librarian at ten thirty—"

"Hang on—"

"Even if that wasn't planted later as an alibi, Raleigh still has over an hour to commit the crime."

Caruthers shook his head. "But he was at Lucy's house."

"According to him, not her." *They are going out of their way to believe him. Jesus, these men.* "There's no evidence of that. We don't know where he is for close to three hours."

"That's not his obligation to prove." Ferris was not smiling anymore. "The burden of proof—"

"Think about all that is going on here." Anne started flipping through her steno pad. "The phony death threats, trouble with his mistress, drinking throughout that night, the phone calls to the house citing the wrong time without a watch, the scrubbed-clean crime scene, his remoteness when the paramedics arrive, the guilt riddling his suicide note, which is practically a confession. And then he broke down on the witness stand because he can't bear it."

"That's all well and good. But circumstantial . . ."

Anne kept driving hard. "What more circumstances do you need before you know?"

"How do you think he did it?" Tamara Robbins asked. She was in Anne's corner.

"I think he went into the house around eleven p.m. He turns off the alarm. She hears him come in and confronts him about the affair. Maybe threatens to call him out in front of his congregation. He strangles her in the kitchen. Drags her to the garage. Cleans up any signs of their struggle. Stages it so that it looks like he's just come home, lifts the garage door, wipes his prints from the handle, backs the car down the driveway, and then he realizes something—"

"Listen, *Mizz* Malone, your theories . . ." Jim Keller leaned back, chuckling. The tone drove Anne batshit. *Goddamn good ole boy.*

"She's not dead. Still breathing. And he leaves her there, waiting for her to die."

"Good Lord . . . ," Carla Mirlo whispered.

Ferris tried to take back the wheel. "Mrs. Malone, why don't we settle down for one minute . . ."

This goddamn eejit dentist is going to split the room. "Fine, but can I ask a question? Since this trial started, how often has Dr. Raleigh gone to visit his wife in the hospital?"

Caruthers shrugged. "I don't think he testified to it."

"If you were betting on it, how often? Once a week? Once a month?" Anne knew the answer from reading the papers. *Not supposed to bring that in, but who else is going to speak for Peggy Raleigh?*

"Maybe they won't let him see her."

"Possible." *They give the reverend every benefit of the doubt while his wife has the bruises from his hands on her throat.* "But if he didn't do it, if his conscience is clear, wouldn't he be taking care of her, praying for her recovery? Even if he cheated on her, wouldn't he be compelled to be at her side?"

Ferris and Caruthers shared a quick look. Keller stared up at the ceiling tiles.

"We don't know that, and I can't believe—"

"I mean, what can you believe? His tears on the witness stand? Who are they for? Peggy? Himself?" Anne flipped her notebook closed. "You know what we do know? That Peggy was strangled so hard it broke her vocal cords. She will never speak to her children again. That I know."

Helen Klais, number eleven, a hummingbird of a North Dallas housewife, spoke for the first time. "Are we allowed to vote? I think we should see where we are as a group."

They took a ballot on the first count of attempted manslaughter. Seven guilty, five against conviction. Split, but the women had heard what Anne had to say.

○ ○ ○

THE OLD AUDITORIUM AT JESUIT WAS A SUNKEN CANYON OF MOLDY RED seats cascading down to a long gray concrete proscenium. Below the truss of lights and before the immediate tumble into the shadows of the audience, Mr. Oglesby had assembled six tables and chairs in a U.

That Friday afternoon, the sophomores acting as heads of state in the Game sat at their assigned places. Dan Malone was perched on the far side of stage left, catty-corner to the Tribunal of Judges— Mr. Oglesby; Mr. Taliaferro, the Jesuit debate coach; and Father Dallanach, the principal. In the void of red seats behind them sat the Vox Populi, the rest of the honors English class. Their vote counted double, as a check and balance against the tribunal, unless, as Oglesby warned them, they acted like idiots and he had to overrule them.

The Game—and the claim to the all-powerful Blaireric—was down to the two final presentations with no clear favorite. Representing the monarchy, Rick had used his thespian skills shrewdly, pretending to be a bonny prince who promised that House Dowlearn would, by royal decree, offer shares in the Blaireric Trading Company to all in his realm. But when it came to why Prince Richard needed divine right to do this, Camelot didn't quite carry the day.

Archbishop Rob McGhee, representing the theocratic state of Salem, gave a C. S. Lewis—inspired homily on the intentions of Our Creator, the voice and spark of human conscience, and declared that the moral good required the Blaireric be treated as a blessing. Even Father Dallanach, who may have nipped into the Cutty Sark at lunchtime, looked lost in these spiritual exercises.

Teddy Boudreaux gave an on-the-nose presentation about how the best and brightest in his meritocracy would harness the power and promise of the Blaireric plant but was tripped up by Mr. Taliaferro's utilitarian criticisms about the useful and the good. Wasn't it obvious that whoever had the Blaireric would maximize their own power? Which was a criticism that toppled Mark Flanagan as well, who gamely argued that every society's resting point was the many serving the few, and that oligarchy was really what all the others pretended not to be. The argument scored with the judges but sailed past the Populi, who frankly found it fun to root against Flanagan as he pounded his fist on the table in true strongman fashion.

So the Blaireric was very much up for grabs when Oglesby nodded at Steve O'Donnell to make the case for communism.

"My brothers . . ." Placing a Che beret with a red star glued to it on his head, Sticky arose from his seat. "Don't be fooled! The Blaireric is not real!"

Oglesby sensed hijinks. "Mr. O'Donnell . . ."

"Judges of the tribunal, my fellow comrades of the tenth grade, don't listen to our teacher. Mr. Oglesby works for the capitalist pigs who built this school to enslave you with their materialistic notions!"

Mr. Taliaferro broke first and started to laugh. And so did Dan and the rest of the sophomores. Sticky reached under his table and pulled a purple caladium out of a Wolfe Nurseries shopping bag.

"Behold the Blaireric. The story of its power, that it will cure all, is a myth."

Father Dallanach, not quite getting any of this, gave Mr. Oglesby a puzzled look. *Is the boy soft in the head? Of course it isn't real . . .*

"The Blaireric holds no such magic powers. It's a fantasy used by the ruling class to keep all of us enslaved and shackled to the ship of state. And today, brothers, I will prove it!"

With that, Sticky tore a bright young leaf off the caladium and shoved it in his mouth. As he chewed, he continued his diatribe:

"The Blaireric is a fraud. The Game is rigged. There is no panacea that will make the world better." Sticky took another caladium leaf and shoved it into his jowl for comic effect. "Could use a little ranch . . ."

Everyone started howling, including an amused-if-drowsy Father Dallanach. Sticky kept chewing.

"But no magic powers, I'm afraid. That's why the nation of

Proleteria should run the world. Because we discovered the truth of the Blaireric and the truth is—" Sticky started to cough. He had taken too much into his mouth. "The truth is unity through strength. Power to the people!"

Sticky pulled his Panasonic boom box out of the Wolfe Nurseries bag—he had the tape queued to the chorus of Billy Bragg's version of "The Internationale." He pressed play and raised his fist.

So come, brothers and sisters
For the struggle carries on . . .

After a few barking bars, the sophomores stood in solidarity.

"That will be enough, Mr. O'Donnell. Well done." Mr. Oglesby clapped, and Stick popped the tape while continuing to cough. He then puckered his whole face and emitted a bolus of Blaireric in an exaggerated spit take.

It was a great presentation.

Stick grinned at Dan. *Shit. I have to pivot off what this godless socialist has called into question,* he realized.

"Good afternoon, I'm President Malone, the leader of Freedonia. And let me begin by complimenting Chairman O'Donnell on exposing some important questions about the Blaireric and the truth about the Game."

Sticky was still hacking up caladium as Flanagan passed him a Dixie cup of water.

"Gentlemen of the jury, tribunes, I don't have any proof about the powers of the Blaireric. In fact the Blaireric is not what the Game is about. And in that regard Comrade O'Donnell is correct— the Blaireric is a red herring."

Dan smiled at Sticky, whose eyes were watering, his face flushed.

"Even if the Blaireric were real, we are still human. Even if everything about the Blaireric made life perfect, we are still imperfect. Like the Blaireric, people have a lot of potential good in them, but even the best, most powerful system can be subject to misuse and human imperfection."

Dan sort of had their attention. Sticky was still chugging water and now sat back wheezing, which prompted more chuckles from his classmates.

"Let me review briefly what options we have been presented today. King Richard asks you to trust him—with the notion that a king has a right to power because he is born better. Are not all men created equal? Is that fair?

"Bishop McGhee, like the old raven Moses in *Animal Farm*, promises the Blaireric like it's Sugarcandy Mountain. Do you believe him?

"Mr. Boudreaux and his meritocrats offer no explanation why they have the right to decide your life for you. Are they more equal than us? And how is that any different than Boss Flanagan's oligarchs?"

As Dan pressed on, Sticky's face was turning all the colors of the revolution. He pushed back in his chair, trying to catch his breath.

"Now, Chairman O'Donnell, well, he looks like he's dying, like part of a failed coup. He wants you to throw off the shackles of the other governments—but then what? The chairman would quickly become Napoléon and yoke us to a new regime of socialistic rules and regulations. The point is that with or without the Blaireric, my fellow leaders promise utopia, but like on Animal Farm, they truly offer dystopia. With or without the Blaireric, none of these governments offer individual rights, opportunity, or true freedom."

Dan tried to look past the stage lights. Was any of this registering with the tribunal? Was Oglesby nodding in assent or dissent? He wasn't sure. All he could see and hear was Sticky gasping and gulping for air. This annoyed Dan, who thought it was still a put-on by Stick, but he had to keep rolling.

"And that includes democracy. In Freedonia, like all democratic states, there is injustice, there is unfairness, there is inequality. But . . . and it's a big but . . ."

And as Dan began his peroration, Steve O'Donnell doubled over and puked into his Wolfe Nurseries bag. The sophomores started bawling with laughter. Then Sticky fell out of his chair onto the hard slab of the stage. His face was purple.

"Oh Lord." Oglesby bolted from his seat.

○ ○ ○

By THE TIME THE PARAMEDICS ARRIVED, IT WAS WELL CONFIRMED that caladiums were quite toxic. Sticky had broken out in hives, and his mouth and tongue were covered in canker sores. Father Dallanach huddled with Mr. Oglesby, explaining with an eerie calm how the school's underlying insurance policy did not cover incidents where the assignment from the faculty encouraged the student to poison himself. The tired, impatient Jesuit then sulked out of the auditorium back to his cave of afternoon scotch. The rest of them stood in a stony, disappointed silence until a freshman cub reporter from *The Roundup* snuck in the back and, sensing a scoop, started whispering questions to the sophomores. Oglesby glared at Dan, who, as editor, sent the freshman to explore the freedom of the press elsewhere. Sticky was stabilized with an epinephrine shot and loaded onto a gurney.

A couple of minutes after Father Dallanach left, Mr. Taliaferro said quietly: "Well, point taken about the powers of the Blaireric. Mr. O'Donnell has proven it to be a fake. I vote for Proleteria."

As Sticky was wheeled out, receiving sympathy high fives along the steps out of the auditorium, the jury of sophomores voted for communist revolution. On his way to Medical City, Chairman O'Donnell had won the Game.

○ ○ ○

ANNE WAS STILL PICKING AT HER TUNA SUB WITH UNCERTAINTY WHEN the foreman abruptly decided the lunch break was over and it was time to resume the debate. Dr. Ferris cleared his throat with a gulp of Diet Dr Pepper and addressed his fellow jurors.

"I can sum up this case in one line: Show me the evidence."

Ferris placed his palm on a written reminder of the jury instructions. Caruthers was nodding like a parakeet. Anne had noticed that the two of them had taken their bathroom break together. *Definitely in cahoots now.*

"I agree with a lot that Mrs. Malone is saying. This doesn't look good. Doesn't sit right."

Ferris kept oozing this serene Arnold Palmer sincerity. A couple of the female jurors turned to Anne, who warily gnawed on the heel of her sub.

"But here's the deal, folks. Judge Samuels has given us a very specific charge. We have to answer one important question: Is there enough evidence to convict the Reverend Raleigh of this crime?

"Direct. Physical. Evidence." Ferris tapped the table with each word. "Let's for a minute agree with everything Mrs. Malone has put forth. Let's say Raleigh typed the death-threat letters, let's say he was having an affair and wanted to kill Mrs. Raleigh. Let's say he disappeared that night and all the phone calls and notes to librarians were alibis. Fine. Oh, and the suicide note? Just further incrimination.

"Then all I have to say is . . ." Ferris searched the faces of the other eleven jurors for eye-to-eye connections. "Prove it."

Anne loudly balled up the butcher paper and napkins for her

sandwich and shot them into the trash. *Literal minded, reductive, and certain.*

"Show me the evidence. Show me the blood on his hands," Caruthers chimed in, a bit too eagerly, and Ferris gave him that friendly fairway wave again.

"Now, it's especially troubling that an ordained minister could lie and commit sin like this, and that can bias our judgment, but we are here to render unto Caesar what is Caesar's. And there is no evidence in Reverend Raleigh's car, in the driveway, the garage, the house, or on his body or on Peggy's body, that he committed this crime. But . . ."

What do you want? A signed confession? Oh, wait . . . we have that. Anne had enough. "If I commit a murder and lie about it and then clean up all the evidence and cover up my crime, am I not still guilty of murder? Can a reasonable person not find me culpable?"

"Yes, but where is the proof?" Ferris smiled like sugar. "That's conjecture."

"Yeah, we don't know," Keller said, practically growling at Anne. He had a pig face as he rooted through the last bites of his roast beef.

What these men don't know could fill a goddamn airplane hangar. Anne knew they were ganging up on her. *The direct evidence is weak. My only shot is motive, opportunity, and the cover-up.*

"Find me one eyewitness who has him in the neighborhood during the window of time Peggy was strangled," Ferris calmly added. "There is plenty of evidence that Raleigh was a philanderer and a liar, but there's zero evidence that he's a killer."

Three loud knocks at the door. Sergeant Redman, the Muscle Beach court bailiff, bounded in with pen and paper. Anne glanced up at the clock. *Already three thirty p.m. That late lunch killed the afternoon.*

"I need to check everyone's personal contacts from their jury forms and then I'll let y'all deliberate for another hour or so. At that time, Judge Sam is going to call you back to the courtroom and end the proceedings for the day and give you instructions about the sequestration."

As everyone processed what was to come, Tamara Robbins piped up: "Wait, we're not going home?"

"No, you will be sequestered at a hotel over the weekend and until you reach a verdict."

Donna Passerine: "But my kids . . ."

Carla Mirlo: "I have to go back to work . . ."

Helen Klais: "My mother-in-law has a heart condition and I take care—"

"I know, folks, but y'all just got to be patient while we make arrangements." Sergeant Redman got a static call on his radio, which he ignored by reaching on his belt to turn down the volume. "There is, however, a shortage of hotel rooms in downtown Dallas so we may be heading out toward the airport. Not sure, but once I reach everyone on this contact list, I'll give them instructions for bringing you fresh clothes and toiletries. Any questions?"

Anne realized this was partly a ploy by Judge Sam. *He wants a verdict. The case has gone on long enough. Lord knows Pat and Dan will return to a feral state in one weekend without me. I just have to ride this out for the next vote. Get to nine to three or ten to two, and then the room will tip.*

Sergeant Redman checked off the names on the contact list and moved toward the door.

"Thank you, folks. Officer Lippett is still posted outside the door. If you reach a decision or need to hear testimony reread, just knock three times. Otherwise expect me around five p.m. to bring you back into court."

When the bailiff left the room, Caruthers sighed with annoyance. "This trial has been a huge ordeal for me and my business."

"Me too," Keller added, all the men nodding whether it was true or not for them.

Yes, all that vital time away from your port-a-john empire in Mesquite.

"Frankly we need to get this thing done." Caruthers folded his arms and leaned back.

The good Dr. Ferris stopped him there. "I think we all feel the same way. So listen, let's get to our assignment here. The law requires the district attorney to prove guilt beyond a reasonable doubt. You probably know what I think, but let me be clear. I'm not voting for Standing Raleigh as man of the year. And I do have my suspicions, but I sure as heck don't think we have the evidence to convict."

The jurors turned to Anne for rebuttal.

"He confessed. The suicide note is a confession. We don't need perfect evidence if—"

"But he doesn't admit it."

"He says everything without saying it." *Because even in confession, he's a coward.*

"I so get what you're after, *Mizz* Malone." Ferris was aw-shucksing Anne to death with his Andy Griffith routine. "I agree he has feet of clay."

"He's not some wayward sheep." *I'm being too shrill, too Yankee, too angry . . .* , Anne thought, *but why does he keep quoting the Bible? Is that code? Why am I doing it now in kind?* "His wife is comatose in a hospital. Peggy's the victim, not him."

"Mrs. Malone . . ." Keller tried to corral her.

"It's not Peggy's fault that her husband has demons. It's not her fault that the Dallas police can't collect evidence—"

And there. Anne had let it slip. Keller jumped on it.

"So you admit there's not enough evidence."

Shit. She had to backtrack. "We know he had the opportunity—"

Caruthers blurted, "No, ma'am, we're talking about direct evidence." He was shaking his head like she wasn't getting it. *Silly, stupid woman.* Anne was enraged.

"Dale is right," Ferris said. "That's our charge here. We have to stick with—"

"The Dallas police just want this to go—" Anne stopped. She could sense the room shifting on her gaffe. *They don't want to hear my theories. They don't want to think about how awful this is. They want to go home.*

Desperate, Anne tried again. "Think about it. If not him, then who? There's no one else who could have done this. They didn't even try to explain how . . ." But she trailed off when this was met with looks of confusion.

"We can only judge the case that was made." Ferris stared Anne down, uncoiling his serpent smile. He had her. "I think we should try voting again."

Anne started to cry but tried her hardest not to. *Why am I so goddamn alone on this?* "What about Peggy? Where's her justice?"

o o o

It was a quarter to five. Ferris tore out twelve pieces of paper. The men wrote their answers to the first charge quickly, folded ballots, and then affirmed each other with side-eye looks. Anne watched down the line. *Please. Please just think about it.* Tamara Robbins glanced nervously up at the clock. Donna Passerine rubbed the anguish on her forehead. Carla Mirlo scratched out her vote and smiled at Pilar Golondrina, who took some sort of cue from that. Helen Klais folded her piece of paper more times than necessary, as if to diminish her decision. And Mary Crane tented her long, pale fingers over her ballot to pray.

I've lost them all. Anne dabbed the tears from her eyes with her sleeve. *Ferris is right about the evidence and the charge. How can I be so sure?* She wrote down her vote and glanced around the room one last time. The women on the jury would not look at her or at each other. *Because there's no killer on the loose. They caught the right guy. He did it. He admitted it. This is fucking insane.*

Ferris gathered the votes in his white Ping golf cap. He then read out each slip as Caruthers tabulated.

But he didn't need to bother. The vote came back eleven not guilty with one holdout.

All the impatient eyes in the room turned now to Anne.

PAT DROVE DOWN A BROILING FOREST LANE, RETURNING ALONE FROM early-morning Mass. The index was going to top out at 98 degrees, WBAP reported. *A Pentecost heat wave, too soon for summer, even by Texas standards.* The cars around him lurched impatiently, heading west, away from the sun. Despite blasting the Cougar's air-conditioning, the air in the car was barely tolerable, the freon cooling his clutched hands on the steering wheel but little else. The car hadn't run right since he had it towed out of that ditch by the river. Shockingly, the fucked-up details of that incident had fallen below his wife's radar. *Thank you, AAA, for your utmost discretion for idiots like me.* The heat pummeled Pat's hangover, and he turned off the torment of the A/C as he felt the sweat pool on the small of his back against the fake leather seats. He rolled down the window in hopes for a breeze, but the air was furnaced by the concrete kiln of the six-lane road. *Ridiculous, it's not even nine in the morning.* As he signaled onto Cox, he could see far to the west an anvil of purple-gray thunderclouds.

Maybe this heat will break. Hopefully before I do.

Pat parked at the top of the driveway, Anne having disappeared in her silver Zephyr to go shopping. Pat peeled himself out of the sweltering Cougar and came into the house. Still no relief. Worried about the air-conditioning bill topping $100 for the month, Anne had adjusted the thermostat a few degrees up past comfort, relying more on weak oscillating fans that creaked back and forth. In the kitchen Pat put on the kettle. Finding the remnants of a bowl of corn flakes in the sink, he hobbled down the hallway and listened at Dan's door. The muffled twanglings of the Beatles came through, and Pat turned to the hall closet and pulled out the electric typewriter, which he set up on a TV tray in the den. The kettle screamed, and he made his instant Folgers. He then sat in the dark den on one of the burnt-orange chairs they had brought down from the Bronx and tried to ignore the thrum of the Smith Corona. *This coffee is not going to cut through.* The plan was to redo his résumé for another round of job listings, and he rolled a blank page under the wheel and popped the carriage down. He typed his name and his address, skipped his date of birth for now, and moved down the line to his education, his career, his life.

I worked for American Airlines for twenty-seven years. What else was there to say, really? *Less is more, let the service speak for itself.* He adjusted the fan to oscillate more in his direction. *Christ, this heat. Like a hammer to my temples and self-defeat its tongs. Where am I even going to send this? None of the airlines are hiring, everyone in the same holding pattern.* Pat typed out the lines for his education. BS, MS, and JD from Fordham. *I have no contacts or network in Dallas; none of these yahoos down here know or trust Notre Dame, let alone fucking Fordham.*

A gust of wind rattled the patio door, and Pat groaned at his first typo: "maintaince" of the Sabre system. Twenty-seven years—and what expertise did he offer that they didn't have with a computer or someone half his age and salary? *Fuck Bob Crandall, fuck deregulation and the greedy unions, and fuck the fare wars and this fucked-up mediocre industry. Why move the whole goddamn operation to Dallas just to cut everyone loose? My loyalty and service are worth less than the piece of paper I'm typing on.* The air-conditioning whirred on. *Fleeing the burned-out, shithole Bronx was a mistake.* He stretched out his left leg, which had fallen asleep. Pat put his head in his hands and stared down at the beige-brown carpet, which was pilled and stained and worn. *Dallas, the Bronx—pick your season in hell.*

The front door to the house screeched open and then slammed shut. *Dan's in a mood. Aren't we all? The boy can't stand to be in the same room with me.* After a few minutes, Pat realized he was alone in the house and what that meant. He stood up and pulled his bum left leg along to the pantry. The weather was changing, and as he walked past the screen door to the patio, a mockingbird swooped from the holly bushes into the screen, crashing with a loud thwack. Pat watched it recover. *Drunk off the rotting berries. Jesus.* The bird flew off, and Pat stared across the yard in complete despair. Through the blur of heat in the alley, a black car fished past the Peñas' driveway. There sat this year's El Dorado, and behind that new ten-foot fence, an in-ground pool. Reshingled roof and new siding last year. *And Abe is a fucking janitor at Kimberly-Clark!* Pat shook his head. *Christ, it was easier when I was poor and knew no better—to have nothing was its own bliss.*

Pat noticed the dark line of thunderclouds had crept farther east. The mockingbird returned to its nest in the holly. *Fuck it.* Pat lurched toward the pantry. There was the bottle of Wolfschmidt that Anne was blacklining, and then there was the bottle Pat had hidden behind the vinegar. He took two long pulls straight from that bottle in the back, his throat burning. Pat gagged, and it strangely reminded him of his own father. *He'll be here before the bad stuff passes through.* Pat felt the anger welling up and took another swig. He was about to start sobbing, as the burn in his throat now scorched his stomach, when a sharp pain ripped through his gut. *Fucking MS.* He doubled over and staggered back into the den, practically crawling toward a burnt-orange chair to lie down on. The bottle of vodka dropped at his feet. The stabbing pain in his side subsided through shallow breaths, and Pat closed his eyes. *He'll be here. Get out of the storm, Jack.* And Pat bolted up from the burnt-orange chair, sheathed in sweat. The phone was ringing.

"Hello?"

"Pat?"

It was Joe Halliday, the COO of Eastern Airlines.

"Colonel Borman is still stuck on a call with the board. Emergency meeting. Bryan and the IAM again. They are in a marathon session, but he passed me a note to call you."

"Okay."

"Colonel Borman would like to offer you the position of director of employee benefits."

"Okay."

"Pat, are you all right there?"

"Yes, sorry. Bad connection."

"Did you hear me?"

"I did."

Halliday then offered him a salary of $85,000 a year.

"That's great. Thank you."

"Let me be the first to congratulate you and offer my sincere hope that you accept. We sure could use your help and expertise."

"Thank you so much. I might need—"

"No pressure. Take a day or two. Discuss with your family. Tomorrow Miss Blaine will call you. Debbie is our executive HR manager, and she can answer any questions you have about the compensation, the stock options, and the transfer."

"Transfer?"

"To South Florida, to Miami."

Pat looked up at the ceiling of his mortgaged Dallas house.

"Of course. That would be great."

"Congratulations, and not to speak prematurely, but welcome aboard."

They hung up, and Pat ran to the kitchen sink and vomited.

Pat's breathing now felt labored, and the pain in his side came back. Just standing there felt impossible. *Thank you, God. I get it. I'm done. I'm quitting. Thank you.* He had a thousand half thoughts but couldn't hold on to one. *Just need one or two more to settle everything down.* He then heard a tapping at the screen door. He thought it was the mockingbird, but then the tapping grew more frequent, and Pat raised his head from the kitchen sink to look outside. Hail the size of quarters pelted the patio. The wind sheared through the trees, and a draft moaned across the attic and the ceiling vents.

Jesus.

The front door flew open and then slammed shut.

"Dan? Pat?"

Pat stepped into the hallway. Anne was drenched and clutching her purse with her fist.

"I was at Tom Thumb and they came on the speakers and said Dallas County was under a tornado watch."

Pat staggered around the kitchen to find the radio.

"There's a huge storm coming, Pat. Where's Dan?"

Before he could answer, an air-raid siren started to wail and blare.

o o o

THAT SAME MORNING, DAN WAS HOLED UP IN HIS ROOM LISTENING TO the spare testaments of *John Wesley Harding* while reading Shelton's account of the motorcycle accident. His mother went out shopping without bothering to bother him. Then his father left for Mass without guilting Dan into coming. *Can't keep track of when one fight ends and another begins.* Alone in the house, Dan wandered room to room. He took two finger-pulls of peanut butter from the jar in the fridge and funneled a handful of Honey Nut Cheerios into his mouth. The house was creepy quiet, like the walls were somehow absorbing sound. Dan settled into the back TV room. Through the window, he saw the dark peaks of clouds rising like a mountain range. Dan flipped around the channels, but it was the Sunday morning block of kiddie cartoons and TV preachers. Bored, Dan thumbed through a mound of his father's papers—junk mail, résumés returned to sender, form-letter replies thanking him for his résumé, want ads from the *Times Herald*, and, below that, a small workbook.

30-DAY CLINICAL TRIAL FOR
HYPOVITAMINOSIS CHOLECALCIFEROL
PATIENT DIARY PATRICK FRANCIS MALONE

The phone rang. Dan extracted his father's diary from the pile and dashed into the kitchen to answer. It was Cady Bloom.

"Hey, Danny boy."

"Hey." *Too cheery for Sunday morning.* Dan was on guard.

"What's happening?"

"Not alotta."

"Same here." Cady hadn't called in a while. There had been a short pink-cloud period when they talked every day. *But not anymore.* "Listen, Dan, you don't really want to go to Spring Fling, right?"

"What?" *Not a prank.* He had agreed to take her to a real dance. Dan started to flip through the diary. His father had written a lot down.

"I'm just saying we don't have to go. Okay?"

"Wait . . ."

"Are you angry about it?"

"I'm confused. What's going on?"

"Sorry, I shouldn't have made a big deal out of it."

"That's okay. We can go do something else."

"Dan." Cady's tone got pouty and impatient. "I'm saying not go together."

"Oh." Dan put down the diary and started paying full attention. "You didn't seem super into it, so let's forget about it."

"Want to do something else that Saturday?"

"Danny, that's not gonna work."

Dan finally started to get it. "Are you going with someone else?"

"No, not really."

"Hold up. Who are you going with?"

"I don't know. Just my girlfriends right now."

It's that Julie Houlihan. Cady's dumping me because Julie told her to, and then she'll set her up with some other guy, so they can all go as a group. Fuck.

"Wait, is this—"

"I gotta go."

And the line clicked, and Dan let the phone slide out of his hand as he curdled with humiliation. He looked around the kitchen in disbelief until his eyes fell back down on his father's medical diary. The following lines popped out at him:

Anne and Dan won't speak to me. I'm all alone and it's my own goddamn fault. I did this to me. Fuck me. Just let me fucking die.

Dan moved into the den and plunked down on a burnt-orange chair. He went back to the beginning of the diary and then skimmed ahead to the bad parts. His father was sicker than he had realized. He also drank too much. Dan closed the workbook. His head and heart tumbled with guilt, and he couldn't think. He heard a car pull up in the driveway, his father's Cougar. He ran to his father's pile of papers and returned the workbook to the stack. He slipped into his own room as his father staggered through the front door. Dan sealed himself off and sank into despair. *Such an awful confession. I didn't know it was that bad.* The MS had left him rotten. He could hear his father shuffling around the house. *It's losing his job. He's depressed.*

Dan put on *The White Album* and turned it up, lying facedown on his bed, but then all he could do was listen to himself go crazy. Cady Bloom had dumped him and he'd never even kissed her. *I'm such a fucking loser.* He pulled a pack of cigarettes from a hiding spot under the mattress and turned off "Helter Skelter." He whispered to no one, "What the fuck is going on?" and then got up off the bed. He ran out of the house and down the driveway, stopping at the concrete wall in front. The storm clouds were much closer, and the wind began to whistle through the trees. *Cady, all those girls, it's like a stupid game to them, everyone trying to rise in the cool rankings. Well, fuck that.*

He had no idea what to do. He lit a cigarette and started pacing along the wall. So many things he couldn't hold in or let go. *Who the fuck do you trust? How do you get close? It's a goddamn mystery and I'm just a pathetic virgin and I don't get why I'm wired like Frankenstein around girls. Is this how I'm built? Like some scared, ridiculous pervert? How did that happen?*

He coughed as the smoke blew back into his face. *And I'm stuck in my own selfish bullshit, while my dad is dying. Fuck, I'm going to lose him.*

He tried hard not to cry. The traffic on Crown Shore was steady. People coming home from church, the wash and yawn of cars going back and forth. *I just need to get out of here.* No one seemed to notice Dan as he stood there holding in his sobs.

Until a black Monte Carlo pulled up to the curb. The tinted window rolled down, and Dan quickly wiped his cheeks on his sleeve.

"Are you okay?"

It was Emma Wesselman. She was driving her father's car.

"No," he blurted.

"What happened?"

"Nothing, leave me alone."

"Well something happened."

"You're not fucking helping."

"Sorry."

And then something in Dan broke and his eyes met Emma's worried smile.

"Where are you coming from?"

"Practice." Emma was always playing basketball up at W. T. White.

"Can we go somewhere?"

Emma looked down at the dashboard and shrugged, and Dan hopped into the black velour of the passenger seat. They turned onto Marsh, then again onto Forest, cruising past the mini malls and drive-thrus, past the car wash, the Korean church, and the library. From there, they meandered back toward Dan's house. The afternoon sun was blazing hot, but the cloud line had crept in, and there was a gust of wind as they cut through an alleyway behind Crown Shore that wound its way toward Truesdell, Emma's street. They stopped and parked on a wide stretch of lawn at the end of the cul-de-sac where someone had planted a small orchard of crab apple trees.

"So what's going on?" Emma asked.

"People are just fucking . . . disappointing."

"Like who?"

"Never mind." Dan flicked his lighter and stared down at the angry yellow flame.

"So what do you want to do?" Emma knew she wasn't going to get the full story. Another blast of humid wind came down the alley, tipping over trash cans. Dan scratched at his neck, sheepish, irritated. He was still coming down off his anger over the

Cady rejection. His fear and grief over his father he couldn't even touch.

Dan looked into Emma's brown eyes as they glimmered. The now-steady breeze caused a cloud of gnats and mayflies to scatter down from the crab trees. *This girl likes you. Has always liked you, idiot.*

"We could watch a movie at my house," Emma offered. She popped the car into park and swung her smooth, brown legs over the wheel and kicked them out the window. The sky was now fully gray, everything thrown under sudden shade. Emma leaned back toward Dan, who was holding her basketball. Dan leaned toward Emma. He was profoundly confused. *Now? Is this happening now?* Just then Emma brought her hand slowly toward his lap.

And tried to steal the ball from him.

She slapped at it, laughed at her own sneakiness, then grabbed at the basketball, but Dan had a solid grip, and they wrestled back and forth, his arm rubbing against hers in all its softness.

"Let go."

"Try to take it."

"Are you coming over or what? It's about to storm." Little shots of hail started pinging the hood of the car.

"I'd like to, but—"

"Come on." She snatched at the ball again with one hand, prying Dan away with the other on his chest. "Stop it. It's my ball."

"Stop what?" He gripped the ball tighter. He was stronger, but not by much, and now they were sitting really close, still wrestling for the ball. Emma tried to tickle the ball free by reaching under his arms; Dan wasn't really fighting back. The wind swirled the branches of the crab trees something hectic. They looked at each other, both frightened, a rush of nerves. And Emma pulled away, unsure.

"Hey, wait," Dan said softly.

"What?" Emma sat back, but she was still there, waiting.

Dan leaned in just as the air-raid siren began to wail and blare.

o o o

EARLIER THAT SUNDAY, ANNE STOOD IN FRONT OF THE FROZEN PIZZAS, the door to the freezer open, the cold, freon-laced air anointing her face, frosting the glass. She pulled out a Totino's pepperoni. The idea of turning on the oven in this heat depressed her, but she had to feed her family something, and this seemed easiest. She lingered in the frozen-food aisle, trying to cool off. In front of the ice cream an old blue-haired crone was licking her thumb as she tried to separate the coupons she'd pulled from her pocketbook. *But for the grace of God go I.* Anne recognized that the store, full of food and fluorescence and Sunday shoppers, was actually a cold, miserable box sitting on an endless torched prairie. *My life in Dallas is a series of moves from one box to the next,* Anne thought, *surrounded by strangers and emptiness.*

She pushed her cart into the next aisle and stared at the rows of cereal boxes. *A hundred choices, more empty boxes.*

The Raleigh trial had ended. Anne had tried to hold out, resisting her fellow jurors, but she had failed Peggy and was still miserable about the verdict. *Another false choice.*

It was too hot, too soon, and Anne couldn't bear the thought of an endless Texas summer. Now that Pat had completed the Irish trifecta—*Drinking too much, lost his job, and sick*—she was losing her grip. With the MS, it was too late to leave him. *What is the greater sin really: to walk away or to resent him?* Anne stood there in the cereal aisle paralyzed by all the choices and downsides. And there was the old woman again, creeping along with her cart and coupons.

After a long, tired pause, Anne walked away from her own cart and headed toward the front of the store. *I don't want any of this. I don't want Pat, this place, the priest, any of it.* In the produce section

an old couple fought like jays over the seedless grapes. *No. I refuse.*
Everyone seemed to be in slow motion, and a checkout girl stared
at her cow-eyed. A fierce wind blasted the electric eye and triggered the double doors to open. Hot air squalled through the front
of the store. And in that moment, Anne didn't have any choices in
her life.

An air-raid siren stared to wail and blare.

○ ○ ○

ANNE DROVE HOME THROUGH THE START OF HAIL AND RUSHED UP THE
driveway into the house to find her husband completely out of it.

"There's a huge storm coming, Pat. Where's Dan?"

The air-raid siren answered before Pat could. Anne dropped
her purse on the kitchen table. The windows strobed with lightning. Thunder tore through the sky above them.

"He can't be outside in this. When did he leave the house?"

Pat shrugged and pretended to look for batteries for the radio
and the flashlight. "He's fine."

Just then the roof was drummed with another barrage of hail.
The wind keened. "He's not fine. He's out there. And you're just
sitting around doing fuck-all."

"Don't start with me."

"Did you ask him where he was going? Jesus, Pat, you're completely fucking useless sometimes."

"Now you're blaming me for the goddamn weather."

The lights went out in the house, and it was very dark inside
and out. The air-raid siren screamed in the distance.

"Shit. Did he take his bike?" Anne grabbed the car keys back
out of her purse. She was shaking with anger. "I'm going to look
for him."

"Wait. I'll go. Give me the keys." Pat stumbled in his first step,
his leg half-asleep and tingling.

"Have you been drinking?"

"Stop arguing with me."

"You can't even walk straight. Christ, Pat. I can smell it on you."

"Stop with all the drama."

"I can't fucking believe you!"

An unnerving gale shook the house. Through the patio screen door Anne could see the trees in the yard, battered sideways. Pat's chin sank into his chest. He had been caught. He put out his hand. "Just give me the keys."

The lights flickered back on for a moment, then went out again.

"You useless piece of shit." Anne turned to go. "You're drunk before noon."

"I'm not fucking drunk! I'm just sick of all your bullshit."

And with that Pat lunged at his wife and ripped the keys to the Zephyr out of her hand.

"Pat, stop . . . please. You can't . . . Listen, we'll both go—"

"I'll find him!"

Pat glared at her with bloodshot eyes, then limped away quickly. Anne threw her head into her hands and started to cry. A blast of hot air rushed into the house as Pat left, slamming the front door behind him. *He's going to kill himself,* Anne thought. But she didn't stop him. She went to the front window as Pat skidded down the driveway and tore off in her car.

Anne didn't know what to do, so she checked that all the windows in the house were shut tight. Five torturously long minutes passed. Anne closed her eyes and prayed. *Lord, I never ask for anything. But this is my hour of need. Please, Lord, deliver my child to safety. Let this storm pass. Please, I never ask—*

The front door swung open, and Dan, his hair tangled with chips of hail, staggered in. Emma Wesselman was right behind him, the wind blasting the drapes off their rods and tossing an oil painting of Manhattan off its nail in the living room.

Dan, his face flushed with fear, shouted at his mother, "This is bad!"

o o o

ANNE OFFERED EMMA AND DAN TOWELS. THEY HAD TRIED TO GO TO Emma's house, but a downed telephone pole was blocking the alley behind Truesdell. The hail stopped and was replaced by quiet and darkness. Dan turned on his father's battery-powered radio, and a chirping noise came through as he tuned it to KRLD. It was the emergency broadcast.

"This is a tornado emergency alert for Tarrant, Dallas, and Collin Counties. Residents are advised . . ."

Anne pulled the flashlight from a kitchen drawer and slapped at the old batteries in its stick until a weak ray of light shone. She looked out again through the screen door. The wind had stopped howling, and the sky swirled with weird tinges of yellow, green, and brown. The backyard held enough hail to mistake it for a hockey rink. A strange gray-blue pall settled over the house, almost like an eclipse. The air-raid siren wound up again. All was still as the thunderclouds moiled silently.

When the air-raid siren wound down, there came a new noise. A buzzing. Like a hive of bees. And it got louder, like a freight train far away mounting tracks. Anne, Dan, and Emma heard it and stared at each other. A noiseless fork of lightning flashed, and Anne pressed against the glass patio door, mesmerized by the unnatural light. And in a moment, the stillness was gone and the trees began to tremble. A pool umbrella from the Peñas' backyard lifted into the air and flew across the Malones' backyard before slamming down on the patio.

"Get to the bathroom," Anne commanded. "Go! Everyone in the tub. The pipes are the deepest thing in the ground. Move!"

The freight train churned louder. Anne turned back and saw a branch of the mimosa tree crack and scrape against the gutter, just missing the glass door she had been standing at. Emma and Dan were two steps ahead of her as they made for the bathroom. The wind gathered in a chorus of terrifying wails. The train drew closer, its grinding, swarming howl deafening. Anne squatted in the tub with Emma futilely holding on to the faucet. Dan was yelling something at her. Anne couldn't hear him as the beams of the house bent and shook with awful wrenching and cracking sounds. The train was tearing in, and Anne couldn't make out what Dan was saying.

"What?" She drew as close to him as she could, one arm braced against the toilet tank.

"Where's Dad?"

Dan yelled something else, but it was too late. Anne just shook her head. The pounding force of the wind tore at the house. The freight train was charging past, and they all looked up, waiting for the roof to fly away. Anne closed her eyes and prayed through the deafening roar.

o o o

THIS DAMN ZEPHYR HANDLES LIKE IT HAS FOUR FLAT TIRES. The gusts and gales of wind shearing against him, Pat struggled to keep the car on the road. *You have to be drunk to drive in this shit,* he thought, and circled the neighborhood, running up Cedar Bend, then down Rosser, on the lookout for Dan. But Pat had no idea where his son might be, and the search was secondary to Pat's fury. Ignoring the dangers of the storm, he was locked into driving himself mad.

"What do you want from me?" he said aloud, alone.

Pat tried to reconcile the hundred ways he had gone astray, and thought of his father. *A drunk, another fool out in a storm*—Pat swallowed hard—*and I'm no better, and maybe worse.*

As he rounded past High Meadow, he saw that a live oak had split to its trunk and hurled a thick arm of branches across the intersection. Pat swerved and braked. As he stopped short, the pain in his side returned. *This shit feels like I've been stabbed. Could it be my appendix about to burst?* Pat took a shallow breath and let the pain pass, then turned onto Marsh Lane.

Clouds moving east; if I head south I can duck past it. The air-raid siren wound up again, and Pat raced down the street, making a futile effort to outrun the storm. As he reached Royal Lane, he drove straight into more hail and sheets of rain. He gripped the steering wheel, feeling flushed and exhausted, the pain slicing through the right side of his gut. *Christ Almighty, what did I do to deserve this?* The windshield wipers couldn't keep up, and Pat had no choice but to pull over. By the time he made it to the intersection at Walnut Hill he knew exactly where to do it.

You weren't looking for Dan. You knew where you were going the whole time.

Pat jerked the wheel into a hard left and skidded into the parking lot for the Hasty Liquor Store.

o o o

TUMBLING OUT OF THE DRIVER'S SEAT, PAT WAS COMPLETELY SOAKED after two steps in the downpour. Lightning flashed and forked, and a crashing thunder rumbled near. He shouldered into the front door, surprised to find it open, the power still on. He stepped into the cool, white fluorescence and endless rows of booze.

The clerk, a bent-over old-timer with a name tag reading SWEENEY, ignored the tempest and recognized Pat as the frequent customer he was.

"Hey there, I was just about to lock her up . . ."

"I needed to get off the road." Pat grinned like a loon, forgetful now, past the pale of his plight. "One hell of a storm."

"Yes, sir." Sweeney gave Pat a stoic squint. And just then the air-raid siren started up again. The blue-black skies drained out, and an eerie quiet gathered. Barely tethered to his wits, Pat pretended all was fine and began to shop. He picked up a bottle of vodka. *This is it, the last one, to celebrate a shitty job offer. Yes, the last one until the next.*

The pain erupted again in his side, sending both Pat and the bottle crashing to the floor. Pat fell hard and was paralyzed by the shock of it. All he could do was look up and down the aisle. Rows and columns of liquor bottles. The calm within the storm was replaced now with the groan of the wind churning, squalling against the windows. Sweeney, the store clerk, moved slowly to the end of the aisle and squinted at him. The power, the lights, went out, and the wind began to holler. Pat lay in the glass shards and puddle of vodka. *This is it. Here it comes. About fucking time.* The bottles of liquor started to shiver on their shelves. Unable to move or get up, Pat lay there in a heap and closed his eyes. All he could hear was the rattle and clink of the bottles, their horrible, dreadful chime.

○ ○ ○

Pat awoke slowly and sat up in the hospital bed. His appendix felt like it could burst at any moment, and he tried not to move his side, which was near impossible. So he lay back down, burning, immobile, in the emergency room at Medical City. He had a terrible hangover, felt bleary, dehydrated, his legs alternating between numbness and shooting pain. The pain in his side was so bad he almost vomited, and he started shivering like he had the flu. The clerk at the liquor store had called an ambulance. Another shot of agony rifled through him as Pat tried to recall what happened. *Did I black out? Looks like it.* His side still tender, his skin rashed and itchy, Pat couldn't get comfortable in the hospital bed. He was shaking with pain one minute and then it would subside. He told one nurse he was in total misery and another nurse he was fine.

After a half hour more of waiting, another patient was wheeled into the room. A guy in his thirties maybe. He smelled awful and lay there unconscious. The nurses were hooking him up to all sorts of machinery. A middle-aged doctor with a crew cut came rushing in, glanced at his chart, and then checked him with his stethoscope. The nurse whispered something to the doctor, and together they fished through the guy's pockets like he was already dead. Turning him over, the nurse found a pint of Old Crow in his back pocket. The doctor opened one of his eyelids and shined a penlight there, and that seemed to jolt him into semiconsciousness. The doctor stepped back and gauged the vital signs now beeping off the machines. The nurse left and returned with the man's mother, who was a sad gray flake of a woman. The doctor interrogated her: How long had he been drinking? All weekend probably. How long has he had diabetes? Several years. The doctor nodded and said something about hepatitis. And Pat realized, yes, his skin was a blotchy yellow, like the filter on a used cigarette. The nurse reported the patient's blood sugar, and the doctor looked put out and said something to the mother about a diabetic coma in a tone that this was all one giant pain in the ass.

Just then a nurse snuck up on Pat, asked how he felt without listening to the answer, and quickly drew some blood. The doctor turned to Pat's bedside.

"Sorry to take so long. That storm made us awfully busy."

Pat could read his name tag now: DR. ROTH. He examined Pat's side and prodded until he found a scarlet surge of pain that made Pat jerk back in the bed.

"Yup, that might be the appendix."

"Does this have anything to do with the MS?"

"Not likely. We should X-ray."

Pat tried to reassure himself that he had extended the health insurance from American for just this sort of scenario, and he was covered. And then he accidentally shifted and, *fuck*, the pain in his side was intolerable. His skin was crawling, and he couldn't sit still but he had to sit still, and *Christ*, this was pure hell.

Later that hour, they wheeled Pat down the hall to be X-rayed. The technician didn't acknowledge his presence, and Pat just lay there like a slab of meat as the guy positioned the machine around his midsection, then stepped out of the room.

Pat was trapped.

He wanted to scream.

Quit crying. Shut the fuck up. You brought this on yourself.

But then it was over and they wheeled him back. The diabetic in the bed next to him was awake now and reading a magazine, his mother resting in a chair alongside. The drug counselor for the hospital came by and murmured through a survey. Pat could only make out every third word, but this guy had taken a whole pharmacy of drugs Pat had never heard of. The counselor talked about the hazardous cocktail effect of drinking and pills on diabetes, and the guy feigned forbearance, but no one believed that, especially the mother, who stared down at the floor and couldn't face her own child. Pat realized this was just the start of a new cycle for this guy. The hospital would dry him out, and then he'd pick up again, and the mother knew that whole big wheel of shit was coming and it would turn him up either back here or at Sparkman Hillcrest cemetery, and she wasn't sure which was worse.

Another doctor, a younger guy, whisked into the room. He didn't interrupt the drug counselor but came over directly to Pat. His name tag read: DR. HOO. Pat almost found that funny. Dr. Hoo grinned, calm and dispassionate, and then looked over Pat's chart, his X-rays and blood work.

"Mr. Malone, how are we feeling?"

"I'm okay, I guess. Just this pain in my side, really."

"Yes, we thought it might be the appendix, right?"

"That's what the other doctor said, yes."

"Well according to this, I'm not sure it's your appendix. Let me see something here." Dr. Hoo reached down along Pat's white belly. His fingers were cool and soft as he poked around. "Any pain here?"

His side felt tight and catchy, like a hernia, but Pat shook his head no.

"Okay. Mr. Malone, looking at this blood work, the liver functions are . . . well . . . they are quite elevated, and that's not good. I think your liver is swollen, and that's the tenderness you're feeling."

He was so matter-of-fact about it. Pat appreciated that.

"Mr. Malone, do you drink?" Dr. Hoo asked quietly.

"Yes."

"Do you drink a lot?"

"Yes. Too much."

"Okay. Every day, including today?"

"Yes."

"You appear to be in withdrawal right now, do you realize that?"

"Yes, I know."

"And you have to stop."

"Yes, I know."

"Especially with the early onset of multiple sclerosis."

Dr. Hoo left it at that. Pat lay back in the bed as the doctor scribbled on his chart, then went about his rounds. Called out for what it really was, the pain in his side disappeared and was replaced with a dull, shameful loathing. Pat studied his lot with sad astonishment—he had put himself here. And he was taking a hospital bed away from someone who was seriously hurt. He cringed at his own pathetic behavior. He got out of the bed and started to put on his clothes. No one bothered with him as he walked out of the room, down the hall, and found a pay phone to call the house and ask Anne to come get him.

o o o

THE STORM PASSED, QUICK AS IT CAME. NOTHING TOUCHED DOWN ON the Malone house or Hasty Liquor Store, but it came close—a twister had pinballed down the six lanes of the LBJ trench as hundreds in traffic ran to the underpasses for cover. Pat had been spared, the heat wave sundered, but major issues remained.

As Pat stepped slow and unsure to the car, he told Anne his appendix was fine and that he had pulled something. *Hernia, sorry for the false alarm.* Anne didn't believe him. His own doctor, Landis, was affiliated with Medical City and would see the results, and the truth would come out. But Pat was wading through deeper shit than that. He was still shaking, his head throbbing. *You are an alcoholic like your father. You put yourself in the hospital.* Even with the air-conditioning on, he was sweating. *You lay down next to a man literally dying from it.* He hadn't eaten all day. Thirsty too. An exhausted wreck. *You have MS.* He took off his hospital bracelet and stuffed it in his pocket. *You'll probably end up with cirrhosis too. You have enough problems. Stop adding to them. You have a wife and child to support.*

For the first half of the drive home, Pat said nothing to Anne, who was seething quietly. *You have to get your shit together. Christ, please. You have to quit.* They drove down Forest Lane until the light stopped them at Midway. Anne turned to him and shook her head like there were no words for her despair. And then uttered feebly: "I just don't know what's going on."

They stopped to pick up the Zephyr at the liquor store on Walnut Hill and drove the rest of the way separately. When they got home, the pain in Pat's side came back and he was short of breath. He needed to lie down and made his way to the back of the house. Dan was there, at the door to his room.

"Hey, Danny boy. Crazy storm, huh?" Pat offered.

"Yeah." Dan smiled with worry as his father hobbled past him in the hallway. He didn't recognize him, or realized he had no memory of what his father was like before he got sick.

"I'm sorry, Dan."

Pat couldn't summon what he really wanted to say.

"I'm just sorry it's never clean."

○ ○ ○

THE NEXT MORNING, MONDAY, PAT TOLD ANNE ABOUT THE JOB IN Miami. On Tuesday, Pat scheduled an appointment with Dr. Landis. On Wednesday afternoon, he dialed the hotline for Alcoholics Anonymous. On Thursday morning, he took the job offer. Late Friday, the machinists' union walked away from the table, and the board of Eastern Airlines accepted the resignation of Chief Executive Officer Frank Borman.

"'THO' MUCH IS TAKEN, MUCH ABIDES; AND THO' WE ARE NOT NOW *that strength which in old days moved earth and heaven, that which we are, we are; one equal temper of heroic hearts, made weak by time and fate, but strong in will to strive, to seek, to find, and not to yield.'"

Oglesby lowered *The Oxford Book of English Verse* and swung his teaching stick, an ancient driver made of persimmon wood nicknamed Carraway, across the blue carpet like a practice cut before addressing the class on his fairway. He was turned toward the windows, stained in a blazing early-summer light, the courtyard fused with green thoughts and clumsy cicadas and june bugs rising on the heat. It was the final day of school and time for one last drive on Gatsby before heading into the clubhouse.

"Gentlemen, what happens when the hero returns? When the war is over and our story ends? Remember back to the beginning of the year: Our hero is on a quest. And a hero, despite his flaws, must be *polytropos* and champion his fate. Consider Mr. Jay Gatsby: Like Odysseus, he has returned home from war. And like the long-lost king of Ithaca, he has endless parties going on in his house. Are there other similarities?"

Oglesby cocked an eyebrow and shifted his weight onto the one-wood. Rob McGhee raised his hand and spoke: "They are both kind of restless and unsatisfied."

"Good, that's right. There are accounts of Odysseus, like this

Tennyson poem, where the story doesn't stop and that take our
hero back out on adventure. What does Tiresias tell him he must
do in order to please Poseidon? Mr. Gilchrist?"

"That he must plant an oar where no man recognizes it from
the sea . . ."

"Correct." Oglesby recited two more lines from Tennyson
without prompt from the book: *"How dull it is to pause, to make an
end, to rust unburnish'd, not to shine in use!"*

He then gave the sophomores the sly smirk that they had grown
to know well: *Who is clever enough to figure this out with me?*

"Did Odysseus know his wife and son? Wouldn't they be es-
tranged all these years later? Why would he perpetuate so much
violence on his return and kill all the suitors? Gatsby also doesn't
fit back into society. His name, his status in West Egg, is suspect.
In pursuing Daisy, he enrages Tom. Like Odysseus, his fortunes
are based on deception, he overreacts and mishandles key situa-
tions, and he is driven by this unrequited longing."

For a final time, Oglesby moved to poke a snoring Jay Blaylock
in the ribs with the driver, but then shook his head and left him
among the lotus-eaters.

"Gentlemen, the hero at rest is a flawed, sad figure. This is
the great irony that Homer and Fitzgerald both realized: when the
hero comes home, he still finds himself in exile."

Oglesby threw back his shoulder and snuck a quick peek at the
classroom clock.

"All right, how dull it is to pause there, but we have fifteen minutes before final prayer service." Oglesby pulled notebooks from
his army bag. "I'm passing back your journals, and we have one last
bloodletting ceremony before I pronounce you upperclassmen."

Oglesby whisked around the classroom, dropping journals,
muttering cryptic insults as he went.

"The marginal Mr. McGhee, who never stayed within the
lines . . .

"Basho Deangelis, the master of the hundred-word haiku. Not a syllable more or less . . .

"To Carthage burning, Mr. Coleman. Using your journal for rolling papers does not impress me.

"Master of the useless arts Malone . . ."

Without further comment, Oglesby flung a yellow spiral notebook to the back row. Dan caught it on a backhand and struggled to read his teacher's rush as any indicator. So he scanned his last journal entries, looking for red pen. Dan had pulled out all the stops: he wrote a wistful, dramatic monologue from the point of view of Telemachus, drew a cartoon about a misunderstood paramecium that saves the universe, and composed a Dylan rip-off ballad (*like questions floating on the breeze*) about everybody being hypocrites, run through a tundish of Gerard Manley Hopkins (*the thorny tendril vined and tangled with my thoughts*). Dan found a check-plus for a C. S. Lewis–inspired essay titled "The Snake Crawled West": "Man brought the snake out of Eden, and discovered what he thought to be the whole world, and once he conquered it, he only then realized that he had been conquered by the snake itself." He also wrote obliquely about his mother and father—in an entry called "Lost in the Supermarket"—with some pain and worry there. Dan flipped to the final page and Oglesby's note: *"Well done. Let's talk about what's next."*

Dan looked up from his desk as Oglesby pulled out his grade book.

"As last time, the top three semester averages are eligible for *Rattus norvegicus* induction. The first candidate, with a grade point of ninety-seven point one, is Mr. Boudreaux."

Despite the chorus of groans, this came as no surprise. Ethan Tsao and his 98 average had transferred to St. Mark's during the spring. The freckle-jowled Teddy Boudreaux leapt out of his seat, beaming at his first-place status.

"With a ninety-six point five, we have Mr. O'Donnell. Please step up."

This was a bit of a shock. Sticky was a stealth ace when it came to tests and papers, and he had won the Game by poisoning himself with Blaireric. The call of his name was met with impressed and envious chimp faces from the sophomores.

"Let's see here . . ." Oglesby stuck Carraway under his armpit and ruled his finger across the grade book. "Mr. Gilchrist has a ninety-five point seven average; come up to the front."

Dan stared down at the remarks in his journal. It was Oglesby's way of telling him he hadn't made the cut.

"Now, Mr. Gilchrist has the third-highest average, but he was also out with mono for four weeks. It also looks like I haven't added all the extra credit in correctly. Mr. Malone . . ."

Dan's heart started to hammer in his chest. *Why are you torturing me?* Oglesby scrutinized him with pale, loveless eyes.

"You have no absences and the best journal marks in the class. You're at ninety-five point four plus extra credit for writing out one thousand and one things to do with a white elephant. So I'm adding you as a fourth candidate for the rites of the rat. Step up here."

Dan waded past the rows of desks as Oglesby read out the rest of the averages, ranking the class from first to hypnagogic Jay Blaylock, dead last. Dan couldn't believe he was in the running— *The trial to get to the trial was a trial.* Oglesby pulled his copy of *Ficciones* and three brown rubber rats from his backpack, aligning them on the teacher's desk like they were ready to assume their places on an Olympic medal podium. Dan was so short of breath he was practically panting. *Pull it together, idiot.*

Oglesby put away his grade book and, with a tap of the golf club on both shoulders, anointed each of the candidates.

"Repeat after me: '*To think, analyze and invent are not anomalous acts, but the normal respiration of the intelligence . . .*'"

Dan mouthed along, wondering what Oglesby's questions would be. He entered a weird hyper zone where he tried to think of everything at once and couldn't focus on anything.

"*'Every man should be capable of all ideas, and I believe that in the future I will be.'*"

Oglesby then saluted the four candidates, each of whom stood up a little straighter, throwing his shoulders back in his Jesuit blue blazer.

"Gentlemen, as you know, the Norwegian rat is more than just an A student. The Norwegian rat realizes that life is a labyrinth but finds the way. There have been years when I have taught a whole class of *Rattus rattus*—all of them falling for traps. Remember rule number seven: reading is paying attention. It's time for the final questions."

"You guys are screwed," Rick said in a stage whisper. The class giggled. Oglesby did not crack a smile.

"Let's start with Mr. Boudreaux. What street is named for the mad general of the Revolutionary War in *The Catcher in the Rye*?"

Teddy plopped his arm on top of his head as if to slap the answer out of his skull. After five long seconds, he shook his head. Flanagan shot his hand up.

"It's too late for you, Mr. Flanagan. And my condolences, Mr. Boudreaux. You may return to your seat."

Teddy Boudreaux went from dejection to rage in two steps—kicking his chair over, to the delight of the whole class.

"Oh boy, Boudreaux's going full Hulk on us." Rick gritted his teeth in fake rage.

"Screw you, Dowlearn," Teddy spat back.

"Gentlemen . . ." Oglesby pointed with his teaching stick for Teddy to pick up his chair and cool it.

"Sit down, clown, this ain't no circus," Rick added.

Teddy planted his chair upright in the blue carpet and slumped in the seat. Oglesby turned away from this nonsense, the class still chittering with laughter at the tantrum.

"Mr. O'Donnell?"

"Ready, sir."

"Then tell me who supposedly dies at the Battle of Shrewsbury."

"Hotspur!" Sticky blurted out with a relieved, if raspy, certainty.

Almost every one of the sophomores nodded his head in agreement. *Trick question*, Dan thought.

"I'm sorry, Mr. O'Donnell, that is incorrect."

"What?" Sticky threw his hands in the air.

"No, that's right!" Rob agreed.

"Silence, gentlemen." Oglesby struck the teacher's desk with a monstrous thwack. "The running commentary ends now. The Norwegian rat must smell the trap. Mr. Gilchrist, are you ready for your question?"

Sticky shuffled back to his seat while Chad Gilchrist tucked his Alex Van Halen behind his ears and nodded.

"What is Boo Radley's first name?"

Gilchrist lit up like he had it.

"Nathan."

Oglesby lowered his eyes and shook his head. "I'm afraid that's his brother."

Dan watched Chad immolate on the wrong answer. He did know it but had misspoken, somehow the answer getting tripped on its way to his tongue. *I'm gonna be sick.* Dan felt truly awful, partly for Gilchrist's mistake but more so that it was now his turn.

"Mr. Malone, are you ready?" Oglesby barked at him.

"Yes, sir."

"What country awards Gatsby a medal during the war?"

Dan shot Rick a look. Rick caught it and grinned with a nod, then turned to Rob, who was halfway out of his chair, ready to high five. Rob elbowed Stick, who grudged out a smile. His crew knew—*I've got this.*

"Montenegro."

"That's not fair!" Teddy Boudreaux swiped the pen, journal, and papers off his desk. "He got the question from the book we just read."

It was a total jackass meltdown. Oglesby turned to address this latest hissy fit. But before his teacher could say anything, Dan grabbed the moment back.

"General Anthony Wayne, Falstaff pretended to die at the Battle of Shrewsbury, and Arthur. Arthur 'Boo' Radley."

Oglesby leaned back on his teaching stick, closed his eyes, and nodded. Rick pumped his fist. The period bell tolled. Jay Blaylock woke up as a red-faced Teddy Boudreaux stormed past him to the jeers of an entire class.

And Oglesby picked up a brown rubber rat off the desk and handed it to Dan.

o o o

JUST AFTER PAT'S TRIP TO THE HOSPITAL, IN A SURGE OF PRODUCTIVE despair, Anne Malone scheduled her own physical checkup. She was healthy as a mare, but the doctor, an icy-handed Baylor grad named Carlson, recommended an annual breast X-ray. He called it a mammogram, which made Anne picture some sort of lactating rodent turned helpless on its side by its mewling litter. Nonetheless, she agreed, and Dr. Carlson's office made her a separate appointment at a hospital for this.

What the good doctor didn't tell her was this procedure literally put her tit in a wringer while a technician lowered an eerie soulless lens that looked like HAL in *2001.* It hurt like hell, but the nurse complimented Anne for precaution and prevention. "Early detection" was the optimistic way to say it, but what Anne really thought was: *With Pat falling apart you would be truly cursed and miserable if you came down with cancer. You* deserve *to be sick.* Which wasn't so much Munchausen syndrome as how miserable Irish people think.

Anne considered her woes as she put her bra back on. And as she got ready to leave, another thought occurred to her: *You're in Presbyterian Hospital. So is Margaret Raleigh.*

The trial had ended seven weeks ago that Friday. Anne had held out for three votes of eleven to one, but then five thirty pushed to six thirty, and the bailiff came back in and announced that the sequester hotel was a Days Inn in Grand Prairie. Everyone was pissed at her stubbornness, and Anne realized she didn't have a chance in hell of changing anyone's mind, so she asked that dickhead dentist who was their foreman for one more vote so they could all go home.

You were weak. You relented. She watched Standing Raleigh hug his smarmy lawyer and Elmer Gantry his way right out of the courtroom. She was ushered in silence with the other jurors to a freight elevator and out the back of the Crowley building. Down a cinder-block hall, they were joined by court officers and clerical staff, everyone scurrying to their cars. Anne ferried the Zephyr around the tight turns of the stygian parking lot, then out into the quivering evening light of Commerce Street, past the media Hooverville, past the protesters who were right for the wrong reasons, across the trickling ditch of the Trinity River, under the roaring Stemmons overpass, looping past the cenotaphless south end of Dealey Plaza, and then, missing several turns for uptown, she pulled over in downtown traffic and retched with sobs for failing Peggy Raleigh.

For the first few days after the trial, Anne tried to shore up her mental defenses by blaming the police and district attorney. There was some truth to that—because Peggy survived the attack, the Dallas PD never worked the case like a homicide, which bereft the D.A. of evidence, and left Anne with a shaky timeline and Standing Raleigh's guilty conscience.

The *Times Herald* and *Morning News* chummed the waters with competing outrage. A few days later it was reported that Lucy Goodfellow had fled town and checked into a holistic healing center in some godforsaken part of California. Then Standing Raleigh disappeared as well, his children abandoned to the custody of Peggy's parents, which left even more lurid unease over the verdict. He later turned up in prison ministry in a different godforsaken part of California. A couple of reporters had called Anne, but marooned in her guilt about the trial, she refused to comment. That left the accounts of the deliberation to the foreman, Ferris, who blathered about the jury being "unified" and the case against the reverend being "unsatisfying," and made it sound like he alone had averted some giant miscarriage of justice. This became the driving force behind Anne's suspicions, and after the immediate weariness of the whole ordeal wore off, she did discover something. There were a lot of Ferris clans in Dallas. A lot of Caruthers too—dating all the way to the early days of the Republic of Texas. Anne returned to the back catalog of *United Methodist Reporter* in Bridwell Library and found that before Standing Raleigh was the pastor at First United, he had been assistant pastor at Highland Park UMC—where Mark Ferris's father, also a DDS, was chair of the finance committee. Raleigh had also served as outreach coordinator at Ridgewood UMC, a church near White Rock Lake, basically built by the Caruthers family.

Anne left her examination room and walked down the hall to the information desk. She then turned on her heel before reaching the nurses' station—asking for Peggy point-blank would raise suspicion. She located the directory by the elevator bank. *Post Trauma. Recovery. Hospice.* The last one sounded right, and Anne took the elevator to the third floor. From there a long hallway led her through two sets of double doors into an older, prewar wing of the hospital. The rooms were larger, with multiple beds in each, like a ward in a TB sanitarium. A nurse walked past with a handful of linens.

"May I help you?" She was young, with half-lidded eyes, maybe not a nurse, but more of a housekeeper.

"I was told Margaret Raleigh was down this hall." Anne tried to sound like she had every right to be there.

"Yes, ma'am, last here on the right." The maid walked her there. Anne followed and smiled a thank-you. She peeked through the porthole window in the door. There were other beds in the room but only one patient. Peggy lay there, her head and neck wrenched to the right on the pillow. Her nose and mouth were covered by a mask and tubing. There was no guard, no attendant. The monitors were muted. The only sound came from the bellows of the respirator.

The housekeeper disappeared down the hall, and Anne stepped into the room. The air was thick and stale, smelling of disinfectant. She noticed Peggy's arms first, atrophied and bowed from disuse. Her hair was darker, overgrown compared to earlier pictures from the paper and the trial. The machine forced her to breathe slowly, in a mechanically labored way, and Anne studied her chest as it heaved and sank. An old bouquet of carnations lay drying out on the windowsill. Anne sat down in the drab green hospital chair. *No more marks on her throat.* Those apparently had healed.

Anne started to pray. She first said a Hail Mary. Then an Our Father. She was about to backtrack to an Apostles' Creed and start a decade of the rosary, just like Sister Michael had taught her at Peter and Paul's. *What was the first Sorrowful Mystery?* She had forgotten. All these years later she remembered so few prayers.

And then Peggy opened her eyes.

Or rather they swung open, like a doll's, and then closed. Her whole body shivered. Then her eyes moved under the eyelids like she was dreaming and her shoulders arched and contorted. Anne sat back unsure, confused. Peggy's eyes opened again and stared right at her. *Is she seeing me?* Peggy's neck spasmed and her eyebrows twitched and she was coughing, a dry hack and gasp muffled by the intubation, her head jerking against the pillow. And despite her eyes' being open, and blinking with each cough, it felt to Anne as if Peggy were looking straight through her. Anne stood up and reached over, placing her hand over Peggy's balled fist. *Is she there? Is she scared?* Anne couldn't tell. But they stared at each other as Peggy's dream seemed to pass, and what was coiled and taut unraveled, and she sank back into the hospital bed, closing her eyes.

Is she seeing him?

Forced to relive that night again and again?

Alone.

Anne withdrew her hand. She too was agonized and alone. And like Peggy, pulled by this invisible string of grief. Anne bowed her chin down toward Peggy, almost touching her forehead.

"Tell me," she whispered.

o o o

PAT MALONE PACKED TWO BROWN HARD-CASE TOURISTERS, ONE filled with his "monkey suits," the other with everything he had scrounged from American in terms of insurance underwriting, applied actuarial science, and employee benefits. Colonel Frank Borman had been decommissioned, but the offer from Eastern stood. In fact, Pat was desperately needed. The new CEO, another union-busting, deregulating hard-ass who "liked analysis," had locked out the mechanics in the IAM. That triggered sympathy strikes from the pilots and the flight attendants. The strikes would end in either a settlement—Pat's job was to threshold the numbers for negotiations—or bankruptcy protection, in which case Pat would have to rewrite the benefits handbook anyway.

And so he was packing, and flying out for Miami that evening.

On top of his dopp kit, Pat placed the AA Big Book and *The Little Red Book*. Since he walked out of the emergency room it had been eleven days and he had gone to two meetings. The first was at St. Monica's and was all fidgety testimonials and one-liners from jaundiced Knights of Columbus types. It was vaguely familiar in a penitential Catholic way that made Pat both sluggish and suspicious: *Welcome to the island of one-armed men, where we sit around and tell stories about how we lost our arms in the shipwreck.*

The second meeting was held at a small Lutheran church in Carrollton, where a mastiff-looking auto mechanic named Herbie came up to him and handed him both books. There was still a jittery one-eye-on-the-door quality to the discussion, but the tone was upbeat with a thank-God-for-small-favors humility. Pat raised his hand for under thirty days but didn't share. He just studied the banners for the twelve steps and twelve traditions, and read a few pages in the Big Book. The good Bill W. seemed to be describing men like Pat's father—unaware and antic salesmen types stuck in Eugene O'Neill plays. And while the meetings didn't hurt, he was still too ashamed and depressed to see their value or seek fellowship. Pat knew he was an alcoholic, he knew the booze had broken him, but he was stuck somewhere between abstinence and sobriety. He had cravings every hour of the day, but once the initial withdrawal was over, half of his conditions from the MS improved. He felt better physically, but his thinking was a fog of aggravation. Even packing seemed overwhelming. *This new job is what I need. Good to have a purpose. A routine. A way to provide.* He had to get away from Anne, who was driving him to drink. He had to get better for Dan. The drinking had led to problems Pat couldn't fathom—*For Christ's sake, I'm deserting my family*—but with stubborn, unyielding dignity he would show his son what it meant to be a man.

○ ○ ○

DAN MALONE HUNCHED OVER THE LIGHT BOX IN THE OFFICE OF *The Roundup,* brooding with impatience. The graduation edition was running late to the printer as Father Dallanach sat on the layout boards. Dan's father was flying out in four hours, and there was no good reason for the holdup. Final sign-off was all that was standing between Dan and summer, and he was sure Dallanach just needed to be goosed. He marched over to the closet that served as the darkroom and knocked. The fussbucket Father Argerlich, the paper's publisher and moderator, was hiding inside.

"In development. What?"

"It's Dan, Father, can I come in?"

Dan heard the blackout curtain pull back and the door unlock. He stepped in to find the tubby priest scowling under the red lights.

"Since you're here, help me with this roll for the alumni news-letter."

Dan picked up the tongs and moved the eight-by-tens of the baseball playoffs against Bishop Lynch from stop to fixer.

"Any word from Father Dallanach?"

"About?" *The oblivious Argerlich—twenty questions every goddamn time.*

"The final issue—are we clear to print?"

"Ah. I saw him this morning in the residence." Popping his glasses onto his pate, Argerlich stooped over a contact sheet and squinted through a loupe. "He didn't make any promises."

"Okay, should we check on it?"

"I'm busy in here."

"Should we call the printer and get a time frame?"

"Patience, Malone. Come back when I'm done."

"Father, it's the last day of school. I'm not trying to come back. I'm trying to go home."

"And I'm trying to develop film. Give me an hour and we'll go up to the principal's office together. Pull the drapes behind you."

Dan ripped the curtain closed and sealed Cardinal Kodak back in his vampire vault. *What a pain in the ass.* He should have just gone directly to Dallanach, who would probably have blessed it with the incense of a Benson & Hedges and been done.

Looking to kill valuable time, Dan left the *Roundup* office and wandered down the Bellarmine hallway to the counselors' wing. There he found Mr. Oglesby tapping with his stick Keisaku while seated at his typewriter.

"Malone, still here?"

"I can't get the Society of Jesus to close the graduation issue."

"The greater glory of God preoccupies us all. Come in. For an honored rodent, you look distraught."

Dan plopped into the low-slung creamsicle-colored chair across from his teacher's desk. In the corner, he noticed the umbrella stand that held all of Oglesby's other teaching sticks. He knew them all now, and smiled at each lesson and lecture they pointed to. *Like the moods of the poet,* Dan thought, *or the magician.*

"Yeah, I have to get out of here soon," he began, and then the following tumbled out: "My dad is leaving."

Oglesby turned from the typewriter. "Where is he going?"

"He has a new job in Miami. He's flying there tonight."

"So, how long—"

"I don't know. I don't know if he knows." Dan hesitated to share more, like he was crossing some invisible line.

"Okay." Oglesby nodded. He saw the line too. "So while I have you here, let's talk about what's next."

Oglesby spooled a new page into his typewriter and, with the occasional glance at his bookshelves, strafed the keys. In under two minutes, he handed the following to Dan:

RATTUS N., MIDSUMMER CAXTONIAN CONSUMPTION:
Heart of Darkness
Frankenstein
A Clockwork Orange
Catch-22
Of Human Bondage
The Heart of the Matter
A Good Man Is Hard to Find
Invisible Man
I, Claudius
Breakfast of Champions

"And since you're a hyperborean, Malone, let me add this last one." Oglesby took the list back and wrote at the bottom in blue felt pen.

Yeats. (A poem a day.)

"Thank you, sir."

"So this summer you're going to read each of these books. And when you finish one . . . here, give me the list again."

Dan handed it back, and Oglesby scribbled down a phone number.

"When you finish a book, call me. I'm around all summer. You call me and I'll have you over for tea, or we'll come meet here in my office, and we'll discuss that book. Sound good?"

"Yes, sir."

"What's wrong, Malone?"

"Nothing, sir."

Dan bit his lip, lowered his eyes, and pressed the fabric in the arm of his chair smooth. He wasn't looking ahead to the summer like he should have. Sure, he would lifeguard and stare at Emma Wesselman lying out on the deck of Glen Cove Swim Club. In the evenings, his crew would cruise Forest Lane. But something felt off. Oglesby rolled forward in his office chair and tapped Dan's knee with Keisaku.

"Listen to me, Malone. You're going to be fine. Remember, you're my Norwegian rat. Okay?"

"Okay." Dan nodded and studied the list of books. *I can do this. I want to do this.*

"Now get out of here, my knight errant. Read away."

"Thank you, sir." Dan got up to go.

And Oglesby was about to turn when he leaned back in his office chair and called after his sophomore.

"And keep writing, Malone. Your journal is your life-force."

Dan walked out of Oglesby's office, where he found a half-lit Father Dallanach loitering in the hall, the layouts for *The Roundup* initialed and okayed. And with that, sophomore year was over for Daniel Malone.

o o o

They took the Zephyr to DFW. As the Malones pulled away from the house, Pat gave a parting glance to his Cougar, parked at the top of the driveway, the dark maw of its grille like the baleen of a beached whale. The evening breeze was scalding. Early June carried on the near-triple-digit heat wave of late May. They merged onto the LBJ and zipped out past the city limits, past the Trinity, out into the boundless airspace of the prairie. The Zephyr coughed cool air at their silence. Despite his new regimen of six cups of coffee and three ginger ales a day, Pat was managing calm. Anne was looking away out the passenger side. Pat took a hand off the wheel and touched his wife's arm, trying to draw her in. She turned and gave an absent smile, and Pat could see it there in her eyes: all of her ceaseless ingrown worry. She was holding on, making a good show for Dan, but Pat knew how unhappy she was. This wasn't a new start. This amounted to a trial separation. This was his exile.

Pat picked up the airport road and checked on Dan in the mirror. He was also staring out the side window, trying to escape this doleful car ride. He seemed strange to Pat, a difference he couldn't quite square, but not the boy he knew. Pat's comfort was that Dan was too wrapped up in his own summer plans—lifeguarding, driver's ed—to really register his departure. But it bothered him that he didn't recognize his own son, a young man halfway through high school, and it was then that Pat knew his anguish wasn't that he was going, but that he had already missed so much.

They parked at the terminal and walked to the gate. Pat checked his bags, and Dan scanned the monitors for the flight. It was on time. Boarding began, and Pat kissed them both on their foreheads and then he hobbled slowly down the jetway. He turned back to wave but couldn't find them. He didn't think they had gone, but like the empty-hearted ancients descending into the underworld, he had disappeared from them. The jetway, which had baked on the tarmac all day, was broiling hot. He made his way onto the plane. Pat was seated in first class, where it took him less than a second to notice the booze cart. Pat opened the tiny nozzle for air above his seat. The Eastern flight attendant came by.

"Anything to drink?"

"Ginger ale, please."

The plane pulled back and taxied. It rumbled onto the runway, the engines screamed, and the plane cleared the ground. As they leveled off, the evening sun burnished the wing and all of Dallas came into Pat's view. He looked down at the tract housing, the glass and steel towers, the golden ribbons of highway, the whole city there below him, glittering like Cibola, which, as we have learned, was nowhere in particular.

ACKNOWLEDGMENTS

Thank you first and foremost to my wife, Susan, whose love saved me.

And thanks to my son, Dan, who will be a sophomore next year. Enjoy it, buddy. I'm very proud of you.

Thank you to everyone at Jesuit College Preparatory School of Dallas. It was a very good time and place—better than I could ever describe it.

Thank you to my high school crew who read this book and gave it their blessing, including Rick Dowlearn, Rob McGhee, Steve O'Donnell, and Will Kelly. (B.J.'s scene got cut, but I promise to make it up to him.) Friends like you make the world spin slow.

Thank you also to my high school teachers David Oglesby and Robert Donahue. It's an honor, sirs.

Thank you to Jake Morrissey, Gerry Howard, Kyle Reeves, and Richard Abate for reading early versions of the book.

Thank you to David Black and Bob Dylan, who both talked me through it.

Special shout-outs to Richard Hauben and Chris Sturiano at Weill Cornell Midtown Center for Treatment and Research.

Sally Kim made this book possible. You are a beautiful person and a true friend. Thank you.

And Gabriella Mongelli, truly an editor's editor. You are gifted—Norwegian rat status hereby granted. I am so grateful for you.

Many thanks to the Putnam team: Ivan Held, Ashley McClay, Alexis Welby, Brennin Cummings, Nishtha Patel, Ashley Hewlett, Ellie Schaffer, Erica Rose, Aja Pollock, and Erika Verbeck.

And thanks finally to my first teacher, my mother, Anne Desmond, who died under suspicious circumstances when her carriage plunged into the Liffey on the tenth of August in the year of Our Lord, 1919.

Just kidding, Mom—I love you.

Miss you, Dad.

SOPHOMORES

SEAN DESMOND

Discussion Guide

A Conversation with Sean Desmond
about *Sophomores*

BOOK
ENDS

PUTNAM
— EST. 1838 —

DISCUSSION GUIDE

1. *Sophomores* follows the experience of all three members of the Malone family. What was your reading experience like as you switched perspectives among family members? Did you identify more closely with one or another?

2. How does Mr. Oglesby's class influence Dan? Do you think Dan's outlook on life and his education is different by the end of the novel? How so?

3. Anne spends much of the novel struggling with her faith, particularly as part of the jury for the trial of Reverend Standing Raleigh. How does Anne's Catholicism influence her view of Raleigh and her relationship with her fellow jurors? Did you find that any of the tensions from the trial filtered into her own life?

4. Pat and Anne both have complicated relationships with their families. How did their upbringings influence them? Do you think those upbringings played roles in how they attempt to raise Dan?

5. Dallas features heavily in *Sophomores*, both as geographic setting and as a community. In what ways does the city's culture, landscape, and history impact the characters, especially given that the book is set during the late 1980s?

6. All different kinds of love are explored in this novel, from teenage crushes to religious faith to the unconditional bond of parenthood. How did you see love expressed by each of the Malones? How does love affect them in return?

7. In addition to losing his job, Pat faces a reckoning when both his MS and his alcoholism escalate. What role do his diseases play in his relationship with his family? Where do you think Pat finds a support system, if he does at all?

8. *Sophomores* is full of missed connections among the Malones. Talk about your favorite moment in which the family comes together. Do they ever find a way of understanding one another?

9. At year's end, Mr. Oglesby gives Dan a Norwegian rat summer reading list. What did you think of his selections? What titles would be on your own Norwegian rat list?

10. Pat, Anne, and Dan all undergo big and small transformations throughout the novel. Do you think people can fundamentally change? Why or why not? If yes, are there specific causes (or people) you think might play a role?

11. What do you think is next for the Malone family? What happens to Pat and Anne's relationship? What about Dan?

A CONVERSATION WITH SEAN DESMOND
ABOUT *SOPHOMORES*

Where did the title *Sophomores* come from?

The word sophomore comes from the Greek for wise (*sophos*) and foolish (*moros*). The Malone family (Anne, the mother, Pat, the father, and Dan, the son) is a classic example of people being too smart for their own good and unable to admit their problems.

You are a twenty-five year veteran of the book publishing industry—how did this background influence your process of writing this book?

I love telling stories. Working as a book editor for so many years, I am drawn to how someone learns to love reading and writing, and what the real work of that is about. And so, inspired by the man who taught me this (Mr. Oglesby, the English teacher in *Sophomores*), I wanted to explain how you become a "book person" and how understanding stories and ideas really matters.

Struggles with alcoholism, disease and faith play a large part in *Sophomores*. What was behind the decision to include such hard hitting topics?

I'm a recovering alcoholic, sober now over nine years. When you stop drinking, you take a look back and wonder: "So how did that happen?" And I realized I was on this path early. My father was diagnosed with MS when I was growing up, but he was extremely determined and resilient about fighting it. And part of that effort was that my family were devout Catholics. Faith was leaf, blossom and bole. I went to twelve years of Catholic school, and on Sunday mornings at St. Rita's, I was the altar boy, my father the lector, my mother the sacristan.

What was the inspiration behind the trial in the novel?

This was a very famous case in Dallas in the 1980s. Peggy Railey, the wife of Reverend Walker Railey, the pastor of First United Methodist, was found strangled in her driveway. The mystery of her attack was shocking, and became this lurid scandal in Dallas society—the investigation and trial received O.J. Simpson-level attention from the local media. Lawrence Wright wrote a chilling piece in *Texas Monthly* about it.

How does being Irish-Catholic impact the lives of the Malone family, and does it play any part in your own?

Great question. I could write a book on this one . . .

The relationship between Mr. Oglesby and Dan, his student, is reminiscent to that of Robin Williams's character and his students in the movie *Dead Poets Society*. Does this comparison resonate with you?

To answer this question I went back and watched the movie again. Boy, is it over the top and I love it. And what it reminds me is that a great teacher is a great performer, and Mr. Oglesby is like that! Also, teenage boys are all sorts of fucked up, and that's okay, that's why English teachers use the great books out there to channel that experience and let young people realize they are normal for not feeling normal.

Why did you decide to set *Sophomores* in Dallas?

My family comes from Ireland (all four grandparents born there), they settled in the Bronx, and my father worked for American Airlines which transferred us to Dallas. So I was in Dallas for grade school, middle school and high school, and it was a fine time, but a foreign land. There are some great books set in Dallas, but I think it's still underexplored as a town with its own culture, history, class lines and divides.

Though it is set more than thirty years ago, what elements of the story have contemporary relevance today?

As I watch my own son work his way through high school (he'll be a sophomore next year), I realize that it's still tough for kids to figure it out. That never changes.

This is your second novel, coming twenty years post your first novel, *Adams Fall*, which was adapted into the 2002 Paramount Pictures movie, *Abandon*. Do you see an on-screen future for *Sophomores*?

Yes. It would be so cool! We could also do a *Derry Girls* like series for Netflix with the sophomores in Dan Malone's class. Rick Linklater . . . call me . . . let's do this!

What's next for you?

Keep reading and writing. It never gets old.

Photograph of the author © Hillery Stone

Sean Desmond is the publisher of Twelve, an imprint of Grand Central, and has been in the publishing world for more than twenty-five years. His first novel, *Adams Fall*, was published in 2000 and was adapted into the film *Abandon*. Desmond lives in Brooklyn, New York.

VISIT SEAN DESMOND ONLINE

🐦 skdesmond1973
📷 skdesmond1973